I dedicate this book to all the mothers.

INTUITION OF A MIDLIFE WITCH

J.C. YEAMANS

RSP

REED SHORE PRESS

Intuition of a Midlife Witch

Newark, DE 19711

ISBN: 979-8-88652-015-6

For content elements, visit the J.C. Yeamans website: https://jcyeamans.com/content-elements/. Please visit the link if you would like more information on the contents before reading this book. There are spoilers.

Cover: Charles W. Clark, Reed Shore Press.
The cover design uses Rosarivo font (designed by Pablo Ugerman) and Photoshop brushes by Brusheezy.com.

Content/Line Editor: Sarah Faeth Sanders

Proofreader: Reed Shore Press

PRONUNCIATION GUIDE

Gwynedd: GWYN-eth
Cockburn: CO-burn
Gorawen: GOHR-a-when
Shailagh: SHAY-la
Aonghas: ANG-us
Tuatha Dé Danann: TOO-a-day-DAN-ann
Cat sith: CAT shee
Nain: NINE
Taid: TIDE
Tylwyth Teg: TIL-with Teg

CONTENTS

CHAPTER ONE

A FRESH START

THE GRAY-SKINNED MONSTER TAKES two steps toward me, muscles bulging, dark, shoulder-length hair swaying with every movement. His gargantuan boots squish into the muddy soil. A whiff of musty earth and rank BO enters my nostrils. I flinch and pinch my nose. When a moonbeam strikes the giant being's scarred face, he turns his head, capturing my gaze with one shiny coal-black eye—the other permanently closed, disfigured. My body stiffens as I clutch my chest, struggling to fill my lungs. A faint voice calls my name. "Ms. Crowther? Gwynedd Crowther—"

"Ms. Crowther?" a woman shouts.

I flinch in the dermatologist's waiting room chair and rub the kink in my neck as I raise my head. The vision I had in June still haunts my dreams, but nothing new has revealed itself. Without using a crystal grid, the premonition will take months or years to develop. Despite my impatience to discover the truth, I've come to accept the future reveals itself when it's good and ready—it's either that or fry my brain with a crystal grid. I peer up at the receptionist.

"The doctor says you may go back now." She gestures toward the doorway.

I swing my purse over my shoulder as I stand, adjusting my jeans and long-sleeved shirt. As I move toward the door, I read the close captioning on the TV screen—breaking news out of Philadelphia.

The reporter announces another kidnapping has occurred, and the FBI is on the case. How awful.

A nurse directs me to exam room four. When the door swings in, my attention immediately shifts to my boyfriend Archie's toned butt, shining bright red with frosty-white blisters full of discolored ink. The doctor spreads a jelly-like healing ointment over the treated area. Archie turns his head toward me, smiling, his icy-blue eyes glinting under the ceiling lights.

"Dr. Cockburn says he needs your approval. Does it pass your test?" He smiles as he gathers bandages to cover the wound.

I wrinkle my nose. "How would I know? I hope it looks better than that after it heals."

"It will take about four to eight weeks," Archie says in his soft Scottish accent. "Aren't you happy the tattoo is gone?"

"Sure I am, but I didn't ask you to remove it." I glance at the dermatologist. "It was all his idea."

"So Dr. Cockburn said." Dr. Patel snickers as he finishes dressing the area. "Call me if it becomes infected. You can schedule a follow-up appointment for six weeks. One more session should remove any remaining ink." He exits the room, suppressing a smile.

After the door shuts, Archie sits up carefully and pulls on his boxer briefs. My inquisition begins.

"Did you tell him why you wanted the tattoo removed?" I ask.

My lover grimaces. "Aye. He asked. He was curious."

"Well, no one forced you to." I roll my hazel eyes. "He appeared amused."

Archie chuckles. "You have to admit. It's humorous thinking back on the incident."

"Funny for you. I had a slight heart attack when I opened the door and caught you screwing Courtney Davies. Of course, I didn't know it was you...or her. I hadn't met either of you formally yet." The image of his butt as he screwed the young, obsessed grad student from behind lingers in my memories like a splinter embedded beneath my skin.

"Which is precisely why I had the tat removed." He pulls on his sweatpants, sliding the elastic slowly over the bandage. "Every time you stare at my arse, you think of her. Don't bloody tell me you don't."

"Well, it's kind of hard not to. That Horned God tattoo is—was—both unique and prominent on your *bum*."

He bends over and kisses me, his goatee tickling my chin. "Are you saying you're going to miss it, my love?"

"Not a fucking chance," I say, patting his other butt cheek. "I wonder what Courtney is doing now."

"Careful, Gwyn. It doesn't hurt yet, but the lidocaine shot will wear off soon. And Courtney took that course with Leslie as an elective. After the semester ended, we never heard from her again. She must have graduated and left the area."

Dr. Leslie Hughes, the chair of the Celtic Studies department and Elder in the Bearsden Coven who is way past Medicare eligibility, kicked Courtney's ass out when we discovered she helped the imposter Audrey Kenilworth infiltrate our witch's circle. But Audrey was under an abusive parental spell and wasn't responsible for her actions. Her mother Edith killed her in retaliation for helping the coven fend off her parents' destructive actions at the fall pagan conference.

I think about Courtney occasionally. Does she ever wonder what happened to her best friend?

"Let's head back to the house. I'm so uncomfortable. Thank you for suggesting a Friday afternoon appointment. I don't know how I would have taught my Celtic Studies classes."

"Told you so. Would you like me to drive?"

He grimaces. "My Tesla? Fawk no."

"I was kidding, but you should teach me how to drive it sometime, in case of an emergency."

"I'll ruminate on that while I'm icing my arse."

We leave the medical office for Archie's cottage style home on Duncan Street. A playful breeze displaces my bangs as we exit the car, but the cool air invigorates me. I inhale the earthy scent of fall, hoping to shake off my worries. When we enter the house, he heads for the kitchen, but I grab his arm.

"Why don't you go into the living room?" I ask. "I'll bring you an ice pack."

"Thank you, my love. You'll find me on the loveseat." He inches toward the russet leather sofa holding his butt.

"Why not sit in the ice packing chair?"

I motion to the corner and recall icing my own bottom there the night I fell at the Old Men oak trees. Well, I didn't actually fall; an evil Sluagh fairy using the tree as a host attacked me.

"Ah, that evening. I remember it well. You told me I was extravagant for owning a Tesla."

I chuckle, and the memory of him standing in the doorway pops into my head—flexing a bicep as he brushed a hand through his ash-blond locks. "Yeah. I can't believe you kissed me after I said that. I'll get the ice pack. Find a seat wherever you want, honey."

"The loveseat will do. I can prop my feet on the steamer trunk."

After filling the pack with fresh ice, I rush to the living room. Archie is still standing, examining his collection of weapons on the wall—a display full of antique flintlock pistols and swords. When he finishes adjusting a random dirk onto its holder, he shuffles to the loveseat to sit. I place the chilly bag under his sore butt. He pushes strands of my chestnut brown hair behind my ear and strokes my cheek.

"I was so hesitant to kiss you that night. Certain you would smash my face with your fist."

"Never. You're too pretty," I say, stroking his whiskers.

Archie frowns. "You're mocking me, witch."

I laugh and bring my lips close to his. "No, I'm not."

I kiss him, and he shifts on the cushion, adjusting the swelling in his pants.

"Don't make this harder for me. You know I won't be up to any intimate shenanigans for a while."

"It's definitely harder," I say, eyeing his bulge. The clock on the fireplace mantel dings the first of three.

"Don't you meet Seamus at the library soon?" he asks, squinting.

"Yes. He's there already stacking books for me to flip through, I bet. No need to cook tonight. I'll bring a plate over after I make dinner at home." I kiss him on the cheek and head toward the front door.

"Thank you, my love." Archie pauses, watching me as I slip on my shoes. "You've spent an inordinate amount of time with him researching for an answer to the vision you had in June. With his possible romantic feelings for you, do you think meeting with him so often is wise?"

"Maybe not, but he's never acted on them. It's only an infatuation. I need to exhaust all the research in every Celtic area. So far, you haven't discovered anything that describes what I saw. Then there's the Welsh literature, too. I try not to get overwhelmed, but there are so many references, and I've got my classwork in Public Policy to complete. I must squeeze in the time whenever I can. Speaking of Welsh lit. Do you think I could bother that new instructor who specializes in Welsh folklore?"

"Dr. Ashley Lewis? I don't know, Gwyn. Her cup is overflowing. She's a widow with a two-year-old boy. Leslie and I are livid the Dean of the Arts and Sciences college wouldn't approve the hire of another professor. Hiring her as an instructor is a wee bit insulting for someone with a doctorate. But she said she needed the work. At least she receives full benefits."

I slip on my fleece jacket and zip it up. "Could I help her out? Do a trade, like watching her son as payment for helping me research the Welsh end."

"Aye. I imagine she'd welcome your offer. But I'd wait until after Samhain. It's less than two weeks away."

"Right. But we have so much left to do. We still must find a spell to close the portal, and there aren't many grimoires remaining to go through. I doubt an incantation is in any of those books. That vision solidifies how crucial it is to eliminate the chance of malevolent supernatural beings from crossing over into our world—not only the Tuatha Dé Danann. Although the threat of Nick's fairy family coming here in search of him has taken up permanent residence in the folds of my brain." If they find out I killed Dr. Evans, Nuada, I'm toast.

Archie shifts the ice pack on his butt and flinches. "I've hesitated to ask. Any new clues present themselves?"

Air rushes through my lips. "No. And they won't. Not without the use of a full crystal grid."

"Aye. Remember what Great-Aunt Gorawen said when we visited in August."

"Don't worry. I'm going to follow her schedule of implementation. But building up to a complete grid over five years will be pointless if that monster arrives before I'm at full potential. I dream about the being once in a while—even today when I dozed off at the doctor's office. It haunts me."

"I can't stop you from doing what you want, Gwynedd. Promise me you'll use a full grid as a last resort. There is no immediate danger."

"My witch's intuition tells me you're right. Of course, it's not fully developed either. But, if it signals a forthcoming danger, I'll need to risk the grid. And that would suck. I promise to tell you if I do, though. Even better, I will use it at your house where you can watch over me."

"Thank you for humoring me, stubborn woman."

I chuckle as I snatch my purse from the oak hall tree. "Not so much now. I can't wait to visit Aunt Gorawen and your family again. The summer there was exciting."

"They enjoyed having you there, too. Winter Session will arrive before you know it. I love you, Gwyn." He blows me an air kiss.

"I love you, tattooless man," I say, turning the doorknob. "See you later when I bring dinner."

I enter the four-story DUB library on Central Campus and make my way to the Celtic folklore section on the third floor. As I climb the stairs lugging my backpack, I glance out the stairwell window at the nearby trees. They're bursting with an explosion of crimson, gold, and rust.

When I reach my destination, I spot Dr. Seamus Duffy, the Irish folklore professor, as he limps to a table with a stack of books near the MDS section of Celtic Myths. He's also the local cat sith witch and my supernatural protector, despite my objections. But what can I do about it?

He drops the books on the wooden surface and sits down. His shiny black hair is pulled behind his head as always, and he's wearing a dark-green button-down shirt, a tie, and charcoal slacks—consummate attire for a professor. Well, at least for him. Archie used to wear T-shirts and jeans. But that was before he changed his attitude. After the attack of the Sluagh, Archie stepped down as chair of the Celtic Studies department.

When Seamus raises his head in my direction, a grin brightens his oblong face. The ceiling light spots his sea-green eyes, making them shine like glass. I wave and rush to join him.

"Good afternoon," I say. "I see you've already found a few books for me to search through. You didn't have to carry them all." I place my purse and backpack on the table, choosing a chair across from him to sit.

"Nonsense," he replies in his sing-songy Irish accent. "I know the lore and can make choices wisely. Why don't you begin with this book?"

He slides the heavy reference toward me, and I flip through a few pages in the text, finding little of help. I glance up to find him staring and shift in my seat.

"Thank you for giving up so much of your time to help me research. I'm so sorry none of the myths have meshed with what I saw so far."

"Can you describe the being to me again?" he asks.

"Sure, but it's been months since the vision kidnapped my brain outside your house. Every time I dream about the monster, the image becomes more blurred." I flip through a few more pages.

"Tell me what you can remember. We'll go from there."

The aroma of decaying pulp and leather in the library triggers the image to return. "He had to be over seven feet tall. Under the moonlight, his skin moved like gray leather. Scars all over. An eye black as obsidian, and the other permanently shut, as if an enemy marred him in a fight. Dark hair that hit his shoulders. Gargantuan boots. And he stank. Or it was fungi in the soil. I don't know. The thing that's imprinted on my retina the most is the image of him staring directly at me with that bulging eyeball." I shudder.

Seamus chuckles. "Sounds horrifying."

"Are you making fun of me?" I ask, tilting my head.

"No. I'm laughing at your description and attempting to keep the mood light. Did you feel threatened by the gray-skinned being?"

"My witch's intuition says no. But I've only known about my witch ancestry for a couple of years. Like the visions, I need to work on that skill. Right now, it's fermenting in my gut."

I push up from my chair and the feet scrape the floor, prompting the students at the next table to scowl at me. I mouth, "Sorry."

"Where are you going, Gwynedd?"

"I'm gonna return this book to the shelf."

The professor stands and reaches for the reference. "Please, allow me. You continue to scour the next text."

"OK. Thank you, Seamus."

While he returns the book, my former classmates and witch friends Spence Huxley and Skye McGowen pass by. Skye's summer tan has faded, but Spence is as pale as always. They're both dressed in DUB polo shirts and dark jeans. Spence's jet-black hair is combed neatly, and the shirt hangs loosely on his lanky body. Skye has gathered her fire-red locks into a ponytail. A coiffed look for the new doctoral students and teaching assistants. Usually, you'd be lucky to catch Spence doing anything more than shaking his head to settle his tresses. I motion to them to come to the table.

"Hey, sis," Spence says loudly. "What's the tea?"

"Shhh," Skye whispers in her husky voice. "There are undergrads studying for exams."

He waves his hands about. "Like they don't talk at the top of their lungs?"

The students at the table turn toward Spence. "Shhh."

He smirks at them and whispers, "I can't help it. It's who I am."

I laugh and gesture at their polo shirts. "I love the formal DUB clothing. Who convinced you to wear them?"

Skye snickers. "Dr. Hughes told him he wears it or no teaching assistantship."

"It's extortion," Spence says, frowning. "I should be permitted to express myself by wearing whatever floats my boat."

"Someone once said to dress for the job you want," Seamus replies, returning to his chair. "Would you prefer to teach in higher academia or to change the oil on my sedan? Both are noble occupations, I should note."

"With how little Dr. Lewis is getting paid as an instructor, I might be better off as an auto mechanic."

Skye laughs. "Hi, Dr. Duffy."

"A good afternoon to you, Ms. McGowen. Did you receive my email with the attachment of notes?"

"Yes. Thank you," she replies. "They will improve the quality of my lecture."

I address Spence. "Who are you TAing for? Archie?"

"One class, but mostly for Dr. Lewis. She needs my help way more than Dr. Cockburn. I mean, she's one of the most intelligent people I've ever met, but her lectures are all over the place. I think

Dr. Hughes assigned her too many classes. It doesn't make sense to overload the youngest instructors over experienced professors." He grimaces at Seamus. "Sorry, Dr. Duffy. But it's true."

"No offense taken," the professor replies. "I agree. Unfortunately, as they say, it's above my pay grade. Now that Dr. Hughes has had to return as chair, she can't take on more than a couple of classes either. The department can barely function under the financial squeeze of the college."

"I'm so glad they approved the teaching assistantships," I whisper. "Considering they wouldn't replace the full professor position. You're both needed badly."

Skye glances at her cell phone. "Spence, we need to go. We have to meet with Dr. Hughes before she leaves."

"You'd think she could have waited until Monday," he replies. "Tanner will beat me home tonight."

"Tell him I said hi," I say.

"I sure will. Dinner will be late!"

Tanner Jones, Spence's partner, works as a financial advisor and often has long hours. The two of them bought my old house a few blocks from the Delaware University, Bearsden campus. We all call it DUB for short.

"Bye, Dr. Duffy," Skye says. "Gwyn, see you at the Fellowship meeting."

"May it be productive," Seamus replies.

"Tell Dr. Hughes I will cook dinner for us tonight," I say. "She doesn't have to rush your discussion."

Spence and Skye dart toward the stairs. The Fellowship of Associated Pagans, the cover name for our town coven, meets on Thursday, and the Elder helps run the meetings. The least I can do is cook dinner for her occasionally.

Seamus and I return to scouring the reference books for any description that fits the being I saw in my vision. I catch him staring at me several times. It could mean nothing. He's socially awkward at best. When my cell phone displays 5:00 p.m., I close the book.

"I better get going. Thank you for giving up your time again to help me sift through these references. With the overload in the Celtic Studies department, I'm sure this is on the bottom of your list of priorities." I gather the textbooks in a pile on the table.

"Nonsense," he says, smiling. "You are much higher on that list than you think. I'll return the books to their proper places. I have some research to complete before I head home."

He put off his own academic work to help me. "I wish you wouldn't do that."

"I have no one waiting for me there, Gwynedd, so I don't mind accommodating your schedule. Before you go, I want to make an offer. Cat sith witches possess an enhanced intuition. I'd be more than happy to help you improve your skills. You could come by for tea tomorrow?"

I slip on my fleece jacket and grab my belongings. "Thank you, but I've got so much work to do before Samhain. Some other time."

He nods. "Have a pleasant evening."

"You, too, Seamus."

When I arrive at the stairs, I turn back. The professor waves. Is Archie right?

CHAPTER TWO

DESTINY

As I MEANDER ON the maze of red paver walkways through the Green, I soak in the colorful pom-poms of burgundy, yellow, and white mums. The Old Men oak trees clutch their turned leaves, refusing to let go. By November, the iconic landmarks on Central Campus will resemble skeleton-like elders watching over all of us. I skip over the fallen acorns, recalling that eventful evening when the Sluagh swiped my legs, throwing me on my ass. That was the first night I saw amber magic shoot out of my hand and Archie kissed me in front of his fireplace.

I grin, remembering how stubborn I was. Yet the Scottish professor refused to let me go home, insisting I drive to his house and ice my butt and the back of my head. Until that night, my life had followed a different trajectory, the path of an Unremarkable—those who aren't *in the knowing* of all things magical and supernatural. Then destiny made its play and won.

Despite the horrendous incidents I've experienced and witnessed since then, I'll never go back. I relish the love and devotion of a wonderful man and the friendships of a devoted witch family. I fully accept my destiny as an ancestral witch and will do all I can to protect my community from the evil the portal in the mound has exposed us to. Of course, that requires me to continue my preparation for the arrival of the Tuatha Dé Danann and the unknown malevolent beings yet to find the aperture into our world.

When I arrive home at Leslie's small Tudor house on Drummond Lane, I nudge the red side door with my hip and enter the mudroom. I kick off my sneakers and hang my fleece jacket on a hook, dropping my backpack and purse on the floor below. Mr. Yeats, Leslie's chimera cat familiar, presents in his human persona wearing his standard three-piece gray suit and spectacles. He glares with his yellow and blue eyes and immediately pounces on me, gesturing to his clipboard with its accompanying agenda.

"Good evening, Ms. Crowther," he says in a thick Irish brogue. "You have arrived much later than expected. Dinner will be late."

"I appreciate your assistance," I say. "But monitoring my every movement wasn't what I had in mind when I asked you to help me stay organized this semester."

Leslie ambles into her yellow kitchen with its outdated countertops and chides him. "At least allow Gwynedd time to catch a breath before you attack her with your schedule of her activities."

"I'm doing as instructed," he says, adjusting his spectacles. "Do not forget the conference with your mum this week as well. As a reminder, Mr. Wolfe is expected. I'll be in the magic room if you need me." He transforms into a chimera cat, half ginger and half black, and scuttles down the hallway.

I wipe my face. "I almost forgot. This could be traumatic for Tyler."

My son has known about my conferencing with his grandparents in the Otherworld but hasn't asked to talk with them. He's still not sure he's ready. Being thrusted into the world of magic scared the shit out of him. But I'm not going to lie. I'm happy to have him practice witchcraft beside me. He's impressed me with his witch training, which he'll need if Nuada's Tuatha Dé family arrives.

"I wouldn't worry about your son." Leslie pushes her silver side bangs off her face, exposing her copper eyes and pallid, wrinkled skin. "He accepted his witch status with ease. Much better than you, I might add."

"Let's not dredge that up. You know, the way you went about it was far from honest. You put my life in danger…and Tyler's."

"I am deeply sorry for my past transgressions. But I won't apologize for pushing you to fulfill your role in the coven." She lays her knobby fingers on mine. "Without you and Tyler, we would have never harnessed the power to fight the Kenilworths and save our town. For that, I am grateful. And for bringing Agnes back to me. I've never been this happy in my life, and I owe it all to you."

I smile, thinking of my hedge witch mentor, Agnes Pritchard. Should the Elder thank me or curse me for bringing them together now so late in her life? They say opposites attract. I pull out a frying pan and a quart sized pot to whip up a quick meal of grilled cheese and tomato soup.

"I'm going to cook us dinner, and when we're done, I'll take a serving of each to Archie."

"Thank you, my dear. I'm so tired. This was a long Friday. It ended with a meeting with the two TAs. Spence and Skye are doing very well, but Spence needs guidance. He's knowledgeable but can go on tangents during lectures. I never worry about Skye." Leslie sets her spindly body onto a kitchen chair and rests her arms on the table.

"Why does that not surprise me?" I say, pouring the soup in and turning on the burner.

"I've spent some time researching the Welsh folklore, but nothing resembles the supernatural being in your vision. Did you have any luck with Dr. Duffy?"

I exhale as I butter the bread and place it in the frying pan. "No. I've not had a lot of time to spend on it with my studies. I have a capstone project to complete this year in order to graduate with my Master's in Public Policy. Seamus has been so helpful, but I think it's more important to finish scouring the remaining grimoires for a portal-closing spell. If we close the opening in the Celestial

Gardens, we'll eliminate that entry into our town. That should be the priority."

"It would please our allies on the council as well. They pressure us monthly on the subject. Elijah says they're extremely frustrated with the coven."

Elijah Jackson, the gentle giant of a man, runs the Bearsden Shelter and serves on the city council. He has had a tough job calming the nerves of the council members who are *in the knowing*. A notification vibrates my phone on the kitchen table. Leslie reads the text.

"It's Ronnie. You should reply to her."

I flip our grilled cheese sandwiches and pick up my cell.

Ronnie: *Don't forget you're going to my birthing class with me tomorrow!*

I send a reply to my best friend, Veronica Baldwin.

Me: *I won't. The date is in my calendar. I'm looking forward to it.*

Ronnie: *Thank you so much for agreeing to go at the last minute.*

Me: *No problem. Not your fault Derek has to work.*

Ronnie: *Yeah. Jamal didn't plan on getting appendicitis.*

Me: *It will be fun. It's been what...almost thirty years since I attended one.*

Ronnie: *Ha! I'm sure the classes have changed! See you tomorrow.*

Me: *I'll meet you there!*

"Ronnie was reminding me about attending her birthing class with her tomorrow. Derek can't go because one of his fitness trainers is in the hospital recovering from appendicitis. You can't plan for things like that."

"Indeed. Life presents unexpected challenges. All we can do is approach them head on." She smiles widely. "I'm so excited about this baby. A new witch being born into the coven is always a day to celebrate."

"Well, let's remember that her child may be born without magical instincts. Derek acts as if he'd be happier if his offspring were devoid of magic."

Derek Young, Ronnie's partner, owns a fitness center. He's a few years younger than her and is an Unremarkable, but he's also *in the knowing*, having discovered our secret when he walked in on Ronnie, Tyler, and me when I was showing my son the powers of Archie's family dirk. He supports her witchery but has reservations about raising a child to be a witch. It's a dangerous path. Who can blame him?

"Witch or not, I am ecstatic for her," Leslie says. "She deserves this blessing."

"She certainly does. Her life was hard. I'm so happy she found Derek. He loves her very much."

I set the soup and sandwiches on the table and sit down across from her. The aroma of melted cheese and butter prompts my stomach to growl.

"This smells wonderful. The perfect meal for a fall Friday dinner." Leslie slurps a spoonful of soup. "Agnes will be sorry she missed this meal with us. I invited her, but she said she wasn't up to the drive. I think she's having too much fun cooking in her renovated kitchen."

"Probably. You've been spending more and more time at her farm. Will you ever move in together?" It's an invasive question, but I rent a room from her. If she moved out and sold the house, I'd be homeless again.

"We both enjoy our independence, but it has crossed my mind. I've suggested she move in here and sell the farm. It's much too big a property to care for, and the land requires immense upkeep. But she will never give up her garden and her...plants."

I laugh, because she's referring to the marijuana she grows in her garden along with other herbs. A hedge witch needs a large garden. As for Agnes staying put, I'm relieved. When she moved in for that short time while her kitchen was being completed, it was a tad crowded in this tiny home. Far too small for three adults and a familiar. I finish the last bite of my sandwich and put my dishes in the sink.

"I better take Archie's dinner to him," I say. "He's starved by now."

"You can't keep your man waiting. I will load the dishwasher. Tell him I hope he's recovered enough to cover his classes on Monday."

"He should feel much better by then. He's icing his butt all weekend." I place his dinner in a bag and head toward the door.

"Leslie, I want you to know I'm not angry anymore. Life's too short to stew over what was meant to be."

She lifts her chin. "Indeed."

As I enter the mudroom of Archie's house, I shout out to him. "I'm here, honey! Don't move. I'll heat your dinner and bring it to you. I assume you're on the sofa?"

"Aye!" he yells from the living room. "Icing again. Bloody good you arrived when you did. I was about to chew on the leather cushion."

"Very funny. It won't take me long."

I warm up the sandwich and soup in the microwave and carry his dinner to him on a tray, placing it on the steamer trunk. Archie removes the ice pack and sits up.

"Mmm. What delicacy you're providing me. You must have slaved over this meal." He winks at me.

"You seriously aren't making fun of my cooking, are you?"

He chuckles and takes a bite of the grilled cheese. "Naw. A simple dinner is fine for a Friday night. We're all knackered after this week. I don't know what we would have done if the college hadn't approved the TA positions for Spence and Skye. Especially for Ashley Lewis."

"I'm glad, too. Still, our school loads have put a dent in our leisure time this semester. I'll be so happy when I graduate. I don't know what to do with my public policy diploma, but at least the degree will be completed. Then I must find a full-time job. I'm thinking I should move out of Leslie's house. Investigate apartments."

Archie takes another bite of his sandwich and sets it on the plate. "You never want to discuss it, but—"

"No. Don't say it." I plop on the loveseat next to him.

"For fawk's sake, Gwyn. We've been together for over two years, if you don't count the few months we were apart. I understand you relish your independence, but I think the reason you don't want to move in with me has more to do with trust. I love you more than I ever thought I could care for a person. You still don't trust me, but you can. I'm not Richard."

"I believe you, Archie. Even after what happened with Laura Lovelace. I understand it wasn't your fault. She cast a spell on you with the help of Nick Evans." I glance at my great-aunt's painting on the fireplace mantel. "Still, there's always a tiny part of me that worries you're under the influence of Aunt Gorawen's picture. How will I ever know for sure?"

He runs his fingers through his wavy locks and growls. "You frustrate me, witch."

"I'm sorry. I wish I could do something to make it up to you."

"Me, too. But I'm too sore to indulge in any extra-curricular activities. My arse burns."

"Why don't we watch a movie in bed on your tablet? You go ahead, and I'll take these dishes to the kitchen."

"A wonderful idea. No need to rush. I'm moving slowly. When you get upstairs, I'd like you to change the bandages for me. It's a bugger trying to replace them on my own arse." He laughs as he heads up the stairs.

"I'll be happy to attend to your fine ass."

"You're a tease, woman."

I load the plate and bowl into the dishwasher, turning out the light as I exit the kitchen. When I get to the living room, I pause. I stare at the painting of my mom. She stands in a field of wildflowers, reaching toward the impending storm.

Did Aunt Gorawen's charmed picture send Archie to me as a protector? Did it influence his love for me? How will I ever know for sure?

CHAPTER THREE

OH, BABY

MYSTIC SAGE, BEARSDEN'S OCCULT store, is bustling with shoppers. Typical for a Saturday, but more so with Halloween and Samhain arriving in the middle of next week. Orange, black, and purple decorations splatter the walls and rubber spiders hang from the ceiling. The entry door dings as it opens, the bamboo chimes clanking when it shuts. Shane Murphy, the owner and my devoted friend, ordered some adult costumes, hoping to lure in students from campus. It worked like a charm—pun intended. After all, we *are* witches.

I ring up customers all morning, both students and townies—the locals—until a lull in the frenzy occurs. The herbs are especially pungent today after Shane filled the baskets, tickling my nostrils as usual. I pinch my nose to suppress a sneeze but snort, anyway.

My boss chuckles. "I'm sorry, darling. Would you like a break? I could run the cash register for a spell while you stock the shelves in the crystals room."

"Nah. I'm OK. Just forgot to take my allergy meds this morning. My own fault."

"How have you been? We've been so busy the last few weeks with Samhain approaching, I've neglected to ask. Has your vision expanded into the next phase?"

I sigh. "No. I've dreamed about the intruder, though. Nothing new. Invades my sleep and scares the shit out of me. Archie and Seamus have been helping me sift through the Irish and Scottish folklore for gray beings, but we've found zip."

He pats his slight paunch. "That's too bad. Keep up your crystal training schedule like your aunt laid out for you. Eventually, the vision will reveal more of itself...safely."

"Yeah, but I don't think the threat is eminent. Better we spend more time at Agnes's house finishing the database. We have very few grimoires left to get through. Unfortunately, we're all so busy. For now, I think we're safe. My intuition has been getting stronger. I don't sense any immediate danger."

"That's good to know. I better go to the back. I'm expecting a delivery soon. Holler if the consumers become violent."

"I will," I say, laughing. "Jeff is supposed to be here in a minute, anyway."

"When he gets here, take a break for lunch."

Shane ambles through the doorway to the storage area in the back, and I tidy up behind the counter before the next wave of vampire and zombie wannabees drag their feet into the store. A ding and a clank resound, and my body buzzes with the warning of a witch. But this magic has a unique flavor. It must be Seamus.

I pop my head above the counter for a peek to find none other than Courtney Davies standing there with a tentative smile. She's as perfect as I remember her, nearly white blond hair, fair skin with a rosy glow, and crystal-clear blue eyes. Instead of the standard T-shirt and jeans of her grad school days, she's wearing a beige dress blouse and a black skirt, her locks gathered in a bun. A tinge of jealousy returns, sparking pounding palpitations.

"Hi, Courtney," I say, fumbling with the pens in the skull mug. "I thought you left the city."

"I...I did," she replies. "But I found a better job back here in Bearsden. I'm working at the town hall in Mayor Devine's office. Someone told me about a grant writing position, and I jumped at the chance to return here. Bearsden felt like home when I was in grad school. I desperately wanted to come back. And Mayor Devine is so nice; she wants the best for the city."

Holy crystals. Hopefully, it's not an attempt to win Archie back. Courtney was so thirsty for my boyfriend, she aided Jeff's cousin Audrey Kenilworth in infiltrating the coven. Helping her allowed the Sluagh to cross over and attack me, an attempt to eliminate me from the picture. I mean, Archie is charming and incredibly sexy. But why go to those lengths over a man who clearly had no interest in her any longer?

"Bearsden is a wonderful town," I say. "I've lived here all my life, so I understand why you would want to return."

"I've been here for a year. In fact, I'm married to John Erickson."

"Oh, the new city councilman. I heard he had a wife. Never imagined it was you." Not in a million years.

"Yes. His day job is in tech, though. I've kept to myself, so I haven't run into anyone, not even Elijah."

The door dings again, and a few students walk in sporting DUB fleece jackets with the scotty dog mascot. A cool breeze follows them in, sending a chill through my body.

"Well, congrats on your nuptials. If you've been here a year, why is this your first time stopping in the store for spell materials? Aren't you practicing magic now?"

She glances at the glass window. Outside, Jeff Williams, the fresh DUB grad and co-owner of Mystic Sage, is shaking hands with Mayor Jessica Devine, a woman with light brown hair in her mid-60s. Another woman, most likely in her early 40s, has joined them. She could be Courtney's older sister—perfect blond strands, rosy complexion, dainty nose.

"I wasn't sure how the coven would react to my return. Also, I knew you worked here and didn't want to make you feel uncomfortable."

That was thoughtful of her. Before, she was a whiny, spoiled brat of a woman. Did she mature after she graduated? She returns her attention to me.

"You have every right to buy at this store. I don't hold grudges." Except for my cheating husband Richard and Shane's ex-girl-friend, Cordelia Davenport. None of us can forgive that witch for pulling a Dearg Due into our world. The vampiric demon killed five young men.

"I'm not here to buy witchcraft materials. I need to apologize for my past behavior. In college, I was immature and selfish. Getting out into the workforce changed me. I only desire to do what I can to help the town."

Wait. Is she trying to lay groundwork to get back into the coven? "I appreciate your apology, but I don't think the Fellowship would allow you to return. We're already at thirteen members again."

"Oh, no. I don't expect anything from them. I wanted you to know I'm here and have no ill feelings toward you or the coven. They don't need to worry about my intent. Please, tell the Fellowship at the next meeting."

"Sure. I can do that." But is she telling the truth?

I knock over the mini iron cauldron a customer left on the counter. It falls practically at Courtney's feet, but she just stands there staring at the witchy decor.

"Would you mind picking that up for me?" I ask, pointing.

She peers up at me. "I'd rather not. It could have broken, and I don't want to be accused of damaging it further."

For fuck's sake. I dash around the counter and retrieve the witchy item.

"Well, I better get back to work. A colleague and I are trying to finish a grant this weekend." She ambles toward the entry door.

"Courtney?" I ask with a tilt of my head.

She stops and turns around. "Yes?"

Should I question her about Audrey? "Never mind. Have a great day."

As the ex-coven witch exits, Jeff enters the store, brushing his taffy brown hair into place. The crisp air has left a pink hue on his skin.

"It's super windy out today," he says. "Leaves are blowing everywhere. So much for raking them into the street yesterday."

"I don't miss that at all. The pile on the road in front of my house was as tall as me. It took a few days to collect and drag them with a tarp, even with Tyler helping. The back yard was the worst. I wonder how Tanner and Spence are handling the mountain of leaves this year?" I don't lament selling my old home, but the neighborhood was full of friendly people.

He lets out a hearty laugh. "Great, until Spence jumped into it. He forgot they raked the leaves to the curb. Wasn't a soft landing."

"Oh, my gods. Is he OK?" I snort as Jeff continues.

"Yeah. But Tanner told him he questions how he is so accomplished academically but lacks common sense."

"It's fantastic you bought the cape cod with red siding across the street, although..." I motion him to lean over the counter and whisper, "You could afford a house like Mitchell Hall."

He smiles timidly. "Oh, I don't want to live in an expensive place. I hated growing up in New Jersey at my aunt and uncle's estate. I'd rather live a frugal life and use my inheritance for good...once they're declared dead, of course."

"Who was the blond-haired woman with Mayor Devine?"

"Alys Morgan, one of the new council members. She's an accountant by day."

"Right. The residents elected her and two others to replace Mayor Manley's cronies. I was elated when the town elected them along with Jessica Devine. The council will get so much done now. I haven't attended meetings since the elections, so I didn't recognize her. Did you know John Erickson, the other new member, is married to Audrey's best friend from grad school?"

Jeff's eyebrows lift. "No. I knew his wife's first name was Courtney, but I haven't met her. Are you sure it's the same woman?"

"Oh, yeah. She just passed you on the way out of the store. I'm surprised you didn't recognize her."

His eyes dart toward the door. "Now that you mention it, she looked familiar. But she appeared older. A far cry from the teenage demeanor she had in grad school."

"Do you think she knows what happened to Audrey?" I ask, biting my lip.

"How could she?" Jeff stuffs his hoodie behind the counter.

"None of the Bearsden Coven witches would have told her, but other covens were at the Delaware Pagan Conference."

"True. Did she say anything to you about her?"

"No. Nothing. I shouldn't have brought it up. Sorry."

"It's all right, Gwyn." He lowers his head. "We can't change the past. You can sweep it under the rug, but the history is still there."

"I wonder if the new councilman knows his wife is a witch? I understand Mayor Devine hasn't divulged the secrets of the Seelie Fae children and the portal in the Celestial Gardens to them."

"Probably not. It's my understanding they aren't *in the knowing*. Courtney must not be practicing witchcraft."

But I sensed her magic was flourishing. "She said she wasn't interested in returning to the coven. You may be right."

"It's been nice chatting, but I've procrastinated long enough. I need to help Shane price tag the new shipments before I take over for you at the cash register."

"Thank you for letting me leave early. Derek had to fill in for one of his trainers. Ronnie didn't want to attend her birthing class alone."

"I'm so excited for her. I hope to have a family one day, too."

"Is it too soon to ask if you're seeing anyone new?"

"You're such a mom, Gwyn, and thank you for asking. I wish my aunt had cared enough to poke her nose into my love life. I've been dating the new instructor in the Celtic Studies department."

"Oh. Dr. Lewis. That's inviting a built-in family. She has a two-year-old. Are you sure you're ready for that?"

"I am, but he's a handful. She's so worn out most of the time. I wish I could help her more, but we're taking it slow. Both of us are recovering from traumatic relationships."

That's for sure. When your last love turns out to be a Celtic vampirish ghoul, you're likely to approach the next relationship with iron gloves.

"Nothing wrong with taking it slow. I'd be in a different boat if I'd done that before." But I love the ship I sailed on.

"Give a shout if I lose track of time."

Jeff rushes to the back to help Shane while I ring up the DUB students' Halloween costumes. I'm happy my young boss is dating again, but is an older widow with a child the best choice?

Ronnie dances around the room, ringlets of crimson hair bouncing on her shoulders, and I rub her back with a tennis ball during pauses. I expected we'd be sitting on the floor, huffing and blowing.

"This is not what I was expecting," I say. "When I was pregnant with Tyler, I did breathing exercises while focusing on an object. Richard came with me reluctantly."

She frowns. "I imagine. Derek hated missing this class. He's so into it. But Jamal has a terrible fever, and Derek preferred not canceling the training sessions."

"I was so excited you asked me. This is fun."

The instructor signals us to dance around the room again and come to another pause. I roll the tennis ball up and down her back.

"Oh, yeah. Right there," Ronnie says, moaning. "It's almost as good as sex."

"Wish I could remember." I laugh and rub the ball deeply into her muscle. "All this pain will be worth it. Take it from an old mom."

"I know, and I can't wait." She exhales, and worry contorts her face. "Gwyn, did you have nightmares about being a terrible mother?"

"Of course. What new mom doesn't? I used to wake in the middle of the night sure I was going to screw him up."

Her signature cackle erupts. "I shouldn't stress over it then. Tyler turned out wonderful. He's become a powerful ancestral witch, too. The coven just approved his level three witch status. You must be so proud of him."

"I'm proud of everything Tyler's accomplished."

"You're a fabulous mother. I hope I'm half as successful as you."

We finish with the last exercise and pack up to leave, exiting into the cool October air. The wind has disappeared, thankfully. As we stroll down Main Street, I admire my friend's glowing, heart-shaped face dotted with freckles, her rounded belly. Only two months left before the baby witch arrives. What a blessing for her.

"Why don't we walk to the Celestial Gardens?" Ronnie asks. "I've not been there in a long time since everyone took turns covering my shifts with the Seelie Fae. They won't come out until way after dark, but I'd like to get a few more steps in today. My OB says I need it for circulation in my legs. Do you mind eating dinner late?"

"No, I can use the exercise, too. Between classes, finishing up the grimoire database, searching for a portal-closing spell, and now trying to search for lore that identifies the being in that vision I had in June, I'm lucky to get a decent night's sleep."

"I feel you. I can't seem to find a comfortable position. Derek has been the best. He sets up all my pillows for me to prop up my arms. Your schedule will burn you out, woman. It has to be affecting your sex life."

I shrug. "Can't do much about it for now. I have to finish my degree. I'm in the home stretch."

"True, but you don't have to spend every free moment with Seamus. You're playing with fire there. And you know it." She crinkles her brow.

"He may have feelings for me, but he hasn't acted on them. Nothing will ever happen. He knows I love Archie."

"Sure, but spending so much time with him doesn't help the situation."

"He's the Irish folklore expert. I don't have a choice."

She scowls at me. "You always have choices. The question is...are you making the right ones?"

"Holy crystals. I almost forgot. Guess who stopped by the store today?"

"Please, don't tax my sleep-deprived brain or my patience. Who?"

"Courtney Davies," I say with a blank stare.

My best friend gapes at me. "What the fuck?"

"Exactly my thoughts when I popped up from behind the counter. But she's married now. Her last name is Erickson."

"Wait. She's married to that young new council member? She had some nerve showing up at the store to talk to you. What did she want?"

"Yeah, they've been married for about a year. She was pleasant. Apologized for how she acted in the past. She seemed sincere."

"Sure, and I'm the queen of the Otherworld," she says, rubbing her back. "She could have grown up. Even a bad witch can redeem herself, but I need more proof than a single apology."

When we arrive at Mitchell Hall, the sun has dipped in the sky, casting a pink hue over the Celestial Gardens. It's serene and calming—just what the doctor ordered. A young woman in her 20s with dirty-blond hair pushes a baby in a stroller, stopping to snap pictures. She notices us and waves. Ronnie grins when the mother leans over to pamper her little one. My best friend will spoil her precious one by Yule, too.

We meander around the fairy water fountains and ornamental boxwood hedges protecting the roses of yellow, pink, red, and black. An earthy smell pervades the area, nearly masking the fragrance of the exquisite flowers. Rose and Alistair Mitchell would be proud of the refurbishment of their gardens. Although they wouldn't be too happy about us destroying their precious hawthorn tree.

I stare at the young plant in the right corner, recalling Ronnie's limp body hanging in the clutches of the Sluagh. The white strip of hair triggered by the trauma of the event snakes through her crimson curls. She slaps my arm.

"Why did you do that?"

"You know why," she says, squinting. "Don't beat yourself up every time you get a glimpse of that tree. Look at me. I'm healthy and having a baby." She rubs her belly, grinning.

I lay my hand on her tummy, and the future witch kicks back. "I'm so happy for you. Is Derek excited?"

"Are you kidding? He lays his head on his restless offspring every night. Talks to the peanut about all the plans he has. He has Wiggles scheduled through high school."

"I bet. He'll be a wonderful father. You found a good one, Ronnie."

"I sure did. That reminds me, he asked me to send a text when I got here. He's going to start dinner." After typing into her phone, she glances back at the young mother, who continues to take pictures with her cell, ignoring her baby in the stroller. "I wish she would leave. It's almost dark. I'd love to say hello to Shailagh and Aonghas."

"You actually miss them?" I ask.

"Yes, the Seelie Fae are mischievous, but they're so sweet."

"Please, don't develop any ideas about adopting them."

"No way," she says, cackling. "One baby witch will be plenty to keep me busy."

I check the time on my cell phone. It's almost 6:30 p.m. "You should get home. She's not leaving anytime soon, and you need to eat."

"Well, fuck," she says loudly. "I'll have to come back later."

The young mom whips her head around, scowling in disgust.

"You know...you may want to curb the F bomb usage in a couple of years. Kids repeat everything you say."

"Yeah. A lot's gonna change after this baby is born." She angles her head toward the woman and shouts, "But for now, let the fucks flow!"

I laugh out loud, and the young mother grimaces at me. Like she's so responsible—taking photos on the other side of the gardens while her baby sleeps unattended.

"Let's go," Ronnie says, yawning. "I don't know how I'm gonna stay awake long enough to eat."

"I'd say drink some of your death coffee, but that's probably not a good idea."

She grabs a lump pushing out the material of her maternity T-shirt. "The little gymnast doesn't lie still now. Coffee would send Wiggles into somersaults."

As we head toward the iron gate, my innards tighten, and an aura overcomes me, spreading throughout my body—all the way to my fingertips. It's not a hot flash, because I'm not sweating. Plus, I've not had one for a couple of months. I glance back at the hawthorn tree where the young mother stands, taking more pictures with her phone. When I turn around, I glimpse a faint movement at the mound.

I scan the back of the Celestial Gardens, darkening with the setting sun. The wind swirls, carrying a clump of dried leaves, and dumps them on the top of the grassy mound. I shiver from the sudden blast of chilly air and zip up my fleece jacket to my neck. The stroller with the woman's sleeping baby rests in front of the portal. Did Shailagh and Aonghas sneak through the opening? It's not dark enough yet for them to cross over. If they did, I'll have to share the rules with them again—not that they'll listen.

"What are you looking at?" Ronnie asks, stopping abruptly.

"Nothing," I say, rubbing my abdomen. "Must be the wind."

We continue on our way. We're almost through the gate when a pain pinches my stomach, as if someone closed a pair of pliers on my insides. I buckle over.

"Are you OK, Gwyn?" Ronnie asks, reaching for my shoulders.

"Help! Please, somebody, help me!" the young mother screams from behind.

Ronnie and I whirl around, our eyes scanning the garden for a malicious threat, but we only see the mother.

"I can't find Daniel. Where's my baby?!"

The distraught woman digs through the contents of the stroller, flipping through the layers of blankets, searching for her missing child. But he's gone. She drops to the ground, tears rolling from her red, puffy eyes.

"My baby! Who stole my baby?"

CHAPTER FOUR

A MOTHER'S REGRET

THE PAIN CLENCHING MY stomach subsides. Ronnie helps me up, and I call 911 as we rush to the devastated mother to console her, my heart pounding against my ribcage. She struggles to breathe as she clutches her baby's blankets against her. My best friend embraces the woman, attempting to calm her down.

"What's your name?" I ask, rubbing her arm.

"Jenny," she replies between gasps.

"OK, Jenny," I say. "I'm Gwyn, and this is Ronnie. Did you see anyone jump over the fence?"

She glances at the eight-foot structure, trembling. "I only saw spinning leaves blowing over the stroller. I was over there near the hawthorn tree." She gestures toward the right corner of the gardens. "This is all my fault. I left my baby alone. Now someone stole my precious Daniel. My husband will hate me for this." She sobs uncontrollably, and I grasp her hand.

"Don't blame yourself, Jenny," Ronnie says, stroking her hair. "We didn't notice anyone in here either. There are wicked people in this world." And in the Otherworld. "Your husband won't blame you."

"The police will be here soon. Don't move from this spot. I need to talk to my friend for a minute." I motion to Ronnie to step away, and I speak to her in a low voice. "Stay with her. I'm gonna look around. Feel out the area."

"It's so dark now, and the lamppost near the house only lights the exit. Be careful," my friend says. "I'll call Derek and Archie."

"Yeah. They must be wondering where we are."

As I walk to the aperture in the mound, I scratch my head. Were the pranksters so curious about the baby they plucked it from the stroller? I lift my hand to examine the area for clues. An amber glow seeps from my fingers, and I shake it out quickly. No sense of the supernatural here. I glance back quickly to make sure the Unremarkable mom missed my magic display. *Phew.* She's staring at the grass beneath her. I scan the right side of the gardens for signs of unusual activity, but the waning moon barely provides enough illumination through the cloud cover to see anything.

As I amble around the back of the mound, a twinge returns to my gut. Is this my intuition trying to send a signal? That's ridiculous. It has to be gas. I grunt as my gaze falls upon the fence. Could someone have scaled the concrete block and snatched her son? But how? Wouldn't we have heard the baby cry? Could the criminal have climbed back over with an infant in their hands?

Sirens blare, signaling the Bearsden Police have arrived. I dart to the iron gate to meet them. After exiting their patrol car, which they parked under a lamppost, street cops Braddock Wilson and Quinn O'Connor run toward me. They're Bearsden's Mutt and Jeff team, except Quinn is a woman. A stocky man in a dark blazer, white shirt, and khaki pants exits a sedan and follows them. I recognize the balding, neckless detective with the Cro-Magnan-like brow ridge. Jack Schmidt approaches us. My stomach twists into knots.

Officer O'Connor addresses me. "Ms. Crowther, were you the person who called 911?"

"Yeah. There's a woman named Jenny back there. Young mom. We were on the way out when we heard her scream. Her baby is missing."

"We?" Officer Wilson asks in his deep voice. "There was someone else with you?"

Detective Schmidt catches up. "I didn't expect you to be here, Ms. Crowther. I'd like to know who was with you as well."

"My friend Ronnie Baldwin. She's consoling the mother," I reply, gesturing to them near the mound.

Detective Schmidt walks toward the lump of dirt with a purpose in his step, and we follow him. All three of them pull out flashlights and turn them on, sending beams of white light scattering in the dark.

"O'Connor. Wilson. Scour the area for footprints. I called for a forensic team, but it may take a while for them to arrive." Jack approaches Jenny, who is still sobbing. He squats in front of her. "Hello, Jenny. Your baby is missing?"

She pants between words. "Yes...someone stole my Daniel."

"How old is your son and can you describe his features?" Jack asks, pulling out his writing pad.

"He's ten months. Has a pudgy face and long, blond hair—almost white. It's so pretty, we haven't cut it. He has blue eyes like an angel's."

While the detective takes notes, Ronnie continues to caress Jenny's back with one hand and rubs her pregnant belly nervously with the other. Officers O'Connor and Wilson roam around the garden, pointing their flashlights toward the ground. They move to the rear of the mound and stride over to the concrete fence.

A man with light-brown hair of medium stature rushes into the garden. "Jenny! Jenny, where are you?"

"I'm here, Dan!" she yells through her whimpering.

Dan darts to his wife and squats to hug her. "What happened?"

"I'm so sorry, Danny," she replies. "It's all my fault."

He strokes her wet cheeks. "I'm sure it isn't."

"You're Jenny's husband?" Jack asks.

"Yes. Dan Hansen. You are?"

"Detective Schmidt of the Bearsden Police Department. Your wife was about to tell us what happened." He takes out his cell. "Do I have your permission to record you, Mrs. Hansen?"

"Yeah. I suppose it's all right," she replies.

The detective fiddles with his phone in the dark while Dan embraces Jenny. Wilson and O'Connor meet with the forensic team that's finally arrived. Ronnie and I shift a few steps to give the detective and the parents space, but for damn sure, we're going to listen.

Jack Schmidt places his cell near the crying mom. "Mrs. Hansen, tell me in your own words what happened."

"I was taking pictures with my phone," she says, whimpering. "I'm an amateur photographer. There wasn't anyone in here. My Daniel is such a good baby. So quiet and happy. He fell asleep, so I didn't want to move the stroller. I swear I did not walk too far from him." She peers up at Ronnie and me. "Then these two women came in and were wandering around. They were being really loud and profane. I worried they would wake Daniel."

My best friend and I lock eyes and shrug. For fuck's sake, we're outside, lady.

"I was so happy when I saw them moving toward the exit. After I clicked a few more photos of the hawthorn tree, I went back to the stroller." Tears roll down her cheeks again. "I pulled back the blankets, and he was gone. Someone snuck in here and kidnapped my Daniel. I'm so sorry, Danny."

Dan Hansen presses his forehead against hers, his eyes welling up with tears. "It's not your fault, Jenny." He glares at Detective Schmidt. "What's being done about this? Why are you just standing here?"

"Mr. Hansen, I shared the description of your son and the circumstances. They sent the AMBER alert. Unfortunately, we don't have much to go on yet. But the local media has been notified."

Detective Schmidt points at the forensic team, who are setting up portable lights to investigate. "My guys are examining the area for clues now."

I don't dare mention I did that myself. Jack would rip into me for disturbing evidence.

He continues his inquiry. "Is there anyone you can think of who might have done this? An acquaintance who desperately wanted a child and couldn't have one of their own? Someone who had malevolent feelings toward you? A stranger who expressed too much interest?"

Both Dan and Jenny search the sky for answers, their eyes roaming in the dark. But the explanation of their son's disappearance hides amidst the secrets of the Celestial Gardens. They say nothing.

"Mrs. Hansen, did you notice anything unusual?" Detective Schmidt asks in a calm voice. "Even the smallest thing could help us figure this out."

Jenny shakes her head and sobs against her husband's chest. Jack motions to Ronnie and me to meet him a few steps away from the grief-stricken parents.

"Ladies, what can you tell me?" he asks. "As I told Mrs. Hansen, the littlest thing could be the clue that identifies the kidnapper. Do you mind if I record your statements?"

Ronnie and I reply in unison. "No. That's fine."

"Great," he replies. "Identify yourself by name before you answer."

"My name is Veronica Baldwin. I can't add anything to what Jenny told you," Ronnie says, protecting her belly with a hand. "Gwyn and I headed out of the gardens while she was snapping pics of the hawthorn tree."

"Same here. Oh, I'm sorry. My name is Gwynedd Crowther. We were almost through the gate when Jenny started screaming that her baby was missing. I called 911, and we rushed back to her. It happened so quickly." I can't tell him about my genuine concern—that the Seelie Fae children may have snatched Daniel.

Jack stops the recording and shoves his cell phone into his pocket. After taking down our contact information, he closes the notepad and presses his lips together.

"Well, that's it for now. I appreciate your cooperation." He hands each of us a card. "Should you remember anything else later, please contact me. Often, insignificant memories find their way to the surface. Witnessing a criminal act is overwhelming. The adrenalin rushes through your body, and while you may think more clearly, it could impair your retrieval as well, depending on the person. I suggest you go home. We'll take care of the Hansens."

We exit the Celestial Gardens as other Bearsden Police officers arrive to tape off the property. Archie and Derek are waiting on the paver walkway where a crowd has formed. Ronnie and I grab their hands and drag them away from the nosy townies.

"How are the parents faring?" Archie asks.

I frown. "They're devastated, of course. Tyler got away from me once in a department store, and I freaked out. He was hiding in the pants rack."

Derek hugs Ronnie. "I can't even imagine. How awful. Are you OK, babe?"

"Yeah," she replies, laying a hand on her baby bump. "My stomach is full of knots."

Her boyfriend kisses her forehead. "I understand you're worried about the recent kidnappings in Pennsylvania. I hope this doesn't mean those criminals have moved into Delaware."

"Let's not jump to conclusions," Archie says. "Let the police complete their investigation. If they determine this case is similar, they will notify the FBI."

My best friend yawns, her mouth opening as wide as a baboon's. "Take me home, babe. I'm sleepy, and I haven't even eaten dinner."

"Great idea," he says. "We'll talk to you later."

Derek and Ronnie head toward the café to pick up her car. Archie and I stroll back to his house on Duncan Street through the Green, lit by the hazy glow of the lampposts. He grasps my hand.

"You saw no one else in the gardens?" he asks.

"No. Only the mother, Jenny Hansen. I was worried Shailagh and Aonghas crossed over and took the baby to the Otherworld to play. I didn't sense any magic residue in the portal area. When I investigated behind the mound, a sharp pain pinched my insides."

"Did you observe the use of witchcraft there?"

I chuckle. "Nah. It was gas. I started putting collagen protein in my morning tea. It's caused bloating."

"Most likely, the baby kidnapping ring has expanded its radius. The media have named them the Baby Nabbers."

I grimace. "That's awful. I didn't tell you about the other shocker of my day. Courtney Davies stopped by the store. She moved away for a while, but she's back. John Erickson, the new young council member, is her husband."

"Husband? Well, I'm glad she found happiness. You don't seem upset about it."

"No. She apologized, and I believe her. I hope she doesn't ask to join the coven again, though."

"I imagine the Fellowship would not be amenable to the prospect. Many still speak of the harm she did at the Winter Solstice Celebration."

As we approach the area where the red paver paths intersect, a woman of medium height with fair skin and mocha-brown hair dashes across the grass, her arms full of hardback books. When she reaches the walkway, she stumbles, and they take flight.

"That's Dr. Lewis," Archie says.

He darts to her, leaving me in the dust. When I catch up to them, huffing, he's helping her pick up the scattered books. The young instructor appears flustered, scrambling on the ground to collect them into a pile.

"Thank you, Dr. Cockburn," Dr. Lewis says. "I tripped on one of the pavers. I hope the references aren't damaged, because I can't afford to replace them."

Archie smiles warmly. "Don't worry about it, Ashley. If any of them are damaged, I'll tell the library it was my fault. They won't mess with me. I was the prior chair."

She brushes leaves and dirt off her long sweater and pants as she stands. "You don't have to do that. I shouldn't have run with my arms full. It's just that I'm so late. The babysitter expected me an hour ago. I lost track of the time."

"You have a massive pile there. Can we help you carry this load of books home?" I ask.

"Oh, I can't bother you," she replies, struggling to contain the stack in her arms. "I'll be fine."

"Ashley, this is my girlfriend, Gwynedd Crowther," Archie says.

"Nice to meet you. A Welsh American."

"Yes. Actually, first generation," I say. "My parents moved here from Wales back in the '60s."

"That's so cool. Do you spell your name with two Ds?" she asks.

"Yeah, and I hate it," I say, laughing.

She chuckles. "Well, I have to go. Thank you again, Dr. Cockburn."

Archie straightens the books in her pile. "May you have a wonderful evening, Dr. Lewis."

"Great to meet you," I say. "I'd love to chat sometime about all things Welsh."

"I'd like that. Good night to you both."

Ashley rushes up the paver walkway toward downtown.

"Does she live in an apartment on Main Street?" I ask.

"Aye." Archie shoves his hands in his pockets. "She lives in a flat over Roots of the Earth."

"Holy crystals. In Nick's old apartment?"

"Aye. You realize the owner has to rent to others, no?"

"Sure. But a Tuatha Dé fairy and a nefarious witch lived there. Who knows what kind of magic residue is floating around in that apartment?"

"True. But she's an Unremarkable. I doubt she'll sense it." He squints at me. "Don't think I didn't catch what you were doing with her."

"What?" I avert my eyes and quash a smile. "I promise I won't bug her a lot about the Welsh folklore. She's obviously tapped out."

Archie exhales. "All right. I remembered I have to pick up a reference I requested through the interlibrary loan system." He inches closer to me. "I miss you. Please find time to spend one night at my house this week."

"I'll try. Thursday after the Fellowship meeting?" I wrap my arms around his torso and slide a hand over his sore butt. "How's your bum?"

He grimaces. "Not good, but I want you to stay over, anyway." He bends down to kiss me. "Tell Leslie I'll see her on Monday."

"I will. Goodnight, honey."

"Sleep well, my love."

I kick off my sneakers in the mudroom and walk to the living room. Dr. Hughes is reading a book on the legends of King Arthur, sitting in the chair by the fireplace with a throw blanket draped across her legs. Mr. Yeats is curled at her feet, purring.

"Hello, Leslie." I squat and stroke the familiar's furry head. "Good evening, Mr. Yeats."

"I heard several sirens earlier. Did you notice where the police cars were headed?"

"Oh, yeah," I reply, continuing to pet her familiar. "The Celestial Gardens. Ronnie and I went for a walk in there, and a young mom was taking pictures of the plants. Her ten-month-old boy was with her in a stroller, but she was wandering around with her phone, clicking away. As we were walking out, she screamed so loud I nearly toppled over. Someone kidnapped her baby."

The familiar pops up, transitioning into his human form and knocking me on my ass. "A kidnapping! How despicable!"

"Ouch, Mr. Yeats," I say, rubbing my butt. "Be careful where you transition."

He grabs my arms and helps me stand. "I apologize, Ms. Crowther. I didn't mean to hurt you."

"Oh, it's OK," I reply. "I have a permanent callus on my tailbone."

Leslie raises her chin. "Did you observe anyone entering the gardens?"

"No. The lowlife must have jumped over the fence and took him."

"That fence is quite high. How could someone manage that?" the Elder asks.

Mr. Yeats adjusts his spectacles. "The criminal would have had a plan. That's how."

"Precisely," I say. "Whoever the criminals were, they were quiet."

Leslie closes her book. "Could the Seelie Fae be responsible? We can't discount them. The infant might have enticed them. Nothing malicious intended."

"Archie thinks it's the Baby Nabbers from Pennsylvania. PA is only thirty minutes away, but to be sure, I'm going to sneak in there late tomorrow. No way I'll get to visit them tonight. The police will investigate into the morning hours."

Mr. Yeats crosses his arms. "Excuse me for doubting your summation, but did you scrutinize the area for...you know?"

"Magic residue?" I ask, blinking. "Yes. I sensed no residuals at the front of the mound. I can't imagine Shailagh and Aonghas took the baby, but I'll question them. As I walked around the rear of it, a strange feeling came over me, a pinching in my gut. But I think it was gas."

Mr. Yeats snickers as he fluffs his tie. A slight smile surfaces on Leslie's mouth.

"Go ahead. Laugh at me," I say, frowning. "I'm still learning how to differentiate between the supernatural and what's related to an Unremarkable status. New skills emerge daily."

"I'll be in the magic room preparing for the night," the familiar says, ambling into the hallway. "May your slumber be restful."

"Goodnight, Mr. Yeats." Leslie places the throw on the arm of the chair and stands, her spindly body towering over me. "Most likely, Archie's assessment is correct. Not everything evil in this world is committed at the hands of a supernatural being. Wicked humans exist as well."

"Exactly." My stomach growls, and I rub it. "It's so late. I better eat something and get ready for bed."

"I left a plate of vegetable lasagna in the fridge. Please, partake. The leftovers will go bad. Your mother's recipe."

"Thank you," I say, grinning. "As tired as I am, I think I will. FYI, Courtney Davies has returned to Bearsden. I thought you should know. She stopped at Mystic Sage to make amends."

"I am aware. I recognized her at the last city council meeting when she approached John Erickson. The Fellowship will be alerted at the next meeting at Agnes's house. Elijah told our allies about the Dearg Due, and they weren't pleased with the news, especially Mayor Devine. She asked to meet at the farm to avoid suspicion."

I nod, grinning. "I bet Agnes was NOT in agreement."

"Indeed," she replies, a faint smile gracing her face. "No matter. We must humor our allies. They have become impatient with our failure to close the portal to the Otherworld."

"Don't remind me." I rub my temples. "They have every reason to stress over the opening in the mound."

"Precisely," Leslie replies. "We must find a spell."

"For sure. Forget dinner. I'm going to bed." I shuffle toward my bedroom but stop. "Leslie, did you ever notice anything unusual about Courtney's magic when she was a neophyte in the coven?"

"Yes. Her acquisition of skills moved at a sluggish pace. Almost purposefully. Why do you ask?"

"Just curious. Goodnight."

"To you as well, Gwynedd."

While I lie in bed, thoughts spin in my head. How many other creatures could have crossed over we aren't aware of? I already know a gray-skinned giant with one good eye is coming, and possibly Nuada's family. What else?

CHAPTER FIVE

OPPORTUNITY KNOCKS

SUNDAY MORNING, I WAKE to the pitter-patter of rain against the windowpanes. The room is dark as a dungeon. I'm not sure it's time to get up, because I woke up several times to the memory of Jenny Hansen's screams. As I stare through the dingy glass at the gloomy skies, my heart races. I can't imagine how she and her husband are coping with the kidnapping of their baby. A notification sounds from my phone.

A breaking news article in my feed shares a few details of the Hansen's "missing" son. Currently, they have no suspects and few clues to go on. They haven't received a ransom note. For fuck's sake. Someone took him. Do they think he jumped out of the stroller and walked away? Technically, I guess he could have. He is almost a year old. No way. He was asleep and strapped in. My phone rings with the tune *Don't Stop Believin'*. Ronnie's name appears on the screen.

I swipe the green icon on my phone. "Good morning, Momma. How did you sleep last night?"

"Terrible. I'm not a mom yet," Ronnie replies, a breathy sigh filling my ear. "I don't even know that woman, but I tossed and turned all night thinking about Jenny and her husband. They didn't sleep either, I bet."

"You only have two months left. Close enough. I woke up all night, too. Jenny Hansen's wails invaded my dreams all night. Did you read the article online about the kidnapping? Well, missing baby."

"Yeah. They have to list him as missing because they don't know what happened. But do the police think a baby could have pulled his strap off and wandered away? Climbed an eight-foot concrete wall?"

"Most likely, they are attempting to keep the FBI from swooping in and taking over their case. Arrogance on their part."

"Well, fuck them. They're wasting time. Jack Schmidt seemed more competent than the average Bearsden detective."

"Hmph. I don't know about that. He didn't figure out I eliminated Nick Evans."

Silence fills the next few seconds before Ronnie replies. "Are you being sarcastic? I don't know whether to laugh or be concerned with your comment."

"Hmph. A little," I say. "Gotta live with what happened."

"I'm glad you moved on from that experience. It could have eaten you from the inside until nothing but shredded flesh remained."

I snort. "Thank you so much for that vivid description."

She cackles into the phone. "You're welcome. What are you doing today?"

"I'm working a few hours this afternoon and evening, then I'm stopping by the Celestial Gardens to talk to Shailagh and Aonghas."

"Oh. So, you think they might have snatched baby Daniel?"

"Nah. But I should ask to make sure. They could have seen the Unremarkables who kidnapped the infant. Who knows how often they spy on us? They could have been hiding."

"Good idea. I feel so responsible. We were right there and didn't notice anyone else in the gardens. Shouldn't we have?"

I recall the pinching in my gut. Maybe it wasn't gas? "I don't know. Those criminals are smart. They have a system in place. But I'm right there with you. It tugs at my heart to watch the Hansens go through this."

"Well, try to have a good day, Gwyn. I don't want to venture out in this weather, but I have a birthing class."

"You, too. Try not to let the dreary day drag you down the rabbit hole of guilt."

"I won't. Talk to you later."

"Bye." I swipe the red circle and tap my fingernails on the glass screen protector.

Shailagh and Aonghas, if you took that baby, we're going to have a little chat about stealing humans.

By the time I arrive at Mystic Sage, my socks and sneakers are soggy. I close my umbrella and rain droplets collect on the floor. My rubber soles squeak with every step as I approach the counter. The aroma of cinnamon and spice permeates the store. Shane must have burned incense. While I wait for Jeff to finish ringing up a customer, my coat drips water into a tiny puddle at my feet. He hands a paper bag to the customer.

"Thank you for shopping at Mystic Sage. Happy Halloween." As the shopper exits the store, Jeff laughs at me. "Did you go for a swim?"

"Very. Funny," I say, removing my raincoat. "My socks and sneakers soaked up the rain like sponges, and I don't have extra shoes with me."

"I'm sorry. I shouldn't have laughed. Give me your jacket, and I'll hang it in the back. There are towels in the bathroom."

"Thanks," I say, handing him my drenched coat. "I wish I had shoes to change into."

"Wet socks suck. I'll be right back."

Jeff dashes to the back of the store, and I stash my purse and backpack under the counter. I sit on the stool and remove my sneakers and socks. I can deal with soaked shoes, but the socks have to go. My boss returns with a hand towel and a box marked with an S.

"Thanks," I say, drying my feet. "What's in your hands?"

He grins and wiggles his eyebrows. "The solution for your shoe dilemma."

Jeff opens the flaps and pulls back the purple tissue paper, exposing unisex zombie slippers. Pointy white teeth border a gaping mouth where you insert your foot.

"You're not seriously suggesting I wear these to work in, are you? Plus, you couldn't sell these slippers after I've worn them all day."

"Consider them your bonus for the week."

"Gee. I don't know what to say?" I stare at the zombie face, one of its eyes popping out. "Thanks?"

He chuckles. "You're welcome. Now put on your slippers and get to work. No one will see them behind the counter, anyway."

I slip my toes into the mouths of the walking dead heads and stand up. "Wow. They're comfy."

"I have a huge shipment of them in the back. They arrived late. I need to get them tagged and on display near the clothing."

"With this heavy rainfall, we won't have many shoppers today. Bring a few up when you've priced them, and I'll set up the display. If anyone comes into the store while I'm arranging them on the shelf, I'll just say I'm modeling."

He laughs. "Sounds like a plan. By the way, I told Shane to stay home today. He's been spending time with a new lady friend, and I figured we could handle the store."

"A lady friend? Please, tell me more," I say, grinning.

"He can tell you himself. Besides, I don't even know her name."

I log in to the cash register. "Speaking of lady friends, I met Ashley Lewis last night. She's sweet, Jeff. A little anxious, but pleasant. She was in a rush to get home so her babysitter could leave."

"Yeah, she called me after she arrived. The babysitter was really pissed. A grad student watches him. Her son, Aidan, misbehaved the entire afternoon and evening. Threw his toys. Dumped his dinner on the floor. She quit. Ashley cried. She doesn't know what to do."

Well, well. But maybe I do? "You know what? I'm booked up this semester, but I could watch her son a few times. I only have a couple of classes because I'm working on my capstone project."

"Wow, Gwyn. That's lit. Thanks so much. I'll tell her."

"You know me...always a mom." And it's a convenient opportunity to ask her about Welsh folklore without robbing her of time she doesn't have to spare.

Jeff cocks his head. "You were walking back late. Did you see the cops gathered at Mitchell Hall? I read the article about the kidnapped baby this morning."

"Yeah. Sadly, Ronnie Baldwin and I were there. Someone scooped up that infant about the time we were exiting the gardens. The mother was taking pictures on the other side."

He shakes his head. "That's so sad. They must suspect the Baby Nabbers ring got him."

"That's what Archie thinks. I've read they can sneak in and snatch a kid in broad daylight. No one can identify them. They prey on mothers feeling safe in a closed environment or in the cover of packed city sidewalks. They must have had a rope ladder or something to get over the concrete wall in the back. It was dark."

"I know. Ashley has been stressing over it. She worries about someone taking off with her kid all the time. I understand the worry about this recent kidnapping, but she's talked about it since I met her."

"She's a single mom. It has to be difficult. At least I'm able to help."

"I appreciate it, Gwyn. Call me if you need me. I'll get these Halloween slippers tagged and bring a load of them to the front." He ambles through the doorway.

For the rest of the afternoon, I meander around the store, dusting and straightening up the shelves, stopping once to add black bat and gray shark slippers to the display shelf. Between the occasional customer, Jeff and I stock the shelves and finish up for the evening. My socks and sneakers are still damp by closing time, but I can't walk home wearing the walking dead on my feet. At six sharp, he locks up, and we leave. I pull on the hood of my raincoat, pop open my umbrella, and make my way to Mitchell Hall.

The rain has lightened to a steady drizzle, but my damp feet are still chilly. I want to sneak into the Celestial Gardens to chat with the Seelie Fae and get home to my warm flannel sheets. As I approach the mansion, I see a woman standing there, statue-like, the rain dripping from the canopy of her umbrella. The wind blows her long, blond hair all over. She'll be combing the knots out of it all night. As I move closer, I realize she hasn't moved an inch. How will I slip past her?

When I reach the front of Mitchell Hall, I recognize her face under the filtered light of the lamppost. It's the new council member, Alys Morgan, who was chatting with the Mayor Devine the other day. If I strike up a conversation, maybe it will prompt her to leave.

"Hello," I say. "The weather is so nasty, isn't it?"

She turns her head toward me, a blank, emotionless expression on her face. "Yes. It's dismal."

"Aren't you Alys Morgan, one of the new council members?"

No response. She stares blankly at the yellow tape blocking the entrance to the Celestial Gardens.

"My name is Gwynedd Crowther. I work part time at Mystic Sage. You've been standing here for quite a while, Ms. Morgan. Are you OK?"

She hesitates, but answers finally. "Yes...and yes." She continues to fixate on the iron gate. "I sympathize with the mother whose child was abducted last night. I don't have children of my own, but I imagine she's hurting. As a member of the city council, I think it's my responsibility to ensure this doesn't happen again in Bearsden."

"I'm glad to hear you want to address this, but isn't it best if the Bearsden PD handles the situation?"

"Pfft. As if they could ever solve any crime in this town."

Way to support the men in blue, lady. But I said the same thing about Jack Schmidt. Alys takes a deep breath and looks away briefly, returning a steely gaze to me. Well, excuse me for having an opinion.

"I better get home," she says. "It was a pleasure to meet a constituent of the town. I hope you'll attend the council meetings."

"Yes, I go sometimes. This is my last year of grad school, so I've been too busy."

"Enjoy the remainder of your evening." Alys walks briskly toward the Raven Pub. I wait until she turns north at the corner.

She's an odd one. What made her want to be the savior of our town if she has no kids? Did she lose a child to kidnapping or murder? Or was she unable to have children of her own? But it's hard to argue with a councilwoman with such conviction regarding our precious ones. Even if she disses our local police.

I check the surrounding area before darting to the gate and pushing under the crime scene tape. The ground is like a sponge from the rainfall, and I sink into the grass as I tiptoe to the mound.

"Shailagh? Aonghas? Come out. I need to talk to you."

The rainfall taps on my umbrella's canopy while I wait for them to appear. The portal lights up, and the Seelie Fae emerge. Their mint-green eyes sparkle through the drizzle as their golden-blond strands skip on a flurry of air.

"Aunt Gwyn, you came on a rainy day. Did you come to splash in the puddles with us?"

I bend down to chat with them. "No. I can't stay. Something bad happened last night. A mother was in here with her baby, and he disappeared. You didn't take the little human from the stroller to play, did you? I won't be mad. But you need to bring him back."

Shailagh and Aonghas trade glances. "No, Aunt Gwyn. Why would we take a human baby? He can't play."

I scan the ground near the fence. The heavy rain has removed any evidence of footprints. I hope the forensic team found them last night. Then I remember. I walked there, too.

"Did either of you see the human who took the baby?"

"No," Shailagh says. "We didn't cross over last night because humans were playing in here with big lights."

"Right. But they weren't playing. They were investigating—looking for clues. I'm wet from the rain and need to go home and change my clothes. I'll come back to play when the weather improves."

"Bye, Aunt Gwyn." They cross through the portal.

As I stand, an aura overcomes me, and I feel a tug in my abdomen in the same spot as before. If this is my witch's intuition trying to send me signals again, it's failing miserably, because it's only giving me gas.

I tiptoe out of the gardens and head for home, thinking about Dr. Ashley Lewis and her toddler. It's been a long time since I babysat such a small child. The inexperienced grad student must have exaggerated. How bad could Aidan be?

CHAPTER SIX

A COVEN'S PLEDGE

MR. YEATS PURRS IN the corner chair of Leslie's magic room. I set the photo of my parents, Rhys and Lowri, on the table. Tyler throws his car fob in the air, catching it as it falls. After repeating this annoying activity several times, I snatch the key midway through one of its tumbles.

"Hey," he says. "Why did you do that?"

"You're making me nervous." I hand it back to him, admiring his coloring—the mirror image of me. "Are you scared to talk with Nain and Taid? You never asked before. I figured you were uncomfortable with it."

"I was." My son shoves the fob into his pocket. "I mean, they're dead."

I laugh while I prepare to burn the mugwort and star anise—double the power for divination. "They are, but your grandparents won't present as ghosts as you'd expect from books and TV shows. You'll see. It's purely magical." I motion for him to stand next to me. "Are you ready?"

Tyler nods. "Let's go for it."

The odor of smoldering mugwort and star anise fills the room. I raise my hand, chanting, and amber magic seeps from my fingertips. When I summon my parents, the outlines of their faces turn golden and protrude from the photo.

Tyler's eyes widen. "Whoa. That's lit."

"You ain't seen nothing yet," I say, intensifying my witch energy.

Their images expand until they're full sized, glittering inches from Tyler's face. He gulps, shocked into silence as he stares at them. Rhys and Lowri Crowther beam at their grandson. A golden tear rolls down my mother's shimmering cheek.

"My grandson is a grown man," she says. "I'm so happy you're here, Tyler."

"Nain, don't cry. I'm ecstatic we're able to talk. I wish I'd done it sooner."

My dad's dazzling smile appears. "It is a glorious day to meet with you again. How are you doing, grandson?"

Tyler grins. "I'm good, Taid. And you? Wait. That was a dumb question."

We all crack up and continue to chat as if they've never been gone, despite the whole golden head presentation. They ask their grandson about his girlfriend, Zoe Wu, and he becomes loquacious regarding his love. I lean against the table and listen while he catches them up on his work, magic skill level, and personal life. My parents deserve the uninterrupted time with him. Mr. Yeats remains in his chimera cat presentation, his tail swaying back and forth. When there is a lull in the conversation, I interject.

"This was great. We should do another family conference soon."

Tyler glances at his cell phone. "I have to get back to work, but I'm down for another meetup."

"Wonderful," Mom says. "We look forward to talking to you again. It's time for your mother to teach you how to conference with your ancestors. Then we could meet without her."

My mouth falls open. "Uh...we'll chat about that later." Much later, because I barely have a handle on this skill myself. Tyler only achieved a level three status recently.

I hug my son. "I'll see you tomorrow night at Agnes's, dear."

"Bye, Nain. Bye, Taid." Tyler waves as he exits the magic room.

"That went splendidly," Mom says, smiling. "I was so worried Tyler would run out screaming."

"I knew he wouldn't. He asked to conference with you. He was ready."

"You should be proud, Gwynedd," Dad replies, his image wavering. "He is a wonderful young man...and witch."

It's the first time one of them has praised me for bringing him into our world of witchcraft. I'm surprised at the effect it has on me. I should stop holding a grudge against them for raising me as an Unremarkable.

"Did either of you expand your witch's intuition when you were young? Try to increase its reach or clarity?"

"I never had any, Gwyn," Dad replies. "But your mother did. The ancestral history."

"Yes, mine was developing well, but then we withdrew from magic. It vanished over the years until the twinges disappeared completely. Occasionally, I'd sense you were in danger. But that could have been a mother's instinct. Even Unremarkables experience that. Why do you ask?"

"My intuition seems to have changed a little. Actually, I don't know if it is a sixth sense. I may just be having GI issues."

She grimaces. "What do you mean?"

"There's been a kidnapping in town. A crime ring from Pennsylvania called the Baby Nabbers appears to have moved into New Castle County. They swiped an infant right from under his mother's nose. Well, she wasn't near the stroller, because she was taking pictures of plants. Ronnie and I were leaving the gardens when it happened, so we didn't witness it."

"How dreadful," Dad says, his brow furrowing. "I hope they discover the scoundrels."

Mom shakes her head. "The mother must blame herself. But she shouldn't. There was no reason to think her baby wasn't safe in an enclosed garden. But what does the kidnapping have to do with your witch's intuition?"

"On the way out, I experienced a sharp pain inside, like someone was pinching me with needle nose pliers. Within a millisecond, the mother screamed her baby was missing. I experienced a lighter twinge when I scouted out the area behind the mound." My shoulders fall. "Oh, hell. It wasn't intuition—just gas."

My parents laugh at my expense, their golden images fading in and out. When they've calmed down, Mom addresses my concerns.

"Dear Gwynedd. I am at a loss to help you with this. As a mother, you will experience greater-than-normal empathy. Those feelings may multiply being an ancestral witch. I wish I could guide you. Have you asked your mentor, Agnes Pritchard?"

I burst out laughing, then snort. "Because she is the epitome of empathy? Or a mother's intuition?"

Mom's face sparkles as she chuckles. "Point taken. Agnes was never a conventional witch, but she was talented. Seek her advice."

"Sure. I'll try to schedule another conference in a week or two. I know you want to talk with Tyler again, but between school and all my other commitments, I may run out of time."

"This question may cause you stress, but I need to ask." Dad's golden hue intensifies. "Have you had any success with the discovery of the monster in your visions?"

"No. But I'm working on it with Dr. Seamus Duffy. Archie continues to delve into other areas of lore, too." I refrain from mentioning Ashley Lewis because I don't even know if she'll have time to help me.

"We look forward to your next call," Mom says. "Please tell Ronnie we wish her well with the remainder of her pregnancy."

"I will. She's eager to meet her little one."

"Every mother's desire intensifies the closer she gets to the end. Until our future conference, be well, Gwynedd," my mom says.

"Thanks, Mom and Dad. I love you."

"We love you, too, Gwyn." Dad's image fades.

Mr. Yeats jumps off the chair and transforms into his human persona, wiping a tear from under his spectacles. "I was so touched by your parents meeting your son. What a heartwarming family reunion. Thank you for allowing me to observe the interactions."

"Thank you for being here in case Tyler freaked out. I would have welcomed your help."

He straightens his vest. "I appreciate the confidence you have in me."

"I do, Mr. Yeats. You have proven yourself. You're not nearly as irritating as you used to be."

He smiles as he fluffs his bowtie, but the corners of his mouth fall flat.

Thursday evening, I rush from my late class to my metallic-blue Prius, zipping up my hoodie as I go. The air is chilly despite the bright sunshine that brought warm temps earlier in the day. But the sky is clear. Stars twinkle across the indigo canvas above as the crescent moon lights their display.

I zip along Manor Road to Agnes's farmhouse where the Fellowship is having their meeting. As I pull up, my high beams illuminate the new white siding and black shutters. The exterior of the hedge witch's home has a fresh appearance after the completed renovations—an amazing transformation from its prior state. The dingy clapboard was rotting away.

I park and discover Archie waiting for me on her newly painted front porch, an exterior sconce spotlighting his gorgeous face. When I reach the top step, he kisses me. I inhale the scent of his woodsy cologne and a calm sets in.

"Mmm. I miss the aroma of your aftershave. You trimmed your goatee, too."

"For later, my love," he says, winking. "I worried you wouldn't make it on time. Everyone is here. Elijah and Jessica Devine just walked into the meeting. It will be interesting to hear what she has to say."

"Nothing great, I'm sure. The allies on the council have lost their patience. If it weren't for Elijah, she wouldn't have waited this long to address us."

We enter the foyer to find Agnes lecturing the young witches about removing their shoes. Her salt and pepper hair cuts across her pale, wrinkled face, casting shadows in the glow of the brand-new light fixture overhead. I look around appreciatively—the coven and our Unremarkable friends converted her outdated home into a modern showcase. Who would think the hedge witch would give a shit?

"I shouldn't have to remind you every fucking time. You take off your fucking shoes at the door. Don't you see the shoe rack?"

Skye bends over to untie her sneakers. "Sorry, Agnes. It's hard to get used to. You never cared before."

"We forgot," Spence says. "So, shoot us with a magic bolt."

She scowls at him as she rubs her back. "Don't tempt me."

"I took mine off the first time I entered." Tanner points to his feet. "But that's because I did most of the refinishing on the floors. I care about my work."

Spence moves his lips silently, playfully mocking his partner. "You're just trying to stay on her good side. It's not like I didn't help. I did a lot of painting."

"Well, I'll give you that," the hedge witch says, rolling her pale-gray eyes.

Tyler glares at her. "We all did, Agnes. You should be more appreciative of the labor we put in. Hi, Mom. Hi, Archie."

"Hello, dear. How are you, Zoe?"

The hedge witch snickers. "I like you, Tyler. You have spunk, like your mom. The rest of you, come on. Get a move on. The mayor is waiting."

"Hi, Gwyn," Zoe says, her big brown eyes shining. "I'm doing great. I got a job working at the town museum. They were excited to get someone with a Celtic Studies background, since the area has so much Welsh and Scottish influence."

Archie interjects. "That's wonderful. Who says a degree in Celtic Studies is worthless?"

Spence and Skye raise their hands, smirking.

Everyone laughs, but Archie scowls in their direction, unamused. We all remove our sneakers and place them on the rack. Chatter from the living room trickles into the foyer.

"Hurry up," Agnes says. "I don't want this meeting lasting longer than it needs to. I need my shut-eye."

She corrals us into her beautiful space for entertaining, which bears touches of both old and new. Not wanting to throw out all the furniture she collected over the years, we put a fresh coat of paint on most of the pieces. We find seats on her refurbished wooden kitchen chairs next to the new sofa and loveseat Leslie bought for her.

I scan the room. Elijah leans on the fireplace where he's talking with Mayor Devine. He towers over her average height figure. Shane arranges pillows behind Ronnie's back on the sofa while Agnes and Leslie settle into the loveseat perpendicular to them. The young witches lounge on the floor, squeezing in wherever they can. Zoe leans back against Tyler and grins at me. Not much can put a frown on her cheerful face—always the optimist.

Trinity Johnson, our coven leader and Director of A Family for All—the local LGBTQ support group—pushes up from a kitchen chair and quells the prattle to start the meeting. A woman in her 60s, she has a powerful presence, and not only because she stands at nearly six feet in height. Wrinkles form in the velvety brown skin on her forehead.

"Hi, everyone. We have plans to finalize for next week's Samhain-Halloween open house. Ronnie, what a fantastic idea you had to engage the community. The more often we invite Unremarkables to our celebrations, the more they will embrace the Fellowship's existence. Who knows when our secret may surface unintentionally? Creating closer connections with them will help us prepare for that possibility."

"Thanks," Ronnie says. "Halloween is a fun time for the town. Better to spend it creating solid relationships with Unremarkables than with the Otherworld."

Trinity nods, her jade-green eyes gleaming. "But first, Mayor Jessica Devine would like to address the coven with her concerns."

Elijah faces us, the ceiling light shining on his warm brown skin. "Before the mayor speaks, I want to remind everyone how supportive she has been. She has kept our secret under wraps, except for Corey Jones and Jeremiah Jackson, of course. But she is concerned about the lack of progress in closing the portal in the mound." He motions to Jessica and sits next to Shane on the sofa.

"I commend the efforts you have made thus far, and I recognize you have forfeited much of your leisure time in your search. However, I can speak for Jeremiah and Corey as well as myself, when I say the threat of other beings invading our town through that portal frightens us. I am grateful you were forthcoming with the information surrounding the...what was it called?"

"A Dearg Due," Elijah replies. "A vampire-like ghoul."

Her already pallid face goes almost white. "Yes. It killed so many young men in our town. You must do more to eliminate creatures from slipping through the opening in the future. The recent kidnapping of that woman's baby. Should we worry another creature has crossed over? Or perhaps the Seelie Fae children took him?"

"I don't think so," I say. "When I asked them about it, they appeared surprised. The police suggest it's the crime ring from PA."

"We understand your concerns," Leslie says. "The Bearsden Coven formed years ago with the sole intention of helping this community, and we continue to abide by our original intent. But we must also acknowledge we may not discover a portal-closing spell in the immediate future. Should beings cross over, we will defend the community from their malicious intents."

The mayor wipes her face with a trembling hand. "That's not comforting when people's lives are at risk."

My witch family is silent, a few coughs and clearing of throats the only sounds in the room. What does she expect from the coven? We're doing our best. Elijah stands and approaches Jessica.

"Thank you, Mayor Devine, for meeting with us. I assure you, we won't stop until the portal is shut. As a member of the city council and director of the town's shelter, I pledge to go above and beyond."

"Thank you, Elijah," she says. "As you always do. The town is fortunate to have you. Well, I guess that's all I have to say. Many thanks for allowing me to speak."

The councilman gestures for the mayor to head toward the door. "I'll walk Jessica to her car."

When they've left the room, the hedge witch doesn't hold back.

"Aww, fuck the mayor and her concerns," Agnes scoffs. "Unremarkables are weenies. We can handle anything that comes across, and we've proven that."

"But our power isn't limitless, my dear," Leslie says.

Shane exhales. "Now, Agnes, she has a right to be frightened. She feels responsible for our town's safety. We may have solved the mystery of the Dearg Due and returned her through the portal, but far too many perished before we did."

"I admire your bravery, Agnes," Archie says. "But this coven made a commitment to serve the greater good long before my arrival—and your return. We must work in tandem with the Unremarkables who are *in the knowing*. And be thankful they haven't revealed the Fellowship's true nature."

"I'm with Agnes." Spence points between himself and her. "We're badass."

She glares at him. "Don't try to butter me up after tramping on my floors with your messy shoes."

"What?" He throws his hands up. "I'm always on your side."

Tanner shakes his head. "Quit while you're ahead, hun. I understand the mayor, though. As long as that portal is open, we're all in danger."

"That's an understatement," Skye adds.

The hedge witch rubs at her back. "Can we get on with the meeting? My lumbar needs mattress time."

"After a brief announcement," Trinity says. "Courtney Davies, now Courtney Erickson, has returned to Bearsden."

Spence throws up his arms. "Are you fucking kidding? How can she show her face after what she did to Gwyn?"

"Yeah, she has some nerve moving back here," Skye says. "Made up all that shit about Archie."

I raise my hand in a gesture to stop. "She apologized to me, guys. We should give her a chance."

"Gwyn's right," Trinity adds. "Courtney works in the mayor's office, so I didn't want to announce this while she was here. I doubt Jessica is aware of Courtney's witch status, and it's not our place to divulge her secret. It appears she has moved on with her life. However, we will keep her on our radar. Hard not to when she's married to a council member. Let's wrap this up."

Elijah returns, and we divvy up chores to set up on Samhain in record time. As Archie would say, "We're all knackered." After taking the chairs back to the kitchen, we put on our shoes and make our way out the front door.

"Mom, I'll text you later this week about conferencing with Nain and Taid again," Tyler says. "I want them to meet Zoe."

"Oh. Are you ready to come face to face with spirits?" I ask her.

"You bet," she replies. "Tyler said it was SO cool."

"We'll chat about it later." I wave goodbye as they step out the door. "Archie, why don't you go ahead? I want to talk with Agnes about...the remaining grimoires."

"Sure. I'll take Leslie home. Have a restful night, Agnes."

Leslie kisses her love on the cheek. "Goodnight, my dear. I would stay if I didn't have an early class in the morning."

Agnes blushes. "Yeah, yeah. You sleep well, too, sweetheart."

What a softie she is under that rough, worn exterior. Like her house, the hedge witch has had a makeover. Once Leslie and Archie leave, I pick her brain.

"Have you ever worked on your witch's intuition?"

She squints at me. "What does that have to do with the grimoires?"

"Nothing. I didn't want Leslie to feel bad that I asked you and not her. According to my mother, she always had a chip on her shoulder about her training. Mom said she envied her ancestral witch background. She was jealous of your witchcraft skills, too."

"Yeah. That's true. But Leslie is powerful now. I let my intuition develop naturally over the years. I wouldn't say it's all that great. The closer I get to death's door, the less I wanna know what's coming, you understand?"

I nod, understanding why she feels tentative about it.

"Why do you want to develop your sixth sense? Aren't your visions stressing you out enough? Do you need the fears of your intuition to finish you off?"

I chuckle. "I don't want it for my personal situation. Recently, I've been having unusual reactions. It happened in the Celestial Gardens the evening of the kidnapping. I haven't had any visions, but maybe my sixth sense could guide me to the identities of the kidnappers. And bring that baby boy home to those devastated parents."

"Shouldn't you leave that to the Bearsden Police Department? Don't you have enough on your plate?"

"So, you won't help me?"

Agnes twists her lips. "For fuck's sake. Call me. But I can't guarantee you'll improve."

I grin at my mentor. "Thanks, you old softie. Goodnight."

"Yeah, yeah. Get the fuck outta here."

Back at Archie's, I'm lying in bed, hoping his sore ass has healed enough for some hanky-panky. My Scottish lover exits the bathroom, donning boxer briefs and a sexy smile. He hops onto the mattress and grimaces.

"Och, I shouldn't have done that. My arse is as pink as a baby's bottom with diaper rash."

I laugh and shuffle toward him. "What a lovely image."

"What did you chat about with Agnes?" he asks, sliding a hand down my back.

"I asked her to help me with my intuition. You don't ever talk about yours."

"That's because I do nothing to enhance it. The future can remain hidden as far as I'm concerned. Look at what your visions have done to you. They caused so much stress."

I play with the springy hairs on his chest. "If I hadn't developed them, you'd be dead."

"Must you always be right, witch?" he asks in a thicker Scottish brogue.

"Aye, professor," I say. My hand searches for him under the sheet, and I find him limp as a wet rag. "No?"

"The desire is there, my love, but my arse is winning tonight." He kisses me. "I'm chuffed you're here with me. That's enough."

Archie turns out the light. I roll over, and he wraps his arms around me, snuggling against my back. As I drift off to sleep, the memory of the gray-skinned creature appears, taunting me with his one bulbous eye. Did he take the baby?

CHAPTER SEVEN

SOMETHING'S AFOOT

THE NEXT DAY, ARCHIE has an early class, and I spend part of the morning at the library working on my capstone project for my master's degree. Our hectic schedules and his sore ass are preempting our love life. I keep telling myself there's light at the end of the proverbial tunnel. If we can make it to the third week of December, we'll have plenty of time to catch up over Winter Session in Scotland and Wales.

When my phone screen displays 11:00 a.m., I throw on my hoodie and exit the library to the Green. Seamus asked me to stop by his office to pick up one of his personal references. I don't want to be late.

As I stroll across the paver walkway toward Stewart Hall, I gaze at the white dome atop the red-brick Georgian building. I soak in the bright sunshine and admire the yellow and garnet chrysanthemums. Their sweet and spicy scent passes my nose. Leaves swirl from the tree limbs, creating a cascade of pink, tan, and orange. Soon, the Old Men oak trees will be barren and cooler temperatures will arrive. But today, it's a warm sixty-four degrees. I'm going to enjoy the pleasant weather while it lasts.

I enter the double doors and make my way to the musty basement where the Celtic Studies department offices are housed. As I amble down the hallway, Archie exits his office with Ashley Lewis in tow. Spence and Skye approach from the other end of the hallway and stop to chat, too. They're all in deep discussion when I reach them. The TAs wave at me while I wait silently for them to finish talking. I notice the young instructor has blue eyes the shade of the ocean. Archie smiles at me as he finishes the conversation.

"Don't worry about the grading. I'm certain Spence and Skye will help you meet the deadline."

The red-haired TA nods. "It's not a problem, Dr. Lewis. The department pays me for the extra hours, and I can use the increase around the holidays."

Ashley shoves a stack of papers into her backpack. "I appreciate your help. You and Spence have been lifesavers. I already lose so much time with my son."

"We're here for you, Dr. Lewis," Spence says. "Whatever you need."

"Thank you all for being so supportive." Ashley turns in my direction. "Nice to run into you again, Gwyn."

"Likewise," I say, the wheels turning in my head. "Anything I can do to help?" Like babysit?

A slight smile curls her mouth. "I don't think so, but thank you for offering."

Spence interrupts us. "Hey, I have a great idea, and you deserve a break. I need to check with Tanner first, but would you be down for dinner at our house?"

"Could Jeff Williams come with me? And my son, Aidan?" she asks.

"Absofuckinglutely," Spence replies. "Actually, why don't we make it a party? Skye, bring Zach. I'll call Tyler and Zoe. Gwyn and Archie, you should come, too, and ask Derek and Ronnie—if she's not too tired. Let's say the Saturday after the Samhain Celebration?"

"Thank you for the invitation. You're all so nice," Ashley says. "I better get home for an early lunch. The new babysitter has a class to attend soon." She darts up the hallway toward the stairs, her backpack swinging over her shoulder.

Spence shakes his head. "Dr. Lewis needs to de-stress. She's wound so tight, she's gonna pop a spring."

"It was a great idea," Skye says. "She should socialize more. Let me know what Zach and I can bring."

Archie nods. "If you want any help with dinner, I'm happy to cook something as well."

"Sure. As soon as I tell Tanner," he replies, grimacing.

Skye motions up the hall. "We better get to class. Let us know which grading to concentrate on."

"Will do," Archie replies as they dart off. "I didn't expect you. Miss me already?"

I stroke his goatee. "Yeah, but that's not why I'm here. I forgot Seamus has a new reference for me—a book from home."

"Ahhh. When will you sleep over again? You barely make it one night a week." He shoves his hands in his pockets. "If you moved in with me, at least you'd bless me with your presence in bed every day?"

I turn my head and exhale. "You know I'm not ready for that."

He pulls my chin toward his face. "Will you ever be?"

"Let me get through this semester. There's too much going on."

"Sure," he says in a thicker Scottish brogue. "I understand. When can I expect you to stay again?"

"I'll text you. Meanwhile, take good care of your ass." I slide a hand over his butt.

He grimaces. "Gwyn. I'm a full professor."

I chuckle. "Like that mattered before. Well, I better get to Seamus's. It's almost lunchtime."

"Have a wonderful afternoon, my love."

I kiss him on the cheek. "You, too, honey."

When I arrive at Dr. Duffy's office, I tap on the door. It swings open, and he steps out, his cat-head cane in his hand and a leather book bag on his shoulder. I step back.

"Wasn't I supposed to pick up a reference today?" I ask.

"Good morning, Gwynedd." He pulls the door shut and puts on his navy-blue blazer. "You are correct. I was in a rush to get to class and inadvertently left it at the house. I'm on the way now. Would you care to take a stroll with me?"

"Sure. I was going home to eat lunch, anyway."

"Excellent." He motions up the hallway. "Shall we?"

While we walk to his bungalow on Drummond Lane, a block from Leslie's small Tudor, we discuss the recent baby kidnapping.

"I was there," I say, frowning. "Ronnie and I comforted the parents. So sad."

"I know. I was there as well." He averts his eyes.

"Of course you were. Listen. You can't keep following me around, Seamus. I understand you feel a sense of commitment to protect me, but you promised to limit your...stalking."

He returns his gaze to me. "I'd had dinner at the Raven Pub and heard the police sirens. A local in the crowd told me what had transpired. The connection I have with you remains. I knew you weren't in danger."

"Well, I feel stupid. I'm sorry I accused you."

"You have not offended me, I assure you." He gestures to his front door as we approach. "The book is in the spare bedroom I use as an office."

After entering the house, Seamus limps without his cane into the bedroom, and I follow. To my amazement, I discover the painting of my mother in a field of flowers on the wall over his desk. I swear the fragrance of lavender exudes from the image.

"You hung the picture of my mom. It looks fabulous there," I say.

He stares at the painting. "Yes. No need to hide it anymore since you learned of my friendship with your Great-Aunt Gorawen.

Lowri Crowther was an attractive woman." He locks eyes with me. "As are you, Gwynedd."

I swallow and my bladder calls. Excellent timing, for once. "Excuse me. I need to use your bathroom."

"Of course. You know where it is."

I dash to the toilet to relieve myself, flinching at the macabre painting of the Dearg Due that hides behind the door when it's open. Another creature that slipped through the portal. How many more will the town endure? I wash up and return to the spare bedroom. Seamus offers the book to me as I enter the room, and I approach him, tripping over his cane. He catches me in his arms, and I peer up at his eyes. A longing remains in them, but what can I do about it?

"Oops. I'm such a klutz." I push away from his awkward embrace and adjust my long-sleeved tee.

"Forgive me. I should have placed my cane in a safer place."

"Tripping is engrained in my DNA. You could have stored it under the bed and I would have managed to fall over it."

He chuckles, and for the first time, I notice a more laid-back demeanor—a lowering of his cat sith armor.

"It's good to hear you laugh. You're always so serious."

"You bring out that part of me, Gwynedd. I buried it deep down years ago." He shifts closer to me and leans on the desk. "I am so incredibly grateful to you for reigniting my soul."

Oh, my gods. This man isn't infatuated. He's in love with me. What am I going to do? *What do I say?* He knows I'm with Archie. I take the book from his hand and move toward the doorway.

"I should get going. Gotta eat lunch and continue with my capstone project."

As I hasten to the front door, I can sense his presence behind me. I swallow again and turn my head.

"Thank you for the reference, Seamus. I'll return it as soon as I have time to sift through its pages."

He smiles warmly. "I am at your service, Gwynedd. Whenever you require it."

I force a smile, exit his house, and head to Leslie's. I can't explain it, but I sense his protective grasp while I stroll home.

This is going to be a problem.

Despite the gloomy skies and threat of rain, Ronnie and I take a hike in North Basin Creek Park on Saturday morning. She has to get her steps in or she can't sleep at night. For now, the temperature trends warmer. I stare up at the ominous clouds. Those threatening skies are going to dump on us any minute. Did we make a mistake?

"I realize you need your exercise, but we're gonna get pummeled shortly," I say, the stones crunching as I step.

"Nah." Ronnie gathers her crimson curls into a ponytail. "We're good until noon. We have two more hours. Plenty of time to complete the loop."

"Ugh. Do we have to hike back on the trail through the bog? With the higher temp, gnats will cover the area. I'm not in the mood for wiping black insect dots off my face."

Ronnie sports a fake pout. "Please? Returning on the same trail bores me. The pests may not be so bad."

"You win. But let's definitely leave the bog side for our return."

"Thanks, Gwyn. I'm so big now, I feel like a whale and waddle like a duck. I don't know how Derek gets it up."

"Oh, stop." I laugh, and my amusement resounds through the forest. "You look radiant. You were always gorgeous, but you're positively glowing during this pregnancy."

"I guess," she says. "Have you had any luck with your search for the monster from your vision?"

"No, but I keep looking. I don't have a lot of time between school and work. And then there's the question of the mound. The coven hasn't met at Agnes's house to finish sifting through the remaining grimoires yet. I doubt we will now. The Celtic Studies department took a hit when the College of Arts and Sciences cut the additional full-time professor position. The single person they added was Dr. Ashley Lewis, and she's an instructor. Leslie, Archie, and Seamus all had to overload their schedules. That leaves very few hours to complete the spell database. I think Leslie has given up on finding an incantation to close the portal."

"I wish I could help, but I'm a little...you know." She points to her bump.

"Don't you dare worry about it. You have plenty on your plate. We may not get to the last of the grimoires until the semester is over. If we can't find a spell by then, Archie says we'll ask his family for suggestions when we visit. Aunt Gorawen couldn't help. She thinks the ancestral witch who wrote the incantation in my family's tome must have left out a step or an ingredient. That's her best guess, anyway."

"Meanwhile, we all worry every day about what could cross over from the Otherworld. Keep looking for that gray-skinned dude."

"I will. Seamus gave me a reference book yesterday at his house."

"That was nice of him," she says, her tone accusatory.

I hesitate to share what happened, but I need to tell someone. Sharing the revelation about the Irish professor with Archie is out of the question for now. He'll say I should limit my interactions with him. If I'm going to have any chance in hell of discovering what the being is, I must have access to all the resources.

"Something happened while I was there. I tripped over his cane, and he caught me. He stared into my eyes like his entire life depends on my existence. I think he's in love with me."

"Oh, I was joking," Ronnie says with a wave of her hand. "We know he is devoted to protecting you. He promised your aunt. You're reading into his reaction."

"No, I'm not. He said, and I quote, 'I am so incredibly grateful to you for reigniting my soul.' Those were his exact words."

Ronnie's jaw drops. "Wow. How beautiful."

"That's your response? What am I gonna do?"

"How should I know, Gwyn? Don't spend more time alone with him than needed, I guess."

"Well, a lot of help you are."

She cackles. "I'm here to please."

We've arrived at the road that connects the trails and walk to catch the path back. I hate hiking in this section because the bog overflows and creates muddy patches when it rains. I haven't been through here for months. The gnats are so thick in the summer evenings, they cover the area like a veil, and I end up inhaling the pests. Not my idea of a leisurely stroll. When we approach the tiny pond, the gnats are, in fact, in residence. However, they are sparse, and we bat at them as we pass the pond full of lily pads. Ronnie gestures at the floating plants.

"I love when the water lilies bloom in the summer. They're so pretty—like white stars on a bed of green."

"Seen through a veil of black gnats. Hard to enjoy the blooms when you're waving your hands all around to keep them out of your eyes, nose, and mouth."

"True. Use bug spray in the future. You don't know what you're missing."

The snapping of wood echoes in the thicket, and I stop. I examine the area on the other side of the bog, but the trees are still, as if frozen in time. Ronnie turns around, grimacing and rubbing her abdomen.

"What are you staring at?"

"I thought I heard something across the pond. Nothing, I guess."

We take a few more steps, and a warm aura overwhelms me, grasping at a spot in my core. I clutch my stomach. The rustling of fallen leaves resounds nearby, and I scan the bog. The water between the lily pads reflects like a sheet of glass.

"Did you hear that?" I ask, touching my flushed cheeks.

"Nope. Nothing. Hot flash?"

"No. I haven't had one for a few weeks."

"Well, your face looks like you ran a marathon."

My gut pinches again, and I rub my stomach.

"You should really go to a GI specialist. These gas attacks can't be good."

"I think it's the collagen I've been putting in my morning tea. Bloating." In my peripheral vision, I'm sure I catch someone running through the trees across the bog. "Did you see that?"

"What?" Ronnie scans the area. "There's nothing in there, Gwyn. Probably deer."

I take a few steps toward the woods.

"Don't you dare go in there," my friend says, squinting. "I'm not in the mood to find another dead body."

I chuckle. "You're right. The deer have multiplied like bunny rabbits. Hunting season will be here soon enough. Let's get back before the rain starts."

We head toward the trailhead, walking at a break-neck pace. Or in Ronnie's case, waddling. When we reach the entrance to the trail, it begins to drizzle. We pull up our hoodies and continue on to Main Street, hoping to get to our cars before the stormy skies dump on us. As we turn the corner at the Raven Pub, we discover Bearsden Police vehicles, their red and blue lights flashing. They're parked on the road in front of the local shipping and packing store next to Mitchell Hall. Ronnie uses her baby bump to push through the throng of nosy townies, and I follow closely behind.

In the center of the crowd is Detective Jack Schmidt, comforting a woman with shoulder-length, blond hair. Officers, including O'Connor and Wilson, question people off to the side. I lean over to a man next to me.

"What happened? She doesn't appear injured," I say, a wrinkle forming in my brow.

"She isn't hurt," he replies. "Someone swiped her toddler in broad daylight on the street when she stopped to check out the costumes hanging outside the thrift store. The mom said she let go of her hand for a few seconds. The sidewalks were really packed this morning—Halloween sidewalk sales."

Ronnie gasps. "Oh, my gods. Someone must have seen who took the child."

He shakes his head. "Happened too fast. One witness said it was a woman with platinum-blond hair. She didn't catch her face."

A twinge snaps inside, and I sense a trail of magic. But there's something different about it. Are the Baby Nabbers using a witch to snatch these poor babies?

CHAPTER EIGHT

A DEVOTED STUDENT

By noon on Sunday, the weather clears, and the high is expected to hit 77 degrees. If it wasn't the end of October, I would pull out a pair of shorts and enjoy the late Second Summer. But I can't find it in me to be excited amidst the tragic kidnappings in our town. As I'm getting ready for work, Archie calls. I swipe the green icon on my phone.

"Good morning, my love. Well, almost afternoon now," he says. "Were you able to sleep?"

"Yeah, but the kidnapping and what I felt last night left me unsettled. I'm sure I sensed magic in the area—different from witchcraft."

"The online news article I read stated no witnesses saw the face of the woman, only her blond hair from behind. Did Ronnie notice any residue?"

"No. But she said her pregnancy is affecting her skills. Her hormones are out of whack. Her baby isn't even born yet, and she's so stressed over these kidnappings."

"Hard not to be. Are you sure you weren't feeling Seamus's presence?"

"No. It wasn't the residue of a cat sith witch." I haven't told him about the Irish professor's most recent comments. He'll advise me to stop meeting with him.

"Your initial assessment is most likely correct, then. A rogue witch."

"My witch's intuition isn't strong enough to identify the source, and I can't take a chance with the crystal grid in the short term. I want to set up a time with Agnes for some training. For all I know, I'm sensing my own magic trail."

"I wish you well, Gwyn. But her tutoring is unconventional."

"I'm not a neophyte now. I can handle what she throws at me."

He laughs into the phone so loudly I pull my cell away from my ear.

"What's so funny?" I ask, irritation straining my voice.

"Remember how the pot episode went? Moderation in whatever she asks you to do is advised."

I chuckle. "Don't worry. I won't make that mistake again. Well, I'd better prepare lunch. I've gotta get to work. Enjoy your afternoon, honey."

"Not likely. I'll be grading. Will you stop by later?"

"I doubt it. I have classwork to finish. But I want to. I love you."

"Have a fantastic day. I love you, too, Gwyn."

I dress in my new Mystic Sage logo T-shirt and jeans, gather my belongings, and walk into the kitchen. Leslie is sitting at the tiny table eating a bologna sandwich and vegetable soup. She slurps a spoonful and rests the utensil in the bowl. Mr. Yeats sits on a chair, his tail wagging back and forth.

"Hello, Gwynedd. Care to join me for lunch?" she asks.

"A quick one. I need to get to work. The incident on Main Street last night ate into my studies. I'm hoping to arrive a little early, so I can leave earlier, too. I must schedule time to plod away on my intuition. Try to enhance it enough to check out any future magic residue."

"The thought of a witch aiding a kidnapping ring is disconcerting. We pledge to do no harm, as you well know. I will warn the coven of the possibility on Samhain before the guests arrive." She consumes another spoonful of soup. "I hear you may do some training with Agnes to increase the effectiveness of your intuition. You're welcome to ask me for help next time. But I understand if you prefer Agnes's tutelage."

"Don't take offense. She became my mentor when I completed my training during the break from the coven. She doesn't follow your academic approach, but I do well when I work with her. Well, most of the time." I chuckle, recalling my initial sessions—when I nearly snuffed out all the pot plants in her garden.

Leslie chuckles. "Indeed. Agnes created the term *think outside the box*. I'm certain of that."

"Her style of teaching is good for me," I say while making a PB&J sandwich. "My entire childhood and marriage were in a box. Look what that got me."

"You have a wonderful son. For that alone, your prior life was worth a portion of time in an Unremarkable world."

I grin as I nudge Mr. Yeats off the chair. "It was. Despite all that's happened, I want you to know I value your support and knowledge. I wish the road getting here hadn't been so bumpy, though."

"Indeed. I appreciate your candor, Gwynedd. Study with Agnes as much as you like. It doesn't offend me."

Leslie takes another bite of her sandwich, and I do the same. It's not the same as having a living mom sitting across the table, but having her here has become a close second.

When I enter Mystic Sage, Officer Quinn O'Connor is speaking with Shane, who's manning the cash register. He pets his snow-white beard.

"I ran out when I saw the commotion on the street. The crowd gathered outside the shipping store blocked me from viewing what happened. I'm sorry I can't add anything to your investigation."

Officer O'Connor finishes taking notes on her tablet. "We have to interview as many people as possible who were on Main Street when the kidnapping occurred. Thank you for your time, Mr. Murphy."

"Anytime, Officer. You have a pleasant afternoon."

She nods and exits the store as I stash my purse under the counter. My boss logs out of the cash register and bemoans.

"Swiped a child in the middle of the day. Unbelievable. It was overcast and had just started to rain. Packed sidewalk. The perfect storm to obscure the criminal from notice."

"Leslie will announce this to the coven on Thursday, but Ronnie and I arrived right after the kidnapping. Magic residue permeated the area. Unfortunately, not enough for me to find the source. My intuition is weak."

Shane's emerald-green eyes widen. "A witch took the precious child?"

"I don't know for sure. I have to work on my skills and figure out if I can increase my radar enough to identify the magic stream. But there would need to be a next time for me to have a trail to follow."

"How unfortunate. I've never had a need to increase my instincts. Accepted what skills I possessed and concentrated on other areas of the craft. I wish for your success, but let's hope you won't need it in the future. The Bearsden Police theorize the Baby Nabbers from Pennsylvania are responsible."

"Well, they aren't releasing any information about what they discovered in the gardens yet. I'll take over now if you want to work on the stock in the back."

"Thank you, darling. I have an appointment with a stack of cardboard."

While he ambles into the crystals room, the door dings. Council member Alys Morgan strolls in and approaches the small toy section. Her pale-blond hair falls to the side as she bends down to pick up a puzzle. She turns her nose up and returns the game to the shelf.

"May I help you find something, Ms. Morgan?" I ask.

"All the toys here are for older children. Do you have any for younger ages?"

"I'm sorry, we don't. There's a specialty toy shop at the other end of Main Street. Try there."

"I came from there. They didn't have anything unique. I'm buying them for the children of a very close friend. Since these kidnappings began, they've all been too terrified to go outside. I wanted to give them something to cheer them up." Alys turns and looks at me, and I'm taken aback by the flash of anger in her eyes. "Someone needs to do something to keep the children of Bearsden safe."

"I agree," I say, at a loss for words. "I'm sorry we don't stock any items that meet your needs. Maybe check online? Lots of toys on the internet. You'll find something."

She smiles sweetly. "Thank you...what's your name? I forget. I'm terrible with names."

"Gwynedd Crowther, but my friends call me Gwyn."

"Have a nice day, Gwyn," she says on the way to the door.

"You, too, Ms. Morgan."

Alys exits the store and heads west on Main Street. Not long after, Jeff enters with Ashley Lewis and a small boy in tow. Although his mother has dark hair, his head is covered in blond ringlets. He's an adorable toddler.

"Hey, Gwyn," Jeff says. "I was working on some spreadsheets at home and stopped by to give the flash drive to Shane. Ashley came with me to discuss your babysitting offer."

YES. Don't act too excited, Gwyn. "Hi, Ashley. I'd be happy to babysit when I'm available. Get my phone number from Jeff and call whenever you need me. Last minute is fine. I'll come if I can." My heart is about to burst with unexpected joy.

"Thank you for the offer," she replies. "I brought Aidan with me so he could meet you."

I squat so I'm eye level with his angelic face. "Hi, Aidan. I'm Gwyn." His eyes shine like pastel-blue sapphires, a lighter hue than his mother's.

He wrinkles his nose and pulls his hand out of his mom's, sprinting to the toy section. He bangs on the skull with flashing red eyes and throws it to the floor. Ashley darts to him.

"Stop that, Aidan! These toys do not belong to you. I'm so sorry. The Terrible Twos, you know."

Jeff jogs over and picks up the merchandise. "Don't worry about it. He's a toddler."

"Two-year-olds can be a handful," I say. "I remember my son at this age. He was a fireball, but he grew into a responsible adult."

She takes a breath. "If you've changed your mind about babysitting, I'll understand. So many grad students have quit on me."

"Well, they haven't raised kids. This is the age when you develop patience and learn how to negotiate with children. It's challenging, but you'll get through this phase. I promise. Call me when you need help."

Aidan stands, his lips pressed tightly together, glaring at me like I'm enemy number one. He needs a touch of discipline, that's all. This will be fun.

Tuesday after class, I drive to Agnes's farm to work on my weak intuition. What a dreary day—blanketed in gray skies with a slightly cooler temperature. But I'll take it. I'm not expecting a lot out of this training, because...it's Agnes. She's never been a mom. The front door is open, so I knock on the wooden screen. The foyer and hallway are empty.

"Agnes? Are you in the kitchen?" I ask, tapping again.

The house is quiet except for a few creaking floorboards as I make my way toward the magic room. That's odd. The door is shut. What is she doing in there? I push on it slowly, and a bouquet of burning incense strikes me—lemongrass, jasmine, and honeysuckle. The graphite Archie put on the hinges really helped. No creaking at all. I peek around to discover the hedge witch with her eyes closed, standing on one foot, a crystal in each hand. How is a woman in her 80s balancing so well? I am impressed. So, I tell her.

"Wow, Agnes! That's amazing!"

"Aghh!" she screams as she tumbles to the floor.

I panic and rush to her. "I'm so sorry. Didn't you hear the door open?"

"Fuck no," she replies, pushing herself up. "Why did you call out while I was meditating? You scared the shit out of me."

I chuckle. "You? Meditating? Can those two elements even exist in the same universe?"

"Oh, fuck you. Have you ever tried to meditate?" She collects the crystals from the floor.

"Yeah. My mind wanders too much. I stress about all the work I have to do."

"Well, that's where we have to begin."

"Why were you standing on one leg?"

"It's supposed to provide focus. Except all I could think about was not falling on my ass."

I crack up and brush debris off her loose shirt. "Are you OK? You're gonna have some bruising."

"Stop fussing over me, Gwyn," she says, pushing my hands away. "For fuck's sake. I'm old, not on my deathbed. Let's work near the table, so we have something to balance against."

Agnes shuffles to the worktable and sets her crystals on the wooden surface with the others. I move next to her, and she passes her hand over the colorful collection—amethyst, labradorite, moonstone, clear quartz, fluorite, sodalite, and others.

"What would you like me to do?"

"Pick two of whatever you want. They all contain energy with various uses. You'll have to try different combinations to figure out what works for you. I told you I never practiced this specifically. It requires super focus. You know I'm a wing it kind o' gal."

I chuckle. "I do. But I have no idea what to pick. I used crystals for a different purpose...to increase the length of my visions."

"It's a crap shoot, Gwyn. You'll have to figure out what combinations work for you to strengthen your intuition. Even then, it may not lead you to this unethical witch who is aiding the Baby Nabbers."

I examine the choices in front of me and decide on fluorite and labradorite. "I'll try these, I guess."

"Those two together are more likely to help with decision-making, but go for it," Agnes says, flinging up her tattooed arms. "Hold a crystal in each hand and close your eyes. Focus on inner clarity. That's what this grimoire states, but it hasn't done shit for me."

I shut my peepers and squeeze the stones in my palms, searching for lucidity.

"Breathe in and out," Agnes says in a scratchy voice. "Absorb the energy from the crystals and find your center."

My abdomen rises and falls as I take air in through my nose and exhale through my mouth. My mind wanders to the Pumpkin House, to the Celestial Gardens, to Jenny Hansen crying. *Focus, Gwyn. Focus.* In...out...in...out...in... My cell vibrates.

"Shit. I forgot to turn the volume down."

I drop the crystals on the table and set the sound to silent. Agnes snatches my phone from me, scowling.

"Hey," I say, retrieving the stones. "Be careful not to crack the screen."

"You'll get it back when we're done." She shoves my digital distraction into the pocket of her long black skirt. "Start again."

I roll my eyes. "Sorry."

For the next hour, I attempt to create more focus using an incantation my mentor recommends. I chant softly, "Ancestors, I call on you for guidance. My intuition is open and waiting for your assurance." Nothing. I switch out crystals, trying different pairings. Sodalite and rose quartz. Nope. Agate and citrine. Meh. I toss them on the table. Lapis lazuli and celestite—only a twinge. To the pile they go. Kyanite and moonstone spark an internal tugging, but it whimpers out. I puff at my bangs.

Agnes squints at me. "Ready to quit?"

"What? I'm no quitter. I'm gonna try these two again."

She snickers. "Good. Just checking. Focus on your breathing again. In...out..."

I recite the incantation one more time while Agnes's voice fades, as if she's whispering in the distance. "That's it. Search for clarity in your thoughts. Find..."

I'm floating in white, voluminous clouds, reaching for passing birds as they fly by. A bright light breaks through, inviting me... My head nods, and I flinch, dropping the crystals to the floor.

"Did you fall asleep?" my mentor asks, bursting out in laughter. "This isn't gonna fucking work."

"I didn't sleep well last night. That's all. Too much on my plate." I pick up the stones and set them on the table. "Meditating with them did not help my visions, either. I promised Archie, Mom, and Aunt Gorawen I wouldn't use the grid again until I've increased my regular practice with them. Even if this doesn't pan out, I'll have more hours clocked. I should go. I have a load of schoolwork waiting for me at home."

My mentor squints at me, pursing her lips. "Follow me into the kitchen."

A wrinkle forms between my eyes, but I do as she says. She opens the cabinet where she stores her Bearsden Poison pot. I sigh.

"Agnes, I won't smoke that again. Ever."

She scowls as she pulls a shoebox out and places it on the counter. "You think I'd waste my good stuff on you after the first time?"

"Then what's in the box?"

She lifts the lid, revealing a gorgeous amethyst geode with a rich purple color. When she lifts the precious gem, the nodules sparkle, hinting at a hidden magic.

"An old eclectic witch gave me this beautiful rock on her dying bed. She taught me the craft and everything she knew. But I had more success with the use of herbs and nature." She opens my hand and places the purple gem in my palm, weighting it down. "I want you to have it. I never had a daughter. Never fucking wanted one, either. But if I'd had one, I would have hoped for a snarky, stubborn bitch like you."

"Gee, Agnes. I don't know what to say? I may cry."

"Oh, fuck that. Don't get all mushy on me. Who knows if this will help you succeed? But give it a go. You can report back to me when we meet after Samhain to sift through a few grimoires."

"You know, my mom should have been my teacher. But I'm glad it was you."

Her eyes tear up, and she clears her throat. "Get the fuck outta here."

CHAPTER NINE

SAMHAIN

By Thursday, I've given up on meditating. I've tried countless crystal combinations, to no avail. I remind myself it's only been a few days, and I just need a break. Instead, I focus on the Samhain-Halloween open house celebration, which I'm beyond excited for. With the lack of time due to schoolwork, my job, and the folklore research, I couldn't pull together a new costume. So, I don my witch costume. I know. So original.

Halfway to the Pumpkin House, I remove my hooded black cape. Samhain weather is supposed to provide cool, crisp air for a mysterious ambiance. A near eighty-degree temp and high humidity hardly sets the tone for creepy. But the surge in warm temperatures will permit the open house to spill out onto the front porch and backyard, a blessing in disguise. We're expecting the Victorian building to be busting with townies and their costumed little ones.

I scuttle across the street in my black high-heeled boots—the worst part about this costume. But Archie won't complain. Elijah is carrying a large cooler up the steps when I arrive. He's dressed as a superhero, and his blue cape gets caught on the screen door.

"Let me help you," I say, grabbing the wooden edge. "You're stuck."

"Thank you, Gwyn. You are certainly ready for the Halloween part of tonight. Wait a minute. Haven't you worn that costume before?"

"Yeah. At the first celebration, actually," I say with a raise of my eyebrows.

He laughs, his bass voice filling the foyer as we enter. "I remember. That's the night it all started for you. Any regrets now?"

"No. Except I wish I'd had time to create a different outfit for tonight. I had to make it slightly less sexy. We must give a good impression. Children are coming, and the city council, too. The kids will flock to you like a magnet, though."

"That's the plan."

Elijah carries the cooler to the dining room where the young witches have set up the refreshment tables. They have on costumes for the occasion and are carrying on like little kids. Spence and Tanner wear pirates' clothing. Tyler and Zoe came as condiments, ketchup and mustard. Skye and Zach are dressed as Frankenstein and his bride. I approach them, wobbling in my high heels.

"Blessed Samhain, everyone. And Happy Halloween. It appears you have everything ready for the open house. Anything I can do?"

"Happy Samhain," they say at random.

I hug my son. "Thanks for showing up early."

"Hi, Mom," Tyler says. "Nah. Most of the food is on the table."

"Except for the candy. I hope we don't run out." Tanner pours chocolate candy bars into a large plastic cauldron and grabs an enormous pumpkin to fill.

Spence turns up a corner of his mouth and adjusts his eye patch. "There better be some for me, matey." He reaches into the cauldron.

"Keep your hands off these treats," Zoe says, slapping his hand. "It's for the kids when they come trick or treating."

Skye snickers as she dumps ice into a cooler. "Don't you feed him, Tanner?"

"His stomach is a bottomless pit," he replies, nudging his partner. "It's his endless fidgeting."

"But you said you like it when I squirm." Spence wiggles his eyebrows.

Zach laughs and shakes his head. "You'll need to tone down the innuendos when the children arrive."

Spence hugs Tanner. "I'm just messing around. I'll be on my best behavior once this celebration gets going. We should have started these open houses after the Mitchells passed away. The town and campus missed their Halloween extravaganzas." He raises his fingers, splaying them into fake fireworks.

"Dressing as a witch, Gwyn? Isn't that kind of...redundant?" Zoe asks, chuckling. "Wait. Didn't you wear that when...you know."

Tyler squints at me. "Isn't your witch costume new?"

My eyes flip back and forth between Spence and Zoe, pinching my lips together.

Spence guffaws. "I remember. That's what you wore the night you cussed your husband out for cheating on you."

I slap his arm. "Spence!" I peer at my son.

"You spoke with Dad?" he asks, his eyes narrowing. "In the Otherworld?"

I grimace. "Well, no. He crossed over here."

Tanner glares at his partner. "Dude."

"I'm sorry. You know I can't control my mouth when I'm excited."

"Why didn't you tell me, Mom?" Tyler asks, frowning at me.

My heart sinks, palpitations thumping loud enough to beat the band. "That was a stressful night. It's how I discovered I was a witch. I'm sorry I didn't explain what happened. Seeing your father was traumatic. We'll chat about it later. I promise."

He turns away from me and fills a platter with more cookies. The rest of the young witches go silent, creating a void as large as the Grand Canyon.

Spence shrugs and mouths, "Sorry, Gwyn."

I gaze at my son, hoping he'll forgive me once I explain. "Well, have fun tonight, everyone. If you need me, just shout. I'm going to help the others."

I approach the parlor, where the older witches are setting up a few children's games. Trinity, as usual, is dressed to the nines in a golden goddess dress with matching gold glitter eye shadow and lipstick, her jade-green eyes glowing like lasers. Shane has on a gnome costume complete with a pointed red hat. Ronnie and Derek have arrived, too. She's wearing an enormous orange pumpkin costume, and her boyfriend has on a scarecrow outfit.

"You two are adorable," I say. "How are you feeling, future mama?"

"Like a whale," she replies. "I've never been this fat in my life. I don't know how handsome here finds me attractive."

Derek bends down and hugs her. "Stop, babe. You're as gorgeous as ever."

Archie chimes in. "He's right. You are radiant."

"You have less than two months left," I say. "Enjoy the quiet time now. Once the baby arrives, the Otherworld will let loose."

She grimaces. "That's supposed to comfort me?"

I chuckle. "Sorry. Being realistic."

"Well, you better be there to quell the chaos," Ronnie says.

I hug her. "Of course I will."

Archie is wearing all black. He's slicked back his hair and applied super-white makeup to his pale skin and red lipstick to his lips. When he grins at me, false fangs appear—sexy. I chuckle and kiss his cheek.

"You look awesome, honey." Especially those bulging muscles through your T-shirt.

"Remember, children will be trick or treating," Trinity says. "We're trying to be welcoming. Not scare the pants off the cherubs."

Archie removes his false teeth. "I plan on joking with them, not threatening to feed on their blood."

"Ronnie, I am so excited about the arrival of your little one." Our coven leader touches her pumpkin belly. "Don't forget about Auntie Trinity when you need a babysitter. I'm at your service."

"Thanks," she replies. "I'll definitely take you up on that. Sooner than later if I can't get any sleep."

"Your gnome costume is perfection, Shane," I say.

He pulls on his beard. "I figured I could put these whiskers to good use. I hear some of the city council members may attend the open house."

"Yeah, a few," Trinity replies. "Please, butter them up. Even the ones not *in the knowing*. We want them on our side in case something else should happen in the future."

Archie nods. "Noted. Gwyn, I was about to go out back and help Elijah. He's setting up more play areas in the yard. What smashing weather we're having today for outside activities."

"Sounds great." I take a step toward the hall.

"Gwyn?" Trinity asks. "Isn't that what you wore the night—"

I silence her with a glare and follow Archie to the back door. Her snickering trickles down the hallway until I exit. Elijah has an area set up for trick or treaters to lob water balloons at the superhero while he runs back and forth. He'll probably welcome the liquid chill in this warm air.

"You're so wonderful to allow the children to have a little fun at your expense," I say.

"I love kids," he replies. "I hope Jasmine and I can start a family soon. We've talked about getting married."

Archie lays a hand on his arm. "That's cracking, Elijah. I'm happy for you both." He peers at me out of the corner of his eye.

"A baby arriving, a future wedding." I glance at Archie. "Our coven is expanding. Leslie will be thrilled with the news. She's worked for decades to keep the Fellowship going."

"No doubt," Archie says, averting his eyes.

Elijah stacks the last of the water balloons and rubs his hands together. "That should be enough. When they run out of balloons, we can play 'catch the superhero.'"

"Brilliant planning," Archie says. "Why don't we go back inside? Guests should arrive soon."

Leslie and Agnes finally show up—the Elder in a doctor's lab coat and the hedge witch wearing black from neck to floor. Is she supposed to be the grim reaper? Because she doesn't have a sickle in her hand. Not that she needs one. Trinity signals for us to gather in the foyer.

"Blessed Samhain, my friends. In a few minutes, we'll open our doors to the town. Please, present yourselves in a positive light. Before we begin, Leslie would like to address the circle."

"On the day of the second kidnapping, Gwynedd sensed a trail of unusual magic. We think a rogue witch may be aiding the Baby Nappers ring out of Pennsylvania. For now, we have no solid evidence. It's merely a hunch. I recommend we remain alert to the possibility. That is all. Enjoy your evening. Let's invite our guests in."

The open house proceeds incredibly well as children and their parents arrive. Some grab their treats and leave, likely skeptical of the Fellowship's true objectives. Others stay to play a few games in the parlor and outside, giggling as Elijah gladly makes a fool of himself running around. The young witches take turns playing with the kiddies while we chat with the parents and other townies—locals who have come for the food and the chance to cosplay some of their favorite movie and video game characters.

Mayor Jessica Devine and a few of the council members arrive, including newly elected Alys Morgan and John Erickson. Courtney is with her husband, who has blond hair similar to Archie's—without the silver strands, of course. Ashley Lewis and Jeff Williams enter, dressed as elves, complete with pointy ears. Soon after, Seamus Duffy walks in dressed as a knight of King Arthur's Round Table. While I'm chatting with Leslie and Agnes in the parlor, a boy in a ninja costume approaches us and points at the hedge witch.

"What are you supposed to be?" he asks in a snarky tone.

Agnes leans over and growls at him, raising claw-like fingers. "Your worst fucking nightmare."

He runs away, crying, and latches on to his mother. She turns her nose up at us, grabs his hand, and they exit out the front door. Leslie huffs at her partner. I jump in before the Elder loses her shit.

"Agnes, you know I support you in being an out witch and not hiding who you are. But you can't treat kids like that and expect acceptance from the community. You're my mentor, but if I hear you use the F word one more time tonight, I'm gonna drag you out of here and take you home." I squint at her, the hint of a hex threat building in my eyes.

Invisible steam exits Agnes's ears, and her mouth wrinkles like a prune.

"You win," she says, her shoulders falling in defeat. "But you owe me."

I chuckle. "So, what's new? I'll be paying you back in the Otherworld at this point."

"Splendid." Leslie pats her partner's hand. "Thank you, dear. I recognize how hard it is to refrain from your colorful prose."

She rolls her eyes. "Yeah, yeah."

About that time, Courtney and her husband approach Archie on the far side of the room. He has been talking with Alys Morgan, glancing at me repeatedly as if he's pleading with me to rescue him.

"I'm going to talk with Archie," I say, spying on their interaction. "I'd like to meet the new council members."

My hedge witch mentor snorts. "Sure. Whatever you say, Gwyn. You're concerned with the blond councilwoman."

"Oh, Agnes," Leslie says. "Don't make trouble."

"Trouble is my middle name."

I give her the bird on the down-low and push my way through the crowd. When I get to Archie, he's shaking John Erickson's hand. I squeeze between him and Alys Morgan.

"Good evening," I say, forcing a smile.

"John, this is my girlfriend, Gwynedd Crowther. She's actually working on a degree in public policy."

He shakes my hand. "Nice to meet you. When you're finished with your degree, you should check the city's job list."

"I'll think about it," I reply. "Hi, Courtney. Thanks for coming. It helps the Fellowship's image to have a council member and his wife in attendance at these open houses."

A sweet smile curls her mouth. "This is fun. The Fellowship should do it every year. I hope you'll consider it."

"I'm sure we will after tonight's success," Archie says, stroking his goatee.

John nods. "I agree, and I bet the city could come up with some funds to help next year."

"Gwyn, this is Alys Morgan. Councilwoman, my better half." He winks at me.

I offer her my hand, and she shakes it reluctantly, her arrogant blue eyes glaring at me. What's she angry about?

"We've met, actually," I say. "I bumped into her in front of Mitchell Hall recently."

Archie shoves his hand in his pockets. "Oh, you didn't mention meeting her."

I shrug. "Slipped my mind, I guess."

"Yes," Alys says. "We discussed the horrible crime in the Celestial Gardens. I mentioned I wanted to address this with the city council. Now two kidnappings have occurred. John, we must pass an ordinance to ensure the safety of the children in Bearsden."

Wrinkles form between John's pale-blue eyes. "I really don't know what we could do, Alys. The Bearsden PD assigned more patrol cars on the roads, and they're investigating both kidnappings extensively."

"We can always do more," the councilwoman scoffs. "If you won't introduce a solution, John, I will."

Archie interjects. "We have an outstanding police department. They are doing as much as they can. This Baby Nabbers ring out of PA has evaded capture. Unfortunately, they are quite skilled."

"Which is why we must act," she says, huffing. "If it were your child, you'd feel the same way. Jessica Devine is here. If you'll excuse me."

Alys ambles toward the mayor, who is chatting with Elijah in the dining room. I look after her, baffled at her response. She doesn't even have kids. How the hell did she get voted into office? She's not personable at all. Oh, now I remember. She ran uncontested.

"So, Courtney tells me she was a member of the Fellowship before," John says. "I told her I was fine with her returning, but she said she didn't want to."

Ha! Because we banned her. *I'm sure she didn't tell you that, dear John, or about being a witch.*

Her eyes fall to the floor. "That's not what I said. I left because I did not belong there."

At least she's telling the truth. I'll give her that. A silent pause captures the moment, and Archie clears his throat.

"Well, I'm chuffed we got to meet you, John. It's good to know the people managing our town. I look forward to working on projects with you in the future. The Fellowship tries to give back to the community as often as we can."

"I'd be happy to work with you all." John pulls out a business card. "Call whenever you're ready to discuss ideas. Courtney and I are trying to make the rounds with as many locals as possible. Nice chatting with you."

They say their goodbyes and squeeze through the packed parlor. A huge sigh escapes my lips.

"That was awkward. How did Courtney act with you at first? I missed that."

"She was fine, Gwyn. I imagine your initial assessment was correct. She's matured and moved on with her life. I'm happy for her."

I glance back at her husband. "And found a younger version of you, Dr. Cockburn. Does that bother you?"

"Why would it? I have you. No one else matters." He squeezes my hand.

Seamus waves to us as he makes his way down the hallway to the back of the house. He must be going outside. I don't blame him in that layered costume. Suddenly, a wave of unusual magic residue overcomes me, triggering an aura. I touch my flushed face.

"Hot flash?" he asks. "I thought they subsided."

"They have mostly. But this isn't a hot flash." I turn around and scan the area, raising my hand inconspicuously to identify the source. But I can't. The feeling dissipates. "An aura took over, but it's gone."

"We'll be cleaning up soon, and I promised Elijah I would join him outside for a while. We should have plenty of time together after the open house." He winks at me and heads out back.

The iced tea I drank has finally caught up with me, so I head to the bathroom. But on the way, I pick up on the trail of magic. Putting my bladder aside, I meander through the foyer to the dining room and into the parlor, following the stream. I stop when I end up outside on the back porch. Seamus is leaning against the railing watching the children play with Elijah and Archie.

"You look spectacular in that witch's costume," he says, his eyes roaming down my torso until they arrive at my spike-heeled boots. "How ever do you manage those?"

I chuckle. "It's a challenge. I bought them two years ago for Halloween. Actually, I was wearing them the night I discovered I was a witch."

"Was that before or after you and Archie became...close?"

"After." I swallow and lower my eyes. "But we split up for a while after the Winter Solstice Celebration. We got back together over the summer." *I shouldn't have told him that. What was I thinking?*

"May I ask what caused the split?" He leans forward on his cane.

I peer up at his haunting eyes but don't reply. Since I'm about to pee myself, I cut the conversation short.

"Excuse me. The iced tea is calling." I point toward the house. "Enjoy the remainder of Samhain."

He smiles warmly. "And you as well, Gwynedd."

I rush back inside to the bathroom just off the kitchen. As I approach the door, the aura returns. I jump when the door swings inward, revealing Courtney.

"I'm sorry, Gwyn. Have you been waiting long? My stomach was a bit nauseous."

I stare at her as the wave of warmth fades. "No. But I do need to go badly."

She exits the bathroom, smiling. "It's yours now."

I dart in and slam the door, barely getting my panties down in time. While I'm washing my hands, a sharp pain stabs me inside. I've got to stop using collagen in my tea. Suddenly, the sound of yelling and footsteps rumble in the distance. I dry my hands on the towel and scuttle up the hallway.

The guests have crowded together on the porch and in the street by the time I exit the house. Trinity is comforting a woman who has collapsed on the sidewalk, sobbing. I shift next to Ronnie. She's clutching Derek's arm.

"What the fuck happened?" I ask, catching my breath.

"She says someone snatched her two-year-old daughter when she turned around to pick up the candy she'd dropped. There were so many people clogging the sidewalk, no one noticed who took her."

Sirens pierce my ears as the police cars pull up. This won't help our image at all. A familiar thread of magic weaves through the crowd cramming the porch, spiraling toward the street. I grab my stomach as the pain pinches inside and observe the anxious townies. They hold their children close, worry contorting their faces—all except for Courtney. She expresses a different sort of angst, both fear and anger present in her eyes. Does she know something?

Chapter Ten

BAD IMPRESSIONS

Detective Jack Schmidt directs Officers O'Connor and Wilson to interview the remaining onlookers, mostly adults without children. The parents skedaddled home with their kids as soon as the police units parked. It's futile. No one saw who absconded with the preschooler. Trinity climbs the steps to the front porch and gestures for the coven to huddle together on one end, away from the ears of Unremarkables.

"This is disconcerting," our leader says. "There were townies standing shoulder to shoulder on the sidewalk. Yet no one saw who took the child."

"I can't listen to this." Ronnie twists her crimson locks. "Derek, take me home." She moves toward the porch steps.

"Goodnight, everyone. The kidnappings are stressing her out. Don't take it personally." He follows Ronnie down, clasping her hand.

"She's right to be concerned," Trinity says. "Gwyn shared she sensed strange magic residue at the last kidnapping. She believes a rogue witch may be helping the Baby Nabbers. The Bearsden Police Department hasn't revealed any of its investigation, either.

It's a hunch, but keep your eyes and ears tuned. Let's clean and lock up. This open house did NOT go as planned."

After splitting up the leftovers, we put all the tables, chairs, and toys away in dead silence. The coven disbands, and everyone exits the Pumpkin House, somber expressions replacing the former joyous ones. Archie and I speak to Tyler and Zoe on the paver sidewalk out front before heading home.

"Goodnight, dear," I say, hugging him. "We'll chat sometime this week. OK?"

He frowns at me. "Sure. I'll call you when I have time."

Zoe smiles as she hugs me. "Goodnight, Gwyn."

"Take care, you two," I reply.

"Don't be so glum," Archie says, patting Tyler's arm. "The kidnapping was not our fault. I'm sure the town doesn't blame us. I'll contact John Erickson this week and have a chat with him about it."

Tyler averts his eyes from me. "Right. Let's go, Zoe. I had a long day and want to get to sleep. Bye, Archie."

"Be careful driving home," he replies.

"Bye." Zoe waves as they walk away.

I put on my black witch's cape because the temperature has dropped a bit. Archie grasps my fingers, and we stroll onto the Green, sharing glances of affection and absorbing the night's event, too, I suppose. We must look like an odd pair, the witch and the vampire. While we weave through the maze of paver walkways and grass, he kisses the back of my hand several times.

"Do you remember me kissing you like this on our stroll through the Green the first Samhain?"

A soft chuckle breaks free. "Of course I do. I'll never forget. Ever."

"You were so hot that night. But then, I always hunger for you, Gwyn."

We turn into the alleyway, and about halfway through, he leads me to the side of Menzies Hall. After guiding me to the brick exterior, he kisses me and slides a hand between my legs. He rubs me through my panties, making me wet. But I won't repeat the act in the alley again.

"Stop, Archie," I say, panting. "Not here. And I thought your butt still hurts."

"Not as much as my front burns, aching for you."

I laugh so loud it echoes in the alleyway. "You should get an antibiotic for that."

He pulls his hand out from under my witch's skirt. "You think you're bloody funny, witch?"

"I am, Dr. Cock-burn," I say, rubbing his swollen bulge through his black chinos.

A corner of his mouth curls up. "You tease."

He kisses me again as I continue to stroke him, but I'm distracted by a clicking in the distance. I want him so badly, but my brain refuses to filter out the sound.

I push on his firm chest. "Somebody's coming up the alley."

Archie peers ahead as the shadow of a tall figure approaches. He smooths out my skirt and steps back.

"It's Seamus Duffy." He crosses his hands over his crotch. "Good evening."

"To both of you as well," he replies, his eyes flipping between us. "I hope I'm not interrupting anything."

Archie clears his throat. "No. Gwyn's high heels were bothering her feet, so she stopped to take a break."

"I thought you went home when the Unremarkables left," I say, stepping next to Archie. "You still have your costume on."

He smiles slightly. "As do you. Perhaps we can walk together?"

"Aye. Why not?" Archie asks, clasping my hand.

As we stroll toward Douglas Street, the crescent moon peeks through strips of clouds, adding illumination to the occasional streetlight. The air turns chilly, and not only because of the cool breeze. I don't think the Irish professor believed Archie's explanation. He knew he interrupted an intimate moment between

Archie and me. And he didn't appear embarrassed by it at all. But I'm more curious why he hung around after, and I can't let it go.

"So, why are you out so late?" I ask Seamus.

"Oh, yes. I failed to answer you," he replies. "I lingered for a while, hoping to gather clues regarding the disappearance of the child. As a cat sith witch, I use my sixth sense to observe and extract information. However, I'm not always successful. Tonight was one of those times."

Hmmm...he has a developed witch's intuition. Good to know. "Do you think magic is involved?"

"Because of the ongoing investigation, the Bearsden Police won't divulge what they have or haven't found. They have no leads at this time. Very suspicious."

"I agree," Archie says. "Gwyn has sensed the use of magic after the kidnappings."

I chuckle. "Or it's gas. I experienced a tightness in my gut but also an aura. In fact, I followed a stream of the residue at the Pumpkin House. It stopped when I walked onto the back porch." Hmph. Where Seamus was standing.

"Interesting." The Irish professor smiles. "Perhaps we can continue this discussion at the library tomorrow at our usual afternoon research meeting?"

"Sure. But the library may not be the most appropriate venue for discussing magic, don't you think?"

We've arrived at Seamus's bungalow, and he turns toward us. "Perhaps you should come here instead? I could make tea?"

Archie squeezes my hand. I get his message, but I need to pursue this.

"That sounds great," I say, pulling on Archie. "I'm exhausted after this evening. Let's go. Goodnight, Seamus."

"To you as well," he replies. "I am sorry for interrupting your private moment in the alley."

He locks eyes with mine and limps on his cane up the front walk. Archie and I continue toward Kent Way to Duncan Street.

"For fawk's sake, Gwyn," he says. "Did you observe how Seamus acted? His comment at the end? He has feelings for you. You want his help to find the being from your vision, but meeting with him most Fridays only encourages him."

I huff and pull my hand from his. "I can take care of myself, thank you very much, and I'm doing nothing that would make him think I have more than feelings of friendship for him. Don't you trust me?"

"Of course I do. But I have to work with him. It's becoming awkward."

We walk in silence until we enter through the front of his cottage. He shuts the door while I bend over to pull off my high-heeled boots. I lose my balance and tumble to the floor, landing on my ass.

I rub my backside. "Ugh. I should have sat on the stairs."

"Let me help." Archie kneels and grabs the heel of my boot. "I'm sorry about before. Meeting with Seamus is entirely your business. I suppose the green-eyed monster was bound to appear, eventually."

My brow crinkles. "Are you referring to Seamus or yourself? Because you know he has green eyes."

"Yes, I am aware. But I'm not referring to him."

"Are you jealous of him? Oh, Archie. There isn't any universe where I'd fall for anyone else. You're my heart."

He pulls my boot off and throws it aside. "Prove it, witch."

My abdomen convulses as I laugh. "Right here on the foyer rug?"

"It is the one place we haven't christened with our lovemaking in this house."

He crawls between my legs, inching up my torso until his face reaches mine. His goatee tickles me, and the warmth of his breath heats my skin. The aroma of his woodsy cologne still lingers and ignites the fire between my legs. I fumble for his pants zipper and pull it down.

"How's your bum, professor?" I ask, caressing him.

"Sore as a sunburnt bottom. But I don't care."

He kisses me, and our tongues intermingle, stroking my desire. But I'm worried all the stress will stamp out the yearning building inside. After tonight's incident at the Pumpkin House, the kidnappings clutter my brain.

I break from the kiss and whisper. "Take off my panties."

"As you wish, my love."

Archie pushes up on his knees and flips my skirt up. As he slips my black lace panties off, a wicked grin stretches his mouth. He unbuttons his chinos and shoves them down, catching his boxer briefs on the way. I stare at this would-be vampire in his white face makeup and slicked back hair, his manhood ready for action, and attempt to suppress my laughter. But I snicker and snort at the sight.

"Why are you laughing?" His eyes dart all around.

"I'm sorry. I looked up at you and realized I was about to get nailed by a vampire."

"Then prepare for a proper nibbling of your neck, witch."

He lowers his body and searches for me, entering with a grunt. Placing his mouth on my neck, he licks and nibbles on the skin, pinching it with his teeth.

"Ouch," I say, grabbing the back of his head. "You better not give me a hickey."

He replies in a vampirish accent, "I want to leave my mark." We pause to chuckle into one another's shoulders, and he whispers, "I cherish how much fun sex is with you. That it doesn't have to be romantic every time. I love you, Gwynedd."

"Mmm...I love you, too, honey."

I slide my hands across Archie's bandaged butt cheek, encouraging him to continue. He pushes into me, each thrust becoming more forceful than the one before. I want so badly to enjoy this, but the embers have died out. My mind keeps wandering to the sorrowful faces of the mothers who lost their babies to evil Unremarkables—and maybe a nefarious witch. His panting becomes irregular until he can't hold back any longer, releasing with a final shove.

"I apologize for the shortness of that session," he says, caressing my face. "It's been so long, I couldn't control myself. Let me catch my breath, and I'll make you writhe with joy."

"No, it's OK. I'm too stressed out to get there."

He rolls off me and rests on his side, stroking my upper arm. "I wish I could do something to help."

"The stress won't leave until everything is resolved. Finding a spell to close the portal. Discovering the supernatural monster in my vision. Graduating. This year is gonna suck."

He arches an eyebrow. "Well, I am a vampire."

He leans down and sucks on my neck. I chuckle and push him back.

"Thank you for trying. But there's even more. Spence spilled the tea on me talking to Richard that first Samhain. In front of Tyler."

"Fawk. What did he say?" He pulls up his pants and zips them up.

"Nothing. I told him we would chat later in the week."

"I realize you'd rather he hadn't learned about the incident, but it's for the best. You should be honest with him."

"He already has mixed feelings about his dad. I didn't want to add fuel to the fire." I roll on my side to face him.

"Speaking of conversations. What did you and Alys Morgan talk about?"

"Och. Nothing consequential. Don't get angry, but I think she was coming on to me."

"What? I hope you set her straight," I say, rubbing his pecs through his T-shirt.

"Aye. I was clear we've been together for years. I don't count the months we were apart."

"She resembles Courtney, a fortyish version, anyway. You can admit you're attracted to her."

He passes a finger over my lips. "I have the witch I want. What will it take for you to believe me? To feel confident enough to move in here?"

"I believe you, but I'm not ready. Please, don't pressure me."

He kisses me, and I ask myself, *Why am I waiting?*

CHAPTER ELEVEN

A MOTHER'S CONFESSION

IN TYPICAL DELAWARE FASHION, a cold front blows through overnight, soaking the ground with rain and sending our warm weather packing for good. By Friday morning, the temperature has dropped twenty degrees. Yesterday, it was too hot to wear my witch's cape. Today, I'm shivering in a long-sleeved tee and jeans. What a way to celebrate the first day of November. Archie cooks us breakfast, and we head to campus for class—him to teach, me to attend.

After my course ends, I rush home in the rain, struggling to keep my umbrella from flipping inside out, and eat lunch. Mr. Yeats scuttles into the kitchen, transforming into his human persona.

"Good afternoon, Ms. Crowther," he says, writing on his clipboard. "I wanted to remind you to schedule training with Mr. Wolfe. To learn how to conference with his grandparents."

Shit. I forgot. "I don't know if it will happen anytime soon. He's pissed at me."

He straightens his vest. "Whatever did you do?"

"Never you mind. Plan on the training happening in the distant future for now."

He drops his clipboard. "Well, if you aren't in need of my assistance, I'll be in the magic room."

"Just as well," I say, placing my dishes in the sink. "I have a research meeting with Dr. Duffy at his house now. Have a pleasant afternoon, Mr. Yeats."

"May the rest of your day be productive, Ms. Crowther." The familiar strides to the magic room.

I put on my fleece jacket, grab my backpack and umbrella, and walk briskly up Drummond Lane to the brown bungalow. When I get to Seamus's, I raise my fist to knock, but the door opens wide before I do.

"Please, Gwynedd. Come in out of this damp, dreary weather." Seamus motions me into the foyer. "Let me take your umbrella and coat."

"Thanks. I can't believe it was warm enough for shorts yesterday," I say, rubbing my arms vigorously. "I'm so cold."

"Then a cup of hot tea is what you need. Please, find a seat at the dining room table, and I'll bring us a pot. The cups and tea bags are already there. Pick whatever you like."

I set my backpack on the floor and sit while he retrieves the teakettle from the kitchen. I choose an Irish blend to try something new. When he returns, limping without his cane, he fills our cups. He places the kettle on a trivet and sits down, smiling at my choice.

"An excellent blend. I hope you enjoy it." After adding honey to his tea, he waves his hand over it, prompting the spoon to twirl. "You don't have to hide your magic here."

I blush and do the same. "Leslie gets pissed off when I display my skills overtly at home. Archie worries I'll forget to hide my witchcraft when I'm around Unremarkables."

"A definite concern, but I imagine you're competent enough not to commit such an error in judgement."

I chuckle. "You don't know me very well, Seamus. I've had my share of fuckups. Like sneaking into your house and hiding under your bed."

He bursts out laughing, and strands of black hair spill onto his forehead. "I had quite the laugh after I left, knowing you were under there."

I bet you did. "Are you sorry I found out you were watching out for me?"

"It was a quandary, I must say." He takes a sip of his tea, staring at me over the cup. "But I'm pleased you know of my existence. I spend less energy on hiding my true nature. So, tell me of your experiences with intuition and the magic you sensed."

I share my experiences with the first two kidnappings, stopping to sip my tea occasionally. Then I elaborate on the prior night's events.

"When I crossed the unusual stream of energy, I followed the residue throughout the Pumpkin House until it ended on the back porch—where you were standing."

I stare into his eyes, hoping to observe any signs of guilt, and the corners of his mouth raise a little.

"You suspect I am the witch employed by the Baby Nabbers? Do you honestly believe I would commit such an evil thing, Gwynedd?" The Irish professor drops his cup on the saucer and chooses a tea bag. "Please, help yourself to another."

"No, I'd have to pee all night." My eyes roam around the sparsely furnished home. "And no. I don't think you are working for the kidnappers."

"What motivation would I have? But I am stumped. How did you sense the residue, but I did not? Curious."

I ponder his question for a few seconds. "Could my magic radar have more to do with being a mom than a witch?"

"Hmmm. A mother's intuition. Could be an accurate assessment. Perhaps I was arrogant in believing I could help you."

"No. I'm grateful you're willing to teach me what you know."

A seriousness crushes his pleasant demeanor. "I can't divulge the ways of the cat sith, Gwynedd. We are a solitary lot."

Well, that blows. "I understand." My gaze falls to my teacup.

Seamus lays his hand on mine. "I am truly sorry. Shall we continue our research?"

I pull my hand into my lap, and he sits back in his chair, a look of embarrassment crossing his visage.

"Sure, but another thirty minutes is all I have. Then I have to meet Archie for dinner. We're going over his research of some obscure Scottish folklore after."

His eyes drop to an open textbook, and he slides it across the table, being careful not to touch me. How can I continue this friendship if he keeps wanting for more?

Archie closes the last reference and sits back on the brown leather loveseat. "Another dead end. We'll keep searching. I don't want to ruin your mood further, but have you spoken with Tyler about your Samhain conversation with Richard yet?"

"No," I say, falling back on the loveseat cushion. "I was letting him stew a bit."

"He'll be at Agnes's in the morning, no? And we have dinner tomorrow with him at Spence and Tanner's house. It could be a delicate situation."

"Yeah. I suppose I should call him now. Can you referee if I need some interference?"

He raises a corner of his mouth. "I doubt it will come to that. But I'll be here if the conversation turns...unpleasant."

I pick up my cell and pull up Tyler's name in my contacts. As I tap the green phone icon, my heartbeat takes off and my hand trembles. I don't care what anyone thinks about me, except for my son.

"Hi, Mom. I wondered when you might call."

"Good thing I didn't wait for you, then. I guess you have questions. Well, ask away." My chest tightens while I brace for his attack.

"I was super angry when Spence blurted that out, but I've had time to think. There must have been a good reason you kept it from me." He breathes into the phone. "Please, tell me you have an explanation."

My heart rate decreases, and I sigh. "I thought the Fellowship was off their rocker. Ronnie and Archie convinced me to join them in their witch's circle for Samhain. A blue haze appeared near the ceiling, and your father's image materialized. At first, I figured someone was playing a cruel joke. Then your father spoke to me."

"Fuck," Tyler says, his breathing becoming erratic. "What did he say to you?"

I glance at Archie, and he shifts closer to me on the loveseat, squeezing my hand and nodding to continue. I grind my teeth.

"He asked about Cassandra. How she was doing."

"What? Didn't he ask about me?" His voice cracks, and he huffs.

"No, Tyler. He wanted to find out how Cassandra was doing."

He growls into the phone. "Well, fuck him. We're both better off without his cheating ass."

"I got pissed and screamed at him. When I mentioned you, he said he wasn't worried about you because you had me. It doesn't change how he felt about you, son. He loved you. I didn't tell you what happened because I wanted you to remember your time with him when he was alive. He's different in the Otherworld. So, now you know why I kept the conversation a secret. You're right, though. I shouldn't have." I tighten my grip around Archie's fingers.

He pants for a few seconds, stopping to swallow. Then he speaks.

"I'm not mad, Mom, but I wish you hadn't gone through that experience. In a way, I'm glad."

My jaw drops. "You are?"

"Think about it. If you hadn't stayed for the ritual... If you had not talked to Dad... Would we even know about our witch ancestry? I would have never met Zoe. You and Archie might not be together. Our lives would have followed different paths. Personally, I like this one. Don't you?"

I gaze into Archie's loving eyes. "Yes, son. I actually do. I'm tired. It was such a long day. Are you going to Agnes's in the morning?"

"Oh, yeah. I almost forgot we're putting in time on the database. Don't forget we have dinner at Tanner and Spence's tomorrow."

"I won't. I love you, son. Goodnight."

"Night, Mom. I love you, too."

I swipe the red icon and fall into Archie's embrace. For a moment, I imagine where my journey would have led me had I taken a right at the fork in the road. What a tedious life it would have been.

Archie stands in the mudroom doorway in a T-shirt and lounge pants, scratching his head. "I don't understand why I can't ride over with you. If you want, I can wait in the kitchen while Agnes gives you some tips."

"I'd be distracted knowing you were in there. You're not even dressed yet." I finish tying my sneaker and shift next to him, wrapping my arms around his middle.

"Give us about an hour. Frankly, I'm not impressed with her suggestions. I mean, she usually wings it when she's practicing the craft. But she really doesn't know what she is doing. It's a bit funny to watch her falter when she's always so competent." If Seamus would show me some of his intuition secrets, I wouldn't need her help.

He kisses me. "Agnes prides herself on figuring things out, even when she fails. I bet she comes through for you."

"Maybe. See you in an hour, honey." I kiss him goodbye and slip on my fleece jacket over a long-sleeved tee.

As I walk to my Prius, I bask in the warmth of the sun's rays. Mid-50 isn't the spring-like temperature we had on Samhain, but I'll take the cloudless blue skies over the deluge we had yesterday. After the short ride to Agnes's farmhouse, I knock on the front door and enter.

"Hey, Agnes." I peek into the living room and kitchen.

She shouts from the magic room in the back, "In here, Gwyn! Trying something new!"

I amble in to find her lying on the rug Leslie bought to brighten the space. A bluish-green crystal rests on her forehead. She's dressed in a loose blouse and knit pants for the practice session. How did she mange to lie down on the floor? Surely she won't get back up.

"What are you doing?" I ask, setting my purse on the wooden table. "Is that labradorite?"

She hisses at me and closes her eyes. "Shhh. I'm trying to activate my third eye chakra."

I tiptoe to my mentor and kneel on the ground while she continues with—whatever she's doing. She turns her hands over, her palms facing up, and summons her magic. But she shakes out the amber glow and grumbles. She removes the crystal and sits up on her elbows.

"Why do you think it's not working?" I ask.

She twists a side of her mouth, adding to the wrinkles on her sun-damaged skin. "I don't fucking know. You need a fuck ton of patience to meditate and align your chakras. Never worked for me. Who has time for this shit?"

I snicker. "Someone with patience."

"Are you mocking me? Ungrateful witch. Here. You try." She passes the labradorite to me.

"I hope the nightly meditation I performed with the amethyst geode helps. How do I facilitate this? Should I clear my head?

Meditate for a few minutes first? Call on my ancestors? Should I—"

"For fuck's sake, Gwyn. You talk too fucking much. I'd forgotten how frustrating it was to teach you." She rolls onto her side and supports her upper body on an elbow.

I laugh and lie down next to her on the rug. "Oh, you love the admiration, you old hedge witch."

"Yeah, yeah," she says, quashing a smile. "Place the crystal on your forehead near your eyes and close them. Try to empty your head of everything. I fail at this part, but maybe you'll have more success."

I attempt to clear the junk from my brain as random thoughts continually invade the solitude. The clutter exits through doors...no, portals into different dimensions. This is amazing.

Agnes continues to offer guidance. "Take deep breaths and hold them, letting the air pass through your lips slowly. Again. And once more. Summon your witch energy and meld it with the labradorite."

I face my palms toward the ceiling, concentrating on the connection. A magnetism pulls my hands toward my head. I want to look, but I'm afraid I'll lose the connection.

"Fuck me," Agnes whispers.

I peek through slits, glimpsing the swirl of energy above me, and open my eyes completely. "Holy crystals."

A faint swirl of amber and white dances above me, connecting the magic from my fingers to the labradorite. And just like that, it disappears.

Agnes moans as she pushes up off the floor. "Fucking beginner's luck."

"Well, it doesn't mean my witch's intuition will be any stronger. Could the daily meditation have helped?"

Knocking on the front door echoes down the hallway, and it creaks open.

"We're out of time, anyway," she says. "Everyone is here to work on the database."

Spence, Skye, Tyler, and Zoe shuffle in. My son walks across the room and hugs me. Richard may have caused me immense grief, but at least he gave me this compassionate man.

"Aww," Spence says. "I'm sorry I caused that rift."

Skye shakes her head. "If you could control what spews out of your orifice, this shit wouldn't happen."

"People like us can't help it." Zoe nudges Spence. "It takes a nanosecond for the words in our brain to transfer to our tongues. It's a curse."

"I have a spell for that, you know," Agnes says. "The incantation is in the fucking database."

Archie and Leslie enter the room in deep discussion with Trinity. Their expressions are wrinkled with concern.

"The coven may want to attend the next meeting," I hear Archie say. "This will affect all of us."

The Elder lifts her chin. "Indeed. Trinity, you'll need to send a group text. We don't have time for a circle."

"What's wrong?" I ask, my eyes jumping from Archie to Trinity.

Our coven leader puts a hand on her hip. "Elijah called. He says Alys Morgan has convinced John Erickson to introduce a short-term ordinance under emergency rules. They want to close off city-owned spaces and...institute a curfew for minors."

"What the fuck?" I ask. "How will we entertain the Seelie Fae?"

"Exactly." Archie brushes fingers through his hair. "They want extra police patrolling the town to enforce the curfew."

Spence crosses his arms. "That's fucked up. I mean, the night is just getting started at 10:00 p.m."

"It is for the Seelie Fae, anyway," Skye says.

Agnes grumbles. "Hmph. Fucking police can't stop the kidnappings if a rogue witch is involved."

"No," I say. "But they will sure get in the way. If we don't show up to play with them on a regular basis, they'll become antsy like before."

Zoe chuckles. "Yeah. Who knows what mischief they'll start?"

"We'll have to cross that bridge *if* it happens," Trinity says.

"What about our allies on the council?" Archie asks, rubbing his goatee. "Can we rely on them to block this?"

"Trinity, you and I should contact Jessica Devine." Leslie glances at me. "But that only gives us three votes."

Our coven leader nods. "I get what you're saying, Elder."

And I do, too. "No. We can't return to the old ways. I won't cast a spell of influence."

"Gwynedd, are you prepared to deal with the fallout if we don't use magic to block this ordinance?" Archie asks.

"Yes, I am," I say. "I'll talk with Shailagh and Aonghas Saturday night and tell them we may not visit for a while. We have to plan other ways around the inconvenience if the city council goes through with the vote. But we'll retain our integrity."

Agnes guffaws. "Fuck integrity."

I scowl at my mentor while the rest of them snicker and chuckle.

"For now, I'll send a reminder text to everyone to show up at the meeting on Monday evening," Trinity says. "Be prepared to speak up. It may be your sole opportunity. We have a couple of hours left to work on the database. Let's get to it."

While we sift through the grimoires, I ruminate over our dilemma. If I increase the strength of my intuition, I'd have a better chance at discovering the source of the random magic. I need to cajole Seamus to teach me his cat sith secrets. But how?

CHAPTER TWELVE

PRANKSTERS WILL PLAY

I STARE OUT THE window of Archie's Tesla on the way to Spence and Tanner's house, contemplating my next steps. Seamus has deep feelings for me, but it would be so unethical to prey on those affections. I can't do it. So, where does that leave me?

"What are you thinking about, my love?" Archie asks, laying a hand on mine.

"Oh, I wonder how Ronnie is doing. I haven't spoken with her since Samhain. The kidnapping really shook her to the bone. I'd feel the same way."

"Understandable. The possibility of an unethical witch assisting the Baby Nabbers would frighten every parent, if they knew."

He pulls up to the curb in front of my old home, right behind Derek's sedan. He's helping Ronnie out of the car. I dash over and give her a tight embrace.

"How are you doing?" I ask. "You were so upset on Samhain, I was afraid to call and bring it up."

My friend smiles. "I'm OK. But I haven't slept well since. I may not stay long tonight."

"Hi, Derek," Archie says, patting his back. "Ronnie, I'm glad you came. It's good to get out. I want you to meet our newest instructor, Ashley Lewis. She hasn't met very many people in town yet."

"Gwyn said she has a two-year-old and is a single mom. I can't imagine how she's managing. Thank the gods I have Derek."

"I'm the lucky one, babe," he replies, hugging her.

"Don't forget," I say as we walk toward the house. "No talk of magic or the supernatural tonight. Ashley is an Unremarkable."

Ronnie zips her lips with a slide of her fingers as Archie knocks on the door. Spence answers, an exasperated look stretching his face. The crash of something fragile resounds in the distance.

"Good. The old people are here." He motions us into the foyer.

Archie scowls at Spence. "I resent that description."

"Dr. Lewis's son is running all over the house. Jeff and Skye have helped her round him up, but...oh, my gods." Spence leans into us, cupping his mouth with a hand. "He's such a brat."

"The boy is two years old," I say. "They're like that. Even Tyler was a fireball."

"Tanner is cooking tonight, conveniently leaving me to watch out for Aidan's naughty fingers."

"He's probably bored with all the adults." A mischievous grin emerges on Ronnie's face. "Auntie Ronnie will entertain him."

"Sounds like fun," Derek says. "I could use the practice, too. Lead the way. We'll rescue you."

Spence waves his hand to follow him into the family room off the kitchen. "Please, before he breaks anything else."

This is the first time we've visited the house since they added this space. What a welcoming area it is, with sofas and oversized chairs centered in front of a gas fireplace. An enormous TV is mounted over the wooden mantel, and a giant fan hangs from the cathedral ceiling. The young couple have breathed new life into my old home.

Spence takes a broom and dustpan to where Skye and her boyfriend Zach are picking up shards from the vase Aidan knocked over. Tyler and Zoe are sitting on an area rug with Jeff and Ashley, attempting to engage the easily distracted toddler.

"Hi, everyone," I say, chuckling. "You're enjoying playtime."

My son glares at me, unamused. "You're funny, Mom."

"Well, I am." Zoe hands a wooden block to Aidan.

"Ronnie and Derek," Archie says. "I'd like you to meet Dr. Ashley Lewis, our new Celtic Studies instructor."

Ashley stands to shake their hands, pushing a strand of brown hair out of her eyes. "A pleasure to meet you. Jeff said you're having a baby, and from the looks of your tummy, the due date isn't far off."

"Yeah. Derek and I are super pumped for our little one to arrive. We didn't want to know the sex. Better to be surprised."

Ashley's son throws a block across the room, frustrated the tower he built has fallen. "No blocks."

"Now Aidan," Jeff says in a calm voice. "We don't throw things."

"He's bored. I'm not a mom yet, but I am aware toddlers have a short attention span." My best friend looks at Spence. "Do you have any boxes in the garage?"

"Yeah, at least one," he replies. "What do you want it for?"

"Get it and bring it here," she says. "And find me some scissors."

"What are you going to do?" I ask.

"You'll see," Ronnie replies as Spence hurries off to the garage.

Archie raises a corner of his mouth, clearly picking up on something I'm not. "Brilliant idea."

Skye and Zach join us in the family room after discarding the glass shards. They sit down next to Tyler and Zoe on the floor, attempting to distract Ashley's son. Tanner enters, wearing an apron.

"Hi, everybody. I'm so glad all of you could come. Ashley, don't worry about the vase. It was a cheap thing we received with some flowers. I should have baby-proofed the house better."

"You're so kind," she replies. "But I still feel terrible about him breaking your things."

"Please, don't. Dinner will be ready soon. Jeff already strapped the toddler seat to a chair. I'll shout when it's served."

Ashley picks up a stray piece of glass and drops it into the dustpan. "Skye and Zach, thank you for cleaning up the mess."

"No problem," they reply.

"He's a toddler," Skye adds. "This won't be the last time he breaks something."

Ashley chuckles. "Very true. Gwyn, I need a babysitter on Monday afternoon. One of the grad students has to finish a paper. Are you available?"

"Sure," I say, eyeing her son.

Tanner ambles back into the kitchen and a whiff of fresh bread trickles into the family room. Spence returns a couple of minutes later with a large cardboard box. Ronnie sets it on the floor. The rest of us observe her, perplexed, as she cuts square holes at random on the sides of it. She bends down next to the bored toddler.

"Hi, Aidan. I'm Ronnie. Would you like to play with a new toy?"

He stares at her for a moment, then replies, "Yes."

"Great. Derek, lift Aidan and drop him in."

"Are you sure?" he asks. "He'll whine if we put him in there. It'll be like prison."

She cackles. "Yeah, but he won't realize he's in jail, because we're gonna make a game out of it."

"Do it," Archie says. "She knows what she's doing."

Aidan whines as Derek transports him to the playbox, but giggles when he lands inside. He pokes fingers through the holes, and Ronnie shoves blocks through them, prompting the boy to do the same. They continue this back-and-forth for a few minutes. Then the young witches take over.

"Great idea," I tell Ronnie. "You're going to be a wonderful mom."

Ashley grins at her giggling son. "Thank you so much. When you've had your baby, we should get together. Our children will only be two years apart. They could be great friends, eventually."

"I'd love to set up play dates down the road," Ronnie says.

"How did you come up with the idea?" Jeff asks.

"You have to think like a kid. Basically, I never grew up. So…" She laughs, and her crimson curls flop around.

"This is so much fun." Spence shoves a block through a hole, prompting Ashley's son to push it back through. "Right, Aidan?"

Ronnie snorts. "Need I say more?"

Tanner shouts from the dining room. "Dinner's on the table!"

"Awesome." Spence presses an eye against the box's hole. "Hey, kid. You wanna eat?"

Aidan giggles as Spence lifts him out of the box. "You funny."

"Very perceptive, young man," Archie says, grinning.

We all crack up as we shuffle into the dining room. Ashley's son acts sweet throughout dinner, sitting next to his new pal, Spence. We chat about everything from the abrupt change in the weather to Ashley's fondness of Bearsden to Ronnie's impending due date. But the conversation turns somber when Tanner brings up the most recent kidnapping and the city council's ordinance vote.

"Play box?" Aidan asks, pointing to the family room.

Jeff pushes up from his chair. "I'll take him." He wipes Aidan's hands and face off.

"You all continue chatting," Ashley says. "I'll play with him. He's my son, after all."

Ronnie wipes her mouth with a napkin, an anxious expression on her face. "Derek, why don't we keep them company?"

"Sure, babe." He follows them into the family room.

When they've left, we continue the discussion in lower voices.

"We should be careful around Ronnie and Ashley," I say. "They're both stressing about the kidnappings."

Tanner leans on the table. "Has the Bearsden PD released any more information regarding the incidents? I haven't read anything, but I follow local online news."

"All the articles I've seen still report no leads," Archie says. "Very concerning when you consider the lack of evidence."

Skye leans on the table. "Except for the single sighting of a woman with long, blond hair."

"Awesome." Spence stuffs a cookie in his mouth. "That narrows the suspect down to about a thousand women."

"Less than that, because not all blondes in Bearsden are witches," Skye adds.

Zach's brow furrows. "What do you mean?"

Spence grabs another cookie and gets up from his chair, turning toward the doorway.

"Dude?" Tanner asks. "Where are you going? We decided no food in the family room."

"Aidan didn't get one yet," he replies. "Don't make such a fuss. The crumbs will fall in the box. No big deal."

"You're quiet, Zach." Tanner stacks a few dinner plates. "Being an Unremarkable, you must have an opinion."

He chuckles. "About the cookie or the kidnappings? Or the possible curfew ordinance?"

"I'd like to know, too," Skye says, grabbing a few glasses.

Archie stands, collecting the bowls. "Let me help you, Tanner. You cooked the meal."

"Thanks for helping, guys. Spence usually loads the dishwasher, but he's too busy playing dad. Any or all of the above, Zach."

"One. The cookie rule is above my paygrade. Two. It's strange there are no leads, assuming they're telling us the truth. They must have a good reason to hide evidence. And three. I don't like the idea of a curfew, but it couldn't hurt to put more cops on the streets—at least until they catch the Baby Nabbers."

I collect the utensils. "But it won't matter if a rogue witch is helping them evade capture."

"Oh, that's what Skye was referring to earlier," Zach says, following his girlfriend's lead. "I thought witches pledged to do no harm."

She heads toward the kitchen. "We make the commitment, but not all witches are benevolent."

Archie lifts a pile of dishes. "Like Unremarkables, there are bound to be a few narcissists in the bunch, unfortunately."

We drop the discussion and take the remainder of the dirty dishes into the kitchen, joining the others in the family room when we're finished. After a few minutes, Aidan yawns, prompting Ashley and the rest of us to relinquish the evening to our kind hosts. Archie drives to Main Street to drop me off at Mitchell Hall.

"Are you sure you don't want me to go with you?" he asks.

"No. They may listen better if I'm alone." I kiss him on the cheek. "I won't be long."

"Could you change my bandage for me tonight?"

"You mean, pull off your boxers and admire your toned ass? Absolutely."

I chuckle as I get out of the car, and he winks at me. I check for pedestrians up and down the street before darting into the Celestial Gardens. Shailagh and Aonghas are already dancing around the manicured shrubs and run to me when they notice me watching them.

"Aunt Gwyn! You're here! Can you play?" they ask.

"Of course, just like every Saturday night. But before we start, I need to tell you something." I hold one of their tiny hands in each of mine. "Remember when I told you someone stole a baby in here? Well, it happened in other parts of the city, too. So, our leaders may create a rule to stop us from visiting you for a while to make the town safe. But it won't be forever. You must be good until I and the others visit you again. Promise?"

"We promise, Aunt Gwyn. Now let's play!" They drag me across the gardens, giggling, and I stay a little longer to hedge my bet. As

I stroll toward the gate to leave, I wave to them. When will I see them again?

"Thank you for babysitting Aidan on Monday afternoon," Jeff says, logging into the cash register. "Ashley needs an experienced mom for a change. She can't work on discipline with him because the undergrad students let him do whatever he wants."

I slip on my fleece jacket. "To be fair, toddlers always push the envelope and then some. I haven't watched a two-year-old in years. It'll be fun."

Shane strolls into the front with tagged merchandise. "Taking off for your hike, Gwyn?"

"Yeah. Gonna be a cold one, but Ronnie needs to get a walk in. As the temperatures dip, she'll have fewer opportunities."

"The baby will arrive soon enough, and then she'll have her hands full."

Jeff nods. "I can attest to that. The way Ashley talks, she's not slept since Aidan was born."

Having met her son, I believe her. "She will certainly be busy. Shane, are you attending the council meeting tomorrow?"

"I suspect I will. We need to make a presence. I'd bet my crystals on townies showing up as well. The ordinance will raise everyone's blood pressure—on both sides of the matter."

"Ashley and I can't go," Jeff says. "She needs help with Aidan so she can grade."

"See you tomorrow at the town hall then, Shane." I wave to my other boss. "Bye, Jeff."

"Bye, Gwyn." He waves at me. "And thanks again."

"Enjoy your hike, darling," Shane replies, waving.

While I stroll to the park trailhead, a cool breeze plays with my bangs and long hair. The sun burns brightly in the baby-blue sky, and not a cloud is in sight. What a great fall day for a hike. Ronnie waves at me in the distance, her crimson curls frolicking in the wind, and I run to meet her. With a little over a month left, her swollen belly has ballooned. She must be so uncomfortable.

"Hey, are you sure you feel well enough to do this hike?" I ask, catching my breath.

"No, but the exercise helps me sleep. Thanks for braving the chilly weather."

I bend my head back, squinting for a moment. "With the sun, the real feel temperature is almost sixty degrees. I'm good."

"Are you OK with going by the bog after the most recent rain? It'll be muddy."

I point to my ankle boots. "I came prepared. We can do the loop."

"Great." Suddenly, Ronnie stops and grabs her belly. "Oh, boy. They've been getting more intense."

"Are you in pre-labor?" I ask. "Frankly, I don't remember mine at all. Should we turn back?"

She blows air through her lips, hissing through her teeth. "No. Braxton Hicks contractions. I'm good. Let's keep walking."

"If you have another, we should go back to the trailhead and have Derek pick you up."

"Stop fussing over me. I already have one momma hen at home."

"Give him a break. He loves you and doesn't want anything to happen to you or the baby."

She grins and her face lights up. "I know. Gwyn, you don't have to answer, but a question has been gnawing at me. Why didn't you have another kid? Did you have problems conceiving, too?"

"No. Nothing like that at all. After Tyler was born, Richard said he wasn't interested in more children. He went and got snipped. Didn't even ask me."

"I'm sorry I asked. Do you wish you could have a baby with Archie?"

I take a breath and exhale. "Sometimes, but he's been a great substitute dad for Tyler. He relies on Archie for advice. I can't imagine having a baby at my age. I'm in a different stage of life. But I am ecstatic for you."

We walk in relative silence, enjoying the sunshine and one another's company. My mind drifts to thoughts of Archie as a dad. How wonderful it could have been if I'd had a baby with him instead of Richard, but I wouldn't have Tyler. Besides, in his younger days, he was sowing his wild oats to avoid settling down. One doesn't need offspring to prove love and commitment, anyway. But deep down, I must need something from Archie, or I would have moved in with him by now.

As we approach the bog, my abdomen tightens. A familiar aura returns, pulling at me like a magnet toward the water. A sense of unexplained urgency overcomes me.

"Ronnie, I can't explain now, but I need to run ahead. Meet me at the bog?"

"Sure. But wait for me there. I don't want to be alone for long."

My legs move as fast as they can, kicking up stones as I succumb to the pull of the magic. My heart pounds deep in my chest, and an amber glow seeps from my fingers. When I reach the bend in the trail, I nearly crash into Courtney Erickson. My mouth snaps shut with a yelp.

"Oh, Courtney," I say, huffing and puffing. "What are you doing here?"

Her mouth falls open. "I'm hiking? Same as you."

"Were you practicing witchcraft in here?" My eyes narrow.

She stutters a bit. "Um...I...no. Why would you ask?"

"Well, you are a witch and you're in the woods."

Courtney chuckles. "So are you, Gwyn. John usually hikes with me, but he's home preparing for the city council meeting. I assume the Bearsden Coven will attend?"

"Yeah. Of course," I reply.

She snickers. "Do you have something up your sleeve?"

"What?" I get what she's implying. "No. We don't cast spells of influence anymore."

"Then you'll have to lobby along with the townies, I guess."

Ronnie arrives a bit out of breath. "Hey, Courtney. Funny running into you here."

"Hi," she replies. "John's expecting me. I better get home."

Our ex-coven member prances down the path in her hiking boots, her pale-blond hair riding a zephyr.

"What a coincidence running into her here," my best friend says.

"Yeah." I stare into the distance at the murky bog. A faint haze rises from the water's surface. *Or was it?*

CHAPTER THIRTEEN

MISGUIDED AFFECTIONS

WHEN I ARRIVE HOME, I nudge the red side door inward and hang up my jacket, kicking off my sneakers. Leslie is cooking dinner in the kitchen. I inhale the aroma of tomato sauce and spices.

"Hello, Gwynedd. I was about to put pasta in to boil. Would you like some?"

"Thank you. I'd love not to cook tonight. I'm tired. This semester can't end soon enough. I need a break...from everything."

She pours small shell pasta into a pot. "You carry too much of the world on your shoulders. More than any one witch should bear. Perhaps you should focus on finishing Fall Semester. Put your research on the being in your vision on the back burner. Archie and I have had no luck. I assume your work with Seamus has uncovered nothing or you would have said something."

"Nope. Without a picture, the monster could fit any of the descriptions we've found. But none of them match a hundred percent. When the gray-skinned giant crosses over, do you think he'd pose for a photo?"

Leslie laughs as she stirs the tomato sauce. "My suggestion would be to ask and make a run for it."

"Exactly my thoughts. I need to concentrate on increasing the strength of my witch's intuition. After my last training session with Agnes, I began meditating with an amethyst geode she gave me. I think it's helped a little, but I can't replicate what happened at her house."

"All things develop in time," she says, placing utensils on the kitchen table. "I noticed you were wearing boots."

"I just finished a hike with Ronnie in the North Basin. We were right around the corner from the bog, and my body reacted to the presence of magic. An aura overwhelmed me, and like a magnet, it dragged me toward the water. I ran as if my life depended on it. When I got to the bend, Courtney Davies appeared."

Leslie dumps the pasta in the strainer over the sink. "Indeed. Was she alone?"

"Yeah. She said her husband had to stay home and prepare for the Monday council meeting. I asked her if she was practicing witchcraft in there. She answered no."

"Did you believe her?" she asks, setting plates of pasta on the table.

"It made sense," I reply as we sit down to eat. "But there was something off about it. When I observed the bog in the distance, a strange haze floated over it. It was odd. But it dissipated by the time Ronnie and I hiked to the water."

"Curious. Are you suggesting Courtney is the rogue witch aiding the Baby Nabbers we've hypothesized about?"

I recall dashing through the Pumpkin House on Samhain, following the stream of magic residue and discovering her in the bathroom.

"How?" I ask. "She was standing on the porch at the Pumpkin House when I ran outside. I was using the toilet right before. But she had a strange expression on her face. Anxious as everyone else, but it was different. What do I know? She probably felt bad for the mom. We all did."

"I'll share this news with Trinity. We should tread carefully around her. She's the wife of a councilman. Please, eat your dinner, Gwynedd. Don't let the worries of the world ruin your appetite. You must remain strong in case your power is needed to protect the town."

I smile at the Elder. "I like you a lot more with this demeanor. Should I thank your partner?"

"Pfft. If it were up to Agnes, I'd be holed up in that farmhouse of hers, letting the coven rot away like a corpse."

"You don't mean that. She's come a long way since you found each other again."

"Yes. She loves me as I do her. But let's be honest. If it weren't for you, she would have never returned to the coven. As much as you didn't want the job, Gwynedd, you are the anchor for all of us." She lays a wrinkled hand on mine and smiles. "I hope you'll keep it."

I don't respond and continue eating. Being an anchor is a heavy burden. I'm not sure I want the position.

After meditation with the geode, I lie in bed, contemplating how I will twist Seamus's arm to divulge his cat sith secrets. Mr. Yeats jumps onto the quilt and stares at me, blinking. I pet his back.

"What am I going to do, Mr. Yeats? How do I convince a cat sith witch to break centuries of rules? Don't answer. It was rhetorical. Scoot, now. I need privacy."

He meows at me, hops onto the floor, and scuttles out of the room. I shut the door and call Archie to fill him in on my suspicions about Courtney.

"Hard to say what it all means. She's a follower, not the makings of a rogue witch, in my opinion. Don't you agree?"

"I guess. But I'm eager to see how things go down tomorrow night at the council meeting." I yawn into the phone.

"You sound exhausted. Get some rest. I'll talk to you tomorrow. Sleep well, my love."

"You, too, honey."

After class on Monday, I rush across the Green to the alleyway, hoping to catch Seamus while he's eating lunch. The sun is shining, and the temperature is nearly sixty. I practice my speech on the way to Kent and Drummond. He has to acquiesce when I tell him about the coven's worry regarding the narcissistic witch.

A neighbor strolls by, waving, as I knock on Seamus's front door. But he isn't coming. Damn. My shoulders fall. He must have remained at school today. As I step off the stoop, he calls to me.

"Gwynedd, I wasn't expecting you. Please, come in."

"Thanks." I enter the house, fiddling with my backpack strap.

"What can I do for you on this lovely day?" he asks, leaning on his cane.

"Yes. It's warmer than expected." My gaze drops to the floor.

"Something is wrong," he says, laying a hand on my shoulder. "Please, you can confide in me. Have you had another vision?"

Whatever words spill from my mouth will play on his affections. But I tell myself I have to do it. For my best friend—to keep her future baby safe.

"No. I shouldn't ask you, but the coven and I are so worried about the children in our town, especially Ronnie's little one that's due in about a month..." I stare into his eyes. He gazes back silently, inviting me to keep speaking, so I do. "Will you teach me how a cat sith witch increases their intuition? Even a tiny morsel of your knowledge could aid me, intensify my skills enough to sniff out the witch who's put money above rectitude. I'm asking my protector for help."

He looks away for a long minute, then returns his gaze. "If I share my secrets, you must promise never to divulge what I show you to anyone—not even Archie." He grasps my hand. "This is knowledge I share only with those I consider special to me."

"Yes. I promise you I won't tell anyone."

He smiles. "I will be in touch when I have a break in my schedule."

"Thank you, Seamus," I say, laying a hand on my chest. "I'm indebted to you."

He gestures to the dining room. "I was about to eat lunch. Would you join me?"

"I would love to, but I have to get home and eat quickly. I'm babysitting Dr. Lewis's son Aidan this afternoon."

"Ah, yes. She has a class at one. You better make haste, then. We can have lunch another time."

"Yes. Let's do that. Have a wonderful day."

"And you as well, Gwynedd."

I step out onto the stoop, waving goodbye. On the way home, my stomach churns. Agnes says there are repercussions for everything we do. Will I regret this?

Standing in front of Nick Evans's old apartment, my chest tightens. I haven't been here since the night I stabbed him with Archie's dirk, turning his fairy body into a mummified corpse. Why did I think I could come here and babysit? My heart beats against my ribcage and my hand trembles as I knock. The door swings in.

"Shh," Ashley whispers, placing an index finger on her lips. "I finally cajoled Aidan to nap. He's been so wired since we moved to this apartment. I can't figure out why."

I take a cleansing breath and enter. "Does he know I'll be here when he wakes? I don't want to scare him."

"Yes. He'll remember you. He's a very smart boy...like his father." Her eyes tear up, and she sniffs.

"Pardon me for asking and tell me if I'm being too intrusive. How did you lose your husband?"

Her eyes dart around the room as if she's searching for the words. "It was a freak accident. He was running and tried to jump an iron fence. But he tripped and fell onto one of the spires." A tear drops from a corner of one eye.

"Oh, Ashley. I'm so sorry. Please, forgive me for making you relive that. I shouldn't have asked you."

"No. It's OK. It happened soon after Aidan was born. I was finishing my doctorate. I've been telling more people since I started dating Jeff. Better to be upfront about my situation."

Ashley squats to zip up her backpack. "Shit. I left a folder in the bedroom. I'll be right back."

As I glance around the living room, I recall my dinner date with Nick. I fell asleep on the sofa. Hers is in the same place. She returns, puts the folder away, and picks up her backpack.

"I have fifteen minutes to get to campus. Thank you so much for watching him."

"No problem. I'm almost sorry he's asleep. I was looking forward to some playtime with him."

"If you're lucky, he'll sleep right through, and he won't know you were even here. Relax or do schoolwork. That's what the undergrads do when they babysit. I'll be back in two hours."

Ashley exits the apartment, and I settle onto the sofa with my laptop. I try to concentrate on my capstone project, typing into the document, but my memories won't let me focus. All the good times with Nick replay in my head—meeting in his office at the Celtic Studies department, laughing together at the Raven Pub, loving gazes shared. The image of his true self as a Tuatha Dé fairy flashes in my brain, and I shudder. When I look up, I flinch at Aidan, who is standing directly in front of me.

"Where Mommy?" he asks, rubbing his eyes.

"She's at school teaching. Your nap should have lasted another hour. Why are you awake?"

"Itchy inside." He scratches his abdomen. "Play with me?"

A grin brightens my face. "Yes. What would you like to do?"

Aidan turns and points at the pile of toys in the corner of the living room. I close my laptop in time for him to grab my hand and drag me over to his playthings. After spending thirty minutes stacking donut rings, sorting puzzles, hammering fake nails into wood, and generally making a mess, he becomes antsy and runs across the room.

"Catch me?" he asks, giggling.

The fidgety toddler darts from one side of the room to the other, stopping to jump up and down on an upholstered side chair.

"Aidan, get down from there. I don't think Mommy lets you do that."

He giggles again, continuing to jump from one cushion to the next, his sapphire eyes twinkling. I gesture to him to sit down, applying my stern face so he knows I mean business, but he continues to hop from one end of the sofa to the other. I've had enough of this, and he's out of control.

"Aidan," I say, holding him by the arms. "You need to sit down."

We collapse onto the cushions, and I hold him still. Ashley has a tiny kid's chair in another corner. It must be for time-out. I clasp the bundle of energy in my hand and guide him to it. I set him on the little seat.

"You need to sit there for two—"

He darts past me and jumps up and down on the cushions again, giggling so hard he can barely breathe. Wow...this kid has had no discipline. My leg shakes as my menopausal bladder calls. How the hell can I use the toilet? He falls on the couch, laughing and pointing at me. Aidan—one. Gwynedd—zero. Shit. *What am I going to do?*

I grab him by the hand again and guide him to the corner. "Time-out, Aidan. Sit in your chair."

"No!" he shouts, stamping a foot. "Play."

He runs around the room, over and under tables and chairs.

"You little imp," I mumble under my breath.

My leg is shaking like a jackhammer, and my bladder is about to burst. So, I do what any impatient witch would do. I raise my right hand, reciting an incantation to corral him, and send a wave of magic at the mischievous toddler. The amber swirls around the boy, picks him up, and carries him to the chair. I chant another spell to lock him in place. He struggles to break free but remains in the seat.

"Ha. You're not going anywhere now, are you? I have to go to the potty, but I'll be right back."

I dash to the toilet in the nick of time, moaning in relief. Aidan's whimpering in the distance tugs at my heart. My actions were a copout. Certainly, Ashley can't use magic to discipline her son.

Once I've done my business and I'm washing my hands, a mournful sentiment overtakes me. I rush down the hallway and turn the corner. Aidan comes into view. For a split second, I see an eerie halo hovering over the boy, green glowing fairy wings sprouting from his back like those of a butterfly. An aura swims over me with a *whoosh*!

When I blink, the image disappears, but a mild aroma of moss remains. I scan the living room, searching for signs of Nuada seeping from the walls. Nothing. Damn the PTSD! Or is the remnant of his magic still present, fucking with my brain?

As I amble to the sweet boy, he frowns at me. With a wave of my hand, I release him from the spell and kneel in front of him.

"I'm sorry, Aidan. I shouldn't have held you in the chair with my invisible hands." What else can I call it? He's going to tell Ashley something that makes no sense. Better I give him a name for the spell that will confuse her.

He glares at me, his face blazing with the redness of fiery fury. "You're mean."

"Yeah. Sometimes adults make mistakes. But you weren't listening to me. You could get hurt running around the apartment. You need to be safe. So, if you dart, I'll have to pull out my invisible hands again. Do you understand?"

"OK," he mutters. Then he yawns and puts his arms up. "Go to bed."

"Ahh. You were just wired up and needed more sleep."

I scoop him up, and he wraps his tiny fingers around my neck. He's passed out by the time I put him on the small mattress. I return to the sofa and log out of my laptop. Ashley will be here soon, anyway.

The deadbolt on the door slides, and the doorknob turns. The young instructor enters the apartment on the balls of her feet and places her backpack on the floor.

"He's still asleep?" she asks, her eyebrows arching.

"Yes, but he woke up from his nap. We played for a while, and he got tuckered out. I put him back to bed." I close my laptop and stand.

She grimaces. "Was he a problem for you?"

"No. I mean, he was wound up, but he listened to me after I spoke with him." *Who am I kidding?* The invisible hands helped, too.

Ashley crosses the room and hugs me. "Thank you so much. I knew he would benefit from a mother with experience."

"More like the stern hand of a grandmother, but you're welcome. I had fun. When Aidan woke, he complained about his stomach. Said he was itchy inside." I stuff my laptop into my backpack.

"He's complained about his tummy since we moved to Bearsden. The pediatrician said he was fine. I think it's a reaction to the move. I'm hoping he'll settle in after a few more months." She's silent for a moment. "Would I be imposing too much to ask you to watch him every Monday afternoon? Until the semester is over."

"Sure. I can work while he sleeps." I put on my fleece jacket, swing my backpack over my shoulder, and turn the doorknob.

"How could I repay you, Gwyn? Please, let me."

I grin excitedly. "I'll think of something."

Chapter Fourteen

A Safe Harbor

"Gwynedd," Archie says. "That was a misguided risk you took. The boy could tell his mother about your wee magic skills. How will you explain yourself?"

"Don't you think I planned an explanation? I called my spell invisible hands. He's two, so he probably doesn't know what the word means. Whatever he tells her, it'll sound ridiculous."

We're on the way to the Fellowship meeting, strolling through the Green. The November chill has returned, sending a shudder down my spine.

"I wouldn't tell anyone in the coven, especially Leslie or Trinity. They'll have a strong opinion on your poor choice. What about what you saw? Are you sure you imagined it?"

I recall the faint mossy aroma. "Oh, yeah. The hallucination vanished when I blinked. Being in that apartment gave me the heebie-jeebies. Brought back so many memories. I don't know why I thought it wouldn't affect me."

"Are you all right? You hadn't been there since..."

"Yeah. I'm fine. The initial shock is over. I'll cope better each time I go. She asked me if I would watch Aidan every Monday. It's the least I can do."

He squints at me. "I know what you're up to. Ashley is so overworked, Gwyn. Promise me you won't steal too much of her time. She has so little of it."

"Is that what you think of me? Of course, I would love to pick her brain on Welsh folklore. But I want to help her out. I like her a lot. At first, I thought Jeff shouldn't date a slightly older woman with a kid. Now I think they belong together. IF it lasts."

"I'm sorry I questioned your true motives." He grasps my hand. "You're so cold. Where are your gloves?"

"I didn't expect the temperature to drop so much. But I have you to keep them warm." I kiss his cheek.

A notification dings on my cell phone—a text from Ronnie.

Ronnie: *Hey. I'm not coming tonight. Tell Trinity I'm sorry.*

Me: *She'll understand. Rest your feet.*

Ronnie: *I know the coven wants to fight this new ordinance, but I hope it passes.*

Me: *I get that. Take care of yourself.*

"It's Ronnie. She's not attending the council meeting. These kidnappings have her so scared she can't sleep. But I think she doesn't want to come because she wants the curfew ordinance to pass."

"No need to add to her stress. The rest of the coven will be there."

We arrive at the city municipal building on Main Street and shove our way through the mass of townies crowding the chamber. Shane was right. This is a touchy topic. Tyler and Zoe wave to Archie and me to come sit with them. They've saved a couple of seats for us. Tanner, Spence, and Skye are sitting nearby. A quick scan finds Leslie and Agnes near the front.

Mayor Jessica Devine taps her gavel and calls the meeting to order. They work through the agenda, discussing the prior week's minutes and move onto old and new business items. The townies grow impatient, babbling over the council members' discussions while others hush them for their rude behavior.

The Fellowship has little to fear because our allies and one of our witches, Elijah Jackson, are there to guide the council to the correct decision.

But Alys Morgan pressed hard to add this ordinance to the agenda. She chats with John Erickson frequently, who is seated next to her. He nods repeatedly. Meanwhile, Elijah confers with our other allies on the council. I scan the chamber, searching for pale-blond hair, and I spot Courtney a couple of rows behind us on the other side of the hall. She taps her fingers on an arm, her chest rising at erratic intervals. When they get to the emergency agenda addendum, Mayor Devine speaks.

"Before we vote on this ordinance, I want to announce there will be no public comment. This is an emergency ordinance."

The crowd erupts. Townies and my fellow witches grumble and mutter obscenities, some shouting at the city council. Not allowing public comment is unusual. I can't believe our allies went along with this. Mayor Devine hammers her gavel several times.

"Order in the chamber. You will remain quiet while one of the council members introduces the ordinance. I now pass the meeting to Elijah Jackson."

I lean into Archie. "Why is he presenting?" I whisper.

"Let's listen to what he has to say before we vilify him."

Tyler leans forward in his seat and faces me mouthing, "What the fuck?"

Zoe's eyebrows leap, and she shrugs.

Elijah angles his head down and adjusts the microphone. "Good evening, residents of Bearsden. I'm sure you are all aware of the recent kidnappings of our precious children. The police have been diligent in their ongoing investigation, but insufficient evidence exists to connect the cases as of yet. Alys Morgan, along with John Erickson, encouraged us to consider this curfew for minors as an added safety measure. We recognize most parents already accompany their young ones, and so far, the kidnappings have occurred with parents nearby. The passage of this ordinance will allow the city to place more officers on the streets to deter those responsible."

"Elijah is supporting it?" I whisper. "Did he share this with anyone in the Fellowship?"

Archie rubs his chin. "Not that I was told. If he told Trinity, she didn't mention it."

I search for our coven leader's burgundy hair in the mass of people and find her sitting next to Shane, who's shaking his head. Trinity's arms are crossed, an epic scowl pulling down the corners of her mouth. I think they're both as surprised as all of us.

Mayor Devine continues her explanation. "During our executive session prior to this meeting, we discussed the dark situation our town is in. If the Baby Nabbers ring is responsible, we must do what we can to keep our residents safe. Is there a motion to pass the ordinance?"

"I make a motion. We vote on Ordinance #535," Elijah says, his deep voice filling the chamber.

John Erickson raises a hand. "I second the motion."

"We have a motion to vote on Ordinance #535," the mayor announces. "All in favor, raise your hand."

Every council member, including Mayor Devine, raises an arm. "Ordinance #535 passes unanimously. Thank you all for attending this council meeting. I'm elated at the community involvement. For those of you who are disappointed by the passing of this ordinance, we will consider a future vote to overturn our decision once the criminals responsible for the kidnappings are arrested. Let's leave on a positive note. The authorities *will* capture them. Eventually."

"I'd like to say a few words," Alys Morgan says. "I introduced this ordinance because I love children. Every precious child in this town deserves to have a safe harbor, and Bearsden should provide one. I appreciate the feedback I received from everyone on the council. Thank you for your support."

The council members and the mayor reply, a chorus of "you're welcome" and "thank you" echoing in response to Alys.

Elijah speaks into the microphone. "I motion to dismiss the meeting."

"I second the motion," Alys says, grinning.

Jessica Devine strikes her gavel. "Meeting is adjourned."

Many residents moan, but at least half praise the vote with applause. Alys Morgan smiles smugly at John Erickson. He searches the townies in attendance. Looking for his wife, I assume. She's still sitting, sighing in apparent relief. I look between them in confusion. Two plus two is not adding up...to anything. If my suspicions surrounding Courtney are true, why would she be relieved at the increase in police on the streets? All four of our phones vibrate, and Elijah pulls out his cell. We get up to leave and shove against the throng of residents to make our way to the exit.

"Trinity sent a group text," Archie says. "She's calling an emergency meeting at the Pumpkin House."

Zoe clenches her teeth. "Oh, no. Elijah's in big trouble."

"I'm sure he had a good reason for going along with all of them." Tyler holds the door open for us. "Perhaps he was the sole no vote and didn't want to have to explain his choice."

I zip up my fleece jacket. "Well, I certainly would like to know why he voted yes, but our council allies voted yes as well. Elijah must have told them our concerns—the possibility of a witch aiding the Baby Nabbers."

"What are you talking about, Mom?" Tyler asks. "A witch could be helping the kidnappers?"

"Whoa. Do you know who it is?" Zoe's eyes pop out. "Is it Shane's wicked ex-girlfriend, Cordelia Davenport?"

Archie glances at me. "Gwyn has a few suspicions."

"My witch's intuition has pointed toward someone, but right now, it's weak and not giving me any useful information. Trinity will probably mention it at the meeting. Before you accuse me of keeping secrets, I wasn't. I haven't discovered anything yet."

Gradually, the residents following us trickle down to zero, and our witch colleagues come into view ahead. When we arrive at the Pumpkin House, we enter the foyer to find everyone standing, Trinity at the front of the small circle.

"Someone else take a head count," she says. "I'm too fucking tired and mad."

That's not a good sign. Elijah isn't here yet. Leslie and Agnes aren't either.

Skye scans the circle. "Nine. One of those missing is Ronnie. She stayed home."

Trinity shifts her weight onto her right foot. "Yeah, she told me. We can't expect much from her for the next couple of months. She's damned uncomfortable. I remember my last trimester. Could not sit on my bottom for weeks. Had to pee every five minutes. Couldn't find a position to sleep in without my arms pinching."

"I'm really glad I don't have to go through that," Spence says, grimacing. "Can't imagine not sleeping. I need my beauty rest."

"Is that what you call all that twisting and turning you do all night?" Tanner asks, snorting. "I'm lucky to get four hours at a stretch."

Skye chuckles. "Why doesn't that surprise me?"

"Now that's the positive about sleeping alone," Shane says. "When my head hits the pillow, I'm out until sunrise. But I much prefer a companion to wake to."

"Aye. My exact sentiments, Shane." Archie smiles at me.

The front door opens, and Leslie ambles in. Agnes and Elijah are right behind her. They join the circle, and Trinity crosses her arms, glaring at our gentle giant witch with a laser-green stare.

"What the fuck, Elijah? I'm so angry, I could spit."

"I am sure he will explain," Leslie says. "Although I must express my disappointment."

Agnes cracks up. "Stop pretending you didn't flip out all the way here, sweetheart."

"Let's give Elijah the benefit of the doubt, shall we?" Archie asks, nodding in his direction.

Elijah rubs his hands together, confidence exuding from his visage. "Before we met in executive session, our allies and I had a private discussion. I warned them about Gwyn's recent intuition feeling. It wasn't enough to convince them the kidnappings are supernatural related, and I agree. Even if an evil witch is helping the Baby Nabbers, Unremarkables are still involved. I realize the increase in police patrol units will hinder our visits to the Seelie Fae, but I think it was the right thing to do."

Leslie nods, a reluctant sigh escaping. "Indeed. Elijah made the correct choice. He would have been a lone vote, which would have brought attention to him...and us. We must move past this and create a plan to visit the Celestial Gardens to keep the children entertained until the police apprehend the kidnappers. It may require the use of masking spells to sneak by the officers on patrol."

"Even with the extra cops on the street, a witch could slip around them," Tanner says.

"You fucking know it," Agnes replies. "Gwyn, Leslie said you have suspicions concerning Courtney Erickson—the council member's wife, and an expelled coven member."

Spence and Skye blurt out. "Courtney?" The young witches share worried glances.

"Yes," I reply. "My intuition tells me something's up with her, but I can't say she's involved with the kidnappers."

"Courtney was such a mess when she was a grad student," Skye says. "But she seems friendly enough. She waved to me at the meeting."

Zoe nods. "Me, too. She looks happier than I ever remember. I can't imagine what reason she'd have for doing something like this."

"Should someone check her banking account?" Spence asks, his eyes widening. "She could have several thousand reasons for it?" He rubs his money fingers together.

Tanner scowls at his partner. "Sure, she screwed up, but give her a break. She has matured and is trying to make a life in Bearsden."

"I'm willing to allow Courtney some leeway on that account," Trinity says. "But we shouldn't give her a total pass, either. Who knows what she's hiding?"

Tyler crosses his arms. "I don't know her at all, so I can't decide if she's trustworthy."

He isn't aware of her time in the coven, either, which wouldn't improve his impression of her.

"What about you, Archie?" Spence asks. "I mean, she made all those accusations against you."

"Aye," he replies, glancing at me. "But not all of them were false."

Shane yawns. "We all have our own opinions about the young woman, but let's be open-minded as well. It's late. I recommend we end this circle and head home."

"I second that motion," Archie says. "Since we're following Robert's Rules tonight."

"Leslie, what say you?" Trinity asks, gesturing to her.

"No need for my staff." The Elder waves her hand. "You are dismissed."

Lying in Archie's magnificent Victorian walnut bed, I contemplate my next steps. I haven't told him Seamus has agreed to instruct me in the cat sith's ways of strengthening intuition. He'd tell me it's a bad idea, and anyway, it isn't his concern. I'm the one trying to improve my skills to root out the rogue witch in town, if one actually exists. While he's brushing his teeth, a notification lights up my phone, and I pick up my cell from the nightstand.

Seamus: *Good evening, Gwynedd. How would Friday at my house work for training?*

Me: *Our usual time?*

Seamus: *Yes. 3:00 p.m. works well. Wear loose clothing.*

Me: *Great. See you on Friday.*

Seamus: *I look forward to our training.*

Archie hops into bed. "Who was that?"

I can't lie to him, but I don't have to tell him everything, either. "Seamus. He's just confirming our regular schedule for Friday."

"Gwyn, you're entitled to do as you please, and I realize you don't want to hear it again. But...if Seamus has romantic affections toward you, spending more time with him is the last thing you should be doing. You should consider taking a break."

"You worry too much," I say, stroking the whiskers of his goatee. "Everything is under control. A pause in our research may not be a bad idea, though. Until after Thanksgiving. I have a ton of schoolwork to catch up on."

He leans down, his lips nearly touching mine. "That will leave more time for...our research."

He kisses me, and the woodsy scent of his cologne entices me as I caress his chest. He slides a hand up my inner thigh.

"Mmm. Explore away, professor."

CHAPTER FIFTEEN

A MOTHER'S INTUITION

SUNNY WEATHER CONTINUES THROUGH Wednesday, providing warmer temperatures than usual for early November. Resident complaints regarding the ordinance have calmed as they accept the new normal. The increased presence of Bearsden Police units is noticeable. As I drive to Ronnie's home, I pass three or four sets of patrols monitoring the area. It's a double-edged sword the town must grapple with—less privacy versus a sense of safety. But are we safe? Not if a nefarious witch is involved.

When I arrive at my best friend's home, Derek is loading his SUV with an athletic duffle bag. I park on the street and walk up the driveway to talk with him.

"Hey, Gwyn," he says, shutting the back car door. "I'm glad you could give her a visit. I am so worried about Ronnie. She's becoming a hermit. The baby hasn't even arrived, and she keeps saying her mother's intuition is sending her bad vibes. Can you talk some sense into her?"

"It's not an irrational fear, Derek. Even Unremarkable moms possess inner instincts that signal when their children are in danger. But I'll chat with her about it." I pat his arm. "Don't worry.

She'll come around once the baby is here. She will be way too busy to think about anything but sleep and changing dirty diapers."

"I hope you're right. I have to get to the fitness center. My cardio class starts in twenty minutes. Thanks, Gwyn."

"You're welcome."

As Derek backs out of the driveway, I approach the front door. I knock briefly and enter.

"Ronnie?" I ask in an elevated voice. "Where are you?"

"In the kitchen!" she shouts back. "I'm making tea."

My best friend sets a kettle on the stove and turns on the burner. At nearly eight months, her belly stretches her maternity T-shirt, and her feet are so swollen, they resemble mini balloons. Frizzy and disheveled crimson curls fall to her shoulders. Dark circles hint at sleepless nights.

"Hey, why don't you let me make the tea?" I ask, placing my purse in a chair. "Sit and prop your feet up."

She rubs her lower back. "This time, I'm taking you up on your offer."

While she sits with a pillow tucked behind her lumbar, I grab a couple of mugs from an upper cabinet and spoons from a drawer. After dropping some stevia in, I place them on the kitchen table.

"What would you like? Peppermint or Ginger?" I ask.

"Peppermint. It's about all I can stomach these days. The scent of ginger makes me want to puke."

"You don't have long now. In a few weeks, you'll say hello to your baby."

The teakettle whistles, and I pour hot water into our mugs. Ronnie waves a hand as she chants, and amber magic seeps from her fingers. The spoons twirl inside.

She chuckles. "I have to do something, or I'll feel useless."

"It's great you're loosening up. Use it or lose it, I say, whether or not Leslie approves."

"Yeah," she says, sipping her tea. "Derek didn't want our child to be raised on magic, but we came to a compromise. I have to wait until our kid is older."

"Probably safer. But if you are practicing witchcraft, you realize it could spark the witch energy in your kid, right?"

"We'll have to figure out how to handle it when or *if* it happens."

"Derek says you've been anxious. 'Bad vibes,' he called them. More mother's intuition warnings?"

"I don't know. Out of nowhere, an overwhelming dread takes over my body, like a tsunami, and I clutch my belly. After massaging it for a while, the sensation fades, but it hangs over me—a guillotine ready to drop." She slides an index finger across her neck.

"Oh, Ronnie. Why didn't you tell me?" I jump up from my chair and hug her.

"I figured it was expectant mom jitters. We all have them, right?"

"Yeah, that's true," I say, sitting in my seat. "Or are these different? You're a witch, too. When did the first one occur?"

"When we hiked in the park. You thought you saw something move in the woods. Do you remember?"

"Holy crystals," I say, my lips parting. "I did, too. Did this sense of dread occur any other time besides recently?"

"Yeah. A little the day we met Courtney on the trail." Her jaw drops. "Is that why you rushed ahead of me?"

I nod. "Something pulled me toward the bog. Then I nearly ran into her. I've had suspicions about her since then. We talked about her at the Pumpkin House during the circle. No one seems to think she's involved. It's a gut feeling I have—my weak intuition."

"What's triggering these feelings? Do you think the kidnappers are camping out in the park?"

"I don't know. But the Bearsden Police are all over the city now. If those criminals are hiding in there, they'll find them. Or frighten them away. But we should share our concerns with the Fellowship on Thursday."

"The patrols can't monitor everywhere twenty-four-seven. The Baby Nabbers have evaded capture all this time." She lays both hands on her belly. "I have a bad feeling."

I lay my hand on hers and squeeze. "The coven is on guard. We'll keep you and your infant safe if they don't capture these kidnappers. Meanwhile, I have a plan. Seamus agreed to teach me some of his intuition secrets—the ways of the cat sith. We're starting on Friday."

"Does Archie know you're doing this?" she asks. "Anyone in the coven?"

I don't reply. Instead, I pick up my mug of Earl Grey and take a sip. Then another.

"For fuck's sake, Gwyn. You're mixing types of magic. Shouldn't you ask someone if it's safe? Or ethical?"

I set my mug on the table. "Do you think Seamus would agree to teach me if it wasn't? How is it unethical? He's a witch. A trustworthy one who saved my life a couple of times and helped the coven when Cordelia Davenport wreaked havoc in Bearsden."

"Hmph. You know why Seamus is helping you. Because he loves you. And that's why you aren't telling Archie."

"I don't want to argue with you. I came to ease your worry. If both of our intuitions are accurate, I need to at least strengthen mine. Agnes met with me twice to work on it. I've been meditating daily with an amethyst geode she gave me, adding other crystals to find the most effective duo. Unfortunately, I haven't discovered the correct combination yet. I've concentrated so much on intuition, I've not practiced with the crystal grid. Aunt Gorawen made me promise to take my time, so that option is off the table."

"Please, be careful, Gwyn." Folds form in her brow. "And I'm not talking about the crystals."

As the rain taps on the windowpanes, Leslie begins our regular Thursday circle with a tap of her Elder staff. "Elijah would like to address the coven before we begin our discussion. Councilman, you have the floor."

He stands to address us. "I want to thank all of you again for understanding my predicament on Monday evening. I was in a tough spot. But that's not my reason for speaking to you tonight. The shelter is going to be very short-handed this Thanksgiving, and we could use as many volunteers as we can get. I understand if you have individual family plans. Any help you could provide would be appreciated. Of course, we'll set you up with a free, scrumptious meal."

Tyler raises a hand. "Zoe and I would be happy to volunteer. Mom and Archie will be there, anyway. An awesome excuse to avoid spending Thanksgiving with my grandmother in Virginia."

Zoe's signature grin brightens her face. "I love playing with the kids. I'm happy to entertain them."

"We missed last year," Tanner says. "Spence and I can come."

"I'd love to help, big man," Spence adds. "Tell us what time, and we'll be there."

Ronnie sticks a finger in the air. "Count me in. And Derek. I'm too close to my due date to go visit my parents this year. It'll be fun to spend it with all of you."

"I can't think of another place I'd rather gather," Shane says, "than with my witch family."

The rest of us, including our coven leader, confirm our commitment with a raise of our hands. All except Agnes. She lowers her head, attempting to hide her prune face.

Leslie nods with a smile. "Splendid. Thank you for providing this much needed assistance to those less fortunate in our town."

"You know I hate hanging out with huge crowds," Agnes mutters.

I glare at her. "You can deal for one afternoon. Besides, we all want you there."

We all stamp our feet, and a rumble fills the Pumpkin House parlor.

"I guess I'll go," she says, rolling her eyes. "But I better get two fucking desserts."

Elijah chuckles. "Agnes, if you come, I will personally serve you as many as you like."

Our councilman sits down, and Trinity takes over the meeting. "You have all read the news by now. This morning, the Bearsden Police concluded their search of North Basin Creek Park. They found no evidence pointing to the kidnappers using the woods as a hideout. Gwyn, I appreciate your warnings, but your intuition must be pointing to something else."

"But I had similar feelings," Ronnie says. "Recently, my motherly instincts have intensified, filling me with an insurmountable dread."

"Couldn't your emotions be anxiety about your future baby?" Skye asks. "Not that I know anything about that."

"Sure," Ronnie replies. "Jump on the 'you're moody' train. I've had enough of that from Derek. I'm in the third trimester. It's not my fucking hormones."

Wrinkles form between Trinity's eyes. "I remember my pregnancy with my daughter. Don't rule it out, Ronnie. But we'll take heed of what you are both experiencing."

"Does it sound like a coincidence to you?" I ask. "We're both getting these signals."

Archie leans forward in his chair. "Perhaps a few of us should investigate the park."

"Don't look at me," Ronnie says. "I'm done walking in there."

"No offense, honey," I say. "But you said your intuition sucks."

The young witches burst out laughing, and Archie frowns at me.

"I don't know what you think you're gonna find in there," Agnes says. "It's a fucking nasty bog full of mosquitos and gnats. Nothing else. My property backs up to the woods. If there were people or supernatural beings hiding in there, I'd have noticed by now."

Skye taps her chin. "Unless there's a masking bubble over the area. If there is one, we'd never realize it. Right?"

"You young witches think you fucking know everything," Agnes replies, smirking.

Leslie attempts to quash a smile. "I trust our youth implicitly because we trained them well. In all my recollections, this is the first time we have had a full coven of witches at level three status. Archie and Gwyn, I recommend you take the young ones with you to obtain a fresh perspective."

"Don't be surprised when you come up dry as a goat turd," the hedge witch adds.

Shane chuckles. "Agnes, you have a way with words like no other."

"Well, I do sleep with an academic," she replies, guffawing. "Must have rubbed off."

We all crack up, and Trinity stands to dismiss us. While we're hanging out on the porch, Archie and I schedule a time to visit the park with the young witches. We settle on Tuesday in the late afternoon after classes. I'm excited about the prospect, actually. Although their intuitions are less developed, they have the skill.

Archie and I stroll through the Green under a blanket of cloud-filled skies. A cold front has moved in, and a slight drizzle wets the paver walkway. I snap open my umbrella, and we squeeze together underneath. When we arrive at Drummond Lane, I stop.

"What are you doing?" he asks. "You're not staying with me tonight?"

"I don't think so. I need to get a good night's sleep. We both know that rarely happens when I stay at your place."

"Aye, but you never complain afterwards." He kisses me. "Do you have an important presentation for class in the morning?"

I can't tell him about my special training sessions with Seamus, but I won't lie to him either. "I'm exhausted. It's best I catch up on my sleep. I'll stay over tomorrow. OK?"

"Do I have a choice?" He kisses me again. "Goodnight, my love."

"Night, honey."

Archie continues on toward Duncan Street, and I dart up Drummond to home. Storm winds blow through my fleece jacket, chilling me to the bone. While the pitter-patter of the rain pings on the top of my umbrella, I tremble, thinking about tomorrow's session with Seamus. It has to work, because I'm out of options.

CHAPTER SIXTEEN

A PROTECTOR'S GIFT

AFTER MY FRIDAY MORNING class, I rush back home and eat a light lunch. Seamus said to wear loose clothing, so I throw on a matching purple yoga shirt and pants. Goosebumps rise on my shivering arms. The temperature has dropped twenty degrees since yesterday. Why couldn't Old Man Winter wait one more day to make an early visit?

I open my family steamer trunk and remove the amethyst geode. I carefully place it in my backpack and head to the mudroom. While I'm putting on my sneakers, Mr. Yeats scuttles in, transforming into his human persona. He buttons his suit jacket.

"Ms. Crowther, it's unusually cold out today. May I recommend warmer attire? A long-sleeved shirt and thicker pants seem more appropriate than..." He examines my clothing from head to foot. "Sleepwear?"

I grimace. "I'm not wearing pajamas. This is what I wear when I do yoga. Although it's usually warmer in there."

"Oh, you're off to yoga?" He checks the schedule on his clipboard. "That's irregular. You usually meet with Dr. Duffy on Friday afternoons."

I put on my fleece jacket and slip on my gloves. "No comment."

"Why are you dressing in yoga attire to attend a research meeting with the professor?"

"Sometimes you ask way too many questions, familiar." I swing my backpack over my shoulder.

He straightens his vest. "I question what is necessary, Ms. Crowther. No more, no less."

"Tell Dr. Hughes I won't be eating dinner at the house tonight. *If* she's even here. She's been spending a lot of time at Agnes's farm lately."

"Yes. It's been quite lonely here as of late."

I lay a hand on his arm. "Don't worry. Dr. Hughes won't ever abandon you."

"Your support is appreciated. May you have a productive afternoon and evening, Ms. Crowther."

"You, too, Mr. Yeats."

I run up the street and hammer on Seamus's front door, jumping up and down to keep the blood flowing. When the door opens, I'm taken aback by his presence. He's wearing a long black tunic that reaches his bare feet. His dark hair is loose and cascading past his shoulders. The gray strands at his temples fall at the sides, shaping his oblong face.

"Please, come in, Gwynedd," he says, gesturing.

As I enter, a blast of warm air heats me, and I strip off my puffer jacket. "It's so hot in here. Is your HVAC system stuck on desert heat?"

"No," he replies, laughing. "It is preparation for the tutoring session."

"Oh. Well, I'm not complaining. Leave it on. I froze on the way here."

He takes my puffer jacket and hangs it in a tiny hall closet off the entrance. The window shades are down, darkening the room. He's moved my aunt's painting from his office. Now it hangs over the fireplace. Several candles are lit on the mantel, where a bouquet of incense burns. Large pillows await us on the floor at the hearth.

"Mmm. What a fabulous aroma," I say, inhaling. "Cinnamon...peppermint. I can't make out the others."

He approaches me, his sea-green eyes standing out in the darkened room. "Frankincense and lemongrass."

"I discern them all, but..." I sniff twice. "I smell lavender and rose, too."

He hesitates. "To aid in relaxation. You will need to rid your mind and body of all stressors to be successful."

"Not promising, with all my knots everywhere. But I have to try."

"Shall we?" he asks, gesturing to the fireplace.

"Wait." I set my backpack on the floor and remove the amethyst geode. "I brought this geode with me that Agnes gave me."

"Excellent," he says as we walk toward the hearth. "Set the crystal to your side for now. We must start with clearing our minds and learning to focus."

He kneels on a pillow and offers a hand to assist me. I place my knees on the pillow, facing him, and set the geode next to me on the hearth. He has a black box near his side.

"Before we begin, can I ask why you're wearing the tunic and nothing on your feet? Why the loose hair?"

"To aid in focus, we must rid our minds of all distractions—anything binding on the body."

I chuckle. "Like jeans or...underwear."

"Precisely," he replies, a faint smile curling his mouth.

I swallow and stare at the floor for a moment. Did he just admit he's naked under his tunic? Kind of strange, but who am I to question his cat sith ways?

"My yoga outfit should work, though, right?" I'm certainly not removing my panties.

"Yes. Your clothing is more than acceptable. Before working with the crystals, let's concentrate on your focus."

"OK. Agnes tried to help me with this, but she's not a model of clarity herself."

"Raise your hands and face them toward me. Close your eyelids. I will guide you. We'll begin with deep breathing."

I gaze into those haunting eyes. "Thank you, Seamus. I know this is very personal for you."

"You're special, Gwynedd. I want to help you in any way I can."

He lifts his hands, his palms facing toward me, and I shut my lids. I breathe in the aromatic air surrounding me and attempt to empty my head of life's worries. Thoughts stream past, from my vision of the gray-skinned monster to the kidnappings and to Ronnie, clutching her pregnancy bump.

"The deep breathing isn't working," I say, opening my eyes. "There's too much swimming through my brain. I'm sorry I wasted your time."

"You're going to give up after one attempt? That's not the Gwynedd Crowther I know so well." Seamus reaches for my hand. "May I?"

I stare at his palm. "Sure. What are you gonna do?"

"I will transfer my focus to you," he says, pressing his palm against mine. "You'll need to keep your eyes open for this. I'll warn you. This may frighten you at first. But I promise, I would never hurt you."

He places his other hand on mine and calls on his magic, sending a tingling sensation into my hands that spreads throughout my body—sensual but not sexual. His eyes radiate as they did in his cat sith state. My heart thumps heavily, but in slow, steady beats, as my mind empties the stressors within. A euphoric emotion strikes me, sending my soul into another dimension. I gasp.

It reminds me of the connection I had with my mom and Great-Aunt Gorawen in Wales, except it's private—between the two of us. Seamus retracts his magic, and the amber glow fades from my hands. Our deep breathing continues, and I swear, I can sense the blood pumping through his heart.

He touches my shoulder. "Are you all right, Gwynedd?"

"Yes. I wasn't scared. That was amazing. I've experienced nothing like it before."

A satisfied smile graces his face. "Excellent. Then you are ready. Hold the geode in your right hand."

I pick up the amethyst and grasp it in my palm while he opens the black box at his side. He removes a piece of clear quartz and lays it in my other hand. The cut gem sparkles in the candlelight.

"You said you had a minor success with combining another crystal at Agnes's home. None since then?"

I shake my head. "Only with the labradorite. I've tried others but didn't even get a spark. My brain is too full of junk."

"We'll try connecting these two while I trigger the focus. When you have success, I will pull back. Be prepared for a powerful force."

I swallow again as I examine the stones. Am I in the correct mindset for this? Oh, fuck it. I can't back out now. "I'm ready."

"Focus as you did before, and I will touch your fingers lightly to trigger a reaction. If you feel overwhelmed, continue to breathe, inhaling as deeply as possible."

I nod, and we begin. I stare into Seamus's eyes, my face reflecting in their glassy surfaces. He strokes his fingers against mine, and my magic seeps out and engulfs me. My entire body is aflame with an amber glow, intensifying until I imagine I may explode. But I suck in air, filling my lungs until they're full and expelling my breath slowly. My head becomes dizzy, and just when I think I'm going to pass out, white fingers of energy discharge from the geode and the clear crystal, merging into an enchanted frenzy.

My lips part, but I'm unable to speak. Seamus pulls his hands away, allowing me to relish in the spectacle of my achievement. He grins at me, rejoicing in his own success. But it's short-lived. My breathing becomes erratic, and I can't sustain my focus. My dizzy head wins, and I fall forward, dropping the crystals onto the floor. He catches me before my face smacks into the brick hearth.

"Gwynedd," he says, concern heavy in his voice. "Can you hear me? Are you aware?"

I peer up at him, unable to form a complete sentence. "Oh, Seamus."

He never takes his gaze from me while I recover my lost energy. I want to say so many things to him. In particular, how grateful I am he's willing to share these secrets of his cath sith magic. When I'm nearly able to speak, my mouth falls open—he kisses me. His lips are full of pent-up passion and months of longing, and a noticeable bulge below his waist presses into me. But I push him back.

"Stop, Seamus. Why did you do that? You know I love Archie."

He stares at me, wrapping a trembling hand around the other. "My deepest apologies, Gwynedd. Your expression appeared to invite me. Then how you spoke... I must have misinterpreted your reaction as affection."

"I care about you, but not in that way. I should go."

When I try to stand, I lose my balance. I get up on the second attempt. I grab Agnes's geode and retrieve my puffer jacket from the hall closet. While I'm tying my shoelaces, Seamus approaches me with the clear quartz in his hand.

"I think we should take a break from our research meetings." I glance at the painting of my mom over the fireplace. "Your af-fections are misguided. You fell in love with the woman on that canvas. She's not me. It's not healthy, Seamus. I took advantage of your affections, and I was wrong to continue meeting with you."

"Please, don't tell Archie. It was a mistake on my part. No need to for everyone to be uncomfortable."

"I can't promise that. I won't lie to the man I love. But I'll make certain he understands nothing happened." I slip the geode into an outside pocket of my backpack.

He stands there, a yearning unfulfilled, and my eyes fall to the floor. This is my fault.

"When will you come again, Gwynedd? Your training isn't complete without the next step, and I don't want this flaw in my social skills to affect the friendship we have."

I return my gaze to him. "It already has. Whatever comes after will have to wait. Let's take a break. It'll be good for the both of us."

"But you still haven't found the being in your vision. How will you discover who he is without my assistance?"

"I guess I won't. But I assure you. He's gonna find me." I open the front door.

"Wait, Gwynedd." He opens his hand, offering me the clear quartz. "Please, take this crystal. My gift to you. It's one of my strongest. You needed more training to increase your intuition to its fullest extent, but you are capable."

I pick up the gemstone and put it in my backpack with the geode. "Thank you for everything."

With a slam of the door, I run to Archie's one street over, shaking from the blast of chilly air. I enter through the front and kick off my sneakers, then hang my puffer jacket on the hall tree. Archie shuffles in from the kitchen as I drop my backpack onto the wooden floor.

"You're here sooner than expected," he says, embracing me.

I pinch my lips, mulling over the decision to tell him the truth or not.

"What has happened?" he asks. "Weren't you with Seamus? For research." His jaw drops. "You found the monster in Irish folklore?"

"No. Not even close to what transpired." I walk into the living room and stand in front of the fireplace. "You're not gonna like what I'm about to tell you."

"What am I not going to like, Gwynedd?" he asks, crossing his arms.

"I was with Seamus." I pause for a moment. "At his house. I asked him to instruct me in his cat sith ways of intuition. He agreed. And—"

"Did you get hurt?" He checks my body from my head to my feet.

"No. Stop fussing over me. I'm fine. The magic made me a bit dizzy. I recovered in minutes. Not like my reaction to the crystal grid. The results were fucking amazing."

He frowns. "What were you thinking, witch? He's a cat sith. His magic could have damaged you."

"Agnes wasn't much help, and I found out Ronnie is experiencing a sense of dread daily—her mother's intuition mixing with her witch energy. I wanted to test if his witchcraft art could strengthen mine enough to help catch the Baby Nabbers. And the rogue witch, if there is one."

He shoves his hands in his pockets. "I don't understand. If you were successful, why are you so upset?"

"I lost my balance when the magic stopped abruptly, and he caught me before I hit my head on the fireplace hearth. When I looked up at him, he misinterpreted my expression of delight at my success and—"

Archie's brow furrows. "And what, Gwynedd?"

"He kissed me." I clench my teeth.

"Fawk, Gwyn. What did you do?"

"I pushed him away, of course. He realized he'd made a mistake and apologized profusely. I told him his affections were misguided and that he'd fallen in love with an image in a painting. We're taking a break from research. I won't be seeing him for a while."

He runs a hand through his locks. "This will make working together *very* awkward. You've made a mess of things. I wish you had asked me first."

"Because I need your permission? You don't own me." I stomp to the foyer in my socks and shove my feet into my shoes.

"Where are you going? Aren't you eating and staying the night?"

I put on my jacket and zip it up. "No. I'm going home to sleep in my own bed."

He strokes my arm. "I'm sorry. Please, don't leave."

"I need a break from the both of you." I open the door. "Give me some space. I'll call you in a couple of days."

"Whatever you want, Gwyn." He kisses me on the cheek before I leave, but the pained expression on his face as the door swings closed stands in stark contrast to his words.

On the way home to Leslie's house, the stress of everything escapes in a scream, and I howl at the moon in the twilight sky. I can't use the grid to expand my vision, and my intuition remains useless. The gray-skinned monster invades my thoughts like an uninvited voyeur. I don't have time for you now, asshole.

CHAPTER SEVENTEEN

UNTIMELY REGRETS

When I enter the kitchen the next morning, Leslie is drinking coffee at the tiny table. She's dressed in a cotton nightgown and robe. Mr. Yeats sits on the floor by her feet, purring and wagging his tail. I'm glad he had a good night's sleep. Agnes slept over because her sewer pipe needs replacing. The two of them made such a racket in bed, I barely got any shut-eye.

"Good morning, Leslie," I say, yawning. "Where's Agnes?"

"She's still in bed. Never been a person to greet the sunrise, as you well know. Actually, I sensed your use of magic last evening when you returned from Archie's. I wasn't expecting you."

After yesterday's fiasco, I contemplate whether to tell them about my training session with Seamus. I prepare a cup of tea and sit across from her, inhaling the jasmine scent. I take a sip and wait for the caffeine rush to kick in. Agnes shuffles into the kitchen wearing a black nightgown and orange pumpkin slippers, the ones Shane put on clearance after Samhain. Her salt and pepper hair resembles a bird's nest—one with less organization.

"Happy fucking morning," she says, grabbing the kettle from the stove.

"Why don't you warm up water in the microwave?" I ask. "Takes less time?"

She glares at me through slits. "You make your tea your way. I'll make mine how I want." She fills up the kettle and drops it on the burner. "What are you doing here, anyway? Weren't you supposed to stay at Archie's last night?"

Mr. Yeats's yellow and blue eyes flip back and forth at us like a sideways pendulum. I take another sip of my tea and stare at the familiar, begging for a solution to my dilemma. He yawns at me. Thanks for nothing, busy body.

"You don't have to answer, but did you have a lover's quarrel?" Leslie asks.

I sigh and drop my cup on the saucer with a clink. "Yes, I should probably tell you both. Although Seamus would prefer I not share what happened."

"This sounds serious," she replies.

Agnes rubs her hands together. "Delicious gossip. Let me get my tea first."

Leslie drops her mug on the table and sits back in her chair. I wait for my mentor to move next to Leslie with her tea and explain what happened at Seamus's house—the amazing connection I had—and his kiss. When I'm finished, Leslie leans forward without a reply and finishes her coffee.

"Don't you have an opinion? I thought you'd be pissed. Archie was."

Agnes scowls at me. "I fucking do. What the fuck were you thinking, Gwyn? His magic is different. So, I'm not good enough for you now?"

"You took a risk practicing the craft with a cat sith witch," Leslie says. "But it was your risk to take, not ours. You have taken many chances in the past but have always had good intentions in mind. Gwynedd, I understand your motives, and you will not get an admonishment from me. But I don't sleep with you."

"Right. Well, at least you're not angry about it." I stick my tongue out at my mentor.

Agnes guffaws. "But now we know who would like the job."

"You're enjoying my fuck up, aren't you?" I ask.

"Damn straight," she replies. "Oh, hell. I'm just messing with you, Gwyn. Poor Seamus, though."

"Dr. Duffy is full of remorse for his actions, I am certain," Leslie says. "I will not make any mention of this to him. It would embarrass him further. But I recommend you patch things up with Archie before your investigation in North Basin Creek Park."

I get up from the table and place my cup in the sink. "Shit. I forgot about that."

"Better plan on some kinky make-up sex. Works like a charm." She winks at Leslie. "Doesn't it, sweetheart?"

The Elder rolls her eyes. "Oh, Agnes. Gwyn, why don't you tell us more about your success while I get breakfast started?"

"Sure," I reply, getting up from the chair. "Agnes, sit down. You're making me nervous standing there."

"Great. My plan worked." She plops in the seat, laughing. "What crystal did you combine with my geode to spark a reaction?"

"It's in my backpack. I'll get it and be right back."

I dart to my bedroom, Mr. Yeats scuttling behind, and retrieve the clear quartz gem. When I return to the kitchen, Leslie is breaking eggs into a frying pan. I set the crystal on the table.

"This is the one I used. I had fabulous success combining the two, but I couldn't get them to work last night. I was missing the trigger."

"What do you mean?" Agnes asks, examining the stone. "You should have ignited the connection yourself."

"I guess I needed a jump start," I say.

She snickers and waggles her eyebrows. "I bet you did."

"Don't tease her, Agnes." Leslie frowns at her.

"It overwhelmed me, and I nearly passed out. But Seamus caught me. That's when he—you know."

My mentor snorts. "I'm sorry. I'm sure it wasn't funny when it happened. But hearing you describe it tickles me."

"I'm so happy I can provide you with entertainment." I get spinach and peppers from the fridge and cut them up.

"How will you pursue this now?" Leslie asks. "Since you won't be meeting with Seamus to learn the next step."

I expel a drawn-out sigh. "I don't fucking know. Keep trying, I guess."

"Gwyn, I'm no cat sith witch," Agnes says. "But I'm happy to work with you for as long as it takes. We can discover the solution together."

"Thanks. I may take you up on the offer. For now, I'll do what I can on my own. I have a project due before Thanksgiving break."

"Gwynedd, do not forget you're an ancestral witch," Leslie says with a lift of her chin. "You have untapped powers you continue to extract from within."

She's right, of course. But for now, all I'd pluck from my witchy innards is gas and an enormous sense of regret.

"Thank you for shopping at Mystic Sage," I say, handing the customer his package.

The young student exits the store with his discounted Halloween merchandise as Shane strolls in with a box of holiday decorations.

"Can you help me hang this evergreen and holly garland?" he asks. "We should have put it up the day after Samhain."

I lock the cash register. "Sure. Personally, I'm glad you were late getting it up. The holidays are so commercialized. On the other hand, I love the vibe of the holiday season. With Ronnie's baby coming, the Fellowship has a lot to celebrate. I wish the police would have apprehended the kidnapping ring by now."

"Darling, I share your sentiments," he says, hanging sprigs of holly with a red bow. "I read in the news feed on my cell phone the Bearsden PD brought in the FBI."

"Awesome, but wouldn't it be great if we could identify their whereabouts? If only I could super-charge my witch's intuition. I tried again last night. Seamus didn't get to the next step in that process, and I'm not going back to ask him. He was so embarrassed."

Shane twirls his whiskers. "After what happened, I don't recommend it either."

"Having finesse with crystals, can you recommend what direction I should go in?" I ask, attaching evergreen to a shelf.

"No idea. My crystal work is purely for spells and healing. It was a risky thing you did working with a cat sith."

I frown at my boss, suspending the last of the holly sprigs. "Everybody is a critic, except for Leslie. Oddly, she supported my decision."

"Stating facts, Gwyn. What will you do about the Seamus situation?"

"I'm taking a break. I suspected he had a crush on me, but I never expected him to act on those emotions. Archie and I had a tiff over the incident. You were married for years. What would you do about it?"

"Every couple argues over the small stuff and important decisions. Your tiff, as you call it, contains a little of both." He pulls out the mistletoe decoration and moves the empty box aside. "It's for the two of you to decide what qualifies as significant and what is trivial. My advice to you? Don't allow either to come between you and Archie. Life is too short."

"It's mostly me. I was pissed he was angry. I thought if I told him the truth, he'd understand. He apologized, but I didn't like how he acted, telling me I should have asked him first."

Shane steps on a stool and hangs the mistletoe on a permanent hook at the door entrance. "A bit of stubbornness returning to the flock?"

"Call me out, boss," I say, exhaling.

He chuckles, his ruby-red lips peeking through the white beard. "Pointing out the obvious, darling. Don't worry. It'll all come out in the wash."

The door dings and Jeff enters the store. "Good morning. Can you believe the temperature may rise to near sixty today? More than twenty degrees since yesterday's high. It's supposed to be in the sixties tomorrow. I just put this hoodie away for the season and had to dig it out again." He glances around. "The decorations are awesome. We should add blue and white, too. Try to be inclusive of more holidays. I'm sorry I'm late. I came from Ashley's apartment. Tough morning."

"Oh, was Aidan a problem?" I ask. "He was improving, I thought."

"No. His behavior has been fantastic since you babysat. Ashley is so thankful. I don't know what you did, but he's listening to us and learning to entertain himself more. Even his sleep is better. It's why I'm late. I never used to need an alarm when I stayed on Saturday nights. I overslept."

"Well, how wonderful for all of you," Shane says, folding the step stool. "Must take a load off Ashley."

Jeff removes his hoodie and stashes it under the counter. "It's a little relief, but she's still so stressed out—partly from teaching and grading. But I think it's mostly over the Bearsden Police Department bringing in the FBI to investigate the kidnappings."

"You'd think that would reduce her stress, knowing they're investigating."

He shrugs. "In my opinion, involving the FBI also confirms the PD's suspicions the kidnappings are connected with the Baby Nabbers. Gwyn, Ashley says she's researching giants in Welsh folklore for you." He crosses his arms. "Really?"

"She offered, Jeff. Wanted to repay me somehow. I promise. I'm not using her. She has enough on her plate. This is a one and done thing."

A customer enters the store with a ding, and Jeff lowers his voice. "I hope so, because she doesn't need to be at your beck and call over your private research project."

"I get your message loud and clear," I say, rolling my lips inward.

Jeff follows Shane into the back of the store, and I grab a duster. I sure hope Ashley finds relevant folklore. So far, every road leads to a dead end.

When I come out of the bathroom, I predict a toy apocalypse will await me in the living room. Instead, the pile of puzzles is merely in disarray, and Aidan is resting on his chair in the time-out corner.

"Why are you sitting there?" I ask, perplexed.

He peers up at me with those angelic blue eyes, giggling. "I get tickles here."

"You're funny, Aidan." I walk over and squat, tickling his belly. "Like that?"

He giggles again. "No. Not in my tummy. All over."

My grin gives way to a flat line as I inspect the walls and the ceiling. I raise my hand to investigate.

"Pweeze, Miss Gwyn. No invisible hands," he says, pouting.

"I won't, Aidan. You've been a very good boy." I stroke his pale-blond hair. "Go to your toys and start stacking a block tower. I'll be there in a minute."

"Yay! I love blocks. I make a big one. We push it down."

He darts to his toys and collects the blocks into a pile while I continue to inspect the time-out corner. As I close my eyes, I recite an incantation to summon my witch energy. I attempt to survey the area for supernatural residue. When my gut pinches, my eyelids flip open. But I discover nothing. I turn around, and there's a bubble of magic surrounding Aidan. The doorknob jiggles, and Ashley walks in, distracting me. I return my gaze to the sweet boy, but the illusion is gone.

"Hello," she says, shutting the door. "How's my sweet angel?"

"Mommy!" Aidan shouts, dashing to her. "We build blocks."

"Great, sweetie. I have to spend a few minutes showing Miss Gwyn a few things before she leaves. Can you build the tower alone for a bit?"

"Aww. OK. I build a big one and make it go down." He returns to his blocks.

"Let's sit at the bar," Ashley says, pulling a reference book from her backpack. "He won't play alone for long. I can't thank you enough for watching him last week. He still has his moments of noncompliance, but since you came, he's more like a regular two-year-old."

"Whatever you can offer is fine with me. You have a busy schedule, and Aidan deserves time with his mother. As I said before, Mondays are a good day for me to watch him. We had fun today."

"It's hard being a single mom and trying to move up the academic ladder. And I'm on the lowest rung as an instructor." She flips open the book to the first note strip. "Why giants? What fascinates you so much about them?"

I suck in my lower lip. "They're unique. One showed up in a dream I had, and I can't get it out of my head." It's not a lie.

"Dreams mess with our minds, don't they? I've had a few nightmares myself lately." She peers at her son. "This one should spike your curiosity. The Canthrig Bwt was a giantess who lived in the county of Gwynedd under a great stone in a small town called Nant Peris."

"Oh, wonderful. That does capture my interest."

"She ate the local children," she says, matter-of-factly.

I grimace. "Perhaps not fascinating enough for me."

She chuckles and flips the pages to the next note. "She was also a witch."

Ashley squints at me, and I swallow my urge to smile. She continues, skimming over giants and giantesses in tales of King Arthur, one of them a red-eyed giant called Rhitta Gawr who held a court in Snowdonia, and the giant of Castell Maelor, who was captured close to his castle.

"His enemies sentenced him to death," she says. "As a final request, he asked to blow his horn several times. He blew with such force, his hair and beard fell out, then his fingers and toenails fell off."

"Uhh, yuck. I assume there aren't any other giants in the Welsh literature?" Because none of these dudes and dudettes resemble my monster giant at all.

"I'm sure there are others I may not be aware of. I concentrated on Arthurian legends in school."

She flips casually past a few pages, landing on a picture of fairies near a lake. They have dainty faces with rosy complexions and blond hair that's nearly white. Exquisite wings sprout from their backs. I press the pages down to inspect the picture more closely.

"What are these? They're enchanting," I ask.

"Tylwyth Teg fairies. Welsh, of course."

"I've never heard of them. Are they malicious?"

Ashley pauses for a few seconds. "No. Not really. The lore says they're mischievous, but they are actually quite sweet." She glances at Aidan, checking on him.

"I've taken you away from your son long enough. They are little for a very short time. You should cherish every minute you can with him." I stand and put on my fleece jacket.

"Thank you again for babysitting. Aidan, say goodbye to Miss Gwyn."

"Bye-bye," he says, waving.

I stare at him and glance back at the time-out corner.

"Is something wrong?" Ashley asks, her brow crinkling.

"No." I grab my purse and backpack and walk to the door. "You have a great evening."

"You, too, Gwyn," she says, waving goodbye.

On the stroll home, I recall the strange illusion surrounding Aidan. Did Nuada's fairy magic continue to thrive in his old apartment? If so, is his essence after the child?

CHAPTER EIGHTEEN

UNCONDITIONAL LOVE

BY TUESDAY AFTERNOON, A frigid blast of air has moved in, prompting me to pull out my puffer jacket again. Despite layering with a sweatshirt and wearing thick jeans, the bitter wind cuts across my face and through my clothes. Winter keeps sticking its fingers into the fall weather like a mischievous child. It may need a time-out, too.

When I arrive at the trailhead of North Basin Creek Park, Archie and the young witches are huddled near the water, chatting. I haven't talked or sent him a text since I left in a huff Friday night. This is the longest period we've gone without speaking to each other since we got back together. I should have patched things up before the hike, like Shane suggested.

"Hi, everyone," I say, getting out of my Prius. "I'll be there in a minute."

I grab my crossbody bag from the passenger side, lock my car, and walk toward them. Archie locks eyes with me, but his expression betrays no emotion. The others wave to me.

"Hi, Gwyn," Zoe says, jumping up and down. "It's so cold, I can't feel my ass."

I chuckle. "You'll warm up as we hike the trail." I hug Tyler. "Hi, dear. Work going well?"

He glances between Archie and me. "Yeah. We're working on never ending updates."

"Why don't we get moving?" Archie asks. "We can chat while we walk."

"Let's not drag this out with chitchat." Skye stuffs loose strands of her red air back into her DUB beanie. "It's too fucking cold."

Tanner, Spence, and Skye follow Archie while Tyler and Zoe join me in the rear. Occasionally, Spence turns around and spies on me. When we catch up with them, the conversation returns to my prior experiences.

"We all have intuition," Tanner says. "But so far, I don't recognize any magic residue here. Do you sense it now, Gwyn?"

"No. Not like before," I reply. "Perhaps when we get closer to the bog."

Spence throws his hands up. "I receive signals all the time, but none of them points in a particular direction."

"I wonder why?" Skye says with a husky chuckle.

"You're hilarious. I bet Zach thinks you're ready for stand up."

"I'm just fucking with you, Spence." She slaps his arm with the back of her hand.

"Skye isn't wrong, dude," Tanner says. "But I love you, anyway."

Spence hugs his partner. "Unconditional love is the best, isn't it, Gwyn?"

My head snaps up. Why is he asking me? "Of course. No matter what mistakes Tyler made growing up, he always knew I loved him."

"I can vouch for her," my son replies. "Except for the time I took the VHS player apart. You were *really* pissed."

I crack up. "I forgot about your 'inspection' of the video machine. Never worked after that. We had to buy a new one."

Archie smiles at the two of us. "Inquisitive. It's why you're a successful ancestral witch, Tyler. Never stop learning. Your power will grow beyond anything you could imagine."

"He shot past me months ago," Zoe says, her puffs of breath turning white in the air. "But I'm holding my own now."

I give her a one-armed hug. "You certainly are."

Spence looks at Archie and then back at me. "So, witches, have you noticed two of us aren't speaking today?"

Our eyes dance around from one face to another, but no one answers him.

"Let it rest, Spence," Tanner says, nudging him.

"No fucking way." He swings a finger back and forth between Archie and me. "You haven't said a word to each other on this hike. Are you guys having a fight?"

Tyler frowns. "Spence, let it go. Sorry, Mom."

"Gwyn and Archie are being cordial," Skye says. "Plus, we're on an important mission today. They're focused on that."

Archie interjects. "Not that it's anyone's concern, but we've been taking a slight break. All couples need their individual space at one time or another."

Spence snickers. "Yup. They're fighting."

I scowl at him. "Can we concentrate on why we're here?"

"Yeah," Zoe says. "Dr. Hughes gave us this assignment, and I don't want to screw it up."

We arrive at the bog, and our footsteps slow. A stream of fog drifts across the warmed pond, a reaction of the recent warm temperatures to the frigid air. The lily pads have turned yellow, and the water is a murky brown dotted with sludge. But the gnats and mosquitos have fled—one point for Old Man Winter's early visit.

"Gwyn, when did you sense magic on the trail?" Tanner asks, rubbing his arms through his jacket.

"The first time, I didn't recognize what was happening. I thought it was gas." They laugh with me, and I continue. "I swore I saw movement in the woods on the other side of the water. The next, well…I told you at the Fellowship meeting what happened. At the bend in the trail, a magnetic pull overwhelmed me, dragging my body toward the bog."

"That's when you ran into Courtney Erickson." Skye gestures to the curve ahead. "About there?"

I nod. "Yeah. I ran and left Ronnie behind. By the time she caught up with me, the magnetism had dissipated. A hazy mist hung over the bog, but I saw nothing else."

"It's not much to go on," Archie says, rubbing his goatee. "Perhaps we should split up."

"On it!" Spence shouts. "Tanner and I will take the left side of the woods behind the bog. Skye, why don't you go with Tyler and Zoe—check out the right?" He peers at Archie and me. "You guys can stay here and…" He swirls his index finger in a circle. "Figure this out."

My jaw drops, and the young witches head into the woods, snickering. Tyler glances back at me and grins. I amble to the edge of the bog and squat, raising my hand to summon my magic. After a few minutes, I lower it. Archie squats next to me.

"You sense nothing?" he asks, facing his palm toward the water.

"No. Not even a twinge. Unless I figure out what the next step in the cat sith's focus training is, I don't think I will."

An amber glow radiates from his hand as he examines the water in the bog, lowering it soon after. He stands and offers to help me up. When I stand, he cups my cheek and warms my cold, pink skin.

"I said it already, but I'll say it again. I'm sorry, Gwyn. You don't have to tell me everything you do, and you certainly do not need my permission. But I wish you would tell me. When you don't include me, I feel alone as a moon that's lost its earth. And I realize that's my shortcoming. Is this pushback because I want you to move in with me?"

Sometimes, he knows me better than I know myself. "Maybe? I'm not saying I'll never consider it. I need to decide on my own terms when."

"Fair enough." He rubs his chilly nose against mine. "I'm selfish. It's not something I'm proud of. I want you with me always. But I'll take whatever time you spend with me and not complain again."

"Like tonight? Dinner and...dessert?" I caress his chest through his wool coat and inhale his woodsy cologne.

"You could twist my arm," he says in a thicker Scottish brogue.

When I push up on my toes to kiss him, whistles and hoots reverberate from the woods. The young witches trickle out of the thicket, laughing. Spence pats himself on the back.

"Aww. Unconditional love. It's the best."

"I agree," Archie says, stepping back from me. "What did you all find?"

Tanner starts. "Spence and I plodded through as far as we could until we hit a muddy area. Didn't find evidence of magic or anyone having been there."

"We're basically confirming what the police found," Tyler says. "No signs of people camping out."

Zoe scrapes her sneaker on the gravel. "We hit mud, too. Literally. If the kidnappers were hiding in here, it wasn't near the water."

"The stretch of fog across the bog is probably due to the weather," Skye says, eyeing the haze. "You guys check out anything besides yourselves?"

The young witches chuckle, and I scowl at her. "Very. Funny. We tested the water but found nothing out of the ordinary. My intuition must have been tracking the residue of someone roaming through here. If there is a rogue witch operating with the Baby Nabbers, the evil person may have visited here. I could have stumbled upon the stream like in the Pumpkin House." A sigh escapes my mouth, creating a cloud of misty white.

"We've done all we can here," Archie says. "I suggest we hike back and get out of this cold. Gwyn and I will report to Trinity and Dr. Hughes."

Back at the trailhead, the young witches get in their cars and head home. Archie walks me to my car.

"Meet you back at the house," he says, winking.

"What about dinner?" I ask. "Do you want to stop and pick up takeout?"

"Nah. I'll whip up something." He kisses me. "A wee taste to hold you until later."

"Mmm. See you in a few minutes, then."

I rush to the small porch of Archie's cottage home. My hand shakes as I turn the lock. Archie runs after me, and we enter the foyer. While he shuts and locks the door, I stuff my gloves in my puffer jacket and hang it on a hall tree hook.

"Why don't I cook for a change—"

He turns me around, pressing his mouth on mine, and pushes me against the foyer wall. I put my hand on the nape of his neck, encouraging him. He hasn't been this passionate in a while, and I enjoy the attention. But my stomach growls so loud it resembles the sound of a hungry tiger.

I come up for air. "I'm sorry. Not very romantic."

"We'll take care of that." He drags me by the hand into the kitchen.

"I said I could cook dinner. What would you like?"

Archie pulls out a chair and pats the seat. "Sit down. I'll get us a wee snack."

He opens the fridge and retrieves a small carton of fresh strawberries, then returns to the table and sits next to me.

"I love strawberries, but it's not dinner," I say.

"No. I wanted dessert first." Archie picks up a single strawberry and outlines my lips before offering its juicy flesh.

"Mmm," I say, taking a bite. "Where did you get these at this time of year? They taste fresh from the earth."

"I don't know. Most likely from California, but maybe Florida. I went grocery shopping before I met you at the park."

He picks another and sucks on it before taking a bite, never removing his sexy eyes from mine. I pick a strawberry from the carton and lick its side. Archie adjusts the bulge swelling in his pants. I chuckle and take a bite of the heart-shaped fruit.

"You win," I say, swallowing. "I was serious. I'll cook us dinner. Aren't you hungry?"

After eating another, he leans over and kisses me again, offering his tongue. "Aye, my love. Famished." He winks at me.

Archie kneels on the floor, slowly unbuttons my jeans, and pulls the zipper down. I stare into his eyes, burning with desire, and bite my lip.

"Right here? In the kitchen? Wouldn't the bed be more comfortable?"

He tugs at my jeans, chuckling. "I'm afraid you'll change your mind before we get up the stairs."

Wrinkles form between my eyes. "Have I been too aloof? I'm sorry."

"You can make it up to me once you're..." He pulls my panties and jeans off. "More engaged."

I chortle as he spreads my legs, sliding his warm hands up my legs. He plants soft kisses on my inner thighs, working his way up my chilled skin. His hot breath warms me, making me wet, and I slide forward on the seat toward him. When he finds me, I lay my hand on the back of his head, urging him to continue. It's been months since I felt this good. Why do I let the troubles of the world take precedence over the joy I have with the man I love?

While he feasts on me, I snatch another strawberry and suck on the tip, matching his prowess as he performs his magic. I enjoy his lovemaking and a few more berries until I can't hold back. I swing a leg over his back, yelping with my release, and throw the remains of the fruit back on the table. He lays his head against my thigh, sporting an arrogant grin.

"Not aloof at all." He kisses my inner thigh.

I run my hand through his locks. "Why do you put up with me and my shenanigans?"

"Because I love you, Gwynedd. You're my heart and soul."

I lean forward and rub my nose on his. "You're my...everything."

He pulls me off the chair, and I fall onto his torso. I kiss him, grinding my body against his groin, swollen and testing the zipper of his jeans. He unzips his pants and pushes them down, hooking the elastic of his boxer briefs on the way.

"Ahh," he moans. "That's much better."

He rolls me over and enters me, starting slowly, and increases his speed with each thrust. At this moment, there are no others in the world. No kidnappers. No supernatural beings. No coven. Only the two of us expressing our passion for each other. If the universe would cooperate, everything would be perfect. Time warps and bends as we make love, so I'm not sure how long it is before Archie grunts with his release. I stroke his firm back while he caresses my face.

"I missed you, stubborn woman," he says, panting.

"It's only been four days. How would you survive a month?"

"Not well, apparently." He rolls off me onto his side. "Gwyn, I truly am sorry about how I reacted to the incident with Seamus. Although I still think it's risky, you should seek his help to strengthen your intuition."

"Oh, hell no. How could I ever train with him again, knowing he's in love with me? Or at least obsessed with my mother's image in my aunt's painting. I'd never have the focus I need. You know, he burned lavender incense. That should have tipped me off. He said it was to relax me."

Archie's brow furrows. "A wee bit alarming, no? Och, I can't imagine he used it to influence you. Do you?"

"I'm not sure. A loner witch with poor social skills seems the type to resort to desperate measures. But I won't embarrass him by asking." I wipe my face. "Oh, my gods. The expression on his face. He wasn't just crushed. He was humiliated."

"Would you like me to talk with him? I'll be cordial about the situation."

"No. He asked me not to tell you. But I told him I couldn't keep this from you. The next time you meet at school will probably be awkward."

"Aye. I won't mention what happened unless he brings up the topic." He caresses my abdomen. "How will you proceed with your intuition?"

"I may ask Aunt Gorawen. I avoided the topic in our video chats because she prefers I increase my use of the crystal grid at a snail's pace. She'd have a strong opinion about me training with Seamus as well. There would be scolding."

Archie chuckles. "No doubt about that. A family trait, no?"

"Hmph," I say, squinting. "Very. Funny."

"I love you." He kisses me again. "Every stubborn, opinionated part."

I sit up straight. "Holy crystals! I almost forgot. Yesterday, I watched Aidan again. For a split second, I swore I saw a magic bubble around him."

"What?" he asks, sitting up.

"I wouldn't have thought anything of it except the first time I saw something strange, too. When I returned from the bathroom, there was a halo over him while he was sitting in the time-out chair, fairy wings protruding from his back. I blinked, and the image disappeared. I figured it was PTSD from being in Nick's old apartment."

"Quite disconcerting. What message does your intuition send you?"

"There was pinching, and an aura wave swept over me. My best guess is there's magic lingering in the apartment. What if Nuada's essence, his soul, is still in there?"

"Ashley should find another place to live. But how do we approach the subject?"

"I'll have to confide in Jeff. He'll have to convince her to move out. But let's see how the next few Mondays go." I roll onto my side, and my stomach growls.

"Why don't we get cleaned up, and I'll cook us a proper dinner."

"Sounds like a plan, professor."

Chapter Nineteen

An Unexpected Miracle

Over three weeks have passed since the new city ordinance went into effect, and as much as I hate to admit it, the extra street patrols appear to have protected the children of Bearsden—no more reports of kidnappings in our area. But the added protection came at a cost. Every time I tried to sneak into the Celestial Gardens to visit the Seelie Fae, a patrol unit happened by. They have to be itchy by now. I may need to use a masking spell to slip in there soon.

I had to put aside my quest for a more powerful witch's intuition to complete a research paper by Thanksgiving. Somehow, I managed to avoid running into Seamus at the library, and it's a relief to be finished and enjoying the holiday, even if it's cold and overcast.

The Bearsden Shelter has fewer patrons this year thanks to the new jobs training program they funded. Having an office directly on Main Street in Mitchell Hall provided much needed access to those looking for employment. But there are always the unfortunate ones who lose their jobs or get evicted from their homes around the holidays. Some people in this world have no conscience, only eyes for the next greedy dollar.

The last time a few Fellowship members volunteered on Thanksgiving, I'd just discovered I was a witch. Unbeknownst to us, an evil Unseelie Fairy called a Sluagh was preying on homeless men in Bearsden that fall. A couple of local drunks crashed the shelter's holiday dinner, carrying in one of its victims. I sure hope no one drops dead bodies on the celebrants today.

Each member of our coven volunteered to help at least a few hours. Even a few of the city council members are here, including John Erickson. Courtney has joined us, too. She's making sure the condiments table remains full. Still suspicious of her intentions, I plan to watch her like a bird eyeing a wiggly worm.

As patrons slide their food up the tray slide, I scoop up mashed potatoes and drop them onto their dinner plates. Archie is working in the kitchen, carving turkeys as they come out of the oven. Better him than me. Leslie, Tanner, and Spence showed up early to bake desserts. Our resident curmudgeon hedge witch has taken a shift, greeting families as they arrive and directing them to their seats.

I point my serving spoon at Agnes. "Whose idea was it to assign her the welcoming position?"

Ronnie snickers and points to Elijah. "It was the sole job that didn't require standing on her feet all afternoon, and she had to swear on her pentacle tattoo she'd watch her mouth."

"She'll never volunteer again after this, councilman," I say, spying on my mentor.

Agnes forces a grin, but the expression isn't fooling anyone. The children cringe and run past her, clinging to the arms of their parents.

"Sure, she will." Elijah observes her. "Agnes puts on a nasty face, but deep down, I think she likes people more than she's willing to confess."

Ronnie snorts. "It amazes me how you remain so optimistic. I commend you."

"Elijah always finds the good in everyone." I recall the reflection of my mentor blowing me a friendly kiss in my car's rearview mirror. "He knows how to read others, Ronnie. Remember, when we needed more..." I stop, remembering to curb what I say in public. "Members. She returned to the Fellowship."

"Damn straight," Elijah says, spooning peas onto a dinner plate. "She'd commit crimes to save us all."

Ronnie snickers. "Like that's a reach for her."

We burst out laughing. Scanning the dining area, I find Shane, Skye, Tyler, and Zoe meandering around the cafeteria tables and passing out napkins. Spence exits the kitchen through the metal double doors, carrying a pan of freshly cut turkey slices.

"Make way for the turkey!" he shouts as he replaces the empty container.

"That you are," Ronnie says, a chuckle breaking free.

Spence glares at her. "Don't think that baby bump gives you a pass."

"I'm messing with you. What are Tanner and Leslie baking back there?" she asks him.

"Apple and pumpkin pies. Can you smell the cinnamon, ginger, and nutmeg wafting under the doors?" He inhales deeply and returns to the kitchen.

"Ronnie, is Derek coming?" Elijah asks. "Not that I expected him."

"Yeah. He kept the fitness center open until 3:00 p.m. He'll be here soon."

"Well, I sure do appreciate him volunteering." His phone vibrates, and he checks the screen.

"Has anyone seen Trinity?" I ask. "Wasn't she coming?"

"Actually, that was a text from our leader," Elijah says. "Her daughter is visiting. She said she would stop by later, around dessert time."

"Of course. She wouldn't miss freshly baked pies." I scoop mashed potatoes onto a patron's plate. "Enjoy your meal, ma'am, and Happy Thanksgiving."

"You know it," Elijah adds. "Someone needs to carry the extra butter over to the condiments table."

"I'll take it if you can cover the potatoes." Any excuse to check on Courtney.

Elijah nods. "Thanks, Gwyn. I appreciate it."

I grab the tub of butter slices and head for the condiments table. Courtney smiles as I approach.

"Thank you, Gwyn. We were running low. People like their butter on Thanksgiving."

"They're putting it on everything, so I'm not surprised." I set the tub on the table and decide to poke the bear. "Have you hiked in the North Basin Creek Park recently? I ask because the Bearsden Police searched the area for the Baby Nabbers a few weeks ago. Did you notice anything unusual? Like near the bog?"

"Uh..." she mutters. "Once or twice. It's been on the cool side for hiking."

I squint at her. "You didn't answer my question."

Her gaze veers to her husband, who is chatting with a couple of council members. He smiles at her.

"I saw the same as you, most likely," she says. "Lots of fallen leaves and barren limbs."

"Sounds about right for late fall." She *still* didn't answer me. "Well, I'm glad you and John could volunteer today. Elijah was short-handed. Enjoy the rest of your holiday."

"You, too, Gwyn. We're happy to volunteer at the shelter anytime."

Shane, my son, and the other young witches are off to the side, chatting, while the patrons eat dinner. Before I return to the food line, I dart over to say hello.

"Happy Thanksgiving. This is the first chance I've had to talk to you all."

"To you as well," Shane says. "Everyone is having a wonderful time. I'm so glad Elijah puts this together every year."

"What were you talking to Courtney about?" Skye asks.

"Asked her if she's hiked in North Basin recently. Did she notice anything out of the ordinary, especially near the bog?"

"What did she say?" Tyler asks.

"Hmph. It's what she didn't say. She never answered my question."

Shane spies on Courtney while she chats with John, who has joined her to help at the condiments table. "Could mean nothing."

"Maybe you scare her, Gwyn?" Zoe asks.

Skye laughs. "Zoe may be on to something."

They all snicker, and I throw them a side-eye. When I glance back at the food line, Archie is serving the potatoes—my job.

"I'm going to take my scary ass and get back to work." I point at my son. "Don't think I'll forget this. Remember, you want me to train you in ancestral divination so you can talk with Nain and Taid."

He chuckles. "Sorry, Mom. But Archie offered to train me, anyway."

"What?" I glare at my Scottish lover. "Well, it's your choice, dear. I'll talk to you all later. Don't forget to get some dinner."

I tramp back to the food line and confront my boyfriend. "Did you tell Tyler you'd—" I stop myself, remembering where I am.

"I'd what?" he asks, cocking his head. "Oh, I think I know what you're asking. I was going to chat with you about the training later tonight. Should I have said no?"

"Or ask me first?" I scowl at him. "It's OK with me if he'd rather have a man show him."

"What are you two blathering about?" Ronnie asks. "I'm almost afraid to ask."

"Nothing like that." I lean over to whisper in her ear. "Tyler wants Archie to teach him ancestral divination."

"Oh. Well, he may want a fatherly figure to train him." She winks at Archie. "I think it's a great idea."

"If it's all right with you, my love," he says.

In the distance, one of the entry doors swings open, and Alys Morgan struts in. Derek follows in behind her and approaches us.

Elijah darts to his fellow council member and introduces her to Agnes. The councilwoman offers her hand, but my mentor crosses her arms and tramps away. Alys takes over her job, greeting a few stragglers as they enter.

"Hello, you two," Derek says, and places a kiss on Ronnie's cheek. "You OK, babe?"

"Yes, handsome. I sit on a stool when I get tired."

"Great way to garner support from our local politicians," I mutter.

Ronnie whispers, "We should be happy she didn't tell her to fuck off."

"She may have," Archie says.

"Who are you talking about?" Derek asks.

Ronnie chuckles and points to Agnes plodding toward us.

"Oh," he replies. "She grumbled a hello when I entered, but the new councilwoman replaced her."

Leslie, Tanner, and Spence break through the kitchen doors, pushing carts with several choices of pies and cookies.

"We'll make room for the dessert," Archie says, pulling out a pan.

"Thank you," Leslie replies. "I suggest you keep some of the main course out for latecomers."

Agnes joins us and inspects the pies. "I've been waiting an hour for this. What took you so long?"

"You know we have to cook them in an oven, right?" Spence asks.

The hedge witch scowls at him. "Don't be a fucking smart-ass. I came for the dessert. So, it better be good."

"We have to prepare multiple desserts, Agnes," Tanner says, placing slices on the food line. "But I'm glad you're looking forward to them."

Ronnie inhales the intoxicating aromas of chocolate, cinnamon, apple, and nutmeg. "Fam, this smells delicious. I can't wait."

"Wonderful job, Leslie." Derek massages Ronnie's back. "Babe, maybe you should grab a slice and get off your feet."

"I think you're right. We'll be over there." Ronnie and Derek pick up two slices of apple pie and head to the far empty table.

"I can't take much credit," Leslie says. "Tanner and Spence baked most of the desserts."

"Doing my service to the community." Spence pats his own back on both sides.

Tanner chuckles. "Would have been more of a service if you hadn't eaten so many of the cookies you baked."

"I only tasted a few to check if they were done," he says, throwing his hands up.

"Sure, dude." Tanner hugs him and kisses his cheek.

Archie lays a hand on Spence's shoulder. "I'm sure Elijah is more than happy to give up a few cookies for your service."

We condense the dinner food for latecomers and place the yummy baked goods on the line. Elijah shouts to the patrons.

"Dessert, everyone! Please take your time. There is plenty!"

The families and single people gather at the food line, along with the few council members and their spouses. Suddenly, the sirens of police and emergency vehicles come within earshot, increasing in volume until they're blaring just outside the building. The murmurs of the shelter's patrons add to the noise as they speculate about the cause, a few people looking around in alarm as the sirens grow even louder. Alys Morgan doesn't appear fazed at the racket, her eyes glued to her cell phone screen. The double doors open with a bang. Trinity rushes in, an elated grin lighting up her face.

"Praise the gods!" she yells. "They've found the kidnapped children! You can't go outside for a while. So, take your time and enjoy your meal." She rushes toward us.

Everyone in the cafeteria roars with applause. Whistles echo around the shelter, a palpable relief settling on the room. John Erickson and the other council members dart out the front doors, except for Alys, who remains oblivious, sitting on the stool. Courtney takes a seat with her dessert.

We hug each other at the food line, whooping in exultation. I search for Ronnie in the cafeteria and lock eyes with her. She's grinning, massaging her belly while Derek holds her close. Agnes wraps an arm around Leslie, smiling. Not many things put a smile on the hedge witch's face.

Spence wipes tears from his eyes. "I'm so happy for their parents. I hope the kidnappers didn't hurt them."

"Let's hope not, for their sakes." Tanner hugs his partner.

Elijah rubs his jaw. "Those kids will have a hell of a lot of trauma, sadly. But at least they're alive."

"It's like a Thanksgiving miracle," I say, touching Archie's arm.

He clasps my hand. "Aye. A blessed day for their parents."

Shane, Skye, Tyler, and Zoe dart to the tray line. The coven gathers in a tiny circle while Trinity catches her breath and fills us in on what happened.

"I got here about twenty minutes ago and found all three of them huddled together outside, the two-year-old holding the baby. Pulled out my cell and called the Bearsden Police right away. I asked the kids if they were hurt, but they didn't answer me—in shock, I suspect. They appeared unharmed...physically. The ambulance is here to take them to the hospital. Their parents arrived, and I came in to tell you all."

"So, the Baby Nabbers dropped them off?" Skye asks.

Tyler scratches his head. "Why? Wouldn't that put them at tremendous risk of getting caught?"

"Indeed," Leslie replies. "The kidnappers could have received warnings the FBI discovered their hiding place and didn't want to get caught with the children in their possession?"

Shane nods. "A perfect explanation. Better to dump them quickly and move on to another city."

"You all don't know criminals very well," Agnes says, grimacing. "Dump them when they could sell them on the black market? You think the FBI scares ruthless people like them? Fuck no."

Zoe tears up. "Why can't we all just be happy the kidnappers returned the children to their families? It's the police's job to figure out their reason."

"I agree," Trinity says, grinning. "I don't know about you all, but I'm gonna grab me a slice of pumpkin pie and go sit over there with Ronnie and Derek. Please, join me and give thanks for this miracle."

Archie grabs a slice of apple pie. "A wonderful idea, Trinity."

"You all go ahead," Elijah says. "I'll check out front and join you in a few minutes."

Each of us chooses a dessert, and we gather at the cafeteria table, laughing and celebrating the joyous news. I realize I'd forgotten to monitor Courtney, my suspicions flying out the window with the return of the children. I scan the cafeteria and find her chewing on the last bite of a cookie, leveling the nastiest scowl at Alys Morgan, who is still sitting on her stool, sporting a shit-eating grin.

What the fuck is that about?

"Are you sure it's safe to visit the Seelie Fae?" Archie asks, leaning on the stair newel in the foyer. "Only two days have passed since the children were returned."

"Bearsden PD canceled the extra patrols. I should be fine on a Saturday night. Besides, someone has to visit them to make sure they didn't create a mess in the gardens while the added police units were shutting us out."

He rubs the whiskers of his goatee. "The ordinance remains, though. How will you handle the curfew?"

"The curfew only applies to children under eighteen. The city council will lift the ordinance at the next meeting, anyway—since the police arrested the Baby Nabbers. Did the news say when they found the kidnapping ring?"

"The Philadelphia Police Department raided an old warehouse in Philly late last night on a tip. Found them with the help of the FBI. They must have dropped the children off at the shelter and returned to their hideout posthaste, hoping to evade capture."

"Were there children being held captive at the warehouse?" I shove my feet into my sneakers and tie the laces.

"The reporter didn't say. Not likely. It would have been all over the news."

I stand and grab my jacket. "I'm sure more will come out as police question the lowlifes."

"Keep your wits about you. Finding you in the Celestial Gardens in the dead of night during a curfew could raise suspicions."

I kiss him. "Please, do I resemble a high schooler or an undergrad? No one has carded me at a bar in years."

"No, but you still tickle my fancy," he says, stroking my chin. "I'll go up to bed and wait for you there. Don't be long."

"I'll only spend a few minutes chatting and leave. But I better go back another night to run around the gardens with them."

I put on my puffer jacket, grab my crossbody bag, and start my trek toward the Green under crystal clear skies. The white vapors of my breath surround me as I stroll along the paver walkways, lit by sporadic lampposts. A single student passes by me, sprinting to a dorm entry. The door slams and reverberates off the red-brick buildings. As the newspapers reported, the Bearsden Police Department disbanded the extra units. Even DUB Police have vacated their additional campus patrols. Visiting the Seelie Fae should be a breeze.

When I arrive at Mitchell Hall, nary a soul occupies Main Street, except for the occasional car driving through. I scan the area, unlock the gate, and enter the Celestial Gardens. Shailagh and

Aonghas spot me from the right side near the hawthorn tree and rush to me, giggling. I sure hope that's not a sign they have been mischievous.

"Hi, Aunt Gwyn," they say. "We're so happy you're here."

Their peachy skin glows under the moonlight as their blond hair dances with the wind. I hug their tiny bodies.

"I am so glad to see you both," I say, my white breath slithering like snakes in the air. "Thank you so much for entertaining yourselves while we couldn't visit you. I'm proud of you both."

Shailagh and Aonghas shrug. "We didn't have to," Aonghas says. "We had children to play with us at night. It was so much fun!"

"What?" I ask, blinking. "Who brought children to play here?"

"We don't know," Shailagh says. "They never came in with them."

"How many children were there?" I ask.

"Three." Aonghas immediately frowns. "But only two of them could play. One was a baby. We rocked him to sleep, then the others ran around the gardens with us."

"They didn't talk much," Shailagh adds. "Or know how to play. We had to teach them."

"How strange. Well, they won't come again. The kidnappers returned those children to their parents two nights ago."

The Seelie Fae giggle. "Aunt Gwyn, they came to play last night."

"Not the baby, though," Shailagh says.

Folds form in my brow. "Last night?"

Aonghas nods. "We played tag. But they still don't talk much."

"Listen, I can't stay to play, but I'll be back sometime this week. Please, let me know if those children come back to visit you. OK?"

"We will. Goodnight, Aunt Gwyn."

"You, too, Shailagh and Aonghas."

As I stroll through Central Campus, a wave of unusual magic overcomes me, and my gut pinches worse than before. The sorcery encompasses me, circling my body from every direction. I survey the area—no sign of Seamus Duffy. But he wouldn't dishonor my request to stay away, would he?

After a few minutes, the strange magic disappears, and I'm left standing in an empty Green, only a cloud of white breath remaining to keep me company. Or is there another lurking close by?

Chapter Twenty

FREEDOM IS OVERRATED

"I say goodbye to you from this position way too often." Archie leans on the doorjamb with his arms crossed, dressed in a T-shirt and lounge pants. "I enjoy our Sunday mornings lying in bed, cuddling. Even more so on a chilly day."

"I get the subtle hint, but thank you for not coming out and repeating yourself like a broken record."

He runs a hand through his hair. "Are you concerned about losing your freedom? Because I wouldn't stifle you if you moved in. Like anyone could stop you from doing what you want."

"No, honey," I say, putting on my shoes. "Even if I lived here, I'd be out the door. I need to visit my best friend."

A corner of his mouth rises. "Aye. You do. Will you mention what happened last night?"

"I don't dare tell her about the strange occurrence on the Green. It'll send her on a downward spiral again. There's no way to know if the magic residue is connected to the Baby Nabbers. If there was a witch involved, she's lost her connection to those Unremarkable criminals."

"There are plenty more lurking in the shadows. If a witch was involved, another group will crop up in no time." He runs a hand through his locks again, exhaling. "What about the children the Seelie Fae spoke of? Disconcerting, no?"

"Yeah, but who are they? Those kids can't be the same ones the Baby Nabbers took. Probably some neglectful parent dropping off their kids to mess around while they go drinking. Wouldn't be the first time parents showed negligent behavior in this town."

Archie nods. "Or the last, but you should tell Leslie. Could be a concern going forward."

My phone vibrates—a text from my young boss. "It's Jeff."

Jeff: *Could you come back after dinner on Monday and watch Aidan?*

Me: *Sure. Do you have something special planned?*

Jeff: *I'd like to take Ashley to a Welsh Music performance on Monday evening.*

Me: *She'll enjoy the music. Those concerts are always lovely.*

Jeff: *Thank you! I need to give you a raise for all you have done for her!*

Me: *You don't have to repay me for friendly gestures. But I won't argue with you, either!*

"He wants me to go back to Ashley's apartment after dinner so he can take her to the annual Welsh Music concert."

Archie cocks his head. "Didn't you go with Nick Evans to one of those?"

"Yeah, but I only saw part of it, remember? You were practicing your *thought intentions.*"

He chuckles. "Aye. I recollect now. You showed up at my house dripping wet...everywhere."

"I was so embarrassed. Two women heard me screaming in the stall."

"But the intention was successful," he says, winking.

A titter bubbles out. "It was. What about the interaction I witnessed between Courtney Erickson and Alys Morgan? Should we alert Leslie and Trinity?"

"And tell them what, exactly? Alys came on to me at the Samhain Celebration. I wager she tried to cozy up to John and Courtney caught her in the act. We know she has a jealous streak. I doubt that has changed."

"Well, he is her husband. She has a right to be annoyed. You may be correct. Alys was sporting an enormous grin of satisfaction, for sure." I finish tying my shoelaces and slip on my puffer jacket.

"Can I enter this day in my online calendar?" he asks with a chuckle. "It may never happen again."

"Very funny, professor." I kiss him and grab my purse from the mudroom hook. "I've got a busy week. But I promise I'll try to pop over some night."

"I'll be here waiting impatiently, my love."

"Love you, honey." I blow him a kiss.

When I open the door, a blast of frigid air hits me like a brick. After the quick drive to Ronnie and Derek's house, I shiver in the near-freezing temperature while I wait to go in. I haven't spoken with my best friend since Thanksgiving. The worry melted from her face when Trinity announced the return of the kidnapped children. With just a couple of weeks left until her due date, she has to be driving her partner bananas.

"Hey, Gwyn," Derek says as he opens the door. "Get in here. It's bitter out today. Your legs must be frozen in those yoga pants."

"I should have worn jeans, but I'm going to the DUB fitness center after my visit. How are you doing? Ready to be a papa?"

An elated grin brightens his face. "I can't wait. Ronnie is in the nursery making up the bassinet and crib."

"Has she slept more soundly since Thanksgiving?"

"Oh, yeah. Except for the discomfort of the baby moving around all night. And her tendons ache."

"Yeah. I imagine they do. A couple more weeks, and she'll not be sleeping at all."

"I'll help as much as I can. I plan on getting the baby in and out of the bassinet for her to nurse. Hopefully, she can fall back asleep more quickly that way. I pass out the minute my head hits the pillow. Once the baby arrives, I'll have to cut my hours back and rely on Jamal."

I enter the nursery as Ronnie pulls the baby comforter over the crib mattress, a celestial moon theme. Rose quartz to encourage bonding between the baby and its parents is scattered around the room. Stars cover the ceiling.

"Hello, Mama," I say. "Nesting, are we?"

She chuckles and massages her baby bump. "You know it. I can't wait to meet this kid."

"Ladies, I'll leave you two alone to chat," Derek says. "I'll be at the fitness center for a while."

Ronnie blows Derek a kiss as he leaves, and I admire the decor again.

"I love the celestial decorations. You created a magical room."

"Wait a minute, Gwyn. You're gonna love this."

She closes the blackout curtains, shuts the door, and turns out the light. The stars on the ceiling sparkle in the dark. She chants an incantation and waves her hand, an amber glow swirling upward from her palm, and they twinkle like the sparkling orbs in indigo skies.

"Does Derek know you're using magic in here?" I ask.

She snickers. "Not yet. It may be my tiny secret with Wiggles. But I don't think he'll mind a little twinkling."

"He'll warm up to the idea. After the commotion of the children's return, we didn't get to chat about how you feel now. You must be floating on a cloud."

She smiles, admiring the sparkling stars above. "I am. And I'm so grateful the universe blessed me with this gift of life."

The corners of her mouth dip, and she grimaces. She lays a hand on her belly, staring at it as if she's experiencing discomfort. I wrap an arm around her shoulders.

"What's wrong, Ronnie? Are you hurting?"

"I realize I have no reason to feel like this. But a sense of dread still clutches at my heart. I can't explain it."

"It's normal to react like this. You're going to be a mom, so you better get used to it. That feeling never leaves. I still worry about Tyler."

"Well, fuck that. I didn't sign up for the continually stressed mom division."

I laugh and give her a squeeze. "You'll find your own path, I'm sure."

"I damn well better. Because I hate this daily dose of doomsday intuition. When does the fun start?"

"Soon, friend. Count your days of independence, because they're flitting away."

Ronnie waves her amber magic at the stars one more time, and they glimmer. "Sometimes freedom is overrated."

Her words remind me of the conversation I had with Archie before I left. She's right. Maybe it's worth the compromise?

Aidan isn't a problem at all Monday afternoon or following dinner when I return. He plays games with me, whining very little. He even entertains himself for a while, to my chagrin. I'm enjoying this new role as a substitute grandmother. I wonder why Ashley hasn't mentioned grandparents on either side, hers or her dead husband's. How odd. But it's not my business. There could be family issues of estrangement, and I won't pry.

My witch's intuition recognizes no magic residue or evidence of Nuada's presence around Aidan. At least for now, he appears safe. Ashley doesn't need to stress over the kidnappers, and I won't have to approach Jeff about the issue. After a quick bath, I put Aidan to bed.

"You were such a good boy today," I say, stroking his blond hair. "And I hear you went to a few play groups with other little boys and girls. Did you have fun?"

"Yes, Miss Gwyn. We laugh a lot. They don't have invisible hands like you."

I chuckle. "No. They probably don't."

"Miss Gwyn? I have invisible hands?" He raises his hand and waves it in the air.

Holy crystals. How do I answer this question? "I don't think so, Aidan."

He giggles. "I think I can." He waves both of his hands around.

Oh, my gods. I should have never used magic to discipline the boy. But I have to humor him now. "You can always try."

"Mommy says I shouldn't." He yawns and stretches his arms.

What a strange answer. He must be confused. "You need to go to sleep now. Goodnight, Aidan."

"Night, Miss Gwyn." He closes his angelic blue eyes and rolls over onto his stomach.

While I wait for Ashley and Jeff to return from the concert, I flip through a few Welsh reference books left out on the dining room table. I pick up a lone book with a tattered spine and skim through stories of fairies, stumbling upon a few about the Tylwyth Teg. One story tells of fairy maidens who dance, make rings, and live under the water. They're enamored with those who have golden hair, sometimes becoming wives of human men. But they must avoid touching iron...

The doorknob rattles, and the two young lovers enter, deep in discussion over the performance. Ashley notices me holding her reference and rushes to me. Jeff's eyes widen.

"What are you doing?" She takes the book from me and presses it over her heart. "I didn't mean to be rude. This is a personal copy of stories my husband gave me."

"I'm sorry. I supposed the book was one of your school ref-erences. But I understand why you cherish it so much. It is a wonderful collection of Welsh folklore, especially the stories on the Tylwyth Teg." My gut pinches, and a slight aura whooshes over me. But my intuition points nowhere.

She averts her eyes. "Yes. My husband wanted me to have the collection because of his ancestry."

"Ashley, I have a few questions about the Tylwyth Teg. If you have time in the future to discuss them with me, I'd love to learn more."

"I...um...I don't think I'll have time until the semester is over. Do you mind waiting?"

"Of course. No rush."

Jeff locks eyes with Ashley. "Gwyn, would you like me to give you a ride home? It's freezing out there."

"No. I don't have far to go, and I need to get my steps in today." I grab my purse and head to the door.

"Oh, I almost forgot," Ashley says with a crack in her voice. "Did Aidan have any trouble going to bed?"

I turn around. "No. He closed his eyes and went right to sleep. He was sweet. I hope you enjoyed the concert."

"It was amazing," Jeff says, messing with his wavy brown hair. "I hadn't heard most of those instruments before."

Ashley places the book on the table and relaxes. "The performances were quite authentic. I was impressed. Were the performers as talented when you attended the Welsh Music concert?"

"Oh, yes, but I had to leave early." I suppress the urge to snicker. "An unusual sensation sent me home."

"That's too bad," Jeff says. "You should go next time."

"I should. Enjoy the rest of your evening."

"You, too," Ashley says. "Gwyn, thank you again for all your help."

"You're welcome. Goodnight."

On the brisk walk home, I think back on my interaction with Ashley. I feel awful, having invaded her privacy. It was an honest mistake, but I'm left with the feeling my intuition is failing me again.

As I pass Seamus's small bungalow, a lamp glows in the living room window. It's been several weeks since I spoke with the cat sith witch, and I've not repeated the success I had that afternoon. But I can't rely on him. It would only feed his obsession. Then again, maybe he's following me, anyway. Could he be the one who left traces of strange magic residue on the Green?

When I enter the house, the living room is empty. As I make my way down the hallway in my socks, voices travel from the office. Leslie is sifting through books and placing them on her old wooden desk. Mr. Yeats stacks them in piles according to some pre-determined organizational scheme. He adjusts his spectacles.

"I don't understand why you are taking all these books to Ms. Pritchard's house. You'll have so few left here."

"Mr. Yeats, I'm spending more time at the farm and need access to my books."

"What's going on here?" I ask, shuffling in. "Are you donating more texts?"

"No," the chimera cat familiar replies. "She's moving the tomes to Ms. Pritchard's farm."

"Oh. Makes sense. You're practically living there these days—now that the city has replaced the old sewer line."

Leslie returns to her sorting. "Yes. Since the danger of the kidnappers is behind us, I'm attempting to...consolidate my life a bit."

Mr. Yeats sets a book in the pile of Welsh language texts. "With both you and Ms. Crowther gone all the time, I'm rarely needed. Why keep me at all?"

"You are indispensable, Mr. Yeats. Perhaps I should give you a list of chores to complete while I'm at Agnes's house?"

Leslie's familiar becomes flustered and transforms into his chimera cat presentation, scuttling out the door.

"Should I go after him?" I ask.

"No," she replies. "He doesn't take well to change." She presses her lips together, staring at the doorway. "You've come from Dr. Lewis's apartment, I assume?"

"Yeah. It was awkward. I was reading a story from one of her books, thinking it was a reference. Turns out, the prized possession was a gift from her late husband. I was mortified. Still, the lore intrigues me. It was all about the Welsh fairies called the Tylwyth Teg. The females were attracted to human men with golden hair, becoming their wives."

"Not only human men but children as well." She picks through the piles of books until she finds a reference and passes it to me. "You may find this intriguing. But I'd wait until you have more time. The tales are addictive."

"Thank you. Did you tell Trinity about the children who've been playing with the Seelie Fae children at night? Does she think we should do something about it? What if they tell their parents about them?"

"Trinity and I agree that it's a definite concern, but we doubt the parents would report anything to the authorities. How could they without being reported to child protective services for leaving their children unattended?"

"That's very true. I'll keep track of how often these children play with the Seelie Fae and report back to you. Thanks again for the book." I walk to the doorway and stop. "Has Seamus talked to you about what happened?"

"He has not," she says. "Give him time to recover from his mistake. You don't have to lose his friendship over the incident."

"I hope not," I say, yawning. "I'm going to bed. Goodnight."

"Pleasant dreams to you, Gwynedd."

I place the Welsh folklore on my nightstand and change for bed. I'm too pooped to practice with the crystals. A good night's slumber could recharge my witch's intuition. But knowing my luck, I'll end up dreaming about the gray-skinned monster again.

Lying in bed, I recall Aidan's words regarding the use of magic. He said, "Mommy says I shouldn't." I sit up straight, my heart skipping a few beats, realizing what he meant. *Holy crystals.* Did Aidan tell Ashley I performed witchcraft in front of him?

CHAPTER TWENTY-ONE

PUZZLING INTUITION

When I arrive at work on Wednesday at ten, Shane is ringing up a customer. I retract my wet umbrella and remove my fleece jacket. It's raining today, but at least the temperature will nearly hit fifty degrees. Not exactly joyous holiday weather, but I'll take it.

Mystic Sage appears festive with evergreen twigs, holly sprigs, mistletoe, and paper snowflakes hanging everywhere. Red, green, blue, and white trimmings set the tone for the coming Yule, and I'm excited for this year's Winter Solstice Celebration. My first one ended with my body bloodied after slaying an evil Sluagh fairy. I left the Bearsden Coven and Archie that night, vowing never to return. But I'm so glad I did. A faint smile curls my mouth.

"Penny for your thoughts, Gwyn," my boss offers, meandering around the counter.

"Oh, I was remembering my first Yule with all of you—the first solstice."

He chuckles. "That memory pasted a smile on your face? You were madder than a wet hen that night. But you returned to us. Any regrets?"

I snicker. "No. I'm happy I came back."

"Ahh," he says, pulling on his beard. "We were so glad you did, darling. Personally, I was happy as a pig in poop."

"You have a way with words, Shane." I glance at the crystals room. "Is Jeff in the back?"

"Hasn't arrived yet. He took Aidan to a play group."

"I'm glad Ashley arranged for him to spend a couple of hours with other children his age. Scheduling a play date was probably difficult for her, but socialization is so important. Isolating him most likely affected his behavior. But I understand why she was cautious."

"She brought him into the store this past week. It was like someone replaced him with a clone."

"Nah. Consistent discipline."

And, as Archie would say, "a wee bit of magic," but I'm not telling Shane or anyone else about my shenanigans with Aidan. What a blunder that was. I walk behind the counter and log in to the cash register after stashing my purse and jacket underneath.

"Your influence probably made all the difference, I imagine," Shane says.

"She was being a bit of a helicopter mom. But who could blame her with the Baby Nabbers ring snatching the region's precious children? I'd have wanted him under close watch, too."

"We're not out of the woods yet. Did you read the news?"

"No. I was too busy with my final class research. What happened?"

He shoves his hands in his back pockets. "The members of the Baby Nabbers refuse to take responsibility for the kidnappings in Bearsden. They say they never came to Delaware. Alys Morgan suggested they leave the ordinance in place for now. Many of the residents who attended the council meeting were hot under the collar."

"Huh. But criminals are liars. They don't want those charges added to their rap sheet. You can't really blame Alys for erring on the side of caution, though."

"Perhaps. But the children are home safely with their parents."

I wince. "Did they say if the kidnappers hurt the kids?"

"The paper stated they were healthy."

"That's good to hear. I hope those kids survive the trauma."

The door dings and Alys Morgan enters wearing a pink wool coat. We wave to the councilwoman as she shuffles to the toy section in her rain boots.

"Her ears must be burning," Shane says under his breath. "I'll be in the back unboxing the New Year's Eve party favors. Holler if you need me."

"Sure, boss. If I hear a popping sound, I'll know you're having an impromptu celebration."

He grins. "Only if my gal agrees to come."

"You're keeping this new lady friend under wraps. Have you told her about..." I glance at Alys, who has an ear turned toward us. "The Fellowship?"

"Not yet, darling. Getting to know her better first."

"Probably best. Go on. I've got the front covered."

"Thank you much," he says, strolling into the back.

When I peer over at Alys, she's picking up the new puzzles for children under age three and examining them with a perfectionist's eye. After her last visit, I mentioned her displeasure about the lack of toys to the bosses. I mean, we aren't a toy store. But Jeff found a few items that fit the store's theme and ordered them for the holidays. I try not to stare, but she is a beautiful woman—and beguiling. Despite her rigid disposition, I wonder how she went this long without snagging a beau. I lock the register and walk over to her.

"May I help you, Ms. Morgan?"

"I can't decide between these two," she says. "What wonderful choices the owners have made."

"Yeah. One of them has a girlfriend with a small child. He had a lot of fun choosing from the catalogue. We're carrying them special for the holidays since we aren't really a toy store. If you're undecided, I could make a recommendation. Who are the toys for?"

Her gaze drops to the puzzles in her hands. "The same two I was shopping for at my last visit to Mystic Sage. My friend's young children."

"You're wonderful to spoil them."

She smiles at me warmly. "I love them so much I almost consider them my own children. Of course I shower them with gifts. What else am I going to do with my money?"

Well, for a start, she could donate a chunk of the green stuff to the Bearsden Shelter. I doubt she'd miss a few thousand. But her ordinance seemed to pay off, so I'll give her that.

She glances at me while she inspects the puzzles. "Isn't your friend having a baby soon? The red-head?"

"Ronnie? Yeah. Right before Yule. So, any day now."

"I thought she might be close. I didn't notice her at the most recent city council meetings."

My best friend was too stressed to attend, but I won't tell her that. "Ms. Morgan, I was against the curfew. In hind-sight, I admit, you made a wise choice. There were no more kidnappings, and now those criminals are behind bars."

"I did what I thought was best for the children of our town. Doing my civic duty. Now we can all rest and enjoy the holiday season." She examines the two puzzles in her hands one more time. "I'm going to buy them both."

"Wonderful. Bring them to the counter, and I'll ring you up."

Jeff enters the store shortly after Alys leaves. I don't know how to approach him about the magic issue. If he told Ashley about the Fellowship, he wouldn't say. He wouldn't have discussed the matter with the coven, either. After all, he's an Unremarkable.

"Hi, Gwyn," he says, pulling off his DUB beanie and coat. "How are you?"

"I'm good." I fiddle with the pens in the skull cup and they slide off the counter—my least favorite pastime. "Shit. If I had a dollar for every time I knocked them over, I wouldn't have to work at Mystic Sage."

My boss grimaces. "I'm not sure how to take that."

I chuckle as I dart around to pick them up. "I'm kidding. Even if I won the lottery, I'd work here for you guys. Once I finish my degree, I'll need to apply for full-time employment. I'll miss seeing you and Shane, but I'll still be a customer."

"I hope so." He hangs his coat on a hook. "About Monday..."

"I'm sorry I read through her special book. It was with her references, but I should have asked first. I hope Ashley isn't mad."

"No," he replies, averting his eyes. "She's just sensitive about the fairy folklore collection." He motions toward the back. "I better go talk to Shane and ask if he needs help."

Jeff darts off to the back as a young woman enters the store with a baby in a stroller. He's acting weird. Did Aidan mention my use of *invisible hands*?

When I glance back at the customer, I'm surprised to find Jenny Hansen shopping in the holiday corner. Her baby, Daniel, was the first Bearsden child the Baby Nabbers snatched. He sleeps soundly in the stroller, but not for long. An ear-splitting cry from her little one breaks the comfort of the silence. She bends over to assuage her infant son, eventually picking him up and bouncing him in her arms.

"Come on, Daniel. You were sleeping so well. What's bothering you this time?" She peers in my direction. "I'm so sorry."

"Never apologize for a baby's behavior. Their cries are the way they communicate."

"Thank you for understanding." Her head bends to the right. "I remember you. You were in the Celestial Gardens the night..."

"Yes. It's so wonderful to see you reunited."

"My husband and I were elated. But since Daniel came home, he's not been the same. He was such a calm bundle of joy—always smiling. Now?" She cuddles him close to her, and tears well up in her eyes. "It's as if someone replaced him with a different baby. We even had testing to be sure he's ours. It matched perfectly. I can't explain it, but..." Her voice lowers to a near whisper. "I don't think he's my Daniel."

My gut pinches, and an aura spreads up my torso. "He experienced a great trauma of being separated from you. Give him time to adjust."

"Doctors and psychologists have told all of us parents that our children are healthy and weren't abused in any way—to give the children time to recover. I've met with the other parents. They have similar feelings. Their young ones are exhibiting behavior problems in daycare or preschool, and they still haven't spoken yet. We are at our wit's end."

Daniel elicits a more intense scream, and she places a pacifier in his mouth. He spits it out. How I ache for this woman and the other parents. To have their children home but face yet another struggle with their behaviors.

"Would you like me to try?" I ask, holding my hands out. "Give you a break?"

"Sure. Thank you. Maybe you can cajole him into taking his pacifier."

She places Daniel in my arms, and I rock him back and forth. I sense the tension in his body. It's as if he's sending me a message, telling me he's in the wrong place. My intuition flares up, prompting my cheeks to flush. What are my witchy instincts trying to tell me?

"There's something terribly wrong." She takes Daniel from me and places him in the stroller, a tear rolling down her cheek. "I'll have to come back later. Thank you for rocking him."

"I hope your situation improves. Take care, Jenny."

She nods and pushes the stroller onto the paver sidewalk, stopping briefly to cover Daniel with a blanket. The townies probably think everything is copacetic with the children's' return. How wrong they are.

I spend the last hour of work tidying up. Fold Yule T-shirts. Straighten up the board games. Dust the shelves. I ring up customers in-between. I love the holidays, but shoppers make a mess of the store. When a lull in shoppers blesses me with a break, I prepare to leave and send Ronnie a text to check on her.

Me: *How are you doing, Mama?*

Ronnie: *Derek and I took a hike yesterday in North Basin, and I lost a glove.*

Me: *I'm sorry, but it's great you took a hike. Get that baby moving.*

Ronnie: *You know it! Unfortunately, the only movement I'm feeling today is from Braxton-Hicks contractions.*

Me: *Where do you think you dropped it?*

Ronnie: *Couldn't be too far down the trail. Took them off close to the parking lot.*

Me: *I'm leaving work. I could stop and look.*

Ronnie: *It would be soaked by now. Don't worry about it.*

Me: *I have my car today. I'll drive there. Not a big deal.*

Ronnie: *You're such a good friend!*

Me: *Get some rest!*

Ronnie: *Thanks, Gwyn!*

Jeff carries boxes in and begins restocking the shelves. He's careful to avoid my gaze as he crouches in front of the herbs. The silence is palpable. When I put on my jacket, he stands.

"Is it four already?" he asks as he walks behind the counter.

"Yeah. I logged out of the register. Will you tell Shane I said goodbye? The Fellowship is having a short meeting this week since we volunteered at the Bearsden Shelter for Thanksgiving. We're making last-minute plans for the Yule Celebration."

"Will do." He logs in to the cash register. "Enjoy the rest of your evening, Gwyn."

"You, too, Jeff. Tell Ashley I have Monday in my calendar."

He smiles awkwardly, and I exit the store. I snap open my umbrella, but the rain has slowed to a drizzle. With twenty minutes left until sunset, the park is gray and gloomy. I hope I don't have to walk too far down the trail to find Ronnie's glove.

I click on my phone's flashlight app and aim it toward the gravel on the park's trail. Her gloves are black. This is like finding an obsidian crystal in a rock bed. I wave my phone from left to right, crunching on the path as I go. Footsteps kick up stones in the distance. I look up.

"Ashley?" What is she doing here alone?

The whites of her eyes expand. "Gwynedd. I didn't expect to cross paths with you here."

This is peculiar. "Jeff is working. Who's watching Aidan?"

"Oh...uh..." She shakes her head. "An undergrad offered to babysit."

"Why are you hiking alone?" And on a rainy day—bizarre.

She chuckles. "You're on the trail by yourself."

"Ronnie dropped a glove here on a hike. I'm fulfilling my friendly duty and searching for it." I wave my flashlight beam. "She's about to pop any day and doesn't need to be out in this dreary weather."

Ashley averts her eyes. "Well, I should get back. The undergrad has to leave soon. Good luck finding the glove."

"Yeah, thanks. Tell that sweet boy Miss Gwyn says hello."

"I certainly will. He babbles about you every day. See you on Monday."

She takes off jogging in the direction of the trailhead and I continue on the path, shining the flashlight to and fro at the ground. Suddenly, my body seizes. A magnetic pulse of magic pulls at me, and tachycardia clenches my heart. Putting the glove quest aside, I run toward the bog, gasping for breath. I reach the water and observe a strip of fog floating above the pond, no different from before. But the unexplainable magnetism continues to drag me closer. The dismal weather has kept hikers away, except for Ashley. It's safe to inspect the area. I chant, summoning my witch's energy, and an amber glow appears.

Using my magic, I examine the bog again but sense nothing new. Could Skye's hypothesis be right? Is there a masking spell over this area? I try one more time with both hands, establishing an intention around Ronnie's baby. The fog shimmers with flashes of silver. The pinching in my gut intensifies.

I rub my abdomen until the sensation subsides and look down at my feet. Ronnie's water-soaked glove rests in a mud puddle next to my left shoe. Did my witch's intuition send me running to find this?

As I remove the dripping clump of yarn and wring out the water, Ashley's surprised expression flashes in my head. Why would Ashley leave Aidan with a busy, undisciplined undergrad for a muddy hike in near darkness? Two plus two does not equal four.

While I recap my experience at the park, I remove my wet socks and lay them on Archie's steamer trunk. He leans back on the loveseat and pulls my feet into his lap, massaging them.

"You think your intuition directed you to the bog for a glove?"

"It appears so. Seems overly dramatic for a weather accessory, but Ronnie really was sad about losing it. Who am I to judge the universe? There has to be some kind of connection related to deep caring. It's why we worry constantly about the people we love. Our sixth sense sends us warnings or answers when we need them."

He wraps a throw blanket around my feet. "Aye. But you would expect it to have the decency to be more accurate."

"You'd think. I wish I could supercharge it like Seamus. But even he couldn't identify the magic residue at the Pumpkin House."

"A witch's puzzle for you to solve, my love."

"I suppose. Oh, I almost forgot. I ran into Ashley on the trail."

His eyebrows arch. "Rather odd. Did she say why she was there?"

"Hiking, I guess. She said an undergrad was watching Aidan, but I know she's had terrible luck in that department before. Seems strange to leave him for a walk in the rain. If she needed some time to herself that badly, she could have called me."

"She probably didn't want to put you out at the last minute. She's been under so much stress at school, and taking care of a child alone adds to the lot. Most likely, she needed a few moments alone."

"I wish things would improve for her. She has a kind soul."

"You improved things for her immensely by helping with Aidan. I'm sorry I questioned your motives."

"Well, I can't lie. I asked her for more information on Welsh folklore, but she said she won't have time until the end of Winter Session. Yule will arrive before we blink, and Ronnie will deliver the baby soon. Also, I have to finish my last class project for my master's degree. Patience has set up camp until then."

A naughty smile erupts on his lips. "More time for me then?"

"What do you have in mind, honey?" I rub his crotch through the throw.

He squirms on the cushion and adjusts his jeans. "A *pop* quiz."

I chuckle. "Before dinner? Sure, start the clock, professor."

CHAPTER TWENTY-TWO

BABY PREP

LESLIE STARTS OUR BRIEF meeting on Thursday with three taps of her Elder staff. "Thank you for attending this circle. Elijah would like to deliver a few words before Trinity takes charge. Your turn, councilman."

He stands, scanning the circle. "I don't have enough 'thank yous' in my pockets to show how much I appreciate your help on Thanksgiving at the shelter. It's been quite a while since we had a full coven volunteer. To boot, we have lots to be thankful for with the return of the kidnapped children. I'm eager for next year's celebration. Perhaps mark your calendars this evening."

He winks at us as he sits, and my fellow witches chuckle as they type on their phone screens. Leave it to Elijah to take advantage of our good spirits while we're high on the recent news. We're family, anyway. Why not spend it together helping those in need?

"At least the threat of those criminals is gone with their arrest," Trinity says, pushing up from her chair. "I don't have many items to announce this evening. Of course, we have the arrival of a baby in our circle soon, and being so close to the due date, Ronnie is not in attendance tonight. I will send out a group text once Wiggles makes his debut."

I raise my arm. "Ronnie wants me present at the delivery. As soon as I know anything, I'll send Trinity the information to share with all of you."

"I'm offended," Spence says, crossing his arms. "She didn't ask me to be there for support, and I thought we were close."

Skye grimaces. "Do you really think she'd want you in the birthing room, her legs spread out with her most intimate parts on display?"

"She wouldn't care, and I'd provide comic relief."

"Don't take it personally, dude," Tanner interjects. "Gwyn is her best friend. She's known her the longest out of anyone in the coven."

"I get it, but my cheering section would have been lit," he says, making pretend explosions with his hands.

Skye laughs. "And the minute her baby's head appears, you'd scream 'alien' and flee the birthing room."

"Well, on second thought..." he mutters.

Everyone cracks up, and Trinity continues. "Most of you have heard about the council meeting on Monday. To recap for those who didn't, the city council chose to wait until next week to vote on removing the recent ordinance. Elijah, do you want to share what happened?"

"Sure," he replies. "Although the Bearsden Police Department removed the additional patrol units from the streets, Alys Morgan thought it best to keep the ordinance in place, especially in light of the kidnapping ring's recent denial about our local kidnappings. They refuse to take credit for them. The authorities believe they're trying to avoid the added charges. There was enough discussion to delay the vote until next Monday. I agreed. Waiting a week hurts no one."

Leslie raises her chin. "Indeed. Mayor Manley's cronies are a thought of the past. These Unremarkables care deeply about our community. I have confidence in them implicitly."

"You put too much faith in people, sweetheart," Agnes whines. "The minute you throw all your trust in them, they come back and bite you in the fucking ass."

Shane shakes his head. "I understand your skepticism. But they have proven themselves."

"Well, we'll see about that, won't we? Two of them haven't served a year yet. Fucking newbies."

"Sure, they're new," Archie says. "But so far, they've won me over, and I have a pessimistic streak."

"Should we attend?" Tyler asks. "And show support?"

Elijah nods. "It never hurts for the community to attend Bearsden Council meetings. Keeps everyone on their toes and promotes transparency."

"Thank you, Elijah," Trinity says. "Anything else before we dismiss?"

A moment of silence occurs in the parlor before Zoe waves a hand in the air. "The Fellowship should give Ronnie and Derek a special gift for Yule, a present for Wiggles. I can organize the collection."

"That's a wonderful suggestion, Zoe," I say. "If you need any help, call me. She has a list of what she still needs."

"Absofuckinglutely," Spence adds. "Wait. They're not gonna actually call him Wiggles, are they?"

Agnes makes a prune face. "No, smart-ass. Sometimes I wonder if you forgot to plugin and recharge during your sleep. You need to load up on some fucking selenite."

He rolls his eyes at the hedge witch, and the rest of us chuckle at their banter. Leslie quashes a smile and takes over.

"With that, I disband our circle. Go in peace." She taps her staff.

After putting the chairs away, everyone trickles out. I approach the Elder and the hedge witch.

"Agnes, are you busy on Saturday?" I ask, glancing at Leslie.

"Not with anything in particular," she replies. "Why? I thought we were going to wait until after Yule to finish the database."

"I want to take you up on your offer. Try to pin down what I need to do to increase the strength of my intuition. I also have a hunch about what is failing me."

"Work with her on Saturday, Agnes," Leslie says. "I have a backlog of administrative paperwork to complete. We will have dinner afterward."

Agnes presses her lips together. "I can't promise you anything, but I'm game."

"Thank you," I say, turning toward the door.

"What do you mean by a hunch?" Leslie asks. "Did something happen we should be aware of?"

"I don't know yet. See you Saturday, Agnes."

When I step onto the front porch, the icy temperature bites my nose and cheeks. Archie is chatting with Zoe and my son amid a cloud of frosty white breath.

"Come by Friday night after dinner, Tyler. We'll start with simple divination and work from there. We can arrange other times as your schedule permits."

"What are you talking about?" I ask.

"Archie wants me to come by Friday night to start ancestral divination," he says.

Zoe lays her head on Tyler's shoulder. "Then he can introduce me to his grandparents. I'm so excited to meet them."

"Sounds like you have a plan." And I'm not part of it.

"Let's go, Zoe," Tyler says, hugging me. "I have to get to work early in the morning, and I can't feel my toes. Goodnight, Mom. Goodnight, Archie."

Zoe waves as they descend the stairs. "Good idea. My ass is frozen like a block of ice. Bye, Gwyn. Bye, Archie."

We follow them but turn left toward the Green. On the stroll back through campus, I sulk over Tyler's decision to start ancestral divination training with Archie. I didn't realize it would bother me so much. I'm quiet as a mouse. He clasps my hand and pulls me close.

"You're too quiet. You're either angry or scheming."

I peer at him out of the corner of my eye. "A little of both, actually."

"You're upset Tyler wants to train with me instead of his own mum, aren't you?"

"I was looking forward to showing him the ways of our ancestors. We became closer once he discovered he was a witch."

"To be fair, you haven't even conferenced with your parents since October. He could have grown tired of waiting to reach the top spot on your priority list."

"Are you accusing me of neglecting my son?" I ask, my eyes narrowing.

"That's not what I said. He's a grown man who doesn't need his mum catering to him. But recently, you have put the welfare of the town and your friend first. And no one faults you for trying to discover where the Baby Nabbers were hiding. I remember a time when you wanted nothing to do with magic or policing the city."

I roll my eyes. "Point taken."

"If it puts you off, I can tell him I'd rather not teach him."

"No. You're a fantastic teacher, and you taught me under a veil of secrecy. The coven could have expelled you."

He grasps my hand again and squeezes. "I would have broken every rule in the Regional Book of Shadows for you, my love. And I still would."

"I love you, Dr. Cock-burn."

He chuckles. "I know."

I throw him a scowl of death as we enter the house. We kick off our shoes and hang up our coats. Archie squints at me.

"What did you mean? A little of both?"

When I enter Agnes's house, the living room and kitchen are empty. She must already be in her magic room setting up.

"Agnes!" I shout from the foyer. "I'm here!"

I remove my shoes and puffer jacket, storing them on the fancy hall tree Leslie had built by a local carpenter. My phone rings as I shuffle toward the magic room. Ronnie's name appears, and I swipe the green icon.

"Good morning. How are you feeling?"

"Fat!" she yells into the phone. "My belly is so tight and low, Wiggles is pushing on my bladder and rear end at the same time. I'm peeing every fifteen minutes, and I can't sit on my bottom. And forget about lying on my stomach. I'm not sure I can last another week."

"Wiggles will arrive when it's time. I assume your manager is running the café now?"

"Yeah. I tried going in yesterday, but I didn't last ten minutes. I'm so bummed. Working was a distraction. Derek went to the fitness center, but he's only logging a couple of hours today. I'll rest with some amethyst."

"Sounds like smart mother-to-be plans. Do you have bloodstone packed in your hospital bag?"

"Yeah. I put three in there. Can't hurt. I want Wiggles to come out healthy."

"Don't worry, Mama. My intuition may be weak, but I sense the delivery will go well. What is yours telling you?"

She cackles. "That I'm fucking pregnant and about to pop. I'm staring at my baby bump right now. Like I needed a sixth sense to figure that out?"

I chuckle. "If only all intuition were more direct. By the way, I washed your glove. I'll stop by later."

"Thank you so much, Gwyn. I can't believe your sixth sense dragged you up the trail to the exact spot where I dropped my glove, although I don't remember removing it there."

"It has something to do with the friendship connection, I think. I concentrated on an intention around the birth of your baby. The fog lit up like a fireworks show, tiny explosions of silver parading over the bog. When I glanced down at my feet, there it was, all wet and muddy." I don't share my suspicion of Ashley Lewis. Archie's explanation seemed accurate. Yet, I still find her presence there dubious.

"What are you doing this morning?"

"I'm at Agnes's. Working with her on strengthening my intuition again. I had more success with Seamus, of course, but I'm not ready to approach him."

"You don't really need to work on strengthening now, do you? Or are you hoping to find the rogue witch who may have been helping the kidnappers?"

I can't tell her about the unsettling sensation around the bog that continues to nag me. She's calm and preparing for the delivery of her blessed baby Wiggles. "I had some minor success with Seamus. Working to increase the intensity and accuracy of my sixth sense could come in handy the next time we're invaded by criminals."

"Sure, but why don't you take a break until after Yule? It'll be here in two weeks."

"Well, I'm here now. I might as well work on it."

"I think I'll take a nap. Wiggles has robbed me of sleep for weeks."

"Call me when you wake up, and I'll stop by on the way home."

"I'll make us some tea—decaf for me. Wiggles doesn't need encouragement to stay awake. Bye, Gwyn."

"Bye, Ronnie." I swipe the red icon and enter the magic room.

"Who were you talking to?" Agnes asks, placing crystals on the floor.

"Ronnie. She's ready to deliver, but it appears Wiggles doesn't want to leave the comfort of her belly."

"Not that I have personal experience, but I've seen many babies born. They come when they're eager to enter this world. And our bodies sense when the time is right. Well, let's get fucking started. I don't have all day. What's this hunch you have?"

I explain what happened at the bog—the magnetic pull and the tugging inside.

"When I examined the area with the intention around Ronnie's baby, the fog became covered in flashy silver discharges. Right after, I found her glove on the ground."

"Interesting. Obviously, your intuition directed you to it. But here's the thing. When this happened before, you weren't searching for anything, right?"

"No. Ronnie and I were hiking. An aura appeared, and the magnetism dragged me to the bog."

The hedge witch twists a corner of her mouth. "Did you cross paths with anyone? Like Courtney Erickson?"

"Not Courtney. The new Celtic Studies instructor, Ashley Lewis. She said she was hiking, but it had to be a short one because an undergrad was watching her son."

"Hmph. In the fucking rain?" She scratches her head. "Silver flashes, you say. I'll have to mull this over. Did you bring my amethyst geode and Seamus's clear crystal with you?"

"Yeah. They're in my backpack."

I remove the crystals and place them on the floor among her scattered ones. I kneel on a pillow and hold one in each hand. "Here's my hunch. The strength of my intuition increases with the degree of my intention, but I think the level of caring I have regarding the person involved increases the intensity, accuracy, and direction of it. I haven't practiced my theory with these two crystals yet. I wanted you to watch me and provide input."

Agnes bends down to kneel on a pillow. "Ugh. My fucking knees. I'm ready to observe."

"Here goes nothing," I say, signaling an intention with the deepest affection I can muster.

A white energy rises from each of them, connecting in the center, and whizzes back and forth toward the ceiling like a ping-pong ball.

"Fuck me," Agnes says, her gaze following the energy's route.

I grow dizzy but fight back the urge to fall, balancing my equilibrium.

"Is this what happened when Seamus triggered you during the training with him?"

"Yes," I say, struggling to keep my body from swaying. "But it was more intense. I can control this."

I suck my witch's energy back into my hands, and the white beam fades. "What's your opinion?"

"What do I think? If the level of affection increases the intensity of your intention, I'd say Seamus Duffy is fucking mad in love with you."

"Oh, fuck," I reply, laying the crystals on the floor.

"Who were you focusing on just now with the stones? If it was Archie, you're in fucking big trouble."

I chuckle. "No. I was concentrating on the affection I have toward Tyler."

"Ha! That's why you could control it. When Seamus triggered the crystal interaction, you were experiencing his love toward you. It's why you couldn't contain it, I would say. But then again, what do I fucking know about a cat sith witch's intuition?"

"If that was step two in the training, what would three involve?"

Agnes's eyes pop out. "I wouldn't wanna fucking find out. Would you?"

My phone interrupts with a rendition of *Don't Stop Believin'*. "It's Derek."

"Hi, is something wrong?"

He chuckles. "Yeah. We're having a baby."

"What? She's in labor now? Why aren't you on the way to the hospital?"

"She's double checking her bag. Hold on, Gwyn. Babe, you've checked your bag at least a hundred times. Let's go! Gwyn is on her way to meet us. I'm right, I hope, because she really wants you there for support." He lowers his voice. "She's not saying it outright, but I think she's scared. I heard her mumble in her sleep about Wiggles being in trouble."

My witchy innards tighten. "Make sure she has the bloodstone crystals. Meet you at the hospital. Everything will turn out fine, Derek. I promise."

"Thanks, Gwyn. I hope so." His name disappears from my phone screen.

"This will have to wait. I'm off to the hospital!" I shout, jumping up and down.

"Fuck, yeah. You go on. I'll send a text to Leslie and Trinity." My mentor puts the crystals in my backpack and passes it to me.

"Thanks. I'll catch ya later. Bye!"

I slip on my sneakers and jacket and run out the door. On the way to the hospital, I call Archie from the car.

"Give Ronnie and Derek my best." A notification sounds on his phone. "Received a text from Trinity."

"I did, too, but I can't have the car read it to me while I'm talking to you."

"She asks you to stay in touch. I'll come to the hospital as soon as I finish a quick lunch. I'll be in the waiting room if you need a break."

"OK. I'd like that. Because..."

"What's wrong, Gwyn?"

"Derek said Ronnie spoke in her sleep about something happening to Wiggles. My witch's intuition is tugging at me. I'm worried, Archie."

"I'll be there if you need my help."

"Thank you, honey."

After several hours, Wiggles refuses to give up the womb, and Ronnie is exhausted. Beads of sweat dampen her face while her crimson curls cling to her skin for dear life. The time on my cell reads 11:24 p.m. Dr. Powell, a middle-aged woman with short gray hair, comes into the birthing room and examines her belly again.

"Ronnie, we've tried to get this baby to turn, but your little one doesn't want to budge. We have to consider a C-section."

"No fucking way!" she screams through labor pains. "I'm gonna do this naturally."

"It's too risky, Ronnie." She addresses Derek. "You need to talk with your partner."

"Give us a couple of minutes, Dr. Powell?" he asks.

Ronnie's obstetrician leaves the room while the nurse stands by.

"Nurse, could you give us some privacy?" I ask, concern contorting my face.

She leaves and I whisper to Derek. "Do you trust me?"

He presses his lips together and nods.

I glare at Ronnie. "I'm gonna take care of this. No arguing. Understood?"

She squeezes my hand. "What are you gonna do?"

"What are best friends for if they can't break a few rules? Right?"

I lay my hands on her baby bump and summon my power with an incantation. An amber glow radiates when I touch her skin. I focus my intention on Wiggles, tickling the little one's butt. I sense movement, and the body shifts inside her belly with a *pop!*

The amber glow fades in my hands as Dr. Powell and the nurse rush back into the room. The doctor glares at her.

"I hope you have made a wise decision," she says.

Ronnie glances at me. "I think I'm OK now, doc."

Dr. Powell examines her belly again, and her eyes widen. "I'll be damned. The mule has decided to turn. Ready to have a baby?"

"Hell, yes," Ronnie and Derek say in unison.

Derek clasps her hand and kisses her cheek. "You got this, babe."

After a few hard pushes and a few grunts and "fucks," Wiggles makes her debut with a head full of strawberry blond hair. After Derek cuts the umbilical cord, Dr. Powell and the nurse check out Ms. Wiggles and clean her up, placing her in Ronnie's arms.

"She has blond hair with a red tint like my mom," she says, kissing the top of her newborn's head. "We're gonna call her Luna."

"I'm so happy for you both. I'll go tell Archie and let you have some time with her."

On the way to the door, Ronnie calls to me. "Gwyn? Thank you."

I grin. "What are friends for?"

As I walk to the waiting room, I'm overwhelmed with relief, but a tugging pulls at my insides. We all couldn't be happier. Is my intuition failing me again?

When I enter the waiting room, Archie is chatting with Tyler and Zoe. The rest of the Bearsden Coven fills the available chairs. Trinity rushes to me.

"Well, don't zip your lips. What's the tea, Gwyn?"

"It's a healthy baby girl! Ms. Wiggles!" I shout. "But they're calling her Luna."

Our coven leader grins. "A fine celestial name."

A nearby nurse admonishes us. "Keep it down, please. There are others in the waiting room."

Zoe laughs. "We're all here for the same mom. We're her family."

The nurse grimaces as the entire coven hoots and hollers, hugging each other. But my smile fades as I clutch my abdomen. Archie takes me aside.

"Is there something wrong with Ronnie or the baby?" he whispers.

"They're fine. Luna was butt first, but I used magic to shift her head toward the birth canal."

His brow crinkles. "Then why the constipated look?"

I glance back at the door to the obstetrics ward. "I don't know."

CHAPTER TWENTY-THREE
A PROTECTOR'S PROMISE

SUNDAY MORNING, I PRACTICE repeatedly with Agnes and Seamus's crystals in Leslie's magic room, focusing on Ronnie and her newborn, Luna. Each time, the white magic snakes through the air like a boomerang. Mr. Yeats stands by, ready to catch me in case I become dizzy from the overpowering energy. Until my intuition kicks in again, I won't know if this work has increased its strength. It's all I can do for now. I set the crystals on the wooden table.

Mr. Yeats collects herbs from the shelf. "A protection pouch is a given. If there is a nefarious witch still out there, a spell prepared specifically for such a person will surely shield Ms. Baldwin's baby."

"That's my hope. Somehow, the bog figures into all of this, but I don't know how yet. Witches do enjoy the woods. She could live near there under a masking spell, like Skye suggested. I appreciate your assistance in preparing the pouch." I collect a few herb jars and place them on the table.

Mr. Yeats grinds the mugwort. "You have more ingredients than I remember. What are you putting in this one?"

"Black salt, cinnamon, rosemary, peppermint, lavender, mugwort, juniper berries, red sandalwood, clear quartz, and black tourmaline chips." I chuckle as I open a jar. "Everything but the kitchen sink."

He straightens his back. "Why in all the Otherworld would you put a sink in the pouch? Clearly, it's too big for the small sack."

I laugh, spilling the black salt. "Oops. It's a phrase."

He scowls at me. "Look at the mess you made. Don't worry, I'll clean up the salt. You have important deeds to complete today."

"Yes, I do. Thank you, Mr. Yeats."

"You're most welcome, Ms. Crowther."

We finish creating the protection pouch and I stuff it in my purse. After a quick lunch, I drive to Derek and Ronnie's house, taxing the speedometer of my Prius. I don't have time to stop before my shift, but the safety of my best friend's baby comes first. When I arrive, Derek is waiting for me at the door.

"What is this all about, Gwyn?" he asks.

What the fuck do I say? I can't tell him the truth. He would worry. And I could still be completely wrong about everything. "I want to leave a blessing in the room. Something special for Luna to help her sleep."

"Sure. She would appreciate you taking the time. You go ahead to the nursery while I'm eating lunch. Would you like something?"

"No, thank you. I ate before I left the house because I have to get to Mystic Sage."

"If you change your mind, let me know."

Derek walks into the kitchen, and I dart to the nursery. I remove the protection pouch from my purse and place it on the diaper changing table. When I summon my power, the amber glow seeps from my fingers. I recite the words, "Elements of fire, water, earth, and air, protect sweet Luna with your care. Keep her safe within your arms and protect her from the witch's harm." I go to the window and tuck the pouch under the pull-down shade valance.

Derek calls from the kitchen. "I've gotta go, Gwyn!"

"I'm coming!" As I rush out of the room, my insides twitch. I glance back at the window. Am I overreacting?

As we're getting in our cars, I wave bye to Derek. My stomach does back-flips the entire way to work. Jeff is bagging a customer's merchandise when I enter.

"Thanks for shopping at Mystic Sage." He logs out of the cash register. "You're late, Gwyn."

I dart behind the counter, removing my purse and jacket. "I'm sorry. Had to stop by Ronnie's house first."

"Oh, is she home? I thought she'd stay another night at the hospital."

"She did, but Derek just left to pick up her and the baby."

He grins. "They must be high on a cloud. Why did you stop by if she wasn't home yet?"

"Uh...I wanted to bless the room before Luna slept there." I hesitate but decide to ask him. "Jeff, is Ashley still upset I read her late husband's book?"

"No," he says, looking away. "She's sensitive about him. Don't let it bother you."

"Phew. That's a relief. She appeared rattled when I saw her at North Basin on Wednesday."

His eyes widen. "Oh, I didn't know she went there that day. Why did you go? It was raining on Wednesday."

"I was looking for a glove Ronnie lost on her last hike there. She was trying to get her pregnancy moving."

He chuckles awkwardly. "It seems to have worked."

"Did you know Ashley was going for a hike?"

"No, she didn't tell me." He messes with his hair and walks toward the crystals room. "I need to work on inventory. Shane wants me to finish up a shipment on his day off."

"OK. I'll be here." He sure ended that conversation abruptly.

The entry door dings and Alys Morgan strolls in. I smile and wave. My phone vibrates—a text from Seamus. My chest tightens.

Seamus: *Good afternoon, Gwynedd. I hope you are well.*

Seamus: *I am embarrassed by my social blunder.*

I plop on the stool behind the counter. That's one way to put it. It would be rude not to reply, and I can't avoid him forever. Immediately, I receive two more texts back-to-back.

Seamus: *Would you consider giving me an opportunity to make amends?*

Seamus: *I value our friendship and I will take whatever steps I can to repair the damage.*

This isn't like what happened with Nick. He's not an evil fairy trying to fulfill a prophecy. To be fair, I took advantage of his friendship and affection. I'd be lying to myself if I didn't acknowledge that fact.

Me: *Thank you for reaching out. I'm willing to talk. When would you like to meet?*

Seamus: *A time that is agreeable to you in a public setting of your choice.*

Me: *Isn't a public place risky for our topic of conversation?*

Seamus: *Yes, but I wanted you to feel safe.*

He certainly is trying, despite how uncomfortable this is for him.

Me: *I trust you. Why don't I stop by your house? Wednesday lunchtime?*

Seamus: *That is most agreeable.*

When I glance up from my cell, Alys is waiting at the counter with a few Yule decorations, clenching her jaw. I slide my phone underneath.

"Sorry. I didn't notice you standing there. I'll ring these up."

"Thank you. I visited the shelter this morning. Elijah Jackson was bubbling over with news about your red-headed friend having a baby girl. What did she name her?"

"Ronnie named her Luna. That comes to twenty-five dollars and sixteen cents."

"What a charming name," she says, pushing her credit card into the terminal. "I bet she has a head covered in her mother's red hair."

"Actually, it's mostly blond. Has a reddish tint to it. She said Luna has her mom's coloring."

Alys grins as she lifts her bag. "What a surprise. Will you attend the council meeting tomorrow evening?"

"I plan to. Elijah said you want to keep the curfew in place. Why not lift the ordinance if the threat of kidnappings has ended?"

"To protect the children of the town, of course."

"I don't think most of the residents will approve. The council should vote to remove the ordinance."

"That remains to be seen." She heads toward the exit. "Have a wonderful day."

"You, too. And thank you for shopping at Mystic Sage."

Alys leaves and the bamboo chimes clank when the door shuts. I admire her for her devotion to the town's youth, but I don't think the townies will agree with her. Many of them want freedom for their older children.

As I gaze out the window, my gut pinches. My intuition tells me freedom may come at a cost.

I tap on Ashley's apartment door. She opens it right away, already dressed in a wool pea coat.

"Hi, Gwyn. I have to dash out. Aidan went down for his nap late, and I'm behind on my lecture for today."

"That's fine," I say, removing my puffer jacket. "You should take an umbrella. It's pouring out."

"Oh, right. With the gloomy weather, he may sleep longer, too. It should be a peaceful afternoon for you." She grabs her umbrella.

"You know I don't mind playing with him. But I brought a book with me to read in case he wanted to play by himself. He does that more these days."

She smiles. "Yes, thanks to you. Gotta rush. I'll be back around four."

I shut the door, lock it, and drop my umbrella on the entry tile. In case Aidan wakes up, I go to the bathroom to relieve myself. I use the last of the toilet paper. When I'm finished washing my hands, I search the vanity under the sink for a replacement roll. Being the klutz I am, I knock a small plastic bottle onto the floor. When I pick it up, I discover dark-brown hair color for touching up roots. Does Ashley color her hair? I place the hair dye back and replace the TP on the holder.

Since I have the time, I plop on the sofa and pull out the tome on Welsh fairies Leslie gave me. As I flip through the pages, I'm intrigued by the exquisite artwork of the Tylwyth Teg. Some possess golden locks with fragile transparent wings while others have hair so light it's nearly white. They have green wings like that of butterflies. Even more have moss-colored faces and pointed ears.

I imagine they exist in the Otherworld like the Scottish and Irish fairies we've come across. Even if the Tylwyth Teg were to cross over, they don't appear to be malevolent. We have more pressing issues in Bearsden than benign Welsh fairies. We must close the portal before Nuada's Tuatha Dé Danann family crosses over along with the gray-skinned, monstrous giant.

The first story covers what Ashley mentioned—their mischievous behavior. A second one tells of the local people setting out milk bowls for the Tylwyth Teg to keep them from causing trouble when the fairies ride on horses in processions to the homes. A third describes the same lore I came across in Ashley's special book her husband gave her, regarding the Tylwyth Teg's fondness of mortals with golden hair and their desire to marry them. But the next tale discusses a malicious side. The fairies steal a tiny child, and the mother has to figure out how to get him back. I sit up on the edge of the sofa, my insides tightening and my heart thumping to beat the band, but I read on.

To prevent mortals from missing their offspring, Tylwyth Teg fairies replaced the stolen children with clones called *changelings*.

"Miss Gwyn."

"Agh!" I yelp, discovering Aidan staring at me.

He pouts. "I'm sorry, Miss Gwyn."

I wrap my arms around his tiny body, chuckling. "It's OK, Aidan. You frightened me. I was reading a story."

He giggles. "I scare you?"

"Yes," I say, taming his disheveled hair.

"You funny, Miss Gwyn. Play blocks?"

"Sure. Go ahead and start a tower while I put this away." I close the reference and place it in my backpack.

While I stack every other block, I urge Aidan to build higher. I stare at his pale-blond hair, blue eyes, and rosy cheeks, and it occurs to me. Is Ashley's natural hair color blond? My witch's intuition stabs me under my ribs. Is she a Tylwyth Teg fairy? Did she steal Aidan from a mother in another town? What about her dead husband?

"Aidan, I need to call my friend quickly. Mommy will be home soon." I move to the other side of the living room and phone Ronnie.

"Hi, Gwyn. You caught me while I'm nursing, so I don't want to talk long."

"I hope you're more rested today. Hospitals are a terrible place to get sleep. How is Luna sleeping?"

"Waking every two hours to nurse. I'm tired and worn out from the delivery, too, but I'm loving each minute of being a mom. I never thought I could love a person so much."

Derek shouts in the distance, "I heard that!"

"You didn't let me finish. Other than you, babe."

"Well, I won't keep you from enjoying this quiet time with Luna."

"Stop by sometime this week. She seems to be growing every minute." She whispers into the phone. "Before I hang up, I know they caught the baby kidnapping ring, but that sensation of dread is still overwhelming me. Should I worry? Or is this typical of a new mom?"

How do I tell her these feelings could be warnings without adding extra worry? My theories may be hogwash. I have no proof of anything.

"I do remember feeling anxious when Tyler was born. Just don't let her out of your sight for a while. Luna is safe with you and Derek." And my protection pouch.

"Thanks, Gwyn. Bye."

"Take care." I swipe the red icon.

The doorknob jiggles, and I slide my phone into my purse.

"Hi. How was Aidan?" Ashley asks, entering the apartment.

"Fine. He's been playing since he woke up from his nap."

"Mommy," he says, darting to her. He hugs her leg. "I'm hungry."

Ashley squats to hug him. I inspect the part on top of her head and swallow. The hair sprouting from her scalp shows about an eighth of an inch of golden hue. I grind my teeth.

"Hey, sweetie. I'll get dinner soon. Go play while I cook."

"Speaking of dinner, I have to leave," I say, slipping on my jacket and gloves. "Gotta pick up something quickly and get to the Bearsden Council meeting." I grab my backpack and purse and rush to the door.

"Jeff says they're going to vote on removing the ordinance tonight. I think it was unnecessary to begin with." She stares at Aidan. "If evil people want your children, they will devise a plan to take them. All you can do is to protect them as well as you're able."

Well, that's morose. "Bye, Ashley."

"Goodbye, Gwyn."

When the door shuts, I lay my hand on its surface and call on my magic, chanting. I inspect the contents of the apartment. A hot aura starts in my torso, spreading throughout my body. I sense the strange magical residue I've encountered before. Is it witch or fairy magic? If it's the latter, is it the remains of Nuada's past presence? Or a Tylwyth Teg?

I arrive late at the city council chamber and sit down in an aisle seat next to Archie. The older witches from the coven are here to observe, although Agnes appears less than agreeable to being there. A bitter scowl has frozen her face. She's sitting with Trinity, Shane, and Leslie. Ronnie's home with Luna, of course.

"Where were you?" he whispers. "They're discussing the ordinance. More like arguing."

"I left Ashley's apartment late and had to get something to eat. I need to tell you what happened while I was there."

His brow furrows. "Something wrong?"

"I'll fill you in on the way back to the house."

Mayor Devine pounds her gavel. "Alys, I understand your concerns. But the parents of high schoolers in the community want their children to have the ease of walking home from their evening jobs on the weekends. They're trying to save up for college, many of them attending Delaware University right here in Bearsden, and their parents simply don't have the time to pick them up every evening. Bearsden has always been a safe town with the exception of the recent kidnappings. Thankfully, those responsible are in custody, and we can return to normal."

Alys pinches her lips together. "This is appalling. Why wouldn't you want to safeguard the children by keeping a curfew in place?"

"I agree," John Erickson says. "Although I don't have kids yet, I say we should err on the side of caution for the town's kids."

Elijah leans forward on the table. "Normally, I would agree with you both, but the threat of the kidnappings has ended. It's time for the ordinance to end."

A few of the other council members nod, and the residents in attendance mutter words of support. As I scan the room for reactions, my gaze falls upon Courtney. She's twisting her pale-blond hair into knots.

Mayor Devine speaks into the microphone. "The night is getting away from us. It's time to vote. All in favor of ending the ordinance, raise your hands."

Everyone but Alys and John vote yes.

"All opposed?" the mayor asks.

John and Alys raise their hands. Alys crosses her arms while John exhales in defeat. Courtney appears distraught, her face wrinkling with worry.

"The curfew is lifted," Mayor Devine announces. "I want to be clear. If our town should experience an issue with severe crime in the future, we will revisit another ordinance like this one. Is there anything else?"

"I make a motion to adjourn," Elijah says, his bass voice filling the chamber.

John mutters reluctantly. "I second it."

Mayor Devine pounds the gavel. "We are adjourned. Have a safe and peaceful night."

When the chamber empties, Courtney waits for her husband to finish talking with Alys, who is clearly furious about the results. Suddenly, my intuition grabs me like a vise grip.

"Archie, I'll meet you outside. I want to ask Courtney a question. I'll tell you why later."

His eyebrows leap. "All right. The Fellowship is going to have a quick stand-up circle outside. Meet you there."

As I approach Courtney, she's putting on her winter coat.

"I wanted to say hello. I haven't seen you since Thanksgiving at the shelter. You appear a little upset. Are you doing OK?"

She lowers her eyes to the floor. "Yeah. Upset by the vote tonight. That's all."

"Voting doesn't always go the way we want it, unfortunately. Nice talking to you."

She peers up at me. "Good chatting with you, too. And tell Ronnie I said congratulations on her newborn. I envy her."

I wave goodbye and push through the bottleneck of residents to the sidewalk. The older witches have gathered away from the crowds on the paver sidewalk, huddled under a fusion of umbrellas.

"Well, that's a worry behind us," Trinity says. "With the ordinance in place, the police could have issued extra patrols anytime they saw fit. We don't need the cops hampering our work."

Leslie nods. "Indeed. We also must keep an eye on the Seelie Fae. They will contain their mischievous streak as long as we maintain regular visits to occupy them."

"I believe it's needed," Archie says. "But at some point, we have to find another solution that doesn't suck up so much of our time."

"Agreed," I add. "But for now, we gotta do it. We can't have them wreaking havoc in the town. We've been lucky so far."

"I'll come up with a new schedule," Shane says. "And share it online with everyone. I actually miss spending time with Shailagh and Aonghas. I've grown quite fond of them."

Trinity chuckles. "Then you can take my shift."

"Can we fucking go now?" Agnes rubs her arms. "My old joints are locking. I won't be able to walk if we stand out here any longer. My ass is freezing."

"Don't be so dramatic," Leslie says. "Mark your calendars for the next Fellowship meeting, and we will finalize the Winter Solstice Celebration plans."

Agnes grabs the Elder's hand. "Finally. Goodnight, all."

On the stroll back through the Green to Archie's house, I share what I read about the Tylwyth Teg, changelings, and my suspicions about Ashley.

"Gwyn, I find it difficult to believe she's a Tylwyth Teg fairy. I work with her closely. So do Spence and Skye. Your theories are all based on coincidences, in my opinion."

I frown at him. "You say all the time you don't believe in coincidences."

"Aye. But what evidence do you have? She dyes her hair brown. Her husband left her a special book on stories of the Tylwyth Teg, and she acted weird about someone reading it without her permission. The kidnapped children are exhibiting poor behavior after a traumatic separation from their parents. You sensed unusual magic in an apartment where a fairy lived and died. And you ran into her on the trail coming from the bog in North Basin Creek Park because she needed a break from her stressful job. All things easily explained. But the most important item is missing from this list, no?"

"What did I leave out?"

"There have been no more kidnappings. Wouldn't she have continued to steal children and replaced them with changelings if she was a Tylwyth Teg fairy?"

"I guess so. But Jeff has been acting strange, too." I wipe my face with gloved hands. "Maybe I'm paranoid."

He kisses me on the cheek. "I commend you for investigating, and I will take note of anything odd she does. However, she's a wee bit busy for fairy shenanigans."

"By the way, Seamus sent me a text. He wants to talk, and I think enough time has passed."

"I'm glad to hear that. It's been quite awkward in the department. No one has mentioned what happened, yet I think he knows we're aware of what transpired in your wee training session."

"Even though my witch's intuition signals something wicked is afoot, I won't ask him about step three in the cat sith training. My work with Agnes last time has built confidence in me. My inner feelings will direct me down the correct path, eventually."

"Aye." He stops and wraps his arms around my upper shoulders, chuckling. "If I'm lucky, it will tell you to pack up and move in with me."

He kisses me on the mouth, stopping my usual rebuttal. But deep down, I know my sixth sense is pointing me toward something more sinister than becoming his roommate.

CHAPTER TWENTY-FOUR

HINDSIGHT SUCKS

AFTER CLASS ON WEDNESDAY, I return to Drummond Lane via the Green and the shortcut alleyway to Seamus's bungalow. Gloomy clouds hang in the sky like a heavy blanket, and the bitter wind bites my skin. I pull my scarf across my face as I tap on the front door, not knowing how long I'll have to wait on the stoop. I was dreading this conversation with him, but now that I'm here, it's a relief to clear the air.

"Come in, Gwynedd. Thank you for agreeing to this meeting."

Seamus is dressed in his usual professor attire, a DUB long-sleeved polo shirt and casual pants, his black hair pulled back in a ponytail.

"Sure," I say, entering. "Where do you want to talk?"

He gestures to the living room. "Is this acceptable?"

"Yeah. Anywhere is fine with me. I told you I trust you."

I recall our training session a few weeks ago as I sit on the sofa. The painting of my mother no longer hangs over the fireplace. A picture of tiny fairies dancing in the woods has replaced it. Seamus sits across from me, leaning his cat-head cane against the arm of the chair. I set my backpack on the floor and unzip my jacket. He wrings his hands while his eerie eyes dart back and forth between me and the fireplace. I break the ice.

"You removed Aunt Gorawen's painting. You didn't have to do that for me."

"I thought it best to not view it daily. It's stored in a closet. Gwynedd, I cannot lie and say I'm sorry I kissed you that afternoon. I will cherish the moment forever."

For fuck's sake. He's starting with *the kiss*?

"My affection for you shall remain with me until my deathbed. But I don't expect you to reciprocate. I understand how much you love Archie. My heart aches knowing you can never return the love I have for you."

How do I respond to him baring his soul? "I care for you, Seamus, and I sensed you had deeper feelings for me than simple friendship. I need to apologize to you."

"Whatever for?" he asks with a raise of his eyebrows.

"I shouldn't have asked you to teach me your cat sith secrets. I took advantage of our friendship, and I'm so sorry."

A faint smile curls his mouth. "Then I need to offer an additional apology as well. I used your desperation to get closer to you. I strayed from my principles, but it will never happen again."

"So, what happens now?"

An unfulfilled yearning wets his eyes. "We remain good friends. My objectives have never faltered. I am devoted to your welfare. Nothing will ever change that."

Part of me aches because I can't return Seamus's deep affection. But if there's one thing in my life I'm sure of, it's my love for Dr. Archibald Cockburn. My gut tenses up, and I bend over a little, rubbing my abdomen.

"Are you ill, Gwynedd?"

"No. My witch's intuition signals me this way sometimes—a pinch inside. Or it's gas," I say with a chuckle. "I'm not experienced enough to decipher the signs." I stare at the fairy painting over the fireplace, thinking of Ashley Lewis. "Seamus? I've spoken to Archie about this, but I want your opinion."

"Sounds like a serious matter," he says, tapping the brass cat head of his cane.

"Let me ask you a question first. I understand your area of expertise is Irish folklore, but what is the possibility of a Tylwyth Teg fairy crossing over?"

"A Tylwyth Teg? Why do you ask?"

"The magic we both observed at the Pumpkin House—the trail I keep picking up on—had a different...flavor is the best description."

"Yes. That's a perfect way to label it."

"I've come in contact with the odd magic residue in other places, like the Green, the Celestial Gardens, on the path to the bog in North Basin Creek Park—and in Dr. Lewis's place. I babysit Aidan on Monday afternoons."

"The residue in Ashley's apartment could be—"

"Nuada. Yes. That's what I believed the first time I encountered it there. Originally, I thought it was PTSD, having not been there since I..."

"Terminated his existence?" he asks. One thing I can say about Seamus. He's always direct.

I swallow and clear my throat. "Yes. I was sure it was residue from his soul, essence, whatever a fairy has. But I experienced it other times as well. The town has returned to normal since the Baby Nabbers were arrested, but my intuition continues to send me conflicting signals. It's not strong enough to point me to the source of my fears. I've been stumbling along, trying to figure out what it's telling me. It's why I came to you. I was worried a rogue witch was helping the kidnappers and wanted to root her out. But now I think those criminals may not have committed the local kidnappings after all. I think a Tylwyth Teg has crossed over from the Otherworld."

"You think Ashley Lewis is a Welsh fairy? You'll need more evidence than magic residue in her apartment. The kidnapped children were returned. Is there any evidence they are changelings?"

"The mom of the infant stopped in Mystic Sage one day to shop for holiday gifts. She said her baby hasn't acted normal since his return. She spoke to the parents of the older two children and found out they have exhibited behavior problems in school. Archie believes trauma explains their emotional difficulties, but Jenny literally said she feels like it's not her baby. Also, I ran into Ashley at the park on the trail to the bog. Again, I don't have solid evidence, only my witch's intuition. But there's something strange going on there. I'm sure of it."

He taps his cane on the floor as if the knocking helps him think. "That's not much to go on, Gwynedd. In addition, the kidnappings ended when the Baby Nabbers were incarcerated."

"I know, but we have to prepare for the possibility, don't you think?"

"Did you tell the Bearsden Coven about your theories?"

"No. I've shared my suspicions with Archie...and you."

He smiles again. "I am honored you are willing to share this information with me. What will you do to confirm your speculation?"

"Keep an eye on her, I suppose." I grab my backpack and stand. "I need to stop by the house and eat lunch."

Seamus leans on his cane as he stands. "Please, let me prepare a quick meal for you. No strings attached. I promise."

"Sure. I could help."

Don't Stop Believin' plays on my phone. Archie's name lights up the screen.

"Answer it," he says. "I'll be in the kitchen preparing our lunch."

"Hi, honey. I'm at Seamus's house. We had a pleasant talk and came to an understanding."

"We'll have to chat about your conversation later." He speaks so fast, his accent garbles the words. "You need to go to Ronnie's straight away. The Bearsden Police should be there by now."

Dread overwhelms me. "Why? What happened?"

"They put Luna down for a nap. When she went to check on her, she was missing."

"Nooo!" My heart pounds against my rib cage. "It's not possible. I hid a protection pouch in the nursery window. I made a special one for Luna since my witch's intuition was bugging me."

"Gwyn, Ronnie put Luna in the bassinet in their bedroom for her nap. She was taken from there."

"Fuck. Of course." I forgot I kept Tyler in our bedroom for the first few weeks. "Oh, my gods. Ronnie and Derek must be devastated."

"She needs you now. Get to her house as quickly as you can. I'll meet you there."

"Please, call me if you arrive first. I'll drive as fast as I can." I swipe the red phone icon.

Seamus ambles into the room, an inquisitive expression on his face. "I sense something dreadful has occurred."

"Someone...or something took Luna."

"What a dire situation." His eyebrows arch. "But now you have your evidence."

I drive as fast as my puny Prius will go and pull up to Ronnie's house, parking behind a police unit. I jump out of the car. Archie is speaking with Officer Quinn O'Connor.

"Ma'am," Officer O'Connor says. "You can't go in there. It's a crime scene. I was just explaining to Dr. Cockburn."

"Ronnie is my best friend," I say, grinding my teeth. "She needs me, so I'm going in there. The only way to stop me is to arrest my ass."

Officer O'Connor frowns at me. "Wait here." She walks into the house.

"Keep it up," Archie says, shaking a finger at me. "And you'll find yourself cuffed in the backseat of her police car, stubborn woman."

"Ronnie needs the support of her friends and family. Her parents are out of the country on vacation because Luna's birth wasn't expected until next week. It will take a while for them to get here. We're all she has."

Officer O'Connor opens the front door and waves us in. Archie and I enter the beachy living room where Detective Jack Schmidt is questioning Ronnie and Derek. The space is always so cheery, but not today. Ronnie's eyes are red and puffy, and her crimson curls spring up from her head in a frizzy mess. Derek has an arm wrapped around her shoulders, holding her tightly against his burly physique.

"I want to read my report back to you to make sure I jotted down my notes accurately. Around eleven, you placed your baby daughter in the bassinet, which is in your bedroom. When you returned at noon, she was missing. The window sash was up, but you said they were always locked. You didn't notice anything unusual other than the open window. Did I get everything?"

Ronnie's lips quiver. "Yes. Luna is a newborn—two days old. You have to figure out who took her soon. She needs to nurse."

"The detective will figure out who kidnapped her, Ronnie," Derek says, tearing up. "He has to."

"I will do my best," he replies. "We have an amber alert out now. I have to consult with the forensic team."

I dart to my best friend and hug her. "Oh, Ronnie. We'll find her. I promise."

"I'm at a loss for words, Derek," Archie says, hugging him. "Have confidence in the police."

Derek sniffs. "I don't get it. How could this have happened? They have the Baby Nabbers in custody."

Because it's not the Baby Nabbers. How do I tell them I had suspicions and hid that knowledge from them? They'll hate me. Archie peers at me out of the corner of his eye.

"I suspect there are others connected with the kidnappings who roam freely," he says. "But the Bearsden Police will do their best to get Luna back."

Derek wraps his arms around Ronnie, and she cries against his chest. I tug on Archie's DUB polo shirt and he follows me to a nearby corner.

"I have to tell her and Derek about Ashley," I whisper. "And we have to alert the coven immediately to devise a plan to find Luna and rescue her. Seamus agrees this is the evidence we need."

Archie rubs his whiskers. "We still don't know it was her, Gwynedd. No one saw Ashley."

My lower lip trembles while I stare at my despondent friend. "We must tell the coven. They can decide what we should do. I'll honor whatever they say."

Archie's phone vibrates several times, and he reads the texts. "It's Trinity and Leslie. I called them on the way here. They sent a group text out announcing an emergency circle for this evening, but they and the others asked to be updated as we learn more."

I check my phone, which has been on silent, to discover several texts and missed calls from Tyler, along with messages from Trinity and the others. One of the forensic team walks into the living room and addresses Ronnie.

"Ma'am?" he asks. "I found this stuffed into the valance in the nursery. Do you know what it is?"

Ronnie glances at me but answers the investigator. "Yes. It's a potpourri to make the room smell nice. If you excuse me, I have to go to the bathroom." My best friend glares at me. "Can you go with me? I'm having trouble sitting on the toilet."

"Sure," I say, swallowing the lump in my throat.

Archie whispers in my ear, "You have to tell her."

I follow Ronnie into the bathroom, and she whisper-shouts at me. "What the fuck is this? Derek said you stopped by before he picked me up from the hospital. You put this pouch in the nursery."

"It's a protection pouch. All these pangs from my sixth sense had me worried. I stuffed it into the valance to ward off a rogue witch. But I forgot a newborn is placed in a bassinet close by the first few weeks. I should have put one in every window. I'm so sorry."

"Why didn't you tell me, Gwyn? I expected more from my best friend. You put Luna in danger." She blows her nose, and her eyes narrow. "This is *your* fault."

The punch hits me straight in the gut—a knife inserting and shredding me into microscopic pieces. "You're right. I should have. But I also didn't want to worry you unnecessarily. The intuition signals triggered more questions than answers."

"So, the witch who was helping the kidnapping ring snatched Luna? Do we know who she is yet?"

I shake my head. "It's not a nefarious witch. It's a Tylwyth Teg fairy who has crossed over. She kidnapped Luna and the other children."

"I'm confused. The kids are home with their parents. If a fairy took them, why would she give them back?"

"Because those children aren't theirs. They're changelings—like clones. The fairy steals the kids she wants and replaces them with duplicates. Jenny Hansen told me one day in the store the young ones were having behavior issues at school, and her infant cries all the time. She said despite having her DNA, she believed the baby wasn't Daniel. At some point, the fairy will return Luna, but that newborn won't be your daughter."

"Do we know who she is?" Ronnie asks, wiping the tears from her face.

I hesitate but tell her. She has a right to know. "Archie and I think it's Ashley Lewis."

"What? The new DUB Celtic Studies instructor?"

"Yes. Lots of circumstantial evidence supports our theory, and Jeff has been standoffish at work recently. I've been asking questions to confirm my suspicions. I think he's figured out I suspect her."

"Would he really hide her guilty ass? We're his family."

"From what I've read, Tylwyth Teg females are attracted to mortal males. Who knows? She could have magical powers over him, and he's not in control of his decisions."

"We have to figure out how to get Luna back, Gwyn."

Ronnie bursts into tears again, and I embrace my friend. She doesn't seem to hold me responsible now, but I blame myself for being so cautious. If I'd told her and erred on the side of safety, Ashley wouldn't have stolen Luna. Unfortunately, hindsight solves nothing. I'll never forgive myself if we can't get her back.

CHAPTER TWENTY-FIVE

FAULTY INTUITION

AROUND DINNERTIME, THE COVEN convenes an emergency circle, minus Ronnie, of course. She's too upset to be of much help, and she's recovering from childbirth. Even a new witch mom needs time to heal. We don't bother with setting up chairs. A standing meeting is all we have time for. When I finish sharing the evidence about Ashley Lewis and the changelings theory, my fellow witches mutter among themselves. Spence is the first to comment.

"That's fucking ridiculous. Dr. Lewis is so scatterbrained. She's lucky to show up to class on time. I mean, she's a brilliant woman—fairy, if your theory is true. But don't you think she would have covered her tracks?"

Skye rocks her head back and forth. "But think about it. She did. If Gwyn's intuition hadn't recognized her magic stream, we probably wouldn't know. It prompted her to investigate further. Dr. Lewis may be acting disorganized as a cover."

"I agree," Archie says. "Gwyn had suspicions early on, and I dismissed them for the very reasons Spence has. If Ashley is a Tylwyth Teg fairy, she would have the cunning to present herself a certain way to avoid suspicion."

Tyler interjects. "That's true. But from what Spence and Skye have told me, Dr. Lewis would have to be putting on an award-winning performance."

Trinity puts a hand on her hip. "Well, clearly, the Baby Nabbers are off the plate, even if it's not Ashley Lewis. Those criminals are in custody."

"Indeed," Leslie says. "Unless some of them remain on the streets, unbeknownst to the authorities."

Elijah nods. "No doubt about it. When one group gets put away, another crawls out of the sewers. Plus, we can't rule out a rogue witch. There are too many variables to know for sure."

"Isn't there an easier way? Why don't we just ask Dr. Lewis if she's a Tylwyth Teg fairy?" Zoe asks. "She'll either think we're joking or she will act *really* weird."

"We can't confront Dr. Lewis without solid evidence," Leslie replies. "We must be absolutely certain of her guilt before we expose who we are. Leveling accusations, we take on the risk of revealing who we are to an Unemarkable. Gwynedd, can you list all the proof for the Fellowship?"

"Her natural hair color is blond, but she's been dyeing it brown to hide her true identity. She was present at the Pumpkin House for the Samhain Celebration. When I read her husband's antiquated book on Welsh fairies at her apartment without her permission, she clammed up."

Agnes's face wrinkles like a prune. "That's not fucking evidence of being a fairy, Gwyn. I fucking lose it if people breathe in the direction of my grimoires without permission."

"No lies detected," Zoe says. "But I think you got more pissed when we sampled your pot from the kitchen."

The hedge witch gapes at her. "When did you swipe pot from my cupboards?"

Zoe scans the circle, clenching her teeth. "Oops." She sinks in her seat.

"I haven't finished," I say. "Jenny Hansen, the mother of the baby who was kidnapped in the Celestial Gardens, stopped by Mystic Sage one day. She was down in the dumps about her infant Daniel because he hadn't been the same since his return. If she didn't have DNA identification, she would have sworn he wasn't her child. She told me the other two kidnapped children were having behavioral problems at school, and their parents didn't know how to handle them."

"That's disconcerting," Tyler says. "They're probably changelings then."

"The evidence appears to suggest that," Archie adds. "But Gwyn has more to tell you."

"I also sensed magic residue at Ashley's apartment early on and witnessed the energy hovering around her son, Aidan. I even wonder if she stole him from a human and made up the story about her dead husband. Recently, I ran into her on the trail in North Basin Creek Park. She was alone and coming from the bog side. When I mentioned it to Jeff, he seemed befuddled by the news."

"But we checked out the pond," Tanner says. "We noticed nothing out of the ordinary there. And why would a fairy hold up there, anyway?"

"True," Archie replies. "But some Tylwyth Teg fairies live in the water. Gwyn went back there again and observed unusual flashes of energy above the pond, glimmering with a silver hue."

"If that's true," Agnes says. "Then those kids are majorly fucked. They'll never return. From what I know of the Tylwyth Teg, they can exist under there forever. And we have no way to go in there to rescue them."

"Agnes, you're the oldest and most experienced here," Trinity asks. "Are there any spells that would shield from drowning? Give one of us enough time to rescue them?"

"I don't fucking know," Agnes replies. "We didn't find any like that in my library of grimoires, although we have many left. I'm a fucking hedge witch. We don't do water. I don't even know how to swim, and at my age, I'd probably drown, anyway."

Leslie pats her partner's hand. "None of us expect you to risk your life, dear. This is a job for the younger witches."

She scowls. "Oh, so now I'm too fucking old?"

"Well, it's kinda difficult to deny that, Agnes," Spence says. "But if we could find a spell, I'm down. I can hold my breath forever. Remember, I grew up near the beach in California. I may not even need an incantation. I'm willing to try. Anything for Ronnie and Derek's baby."

Shane raises his hand. "Let's focus, everyone. It may not come to that. First, we decide how to confront her. She is likely to flee, and then we'll be up the creek without a paddle in the deepest shit we've ever encountered. We will never discover where she's hiding the children, including baby Luna."

"The solution is to ask her directly," Elijah says. "We'll have to invite her to someone's home, where we'll be waiting for her. Ready to stop her from fleeing."

For the next few minutes, we throw ideas back and forth, most of which require her to come to us as a group. We're losing time.

"May I offer a suggestion?" I ask. "Since I have a close relationship with Ashley, let me approach her. I could question Jeff first. But that would be risky if she has some sort of fairy power over him. I should go to her alone and ask her directly. Appeal to her motherly feelings. I'm a mom, and she looks up to me. I'll tell her we aren't angry, but she needs to return the children to their parents."

Trinity nods. "Sounds like a plan to me. Since there is a slight risk we could expose ourselves to another Unremarkable, we must vote. Should Gwyn confront Ashley Lewis?"

Every single hand raises. The decision is final. I will confront Ashley and hope for the best. For Ronnie's sake, I cannot fail.

Our coven leader shakes a finger at me. "Gwyn, we are counting on you. When will you go to her?"

"Right away. The longer we wait, the more difficult it will be. I'll keep you informed." I scan the circle. "Be on the ready. If she flees, we'll have to go after her using the spells we have at our disposal. Wing it, like the hedge witch."

"So, I'm not too fucking old after all," Agnes says, sarcasm lacing her voice.

"We'll need everyone," Archie adds. "Ronnie can't help, so we're not at full capacity as a coven."

"But we have three ancestral witches," Tyler says. "And all the young ones have attained the third level in their magic skills. We're stronger than ever before. We can do this."

Skye stands with her arms crossed, a look of bewilderment on her face.

"You don't appear convinced," I say. "Can't our magic fight that of one Tylwyth Teg fairy? She isn't a Tuatha Dé."

She taps her chin. "I don't understand why no one has mentioned the fact that Jeff Williams has brown hair. Don't Tylwyth Teg fairies favor blond males? Why did she choose him?"

"I didn't even consider that," I say, biting my lower lip. "But Luna doesn't have pure blond hair either, and Ashley snatched her from her bassinet. Jeff's hair is on the lighter side. Some might call it dirty blond. But does it have to be pure? We know the lore but not the reality of their realm."

"It's the sole element of contradiction," Leslie says. "And time is of the essence."

"I wholeheartedly agree." Trinity takes a cleansing breath and locks eyes with me. "Gwyn, this all rests on you. Don't fuck it up."

Shane pulls on his whiskers. "Aren't we forgetting something? If we're correct, what do we do about her? After retrieving the children, we can't allow a Tylwyth Teg to remain in our world."

"One step at a time, Shane," Trinity replies. "One fucking step at a time."

We disband, and Archie walks me to my car. The icy air sends a chill down my spine—or is my intuition finally sending confirmation of my assessment concerning Ashley? The coven stands huddled on the porch in the distance. They'll remain at the Pumpkin House awaiting my report, prepared to fight for the children of Bearsden, and Luna, one of our own. Tyler mouths the words, "You got this, Mom."

I get into the driver's seat of my Prius and Archie shuts the door. I push the button to lower my window.

"Should I wait outside Roots of the Earth? In case she takes off running?" he asks.

"No. She may detect your magic in the area and could feel threatened. This is one time I have to fight alone—for Ronnie and Luna."

"Would having the dirk in your possession convince her to comply?"

"She'd take off for sure. I have to appeal to her motherly side."

"Aye. I have faith in you, Gwyn. If anyone can convince her to bring back the children, you can. Good luck, my love."

I stand in front of Ashley's apartment, considering what to say to her. I have but one chance to convince her to return the children to their parents. The last time I confronted a fairy here, I killed him with Archie's dirk. Now, I must fight with words. I tap on the door, waiting for a minute or two before it swings in.

Ashley gapes at me. "Gwyn? Why are you here? It's late."

"Yeah. I know, but something terrible has happened. I thought you should know."

"Oh. Is Jeff hurt? Please, tell me."

I shake my head. "No. He's fine. I mean, I think he's OK. I haven't seen him since my last shift at Mystic Sage."

"Come in." She glances at Aidan, who's sitting in the toy corner wearing pajamas. "He had a nightmare, so I'm letting him preoccupy himself for a few minutes before I put him back to bed. We can talk on the sofa."

When I sit down, Ashley chooses the cushion at the other end. I hesitate for a moment, staring at Aidan. I examine his blond hair and fair features. Who are his actual parents, and where did she snatch him from? He must have been a baby.

"What's so urgent you couldn't wait until the morning?" she asks.

"Someone has kidnapped Ronnie's daughter Luna."

Her eyes widen. "Oh, no." She wrings her hands, conspicuously not mentioning the Baby Nabbers at all.

"Obviously, it's not the kidnapping ring out of PA. But we think we know who did it."

She shifts on the cushion while her eyes wander around the room. "Who is it?"

When her gaze returns to me, I take the leap. "Ashley, we know who you are."

"What?" she asks, squinting. "Who do you think I am?"

Be careful how you say it, Gwyn. "We, the Bearsden Coven, know you're a Tylwyth Teg fairy. I found the hair dye under the sink."

Her jaw drops, and then she laughs, starting with a chuckle and ending with full-blown guffawing. She clutches her abdomen, patting it until she calms down enough to talk.

"Gwyn, I'm not a fairy. Have you lost your mind?"

Fuck. I swallow. Twice. I've made a gargantuan mistake. Or have I? I chant to summon my magic. The amber glow radiates from my fingers, and I test the room for residual magic. *Yes.* It's floating throughout.

"Oh, my goodness!" she shouts. "Jeff told me about your skills, but I didn't expect it to be so powerful."

"He told you about us, then?" I ask, lowering my hand as the glow dissipates.

"Yes. Of course. He loves me and Aidan. We confide in each other."

"Sure, he did. Ashley, I know you have love for those humans, but I'm pleading with you as a loving mom. Please, give the children back to their human parents. Return Luna to Ronnie and Derek."

She shakes her head several times. "I can't give them back, Gwyn. Because I'm not a fairy."

I wrinkle my nose and squint. "I'm confused."

She gazes at Aidan, still playing quietly in the corner. "But he is. Well, half of him, anyway."

Holy crystals. My lips part, words failing me as I wait for her to explain further.

"His father was Tylwyth Teg. His name was Emrys. I met him in PA, where I was finishing my Ph.D. He was monitoring a landscape design project at the college I attended. When I passed by one day, he started up a conversation. He stopped me every time I passed by. He was so handsome and charming—but mysterious. We were together for months."

Ashley pauses, glancing at Aidan. "When I asked him about his family and his past, he evaded the questions. One day, I followed him home as he left campus and peeked into his house window. I saw his wings sprout from his back and froze, imagining I was hallucinating. He caught me staring at him through the glass and ran outside, begging me to come in so he could explain. He confessed about being a fairy and pleaded with me to stay with him. That's when he asked me to marry him."

I have to interject. "Did he cross over through the portal in the Celestial Gardens?"

"Yes. He was sent to find a few Tylwyth Teg females who snuck over—to force them to return to their realm in the Otherworld. He created a human cover as a landscape designer while he searched for them. But then he met me, and we fell in love. Knowing we may only have a few months together, I got pregnant right away. I had Aidan nine months later. Emrys was so overjoyed, he made the decision to stop looking for the others and remain in our world." She tears up. "It was an accident that he fell on that iron spire. It was a nightmare when the police found his body mummified. The forensic team could never explain it. But I knew."

I rub my temples. "Shit. Give me a minute. I have to process this. So...Jeff told you about the Bearsden Coven. All this time, you were aware we were witches?"

"Once he discovered the truth about Aidan, he told me about your existence, in case I needed your help."

I lecture her, a scolding tone in my voice. "Both of you should have told us about the Tylwyth Teg invading our world. You knew the dangers. Now a fairy has stolen Luna and the other children. We could have taken precautions—searched for the fairy."

"I'm sorry. I realize that now, but I truly thought the Baby Nabbers ring was kidnapping the children. For two years, I've been worried about my son exhibiting magical powers. Luckily, he never did. Then I went for a walk with him in the park. When we stopped at the bog to throw stones in the water, something mysterious happened. The misty fog hanging over it shot a stream of something at him. I screamed and shouted at the perpetrator to stop. Then I picked him up and ran home. After that, strange things started to happen."

"He sprouted wings?" I ask with a raise of my eyebrows.

"Oh, my goodness. You saw that?"

"Yeah. But I thought it was because of... Ashley, a Tylwyth Teg must be living in the bog and hiding the children there. When you got close, she must have detected Aidan and made a connection of some kind. Being near fairy magic isn't a good idea. In fact, you need to know a prior tenant of this apartment was a Tuatha Dé Danann. You should get out of your lease and move. Make up some kind of shit excuse."

She scans the apartment. "I'll pack up right away. Jeff will help me."

"If you can't get out of the lease, don't worry. I'm sure Jeff can cover the rent."

She tilts her head to the right. "He has that kind of money?"

I chuckle. "Oh, yeah."

I stand and walk to the door, Ashley on my heels. I glance back at Aidan. "You were never worried about the Baby Nabbers snatching your son. You were scared the Tylwyth Teg would scoop him up and take him back to the Otherworld. It's why you dyed your hair brown, isn't it? To avoid attracting more of them to you."

"Yes." She strokes her brown hair. "The threat has followed me everywhere. Emrys warned me of the danger. It's why he left me that book as a reference. It contained stories to help me identify other Tylwyth Teg."

"Do you know who she is?" I ask.

"No. She's cunning and may not have revealed herself to anyone. Most likely she's hiding in the bog—their safe place. I tried to communicate with her that rainy day in the park, worried she would come after Aidan. I figured no one would be there."

"Did she answer you?"

Ashley shakes her head almost imperceptibly. "No. I don't think there's a way to retrieve the children. You and the Fellowship, the coven, must figure out how. Please, find the Tylwyth Teg fairy and send her back, so she can't do this again."

"We will," I say, laying my hand on hers. "I don't know how, but we'll figure it out. Is there anything in your husband's book that could help us?"

"No. I've read the stories over and over." She grabs a tissue and blows her nose.

"Read it again. If you find something, call me," I say, standing. "I'll be in touch."

I wave goodbye to Aidan as I head to the door, and he smiles at me. On the way back to my car, I send a group text to the coven.

Me: *My witch's intuition fucked up. Ashley isn't the Tylwyth Teg fairy.*

I take a cleansing breath. This will require several texts to explain.

Me: *You'll never believe this.*

On the drive back to Archie's house, I call Ronnie to update her. Her name lights up the dashboard screen.

"Gwyn. Do you have Luna? Please, tell me you got her back?"

"No. I'm sorry, Ronnie. I confronted Ashley Lewis, but she isn't the Tylwyth Teg fairy who took her."

"What? Then who is it?" Ronnie asks, crying into the phone.

"We don't know. She doesn't know, either. But we're fairly certain the fairy is hiding in the bog."

"Our intuition was correct about the area all along, then. Who could it be?"

"Ashley isn't a Tylwyth Teg, but her son is half fairy. The residue I sensed in her apartment didn't belong to Nuada. Aidan's power was sparked by coming in contact with magic at the bog. His father was here to corral a few fairies and take them home."

"Shit. There's more than one of them here?"

"Yeah, but Ashley believes this one is just hiding in the bog. She tried to communicate with her but got no response."

"How is Derek?"

"He's in the bedroom, lying down with his hand on Luna's bassinet. I cry every time I'm in there. He feels helpless being an Unremarkable."

"He's not alone. The rest of us aren't sure how to fight a Tylwyth Teg fairy."

Ronnie sniffs. "Bring Luna home, Gwyn. A piece of me will be lost without her."

"I promise I will. But we can't do anything else tonight. It's too dark. We'd be fighting blindly. The coven is meeting at sunrise in the park to avoid hikers. Plus, the temperature will be in the teens."

"I won't sleep until she's back in my arms."

"We'll get her back, Ronnie. Try to sleep. You'll need your energy in the morning when we return her to you."

"I trust you all, but I can't stay back at the house twiddling my thumbs. I need to go."

"Rest the best you can, then. You'll need your energy. Bye, Ronnie."

The phone goes silent as I'm pulling into Archie's driveway. He's waiting in the foyer when I enter.

"You spoke with Ronnie?"

"Yeah." I fall into his arms.

"We'll figure out a way to puncture the barrier at the bog. Spence says he'll dive in and search for the fairy's protective bubble and retrieve Luna."

"What if he can't? I shouldn't have messed up my training with Seamus. If I'd convinced him to share his secret about the third step, I could have prevented Luna's kidnapping. I might have figured out how the bog was connected and that a fairy was hiding the children there."

"You're being too hard on yourself, Gwyn," he says, kissing the top of my head. "You did the right thing regarding Seamus. If you had let things continue, you would have crossed a line. Using people isn't in your skill set."

"I won't sleep a wink tonight," I say, peering up at him.

He offers me his hand. "We have to try. Let's get as much shuteye as we can. The coven needs to be at full capacity."

"Ronnie's going, but she won't be much help in her weakened state."

"Then we'll fight harder."

While I'm lying in bed, I gaze at Archie's family dirk in the glass case. Do I have it in me to kill one more time?

Chapter Twenty-Six

TO CATCH
A FAIRY

The moon is still shining through the front bedroom window when I wake, but a hint of sunrise peeks through pink skies. I barely slept, but adrenaline rushes through me like the first sip of hot cocoa, prompting my heart to pump faster than usual. I check my phone for the weather and discover a text from my crimson-haired best friend.

Ronnie: *We barely slept. Derek is coming, too.*
Me: *OK. Tell him he'll need to be careful. He's an Unremarkable.*
Ronnie: *He doesn't care. He's helped us before.*
Me: *Meet you there.*

I roll my head right on the pillow and find Archie dead to the world. I go into the bathroom to wash up and get dressed. When I'm finished, I tiptoe to his side and reach behind the headboard. I turn the key and remove the dirk from the glass case.

"What are you doing?" Archie asks in a thicker Scottish brogue.

I sit on the bed next to him, the dirk resting in my hand. "I couldn't sleep any longer. We have no idea what powers this Tylwyth Teg has. I'm going to go early and check out the area."

"Killing Nuada left you quite shaken. Are you sure you're capable of taking the life of another fairy?"

"Fuck, yes. She took Ronnie and Derek's baby."

He sits up in bed. "That's very true. But what happens if your PTSD is triggered? I should go with you."

"You don't think I can defend myself?"

He clasps my hand. "I do, but you're a single witch, Gwyn. Fighting against a fairy with unknown powers. I almost lost you once. Please, let me go with you."

I squeeze his hand. "Sure. But you need to get ready quickly. The sun is almost up. I want to arrive at the bog before the rest of the coven shows up. I could detect the magic there by increasing my energy level. Together, the two of us could analyze irregularities in the protective shield she's placed over the water. We could prepare a more efficient plan of attack."

"Aye. I'll get ready in a jiff." He jumps out of bed and darts to the bathroom.

"I'll carry the dirk in my backpack," I yell to him.

I empty most of the contents and place the dirk in the computer slot. As I slip my arms through the straps, I recall the moment I stabbed Nick Evans and shudder. *Damn it, Gwyn. You can do this. You have no choice.*

Archie parks his Tesla as close to the trailhead as possible. When we exit the car, the bitter air hits me like a block of ice. I pull up the hood of my puffer jacket, slip on my gloves, and we walk toward the trailhead.

"This polar vortex could have waited one more day to dip into Delaware," he says, pulling his DUB beanie over his ears. "This fairy may be immune to the cold. That's one shot against us."

"We fought a fairy in frigid temps before. Remember?"

"Aye. You fought for Ronnie that night as well." He grabs my gloved hand. "You're a devoted friend."

"I may have killed the Sluagh, but the coven fought as a team. I wouldn't be here if they hadn't."

"And we'll do it again."

North Basin Creek Park appears frozen in time. Barren, lifeless, tree limbs reach out over the path as if they're pleading for help. As we approach the bend in the trail, a woman with blond hair appears on the path quite a distance ahead of us.

"Shit," I whisper. "I think that's Alys Morgan. Who the fuck takes a hike on a day like this, so early in the morning?"

"Actually, I'm not shocked. If anyone were to walk in the park in freezing temperatures, it would be Alys—a woman with a stiff demeanor."

"She's gonna fuck up everything."

"We'll have to wait until she finishes her hike. I doubt anyone else will have the desire to brave this nippy weather."

Alys disappears around the bend, but we continue on the trail, giving her time to get way ahead of us. Once Archie and I arrive at the bog, we can hide in the woods until she doubles back, unless she takes the loop, and then we won't cross paths with her again at all. But how will we know for sure she's chosen to return via the other side? Oh, who would believe her, anyway? A fantastical story about witches fighting a fairy in the water?

We turn the corner and nearly jump out of our skin.

"Why are you two following me?" Alys asks, a stern expression on her face.

I glance at Archie. "Uhh...same as you, I guess. Racking up some steps. I couldn't sleep, so we threw on some clothes and headed down here. Didn't expect to run into a member of the council in the woods."

"I'm an early riser. Out here every day," she says. She looks at Archie and her icy expression melts into an amorous smile. "Good morning, Dr. Cockburn. So nice to see you again."

For fuck's sake. We don't have time for your flirting.

She squints at me. "I know you. You're that cashier at Mystic Sage." She turns her attention back to Archie. "I'm surprised a man of your academic stature would date a cashier."

I roll my eyes and bite my tongue, resisting the urge to remind her we've met several times outside of Mystic Sage.

"Unfortunately, you know nothing about Gwyn. She's a very accomplished woman. In one more semester, she'll receive a master's degree in Public Policy from Delaware University at Bearsden." He smiles at me. "I'm very proud of her."

Alys glances at me and smirks. "Well, if you don't mind, I would like to finish my morning walk in solitude and silence."

"We apologize for interrupting your ritual," Archie says. "Gwyn and I will head back to the car and come back later when it's not as chilly."

I give Archie a what-the-fuck look. Did he forget why we came?

"Well, aren't you so kind, Dr. Cockburn?" She bats her eyes at him. "We should chat sometime about your Scottish heritage. I've always been interested in learning more. Could we meet for coffee?"

He clears his throat. "I'm quite busy at this time of the semester. Perhaps, during Spring Semester."

"Wonderful. I look forward to it. Have a good day."

Alys turns and continues on the path, and Archie heads back toward the trailhead. I rush to maintain his pace.

"What are you doing? Did you forget why we came?"

"No, Gwyn. But we can't attempt to break the protective shield over the bog with Alys nearby. She's too into everyone else's business. It's probably why she ran for city council so soon after moving here. We might as well go to the trailhead and wait for the others to arrive."

"Ugh. She ruined everything. And holy crystals. The way she flirted with you right in front of me. Inviting you on a date as if I weren't even there. Aghhh. What a bitch. I'm sorry I was so nice to her in the store."

He laughs at me. "You're jealous. I'll admit, I love seeing you so protective of me." He stops for a moment and kisses my cold, rosy cheek. "But you needn't worry about other women anymore. Those days are far behind me."

"Not to burst your bubble, but it's more about her audacity. I'm criticizing her behavior. Who can blame her, though, right?" I kiss his warm lips and rub my cold nose on his. "You're dashing, blond, toned from the top to the"—I cup his crotch—"bottom."

He raises a corner of his mouth and removes my hand. "We better keep moving or my manly goods will freeze off and you'll not have them to service you later."

"Promises, promises," I say with a snicker.

While we walk, I recall Alys's amorous advances again. "I wonder if she has a thing for Scots. Or blondes."

A sharp pain strikes me in the gut, like a dagger shoving directly into my abdomen, and I double over. A magnetism overwhelms me like before, drawing me back toward the bog. I stop in my tracks to process the signals from my intuition and peer up the trail.

"What's wrong?" he asks. "Are you all right? Please, tell me you don't have to pee."

I stare at him as our misty white breath surrounds us. "Blondes."

He cocks his head. "What about them?"

"Not them. Her. Alys must like men with blond hair."

"How did you come to that conclusion? I'm one man. You have no knowledge of her prior relationships. And who gives a fawk what she favors in men?"

"True. But Archie. Tylwyth Teg fairies crave human men with blond hair. Remember?"

His eyes widen. "Shite." But his expression relaxes, and he frowns. "There's one problem with your theory, my love. When the kidnappings occurred, she was the one to introduce the ordinance. She was extremely adamant about its passing. Why would a Tylwyth Teg fairy do such a thing?"

"To cover her ass."

"But what other evidence do you have? Taking a chance at confronting Ashley was one thing. Accusing a councilwoman who is most likely an Unremarkable? That's a right dodgy risk to take, don't you think?"

"Archie, she came into the store several times to buy toys for a couple of young children. Said they were for kids of a dear friend. Recently, she showed up again and brought up Ronnie's pregnancy. She asked about the baby's hair color...if it was red. When I told her it was blond with reddish highlights, her face lit up."

"Fawk."

"Exactly. The cherry on top? My intuition just hit me with the strongest pang I've ever experienced, and a magnetic pull is tugging at me to go back."

Archie stares at the empty path ahead. He grabs my hand, and we run as fast as we can toward the bog. Our lungs struggle to function in the frigid air, but we have to catch Alys before she passes through the protective shield she's created. I trip over large rocks protruding from the trail, and he pulls me up. We jump over a fallen tree blocking a section of the path and push through low hanging limbs.

Once we arrive, we scan the area for her, gasping. My lungs burn from the icy air. We examine the area. The strip of hazy white cloud hangs over the water like a protective bubble. No sign of Alys. Archie darts back and forth, inspecting different sections of the woods around the bog while I use magic to heal my aching chest. He shakes his head and returns to the pond's edge where the lily pads lay dormant.

"We're too late, I'm afraid," he says, panting. "The coven will be here soon, and we can attempt to pierce the shield."

"If my intuition had been more accurate early on, we could have saved the children sooner."

"I think your sixth sense was more than efficient. It's not a perfect system, Gwyn. It certainly zeroed in when we desperately needed it."

"We should try to pierce the shield together. Combine our energy. It's worth a try."

"I'm hesitant to poke the bear, Gwyn. We should wait for the others."

I raise my hand, chanting, and a brilliant amber glow seeps out. "If you don't help me, I'll attempt it by myself."

"Stubborn woman," he says, scowling.

He lifts his hands. They radiate intensely as he turns his palms toward the foggy mist over the water. I place my left hand next to his right. We combine our energy and throw a magic fireball at the fog, attempting to slice into the outer layer of the barrier—enough for one of us to slip through. It bursts on impact, sparking a rainbow of explosions, but the shield appears intact. At the very least, we've confirmed the shield exists.

Suddenly, a beam of white light descends from above. It's coming from Alys, who is flying right at us, glowing with green and purple butterfly-like wings fluttering behind her. The stream of magic strikes Archie, throwing him into the thicket of the woods.

"Archie!"

CHAPTER TWENTY-SEVEN

COUNCILWOMAN EXPOSED

"You won't take my children!" Alys shouts, barreling toward me.

She throws another bolt of fairy magic, but this time, at me.

I scream so loud, my voice distorts. "They aren't your babies, you bitch!"

Palms up, I summon my power and chant a protection spell. My heart pumps blood through my veins so fast, I swear it's going to split open my rib cage. The beam of white light bounces off me as she passes by. I call forth my energy, forming an amber ball of fire the size of a basketball, and hurl it at Alys as she disappears into the shimmering fog. But my enchanted spherical weapon ricochets off the shield.

I rush into the thicket of woods, pushing vines and tree limbs aside to find Archie. He's stirring in a clump of dried leaves, rubbing his head. *He's alive.* His coat is torn and blood seeps from a cut across his cheek and chin, the one without the scar. I exhale and run to him.

"Are you OK?" I ask, inspecting the abrasions on his face.

"Aye. But I'll have a few bruises. Nothing a little healing magic can't remedy." A blood droplet rolls down his cheek, and he wipes it with his glove.

"You have a deep cut. I should heal it, or you'll have a scar." I chant, calling on my magic.

"No time for that. Besides, it'll match the one on the other cheek. Where's Alys?"

"I failed. She's in the bog. I couldn't stop her from seeking refuge within the protective bubble she's created."

"You're unharmed, though?"

"Yeah. I had time to cast a protection barrier spell before she hit me, too. I threw a magic fireball at her, but she got through the shield before it reached her."

"She must have sensed we were coming back. Caught me off guard, but it won't happen again." He pushes himself up and wobbles. "Shite. She walloped me good."

"Can you fight? Maybe you should sit for a bit?"

He stands straight and wipes his cheek again. "Those children don't have time to wait. Let's get going."

We retrace our steps out of the woods, our feet crunching dry leaves and sinking into the damp mulch below. When we reach the trail, the rest of the Bearsden Coven is huddled together in front of the bog, dressed for the icy temperature in winter coats and hats. Ronnie and Derek are just arriving. My best friend plods along with her boyfriend's help.

"There they are!" Shane shouts.

Elijah points across the trail. "Near the woods!"

My fellow witches and Derek approach us with questioning looks.

"What have you been doing?" Leslie asks. "We saw your car in the parking lot and expected to find you here waiting for us."

Agnes scowls. "What the fuck? You really thought you had time for a quickie in the woods? Now?"

"Your head is always in the gutter, Agnes," Spence says, chuckling.

She snickers. "I call it like I see it."

I grimace. "What? For fuck's sake, Agnes. No. That bitch struck Archie with a bolt of fairy magic. Sent him flying into the woods."

"And he's still standing?" she asks. "Don't fuck with an ancestral witch, I guess."

The young witches run to him, asking him overlapping questions and checking his wounds. "Are you hurt badly?" "How strong was her magic?" "Where is she?" "Should we prepare for her to attack again?"

"You're bleeding," Tyler says, chanting to summon his magic. "Can I heal you?"

Zoe raises her hand. "I wanna help, too."

Archie rubs his rib cage. "No need. I'm a wee banged up, but I'll heal."

Trinity pushes the young ones aside. "Give him room to breathe. Archie's weathered worse than this."

Derek removes a rib brace from his backpack. "This will help until there's time for magic healing."

"Thank you." Archie pulls down the zipper of his coat. "I may need help with the wrapping."

"No problem," he says, pulling the brace around his torso. "I can't thank you all enough for trying to get Luna back to us."

Ronnie scans our impromptu circle. "I'm not at full strength right now, but I'll do what I can."

"We certainly can use you," Trinity says. "But remember, Luna needs you. Stay as far back as you can from the thick of it. I would like answers about the fairy, though. Besides the wings, how will we recognize her? Blond hair and fair complexion, I assume."

"You bet," I say with a nod. "But hold on to your beanies. It's Alys Morgan."

"Alys Morgan?" Skye asks, a perplexed expression freezing her face. "The councilwoman?"

Elijah gapes at me. "Are you sure, Gwyn? The fairy must resemble her. I worked with that woman every damn week. I noticed nothing about her that would point to being a Tylwyth Teg."

"The councilwoman does keep to herself," Shane says. "But I noticed nothing suspect when she came into the store."

"Aye," Archie replies. "It's definitely Alys. She was walking on the trail when we arrived to check out the bog. We turned back to meet you at the trailhead to give her time to finish. But Gwyn had an epiphany on the way after Alys spoke to me."

Leslie tilts her head. "What earth shattering words were they?"

"She hit on him again, right in front of me," I say, frowning.

Spence guffaws. "That was the revelation? If making a pass at Archie is the sole qualifier, then we have hundreds of Tylwyth Teg living in Bearsden."

"Very. Funny." I throw him a side-eye.

Agnes growls toward the pond full of lily pads. "Well, we better not have a ton of them. One is fucking bad enough."

"I agree," Trinity says. "Get on with it, Gwyn. We can't go making accusations willy-nilly against a councilwoman."

"Well, how's this for evidence?" I ask, frustrated with their line of questioning. "When Archie and I threw a fireball at the eerie fog hovering above the pond, Alys Morgan flew down from the trees, glowing with green and purple wings flapping like a bird behind her back. She struck him with a bolt of fairy magic and sent him into the woods. Next, she came after me, but I had time to cast a protection barrier spell."

Tanner gapes at me. "All this time, she's been hiding and working to obtain a place on the council to manipulate us."

"Well, I do declare," Shane says. "Alys put up one helluva front. I never imagined she was responsible."

I shake my head. "Of course not. She pretended to care about protecting the Bearsden children because she wanted them for herself."

"I've had an excellent working relationship with her," Elijah says. "Should I try to reason with her?"

Archie shakes his head. "Not in her mental state. She's not willing to negotiate. In her mind, those are her children now."

"What a narcissistic bitch," Spence says. "Conniving, too. She would have loved ex-Mayor Manley."

Tanner glances back at the misty fog. "Did you pierce the protective bubble at all?"

"Naw," Archie replies. "And I didn't get another opportunity after Alys attacked. Gwyn had no success alone either."

"Gwynedd, what can you tell us about the protective bubble she's created?" Leslie asks.

"It was impenetrable, even with Archie and me combining our energy," I reply. "I hurled as large a sphere of magic as I could form at her, but I missed. She's protected by the barrier now. Plus, we have no idea how to get the children out of there once we break its seal."

Zoe taps her lips, deep in thought. "Could the air bubble Alys is hiding the kids in float to the top?"

"Wouldn't it be great if it were that easy?" Tyler asks. "But I suspect it's more complicated than we can imagine."

"Only one fucking solution," Agnes says. "We gotta form a circle and combine our energies. Create a magic laser beam."

Skye eyes the hazy strip of white mist. "I'm getting bad vibes about this plan. Do we even know what will happen when we pierce the bubble?"

"What if it hurts the children?" Ronnie asks, wringing her hands. "Our Luna."

Derek wraps a burly arm around her. "They'll be careful. You can do this without hurting the children, right?"

We glance back and forth between us but don't answer him. The truth is, we don't know what will happen. In the distance, the crunching of gravel echoes in the woods—an uneven rhythm in the steps. Trinity puts her fists on her hips.

"In the name of all the gods, who is coming up here on this frigid morning?"

Seamus Duffy turns the corner, wearing a long black winter coat and limping with his cane. That hike from the trailhead must have been hard on him. He waves as he approaches, his eyes searching for me. A faint smile curls his mouth when he finds me in the circle.

"Dr. Duffy, you should not be here," Leslie says. "This is not your fight."

Trinity approaches him. "I appreciate your desire to help, but you shouldn't get involved."

Archie walks to him, holding his side. "How did you know we were here? Did someone contact you?"

"No," he replies, staring at me. "I was alerted to danger in our midst."

Archie glances at me. "Oh, right. Still, you should not be here. Gwyn is fine and can defend herself."

"Gwynedd confided in me about her suspicions of a Tylwyth Teg's presence in Bearsden. I assume you have found her here, taking refuge in the bog."

"Aye. Turns out Alys Morgan is the culprit. We're about to form a magic laser to pierce the protective layer. If we can create an opening big enough, one of us can attempt to go in there and rescue the children."

"The councilwoman? That is certainly unexpected." Seamus limps to the bog and chants. His hand radiates magic, more yellow than amber. "And how do you suppose you'll retrieve these children living within the air bubble? Will they not drown before you pull them out?"

Ronnie darts to the side of the pond, her frosty breath expelling as she pants. "He's right. Luna will drown. I sense the danger throughout my entire body." She hugs herself, squeezing tightly.

My sixth sense tugs at my insides as well. "We must consider Ronnie's instincts. Mine is sending signals, too."

"What are we gonna do then? Nothing?" Trinity asks. "We have to try, at least?"

Agnes approaches the bog and raises her hand, an amber glow emanating from her palm as she chants. "I sense a weakness in the far right of the fog where the haze swirls in and out. We can break through the barrier there without affecting the rest of the bubble. I bet my life on it."

"I realize I'm an Unremarkable and can't gauge the effectiveness of your magic," Derek says. "But my Luna is in there. Please, don't do it unless you're sure you can without hurting her and the other kids."

"Not to rain on your parade, Agnes," Tyler says. "But what do we do after we break the seal? The children are safe in the fairy's bubble chamber, or whatever you want to call it. But who's gonna get them out?"

Skye nods. "I don't know if it's intuition, but those nasty vibes are giving me an unsettling sensation again."

Spence shoots his hand up. "Me. I told you already I can hold my breath as long as a deep-water diver, and I swim fast. I'll get them out. Screw your bad vibes."

"I care about getting Luna and those kids out as much as everyone else here," Tanner says. "But the temperature of that water is almost freezing. You'll get hypothermia. Please, don't do it."

Spence hugs his partner. "Chill. I'll be fine."

Leslie observes the silver sparkles shimmering over the water. "As the Elder, I am going to make the final decision. We should attempt to break the seal on the far side of the fog. If the children should perish, I will take full responsibility. Spence, if you are willing to risk your life to save them, I won't stand in your way."

Tanner's face grows sullen as he looks at his partner. The rest of us lower our heads. My intuition tightens in my abdomen again. But what else can we do?

Archie lays a hand on Tanner's arm. "The two of us can be prepared to cast a healing spell once he finishes."

"We'll all be ready to help," Zoe says. "We can do this together."

"But we need Ronnie and Derek's blessing." I wait for my best friend's response.

She tears up and nods. "Derek, I think we have to try. My intuition tells me not to, but we can't leave Luna in there one more minute."

"OK." Derek wraps his arms around her. "You're the witch. I have to rely on your judgment."

"Let's do it now, then, witches," Trinity says. "Seamus, we'll gladly accept your help, if you're still offering."

"My pleasure," he replies. "May I recommend we form a line along the perimeter of the pond? Ms. Morgan will have more difficulty attacking the coven that way."

"You mean it will be difficult to kill all of us at once." Archie says.

"Precisely," he replies. "But we are many. Each of us should prepare to back up the person on your left and right. You'll need to respond quickly."

Leslie glances at Agnes. "My dear, we should not stand together. We are experienced, but our reflexes aren't what they used to be."

"Speak for yourself, sweetheart," the hedge witch replies. "I survived an attack by the Kenilworths—ancestral witches to boot. I can fight off one pathetic Tylwyth Teg."

"Let's form our line of attack, everyone," Trinity says, motioning toward the pond. "Ronnie, I understand you want to fight, but Seamus can replace you in the circle. Derek can't defend himself against a Tylwyth Teg with a mama-bear attitude. Take cover near the forest. If Alys sees you here, she could lash out even more."

My best friend makes eye contact with each of us. "Good luck. Bring my Luna back to me."

I lock eyes with her. "We won't stop until we get her. I promise."

"Don't worry, Ronnie," Spence says, removing his coat and shoes. "I'll bring her back." He kisses Tanner. "Be ready to warm me up, hon. I'm gonna need it."

"I love you, Spence," he replies. "Don't do anything stupid. Just get them out of there."

Derek clasps Ronnie's hand and they walk toward the forest. They find a large rhododendron and kneel behind its glossy green leaves, rolled up like cigars in the icy temperature. Spence stands at the water's edge, shivering and rubbing his arms.

We line up shoulder to shoulder along the bog—Archie on my right side and Seamus on my left. Raising our hands together, we face our palms toward the silvery strip of fog, chanting to summon our power. As our magic intensifies, we interlock our beams of amber until all thirteen connect to form a thick central laser, as Agnes suggested. A buzzing like that of a motor echoes through the park. Holy crystals! I hope the townies can't hear this.

"What now, Agnes?" I ask. "Do we set an intention on the weak part of the barrier? Does one of us decide where to focus it?"

Agnes shouts over the roaring hum. "I don't fucking know. I told you I wing it. Witchcraft isn't an exact science. Seamus, do you have a suggestion? We can't blow this."

Wow! The hedge witch is asking for help. That's a first.

"Yes," he replies, gazing into my eyes. "Gwyn should set the intention. Everyone, clear your minds and focus on the energy beam."

Archie nods at me. "Do it, Gwyn."

I search for the spot where the fog appears to open and close, gyrating to the left and right. If I set my intention in the center-most position where the swirling stops and moves in the opposite direction, I should break the seal.

"I'll count backward," I yell. "Three, two, one. On one, give me all you've got."

The magical laser intensifies, the amber glow thickening into a wide beam of energy. I filter out everything around me—the trees, the foggy clouds of our breath, the gloomy skies above, Archie, Seamus, the others. I may have one chance to do this before Alys attacks.

"On my mark!" I shout over the humming. "Three. Two—"

"NO!" a female voice shouts behind us. "You'll kill the children!"

We snap our heads around. It's Courtney Erickson, and her husband John is with her.

"Stop! You don't need to break into her protective bubble. I can pass through the shield and retrieve the children."

We lower our hands, and the amber laser beam dissipates as Courtney rushes to us. Leslie addresses her.

"How is it possible for you to enter through the barrier? Do you have knowledge of a special spell?"

Courtney stares at me, pleading with me to decipher the puzzle for Leslie. Because for some reason, she can't answer the Elder. I inspect her pale-blond hair, blue eyes, and fair complexion. I look at John, his head covered in golden locks. The frigid air has numbed my cheeks, but not my brain.

"Because she's a Tylwyth Teg."

CHAPTER TWENTY-EIGHT

TO SAVE THE CHILDREN

"Fuck me," Agnes says loudly, breaking the shocked silence of the coven members.

Archie whispers in my ear, "Well, that explains her early obsession with me."

"Sure does," I whisper back. "And the variance in her magic. My stronger intuition must have sensed the difference. Seamus's did, too."

Everyone else gapes at Courtney, creating a cloud of hazy white. Still running in place to keep the blood flowing through his body to stay warm, Spence remains ready to lunge into the icy pond. Ronnie and Derek join us from behind the shrub, Ronnie's expression set to kill as she looks at Courtney. John wraps an arm around his wife, worry distorting his face. Agnes begins the inquisition.

"Another fucking fairy? How many Tylwyth Teg crossed over through the portal into Bearsden?"

"I don't know for sure," Courtney replies, clinging to her husband. "But the gateway in the Celestial gardens isn't the only one in the country. Hundreds could be living here now. Please, don't be angry with me. I want to help."

"There are more fucking portals?" Agnes asks.

"We'll deal with that issue later," Leslie says. "We must focus on the task at hand."

Trinity pounds the dirt as she approaches Courtney. "You've lied to us since the fucking beginning. Pretended to be a novice witch. Helped Audrey Kenilworth infiltrate the coven when she was under the influence of a hex cast by her mother. It's why you were expelled. Why should we trust you now?"

The young witches shout at Courtney at random, reminding her of all her past deceptions. Who can blame them? She invited this condemnation. Tyler remains silent, having not been *in the knowing* of his ancestral witch status during Courtney's past transgressions.

John yells back at them. "I understand Courtney fucked up in the past. But Alys threatened to out her if she revealed Alys was kidnapping the children. I didn't have any choice but to vote as she asked and appear to support her. We remained silent until Courtney couldn't live with the guilt anymore."

Ronnie stamps toward Courtney, her face twisted in rage, and gets right up into her face. "Alys took my Luna. How do we know you won't turn around and steal more children like she did?"

"Indeed," Leslie adds. "You are Tylwyth Teg. It's in your nature."

"I won't because..." Courtney lays a hand on her coat above her lower torso. "I'm pregnant. Please, let me help you get Luna and the other children back."

Seamus limps over to the newly outed Tylwyth Teg and lifts his hand, a blue glow emanating from his skin. Courtney flinches as his magic passes over her.

"I sense truth in her words," he says.

Courtney pulls her arm from around John and points at the shimmering fog. "I am telling the truth. I can fly through the barrier and grab the children one at a time."

A warm aura rushes through me, my witch's intuition confirming her statement, and I unzip my coat. "I believe her. Tell us what to do, Courtney. You can't possibly pass through the shield without Alys noticing. She'll attack you and the children before you free them."

"You'll have to blast the shield with magic. Irritate her enough to come out."

Zoe's eyes widen, and she waves her hands in the air. "Whoa! Stop! I thought that was bad?"

"Exactly," Tyler says. "We could hurt the children."

"If you pierce the weak point in the barrier, you could. The rest of the surface should hold," Courtney replies.

Shane inspects the area where the fog swirls in and out. "That should be easy enough to avoid."

"Sounds like a plan," Spence says. "Can I put on my fucking coat and shoes now?"

Tanner runs to him and helps him into his coat sleeves. "We should throw magic bombs at her one after the other—big enough to piss her off, but not enough to damage the shield."

Archie rubs his goatee. "Aye. But we should prepare for her wrath as before. She'll come after each of us."

"Ronnie, you and Derek go back behind the shrubs for protection," Trinity says. "But be prepared to help with all the children."

"We can do that," she replies.

"Absolutely." Derek grabs Ronnie's hand, and they return to their shelter behind the rhododendron.

Skye approaches the right side of the bog. "Why don't I act as a liaison? When Courtney brings the children out, I'll run them back to Ronnie and Derek?"

"Perfect," Archie replies, motioning to us. "Let's prepare, everyone."

John kisses his Tylwyth Teg wife. "Be careful. Alys could come after you."

"Don't worry," she says, cupping his cheek. "I can handle her. I'll hide behind that enormous oak tree until the coven creates a distraction."

Courtney removes her coat and calls on her wings to expand from her back. Glowing in green and purple hues, they lift her off the ground, and she floats toward the strip of hazy white. No one can deny her unique beauty. Who can blame John for falling in love with such an exquisite creature? Even if she is a lying bitch.

We line up as we did before, except this time, I pull out Archie's dirk and shove it under my belt. I don't want to kill Alys, but she may give me no choice. Courtney signals she is ready as she hovers above the entry point.

Trinity addresses John. "Councilman, we need someone to monitor the trail for Unremarkables."

"I'll start up the trail immediately." He stares at his wife from a distance, pressing his lips together. "Good luck, everyone."

"I suggest we start on the left," Elijah says. "Blast the shield every five seconds. Once we get to the end of the line, repeat as often as we have to until Alys surfaces."

"And then what?" Tyler asks. "She's gonna come after us."

"We'll have to defend each other as she attacks," Archie says.

Trinity raises her hand, an amber fireball burning inches from her palm. "Tanner, you're at the far left of the line. Whenever you're ready."

We all chant, forming balls of fire in each hand and wait for Tanner. He raises his arms above his head, and we follow his lead.

"May the gods be with us today!" he shouts.

Tanner throws the first blast of magic at the barrier, and it explodes as it bounces off the surface, splaying outward with rays of yellow and burnt umber. One by one, we follow suit, throwing our energy bombs into the silvery fog. Our fire balls paint the space above the pond with fireworks of russet, amber, and bright yellow. The air fills with smoke, and we cough and hack as it drifts back to us.

Courtney flies back and forth to avoid the streams of fire, but a stray ember falls on her wings, singeing an outer edge. She waves at us to continue, and we sling our magic bombs at the fairy shield. After five minutes of this, my upper arms burn and my ears ring from the explosions. I may be an ancestral witch, but my body tells me I'm menopausal and shouldn't have skipped the fitness center last week.

"It's not working!" I shout over the hissing and crackling. "Should we try something else?"

"No!" shouts Agnes, hurling another blast of magic. "She can't put up with this indefinitely. At some point, she'll get pissed off."

"I agree!" Elijah yells. "If I know Alys, she's fuming about now. She has little patience."

Spence throws another sphere of fire. "I don't know. She appears to be just fine with us wasting our time."

"Keep at it, witches!" Trinity yells. "We can't stop now!"

"Look!" Zoe says, pointing to the left of the pond. "The fog is separating."

Alys emerges and flies straight up, her wings flapping a mile a minute. Her usual rosy complexion is red as a pomegranate.

"She's madder than a wet hen," Shane says.

"Or a protective mother," I reply.

Zoe calls up a magical burning sphere. "Look out! Here she comes!"

"Prepare yourselves, witches!" Trinity shouts.

Alys flies toward us. "I don't want to hurt you, but I can't allow you to take my children! I will kill you all first."

She waves her hand from left to right and her fairy magic blows each of us back toward the trees like dominoes. My back slams against a pine tree with a trunk the size of a compact car. The evil councilwoman retreats into the trees behind the bog. Tyler's screams echo from the left side of the trail.

"Mom!" he says, dashing to me. "Are you OK?"

I roll over and try to get up. "No. The pain in my lower back has returned. Screw that bitch."

Archie arrives and helps me stand. "Your mum is made of tough stock. She'll heal."

"Gwynedd, are you hurt badly?" Seamus asks. "The defensive use of wind was unexpected."

"No. I'll be black and blue for a few weeks, though. Are you hurt?"

"Merely a few abrasions," Seamus replies.

The others slowly rise, dusting off their clothes. I glance over at the shield where Courtney was floating. She's nowhere to be found. Alys emerges from the forest, blowing air at us with such speed that we have to drop to the ground and clutch at the protruding rocks buried in the dirt. Limbs, stones, and other debris graze the skin on our faces, leaving lacerations. Blood seeps from the wounds and rolls down our cheeks.

"Leave before you suffer the consequence of your evil actions!" the narcissistic Tylwyth Teg yells as she flies back into the cover of the trees.

Courtney appears at the weak spot in the shield and flies toward the edge of the pond, snuggling a baby. The newly outed Tylwyth Teg floats down to the ground and passes the little one to Skye. The young witch darts back to the woods, her fire-red hair streaming behind her, and places the child into Ronnie's arms. My best friend cries tears of joy. Luna is safe in her mama's embrace once again.

Courtney turns and jets back to the shield to retrieve another child while the rest of us prepare for the next attack from a mother enraged.

"We must fortify our stance," Leslie says. "Come together as one."

"Yes!" Agnes shouts. "We'll combine our magic like before, except this time, cast a protection barrier. When she turns around to head back into the forest, we attack."

"Brilliant, Agnes." Archie motions at the coven. "Quickly, before she returns."

"Raise our hands as one, witches," Trinity says, gesturing.

As we wait for Alys to return, Courtney passes through the shield and places the other kidnapped baby into Skye's arms—Jenny Hansen's son Daniel. Just as Courtney passes back through the shield, the councilwoman heads in our direction again. She must be losing patience, because she targets the coven with a bolt of fairy magic like the one she used to attack Archie and me. But this time, we are prepared. We combine our witch energy, creating an amber halo above us. The Tylwyth Teg's lightning strikes our barrier and ricochets into the woods, starting a blaze. Alys retreats once more.

"Fire!" Spence shouts into the rafters of the forest.

"I'll put it out!" Tanner runs to the burning flames quickly taking hold in the dry leaves and casts a spell for a contained downpour.

"I'm going to lend him a hand. You'll be all right, Gwyn?" Archie asks.

"Yes," I reply. "Go help him before it triggers the fire department to respond."

"Here comes Courtney with the third child," Shane says. "The two-year-old girl."

Courtney sets the golden-haired girl onto the muddy ground and flits back to rescue the last of the kidnapped children, the toddler who was snatched in broad daylight. The little girl wraps her short arms around Skye's neck as she picks her up and darts to Ronnie and Derek. Derek takes the crying little one and positions her behind the wall of rhododendrons.

Alys appears again, more enraged than ever, her face resembling the crimson hue of Ronnie's curly hair. Who knew a fairy's complexion could flush so severely with anger? I pull out the dirk because we may not have another option but to eliminate her. She heads toward us, her arm raised.

"I warned you!" she screams. "The children are mine!"

She propels her fairy magic with the force of a missile, and we barely get our halo barrier up in time. The impact pushes us to the ground again, adding to our accumulation of abrasions and bruises. She glares down at the bog and dives back through the fog. I shove the dirk back into its leather sheath.

Archie and Tyler dart to me about the time Seamus is helping me up.

"Thank you for looking out for Gwyn when I'm not around," Archie says.

Tyler dusts off my clothes. "Yes. Thanks, Dr. Duffy."

Seamus smiles. "My pleasure."

"For fuck's sake," I say. "You all act like I can't take care of myself. I'm middle-aged, not on death's doorstep."

Elijah gestures toward the portal in the shield. "Courtney's taking a lot longer than before to return with the last of the children. I'm fearful something's gone wrong in there."

"I'm afraid you're right." Trinity gestures toward the bog. "There they are!"

Alys and Courtney shoot up through the shield, flipping and tumbling in the air. Courtney has one arm wrapped around the remaining toddler, the other struggling to block Alys's grasping reach.

"Attack Alys if you can!" Leslie shouts. "We must save all the children!"

We send precise blasts of fire magic at Alys, attempting to strike her wings. After several attempts, one of the magic missiles sets her fluttering appendage ablaze, and she takes a nosedive to the water's edge. Agnes quickly casts a sleeping spell over her, and the councilwoman collapses on the muddy bog perimeter. Courtney stabilizes her flight and floats to the ground, passing the toddler to Skye.

"Ha! Take that, you fucking narcissistic fairy," Agnes quips. "Enjoy your rest. It's gonna last a while."

Spence darts to Alys and stares down at her crumbled body. "How did you know the spell would work on a Tylwyth Teg, Agnes?"

"I didn't. Fucking lucky, I guess." She bursts out laughing.

I chuckle at my mentor. "Luck seems to stalk you."

She snickers. "Not luck. Karma, Gwyn. But I'm OK with it."

We all crack up as we huddle around Alys.

"What are we gonna do with her?" Zoe asks, staring at Alys's limp body.

Shane twists his beard. "I suspect we'll have to banish her back to the Otherworld."

"Someone should run up the trail to tell John his wife is safe and he can come back," Archie says.

Courtney walks toward us, her wings contracting within her back and her pale-blond hair dripping onto her wet clothes. "I told you I could save the children." She lifts her winter coat off the ground and slips her arms into the sleeves.

Ronnie emerges from behind the shrubs with Luna swaddled under her coat. Derek and Skye follow with the other children. My best friend approaches Courtney.

"Thank you. I don't care what anyone else has to say. You have redeemed yourself in my eyes."

Derek wraps an arm around Ronnie and Luna. "Ditto. You're OK in my book."

"You're welcome," she says, eyeing the expressions on my fellow witch's faces. "Please, don't send me back through the portal. I'm having a human baby. I'll never have a reason to covet another."

John runs to his wife, panting, and hugs her. "Are you hurt? Is the baby safe?"

She kisses him. "Yes. We're fine, John. Agnes Pritchard cast a sleeping spell on Alys."

My hedge witch mentor scowls. "Fucking great. How many more half-breed fairies are out there?"

"That's derogatory, don't you think?" Tanner asks. "I never expected a response like that from you, Agnes. As long as they remain hidden, what does it matter how many are living among us?"

"Doesn't," she replies, shrugging. "As long as they don't resort to kidnapping human children. It's not about bigotry. Just makes our job as a coven much harder if we have to monitor them."

I recall the days when Courtney coveted my man, but the woman standing before me now seeks redemption. "I agree. There's no reason we should banish her. She put her own existence at risk."

"Gwynedd speaks for all of us," Leslie says. "We welcome Courtney into Bearsden."

John exhales a frosty breath. "Thank you, everyone. Courtney is part of my life now. What can I do from here on to make amends?"

"You'll have to take Mayor Devine aside and explain what happened here today," Elijah says. "Fess up."

"I will," John replies. "But she may not believe me."

"If you need me to back you up, tell Jessica to contact me." Elijah fist bumps the councilman.

John and Courtney take off up the trail, leaving us to clean up Alys's mess. Seamus grabs his cane.

"I will join the councilman and his wife on their walk back to town."

Archie shakes his hand. "Thank you for your help, Seamus. Let's hope your assistance won't be needed again anytime soon."

"I speak for all of us, Dr. Duffy," Trinity says. "You are welcome in our coven if ever you should choose to leave your solitary status behind you."

"Ditto," Shane says. "Come by the store this week. I'd like to thank you by offering anything you need from our stock."

"You're most welcome," he says, catching my gaze. "I wish you well with the tasks ahead of you." He starts up the path.

Ronnie passes Luna to Derek and approaches me. "I'm sorry I got so angry with you."

"You had a reason to be," I say, hugging her. "I should have told you about my suspicions."

"You helped bring Luna back to me. That's all that matters now."

Skye picks up the toddler. "What do we do with the children? We have to return them to their parents without them knowing."

"But won't they remember what happened?" Tyler asks.

Leslie observes the children. "We'll have to cast a spell of lapsed memory on them."

"Who will sneak the wee ones into their homes?" Archie asks.

Trinity addresses the young witches. "Can I rely on you youngins to return the three kidnapped children to their beds tonight?"

"What do we do with the changelings?" Skye asks.

"Hide them in the Pumpkin House," Trinity says. "Elijah, Archie, Shane, you'll need to sneak Alys's body into the trunk of my car. I'll park it at Agnes's farm until later. We'll all meet up in the Celestial Gardens tonight. Make it late—around midnight."

"Splendid," Leslie says. "You all have your assignments, except for Ronnie. You should go home and tend to Luna. The rest of you, we gather in the dead of night."

Later, under indigo blue skies, the coven's plan unfolds. The young witches exchange the human children for their changeling clones after their parents are fast asleep, cloaking themselves with a spell to complete their task. They meet up with the rest of the Bearsden Coven in the Celestial Gardens under the illumination of the full moon.

Bitter winds cut across my face as my fellow witches gather at the mound with the changelings and a still-unconscious Alys Morgan. The poor clones are shaking, cold and confused by being snatched from their temporary homes. But they must go to the fairy realm in the Otherworld. Agnes pulls up a hex from the database on the phone Leslie bought her, and we recite an incantation to banish her.

"Spirits of the Otherworld, receive this Tylwyth Teg in haste. Never to return to Bearsden, Alys Morgan is banned and disgraced."

We repeat the incantation while Elijah and Archie push Alys through the portal, which sucks her in with a *whoosh*.

"That was fucking awesome," Agnes says. "Good riddance, bitch."

Trinity approaches the portal. "Gwyn, now would be an excellent time to ask the fae children for their help."

"Sure." I call on the Seelie Fae. "Shailagh. Aonghas. I have some friends for you to play with."

The opening in the mound turns bright white and the Seelie Fae cross over. "Aunt Gwyn, you found our friends!"

"Yes. Would you like to help them find their way back home to the Otherworld?"

They giggle and dance. "Yes! Yes! We can play all the time!"

"Wonderful," I say, motioning to Skye, who's holding the baby.

I guide the older changelings to the portal, and Skye passes the baby to Aonghas. He giggles at the infant. Shailagh clasps the hands of the others, one in each hand. The Seelie Fae approach the aperture.

"Thank you, Shailagh and Aonghas," I say.

We wave goodbye as the Seelie Fae guide the changelings through the portal. I sigh, knowing this is not just the end of one saga, but the beginning of a whole lot more headaches for the coven. Once the mayor learns about the invasion of Tylwyth Teg, she and our allies on the council will pressure us more than ever to find a spell to close the gateway in the mound.

Suddenly, an aura stronger than I've ever experienced washes over me. I become dizzy as the vision plays out in my head...

Fairies, one after another, cross over through the portal, moving so swiftly I can't identify who they are. Like a turnstile, they pass through back and forth with no one to stop them. Are they Tylwyth Teg? Tuatha Dé Danann? Seelie? Unseelie? The gray-skinned monster appears in a flash and blinks at me...

I wobble, and Archie catches me. The others huddle close, concern gripping their faces. "Gwyn, are you OK?" "Did you pass out?" "Did you trip?"

Tyler rushes to me. "Mom, should you go to the hospital?"

"What happened, Gwyn?" Archie asks. "Why did you lose your balance?"

I stare into his icy-blue eyes and then scan the faces of my friends. "We have to close the portal. More of them are coming soon. And not just the Tylwyth Teg."

Chapter Twenty-Nine

CHANGE IS EASY

A WEEK HAS PASSED since we banished Alys Morgan and returned her, along with the changelings, to the Otherworld, but the days flitted by like months had passed. The local paper reported complaints of *popping sounds* in the North Basin Creek Park. By the time the Bearsden Police arrived to check out the area, they found evidence of a recent fire—nothing more.

The Bearsden Coven couldn't risk another missing person report, begging questions from the curious Detective Jack Schmidt. Mayor Devine wasn't thrilled about what transpired in the clandestine gathering but agreed to falsify paperwork to coverup Alys's disappearance, anyway. John wrote up a letter of resignation from the missing councilwoman and created a power of attorney to close out her bank accounts and settle up with her landlord. As far as the public knew, he and Alys were good friends. Since she had no other acquaintances, who's going to miss her? Certainly not the townies she pissed off.

Ronnie is back to worrying about running out of diapers and getting enough sleep, although the knowledge of Tylwyth Teg fairies living in our world ferments in the back of her mind. We've heard rumblings of the kidnapped children's behavior improving with such speed, their parents may stop therapy altogether. The situation could have ended so much worse. I wish my witch's intuition had worked with more accuracy. We could have discovered Alys's true identity sooner.

The Fall Semester has ended, and I'll finish my master's degree in May. I'll have to stop working at Mystic Sage and find a full-time job. I should begin searching for my own place, too. The proceeds from the sale of my house have collected a fair amount of interest. But should I buy another place? I imagine Leslie will be a little sad to see me move out, but not as much as Mr. Yeats.

Jeff Williams enters the front of the store carrying a box full of children's puzzles to replenish the shelf. With the holidays upon us, last-minute shoppers wiped out the store. I finish ringing up a customer and smile at Jeff as she turns to leave.

"Thank you for shopping at Mystic Sage, and enjoy your holiday," I say as the shopper exists. "Boss, would you like some help while the store is empty?"

"Sure," Jeff replies, dropping the box on the floor. "I hate putting these tiny stickers on. Somewhere there's a price tag demon, and he's getting even with me."

I chuckle. "For what? Loving a woman and her kid?"

"No. They're the best things to happen to me since..." His voice trails off, his eyes growing misty.

"I'm glad Ashley and Aidan found you." I lay a hand on his shoulder. "You needed them as much as they did you."

He lowers his head. "I never apologized for keeping her secret from you. I was worried about how the coven would respond. She was sure the Tylwyth Teg fairy, whoever she was, would take Aidan, and she couldn't trust anyone else."

"An apology isn't necessary. You had every right to protect them. Ashley told me she didn't know who the fairy was, and I believed her. She came clean about Aidan, after all."

"She's befriended Courtney Erickson since she's having a half-human, half-fairy baby, too."

A faint smile curls my mouth. "Everyone should have a friend they can trust. Someone who understands their life experiences.

You knew Courtney went after Archie early on, right? It's why she helped Audrey infiltrate the coven. I never imagined she was a fairy, though."

"Audrey told me after she got rid of the hex her mom put on her. But I don't think she was aware of Courtney's fairy background."

"Well, it doesn't matter now."

"No. But...do you believe Courtney after all that's happened? Should Ashley trust her?"

I take a cleansing breath. "At some point, you have to use your best judgment. Courtney has a unique situation, just like Ashley. They need to trust each other so their half-fairy babies can survive in an Unremarkable's world."

The front door dings and Shane strolls in, bringing with him a gust of icy air. "Blessed Yule, my friends. Well, technically, the solstice doesn't occur until the early morning hours on Sunday, but we're celebrating on Saturday evening at the Pumpkin House. Jeff, why don't you bring Ashley and her son? Other children will be there."

"I planned on it," he replies. "Sounds like a lot of fun. I'll be right back. I left the tag machine in the back."

Shane removes his coat and hat. "How are you today, darling? Everything right in the world for once?"

"For the time being. But as long as that portal is open, I won't sleep well at night. Not that I sleep all that great, anyway. Menopause is the gift that keeps on giving."

He laughs as he walks behind the counter. "I'm sure I can't relate and never will, I'm happy to say."

A chuckle breaks free from my mouth. "I bet you are." After slipping on my puffer jacket, I grab my purse and head toward the door. "See you at the Winter Solstice Celebration. Any chance we'll finally get to meet that Unremarkable woman you've been hiding?"

"Perhaps, darling," he says, pulling on his whiskers. "Where are you off to now? Home?"

"Yeah. I may take a nap before dinner. Archie said he was preparing something special. I want to stay awake to enjoy the meal."

He wiggles his eyebrows. "And after?"

"You're bad, Shane," I say, squinting.

A mischievous grin peeks through his white beard. "Have a wonderful evening, Gwyn."

I chuckle. "You, too, boss."

When I step onto the red paver sidewalk, I pull up my hood. The sky is as blue as a clear summer's day, but the bright sun barely cuts through the December chill. I soak in the holiday decorations on Main Street as I head toward the Green—large white snowflakes sparkling with silver glitter and evergreen trimmings topped with puffy red bows. For now, all is right in our world. As close as it gets for Bearsden, anyway, a town with an open portal to the Otherworld.

When I turn into the alleyway shortcut to Douglas Street, I discover Seamus walking ahead of me at the far end. I run to catch up with him.

"Hi. Would you like company on the way home?" I ask.

The Irish professor nods with an enormous grin. "I would love to have you join me, Gwynedd."

"On behalf of the Bearsden Coven, I want to thank you again for assisting us in the rescue of the town's children. From what I've heard, the children's behavior has returned to normal."

"I will always be at your service, Gwynedd." He averts his gaze for a moment, then looks back at me. "However, I'll be at a distance come Fall Semester. I've applied for a position in Northern Ireland."

"Oh. Did you tell Dr. Hughes? And Archie?"

"I have not as of yet. I would appreciate you not mentioning the news to them. My letter of intent should arrive in a few days by snail mail."

"Why did you change your mind about staying?" As if I need to ask.

"It's time for me to return home, and clearly, you do not require my protection."

I chuckle at his realization, and he smiles warmly. We've arrived at his bungalow rental home, and he gestures toward the house.

"Would you like to come in for some hot tea? Warm up after the chilly walk here?"

"I would love to, but I have to get home. Archie is cooking dinner for me, and I need to freshen up." I stare fondly into his sea-green eyes. "It may surprise you, but I'm going to miss you when you leave."

"Those words warm my soul, Gwynedd. But remember, I visit Buckley a few times a year. Perhaps we'll cross paths when I stop by your Aunt Gorawen's estate in the future."

"That would be lovely." My heart twitches a little at the idea of not seeing the cat sith witch in Bearsden.

"Ms. Johnson and Dr. Hughes have invited me to assist in the completion of the grimoire search on Sunday at Ms. Pritchard's farmhouse."

"I didn't know Trinity asked you. We can certainly use another body."

"Have a wonderful dinner and evening. Give Dr. Cockburn my regards."

Seamus tips his cap and limps to the stoop, turning to wave before entering the house. I continue on to Drummond Lane. When I get near home, I notice Tyler's sedan parked in front, as well as Agnes's old jalopy. Why did he stop by? He knew I was at work.

I nudge the red side door and push into the mudroom, relishing the warmth. Voices trickle down the hallway while I remove my puffer jacket and gloves. I kick off my sneakers and shuffle toward the magic room, catching part of a conversation.

"I'm agreeable to any terms you would like to propose," Leslie says.

"Then I'm decided," Tyler replies. "It's a no brainer."

I enter the magic room to find Agnes, Tyler, and Zoe cramped together around the old wooden desk where Leslie is sitting. Mr. Yeats stands in the corner, adjusting his spectacles and bowtie. He appears flummoxed. Stacks of boxes are piled nearby. He's not the only one who's perplexed.

"Mom," Tyler says, his eyebrows arching. "You're back already."

"Yeah. I'm actually getting home a little late. I walked back with Seamus part of the way."

Zoe's eyes hop from Tyler to Agnes and stop at Leslie. "I'm sure Dr. Duffy appreciated the company."

"Why are you guys here?" I ask my son and his love. "Were we supposed to eat dinner together? If so, I forgot. I'm eating with Archie tonight."

The shelves are barren except for a few pieces of paper and dust bunnies clinging to the corners. Agnes stares at me from the corner seat, her lips twisted into a don't-ask-me expression. Leslie pushes up from her desk chair.

"We have exciting news to share with you, Gwynedd. Wouldn't you agree, Agnes?"

My hedge witch mentor grimaces. "For us. Who's gonna fucking tell her?"

"Tell me what?" I ask, observing their roaming eyes.

Mr. Yeats moves forward, huffing. "Dr. Hughes is moving into Ms. Pritchard's farmhouse. And she's forcing me to go with her."

"Now that's just not fucking true, you ungrateful familiar," Agnes says. "You can stay here if you want. Your fucking choice."

"Why would I remain in this house if my witch is leaving? I am Dr. Hughes's assistant, not Mr. Wolfe's."

"What the hell are you talking about?" I ask. "Why would you become Tyler's familiar?"

Mr. Yeats crosses his arms. "Because Mr. Wolfe is buying Dr. Hughes's house."

My eyes bulge. "What the fuck?" I ask my son. "Is the familiar making this shit up?"

"No, Mom," Tyler replies. "Dr. Hughes asked me about buying her house. I told her I didn't have that much money saved up. So, she's going to hold the mortgage herself."

Zoe clenches her teeth. "We should have told your mom when Dr. Hughes first asked you about buying the house."

"Fucking right, you should have," Agnes says. "Gwyn, I wanted to tell you all along, but sweetheart here thought we should wait until Tyler was sure he was comfortable buying a house."

Tyler walks forward and hugs me. "Be happy for me. I'm finally settling down with Zoe. You'll still have the spare bedroom. We wouldn't kick you out."

My jaw drops. I can't muster one word of response.

"Gwynedd, Agnes and I have lived apart for far too long," Leslie says, wrapping an arm around her partner. "When she suggested I sell the house and move onto the farm, I knew it would be terribly unfair to sell to a stranger, knowing you would have nowhere to go. When I approached Tyler and Zoe about buying my home, he had to ruminate over the offer. He decided just a few minutes ago."

Apparently, I was wrong. I have at least one word to comment. "Fuck." I turn around and head toward the mudroom.

"Where are you going, Mom?" Tyler's voice echoes down the hall. "Don't be mad."

"Of course she's fucking angry." Agnes shouts after me. "Gwyn, you can always move in with us at the farmhouse."

I throw on my puffer jacket, grab my purse, and head over to Duncan Street, slamming the door as I leave. When I enter Archie's house, the aroma of fresh bread and something scrumptious fills my nostrils. Whatever he's cooking prompts my stomach to growl. I kick off my shoes and dart into the kitchen. I slide my fingers across his torso from behind.

"Gwyn, I wasn't expecting you for another twenty minutes."

He turns around, and I plant my lips on his delicious mouth, offering my tongue. He reciprocates without hesitation, then pulls away for a breather.

"Well, good afternoon to you, too, Ms. Crowther."

I reach around him and turn off the burners and the oven.

"What are you doing? Dinner has at least thirty minutes left."

I grab Archie's hand and drag him up the stairs into the bedroom without a word. Once in inside, I shove him on the bed and pull off his shirt. I slide my fingertips across his firm pecs and rub his nipples with my thumbs. He sits up and pulls me to him, kissing me as he unhooks my bra underneath my blouse. I whisk both of them off and toss the tops to the floor. The bulge in his pants begs for freedom. I rub him through his jeans, and he moans.

"Whatever in all the Otherworld has gotten into you, witch?"

I unzip his fly and tug at his jeans and socks. "Does it matter?"

He raises a corner of his mouth. "Not one fawking bit."

After I yank off his pants and boxer briefs, I stand back to admire his physique. I could gaze at him like this all day—every day—for the rest of our lives together. Wake up next to him each morning wrapped in his arms. I strip off the last of my clothes and climb onto the bed. He shifts back, giving me the clearance I need to straddle him, and I moan as he enters me. He clasps my shoulders and pulls me down to kiss him.

I recall our first night together. I shook nervously as he touched me—so new and exciting. How could this gorgeous man want me? A naïve older woman who could barely get out of the bed in the morning. Now, our lovemaking is comfortable. He fits well against my body, and his caresses titillate my skin as much as the first night he made love to me.

Archie rolls me over onto my back and moves slowly, as if he's savoring every moment. He runs his fingers down my side while grazing my neck with his lips. I grasp his hand and call on my magic. An amber glow radiates and spreads throughout our bodies, prompting him to move faster. I cup the sides of his face and gaze into his clear-blue eyes.

"I love you, Archie."

"And I will never love another, Gwyn."

He kisses me passionately, gasping for air as he increases his speed. I slide my hands across his butt, encouraging him further. When I cry out with my release, he follows, grunting with a final thrust. He lays his head on the pillow next to me while I stroke his back.

"What brought this on, Gwyn? You've not said a word."

A hearty laugh erupts as I catch my breath. "I was super pissed and had to let off some steam. Are you complaining?"

"Fawk no. But I assume it's not me you were all hot and bothered about."

"Oh, I think I was, don't you?" I pinch his butt.

He laughs and rolls off of me onto his side. "Decidedly so."

"No. I'm not mad at you. I just found out Leslie is selling her house and moving in with Agnes. And get this. Tyler and Zoe are buying her place."

"What the fawk?" he asks, wrinkles folding between his eyes.

"Yeah. Exactly what I said before I darted out of the house. I was so mad they kept it a secret, I couldn't respond. And to top it off, Tyler offered to let me stay in the spare room, like I'm some sort of geriatric charity case."

He chuckles as he strokes my cheek. "And your first reaction was to come here and have sex with me?"

"Yes," I say, fondling his chest.

"I feel so used." He snickers and kisses me. "What are you going to do?"

"Tyler and Zoe want me to stay, but it was incredibly awkward when I lived with him before."

I shift to my side, panting, as my heartbeat slows. While my hand rests on his firm chest, his heart beats under my touch, always steady and dependable. I press my lips softly against his.

"How would you like a roommate?" I ask, batting my eyelashes.

A wide grin stretches his goatee. "In the words of Spencer Huxley, 'Absofuckinglutely.'"

CHAPTER THIRTY

AN UNCERTAIN FUTURE

"ARCHIE!" I SHOUT INTO the stairwell. "What are you doing? We're supposed to meet up with the others at the Pumpkin House by five to set up."

His Scottish accent echoes in the upstairs hallway. "I'm coming! Finishing up now."

He runs down the stairs in his socks and slips, falling on his butt. I dash to him.

"Are you OK?" I ask, touching his back.

He grabs the railing and pulls himself up, rubbing his bottom. "On the cheek where I had the tattoo removed. A brilliant bruise to match the remnants of the ink, I bet."

"You should know better than to rush down steps in your stocking feet."

"Well, which is it?" he asks, grimacing. "Are you overly concerned about my well-being or scolding me for my clumsy habits?"

I scowl at him. "Fuck you."

He laughs and slides a hand around my waist, pulling me toward him. "I plan to, my love. Every night if you'll have me."

I kiss him. "You're way too happy about me moving in. What were you doing up in the bedroom?"

"Rearranging the closet to make room for your clothes." He sits on the bottom step and puts on his shoes. "We may have to store summer attire in the spare bedroom."

"It's not like I'm a fashionista. But I'll probably have to buy new clothing when I get a job at the end of Spring Semester."

"Don't forget Tyler is coming by Sunday to attempt his first conference with your mum and dad. Zoe is joining him. You're not upset he wants to meet with them without you present, are you?"

"No. I'll drive to Ronnie and Derek's for a visit. He doesn't need me breathing down his back. Thank you for being such a great substitute father to him." I zip up my puffer jacket and slip on my gloves.

"It's not an inconvenience. I enjoy my time with him immensely." Archie puts on his winter coat and cap. "Are you sure you want to walk to the Pumpkin House? It's a wee nippy out tonight. Dropping below freezing."

"It's silly to drive such a short distance. There isn't much wind."

"Let's brave the cold, then."

We stroll through the Green with a purpose, and as usual, Archie has trouble keeping up with me. The air nips at my face, and I'm eager to get to the Pumpkin House to set up for the Winter Solstice Celebration. He grabs my hand, slowing me down.

"Can we at least enjoy the walk together? We'll arrive soon enough."

"Tyler and Zoe should be there already. I want to chat with them before we open the doors to the community."

"I thought you spoke with them and smoothed things over?"

"Oh, I did. They want to discuss getting some of my old furniture out of the storage unit. I held onto a few things for a new house. Looks like I won't be needing any of it."

He squeezes my hand as we ascend the steps to the porch. "You're absolutely certain you aren't moving in with me just because Tyler and Zoe are buying Leslie's house?"

"Yes. If I weren't ready, I would have looked for an apartment. Let's talk about the rest of the move later at home."

"I like you calling my house your home."

"Me, too," I say, turning the doorknob.

The young witches are busy setting out refreshments on the tables. Shane and a woman near his age are chatting with Ronnie and Derek in the parlor. My boss is finally introducing his secret love to us, but I have a feeling he's not divulging our witch status. Courtney Erickson, Jeff Williams, and Ashley Lewis arrive and join them. Mesmerized by Ronnie and Derek's daughter Luna, Ashley's son Aidan can't take his eyes off of her. I hope it's curiosity and not a sign of his Tylwyth Teg ancestry. I approach Tyler and the others in the dining room while Archie goes into the parlor.

"Hi, Mom," my son says. "Did you remember to bring the key to the storage unit?"

"Yeah." I remove the tiny piece of metal from my purse and hand it to him. "Take whatever you want. I may sell what's left and stop paying the monthly bill. I'll transport any personal items to Archie's."

"Do you care if I paint the furniture?" Zoe asks. "I want to go wild." She splays her hands in the air.

I chuckle. "Sure. Knock yourself out."

Skye nudges me. "Tyler said you're moving in with Archie. Congrats."

"Thank you. Zach coming tonight?"

"Yeah," she replies. "When he's done at work."

"It's about fucking time," Spence says, hugging me. "You're like an old married couple already."

"We are. Well, middle-aged at least." I remove my jacket and gloves and stuff them under a table.

Tanner throws Spence a side-eye. "Dude, that'll be us soon enough. I'm happy for you both, Gwyn."

"Thanks. It felt like the right time, if there ever is one. Speaking of old, where are Leslie, Agnes, Trinity, and Elijah?"

Skye motions toward the hallway. "In the back room. Mayor Devine and John Erickson came early to talk with them. Sounds more like a set of demands than a conversation, though."

"Really?" I ask, glancing into the parlor. "I should tell Archie."

As I approach the parlor, Aidan runs to me, hugging my leg.

"Miss Gwyn." He points to Luna. "It's a baby."

I smile at Ronnie and Derek. "Yes. It is. A beautiful little girl." I glance at Courtney. "Hi, I'm so glad you came."

"I am, too," she replies. "John came with me. He's in the back."

"When Luna gets old enough, the two of you can play together," my best friend says. "Would you like that, Aidan?"

A bashful smile shapes his mouth. "Yes. I want to play with other girls and boys like me."

"You do, Aidan," Ashley says, averting her eyes. "We have a play date set up for this week. He didn't remember."

Jeff interjects. "But Mrs. Erickson is going to have a baby, too. You'll have plenty of friends."

"Be patient, Aidan," Courtney says. "My baby will arrive in a few months."

It appears he will have friends *like him*, and those are just the ones we're aware of. I gesture to Courtney to follow me to a quiet corner of the room.

"Are we OK?" Courtney asks. "I want to have a fulfilling life in Bearsden. You don't need to worry about me."

"Yeah, but don't expect us to be great friends. You fucking lied to everybody about everything. But you saved the children, and for that, I'm grateful. I have a few questions, though."

She nods. "Ask me. I'll tell you anything you want to know."

"Why didn't the coven sense your fairy magic before? I only noticed it a few times when you returned to Bearsden. I'm assuming that's due to my improved intuition. But you'd think one witch in the coven would have discerned the difference."

"Audrey cast a masking spell to cover my fairy magic. She wanted my help to infiltrate the coven because she knew she'd have trouble finding a witch who would do harm to others. I agreed to do it if she helped me get Archie back."

"Wow. She knew you were a fairy."

"Yes. She sensed my magic when I crossed over into Bearsden. I discovered this new portal and came through alone. I hid at first, observing the humans in the town. One day, I saw Archie walking through the Green. He was so handsome. I created a human persona right away and enrolled at DUB to be closer to him." She smiles mischievously. "And it worked."

I scowl at her, and her smile falls flat.

"Then you showed up. Well, you know the rest. But that's all behind me."

Audrey never told us about Courtney's true identity, and she remained true to her fairy friend until the end. Does Courtney know what happened to her?

"Courtney, did you stay in touch with Audrey after you left Bearsden?"

"For a while. She told me she was sorry for using me. That her mother had hexed her and was forcing her to go after you and the coven. The last time I spoke with her before I left town, she was trying to get out from under her mother's hex. Do you know if she was successful?"

"She was. She apologized to me and the coven for what happened. Courtney, Audrey's parents tried to kill all of us in the coven for interfering with their business. They almost succeeded, but Audrey killed her mother, saving us all. Unfortunately, her mom threw a wave of magic at her right before she died." The corners of my mouth fall. "She killed Audrey."

"I didn't know that." Courtney's eyes tear up. "I wondered why she never returned my calls or texts."

"I'm sorry, even though your original arrangement wasn't based in good intentions. Audrey was a good person, controlled by an evil witch. You've redeemed yourself, too. She'd want you to move on and be happy."

The Tylwyth Teg fairy wipes the wet from her eyes. "I will. I mean, I am."

"We should get back to the others before they start gossiping."

I begin walking back, and Courtney follows me.

"Thank you, Gwyn. You didn't have to be so understanding."

I smile at her. "No, I didn't. Take care, Courtney."

She makes her way into the dining room and I go back to my friends. Archie has joined them.

"Gwyn, Archie asked if I could pick up your steamer trunk tomorrow morning," Derek says. "It won't fit in his Tesla."

"Or my Prius," I say. "Thank you for moving it for me."

"Not a problem. You should come for dinner sometime this week. I'll cook."

"Sounds wonderful," Archie says, nodding toward the back room.

Shane walks over to me with his lady friend. "Gwyn, I'd like you to meet Julia. I've told her all about you."

"So nice to meet all of you finally," she says, shaking my hand. "I was beginning to think Shane was ashamed of me."

"It's a pleasure to meet you as well." I peer at my boss out of the corner of my eye. "He was probably being protective of you. The members of the Fellowship can overwhelm people. Shane has been so happy these last few months. You're the reason for that, I'm sure."

Archie clasps my hand. "If you'll excuse us, we're needed for a brief meeting."

Shane nods. "We'll chat again during the open house."

We rush to the back room. Archie whispers in my ear as we walk. "Your boss said they've been arguing back there for over twenty minutes."

"Yeah, Skye and the others told me, too."

Archie pushes the door in. Mayor Devine stands with her arms crossed and a glower etched on her face.

"I'm done talking about this," she says, walking away. "You find a spell to shut that portal. John, I demand you stay on top of this. I can't be the only one carrying the load for the safety of this town. The other council members who are *in the knowing* refuse to listen anymore. It's too much stress for all of us. Do it." She exits the room.

Agnes opens and shuts her mouth, mocking Jessica Devine. "Who the fuck does she think she is?"

"She's the mayor, Agnes," Elijah says. "And she has a right to vent. Unremarkables weren't supposed to shoulder the burden of the supernatural in our town. That was the job of the Bearsden Coven."

Trinity exhales heavily. "Damn straight. We kept the coven hidden for over thirty years. Now we're confiding in every person we love. Eventually, the truth will get out."

"Not if we close the portal," Leslie says. "Tomorrow, we all meet at Agnes's farm to finish up the grimoires. If we don't find a portal-closing spell, we'll have to seek out other witches here and abroad for help."

"Aye," Archie replies. "We may need to research ancient tomes in Britain to find one. My family has offered assistance."

"Trinity, you'll let the young witches know they're expected tomorrow?" I ask.

She types into her phone. "Group text is already sent. Except for Ronnie. She needs to stay home with Luna."

Notification sounds ring within seconds of each other.

"Just fucking great," Agnes says, grimacing. "They better not sneak into my Bearsden Poison again. There are hexes in the database now, and I know how to cast them."

Leslie rolls her eyes.

Trinity slams the last grimoire shut and drops it on the table. "That's it, witches. We've exhausted the search here. I know this isn't how you wanted to spend your solstice morning. Unfortunately, we came up dry. Thank you again, Dr. Duffy, for lending a hand."

"You're most welcome," he replies. "I will inquire through contacts at home, but I've never come across a spell to close a portal before."

Agnes crosses her arms. "We tried one, but it didn't work. Don't fucking know why. We found another one, but they don't want to use it."

He cocks his head. "I'm befuddled. Why haven't you tried to cast this spell?"

"Because it requires the use of a human sacrifice," Spence says.

"How unfortunate." Seamus grimaces as he sits. "That presents a problem."

Agnes growls. "No, it doesn't. If we—"

"Don't say one more word, dear," Leslie says. "Or you'll find yourself alone in this house again."

My hedge witch mentor presses her lips together. Her face turns beet red. We all crack up as Trinity places the last grimoire on the shelf.

"You all can go on home," she says defeatedly.

Archie closes the file on the computer. "It's not a complete loss. We have a searchable database of every spell in this library."

"Indeed," Leslie says. "Research is never useless. And we have Agnes to thank for her cooperation."

She huffs. "Yeah, yeah. Now you all can get the fuck out of here."

Trinity snickers. "Elijah, you'll have to tell the mayor we did our best, but we'll continue to search."

"Will do." He puts on his coat. "Shane, would you like a ride?"

"Thank you kindly, councilman," he says. "Gwyn, are you working extra hours at the store?"

"Yeah. It's gonna be a busy day." My shoulders fall. I didn't expect to find another incantation to close the portal, but the letdown is real.

"I'm going, too," Trinity says. "Charlie is cooking brunch as I speak. Merry Yule."

Our coven leader, Shane, and Elijah exit the library. Skye, Tanner, and Spence follow them out, saying, "Merry Yule, everyone."

"Merry Yule," we reply.

"Gwyn, why don't we go?" Archie asks, grabbing his jacket. "I'll make lunch before you have to go to work. Seamus, we can give you a ride back."

"Thank you," he replies. "I'll retrieve my coat."

"Lunch would be great," I say. "Leslie, I'll be in and out this week to move my clothes and other belongings. It shouldn't take long."

"Perhaps I can prepare dinner one more time at the house. Tyler and Zoe could join us."

"How about I make dinner?" Zoe asks. "I should get used to the stove."

"Outstanding," the Elder replies. "I'll contact you later in the week."

"Sounds great." Tyler lifts a tome from a shelf and blows dust off its edges. "Wait. Why didn't we go through this grimoire?"

Agnes shuffles over to my son and examines the tome. "Because it isn't a grimoire."

Tyler sets the worn leather-bound book on the table and flips through a few pages. "Looks like a journal of some kind. Where did you find it?"

"I don't fucking know. I'm old. Picked it up somewhere in the last fifty years." She scratches her head. "Oh, I remember. The ancient crone I studied with gave it to me on her deathbed. Gwyn, the same witch who gave me the amethyst geode. I had no use for it since it was written in a foreign language, but I kept it, anyway."

My son sits down and turns a few more pages. Zoe plops into the seat next to him.

"This is so cool," she says. "If I'm remembering my Irish class correctly, this is old Irish Gaelic."

Leslie approaches them to view the tome. "Very perceptive, Zoe. You were always an excellent student."

Seamus appears intrigued and limps on his cane to where they are sitting. Tyler flips through a few more pages.

"We really need to go soon, Gwyn," Archie says.

"OK," I reply as I zip my jacket. "Tyler, can you take the professor home?"

My son lifts his head, his eyes as big and white as billiards cue balls, and his jaw drops. Zoe covers her mouth with a hand. Seamus motions to me.

"You may want to examine this, Gwynedd."

"What's wrong?" I ask, darting to them.

I stare down at the frayed pages, which display a hand-drawn sketch—a giant with massive muscles and one bulging eye. My skin crawls with immediate recognition. "Fuck. It's my monster." I gesture to Archie to join us at the table.

Seamus examines the writing under the drawing. "Zoe is correct. Kudos to your excellent memory of your studies. It is, in fact, old Irish Gaelic."

"Can you translate the description?" Archie asks, staring at the image.

He reads the hand-written words and nods. "It says it's a Fomorian."

Agnes leans over the book. "What the fuck is a Fomorian?"

"It's written they were the enemy of the first Irish settlers. Monstrous giants. A violent supernatural race in the Otherworld. But I don't recall paintings depicting them like this. If I had, I would have told you, Gwynedd."

"But why would I have a vision of one crossing over through the portal in the Celestial Gardens?" My heart pounds in my chest, and I grasp Archie's hand.

Leslie locks eyes with Seamus, and he nods at her. The Elder touches my shoulder.

"Because Fomorians are also the enemy of the Tuatha Dé Danann."

"Fawk," Archie says, squeezing my hand.

My hands tremble as an aura rushes over me like a tidal wave. I clutch my abdomen, and a sudden sureness fills my chest. I stare into Archie's anxious eyes.

"They're already here."

Acknowledgments

Thank you to my son for all the tech support and setting up my online book shop.

Thank you to my daughter for her continued consultation on Welsh pronunciations.

To my book cover designer Charles Clark. My books would be naked without you.

Special thanks to my editor Sarah Faeth Sanders. You took my book and smoothed out all the wrinkles!

To my ARC Team. I can't thank you enough for your continued devotion to my books.

About the Author

J.C. YEAMANS is an author of PWF Urban Fantasy and other paranormal fiction. A former public school teacher based in Lewes, Delaware, she writes about all things witchy to find the inherent magic in life's journey of discovery and love—all while making blunders along the way. As the owner of Reed Shore Press, she also publishes fiction and nonfiction works for others. Her prior career revolved around the performing arts. She is married and has two adult children. When she's not putting pen to paper (or more aptly, fingertips to keys), she spends time biking, hiking, and weightlifting.

Sign up for J.C. Yeamans's newsletter at jcyeamans.com to download A Trinity of Witches, a free backstory to The Bearsden Witch Series.

OTHER BOOKS

The Bearsden Witch Series

Secrets of a Midlife Witch
Schooling of a Midlife Witch
Stalking of a Midlife Witch
Trials of a Midlife Witch
Intuition of a Midlife Witch
Resolve of a Midlife Witch
(Late Fall 2024)

www.ingramcontent.com/pod-product-compliance
Lightning Source LLC
Chambersburg PA
CBHW021412010826
48972CB00014B/1771